Also by Joan Aiken

If I Were You
Mansfield Revisited
Foul Matter
The Girl from Paris
The Weeping Ash
The Smile of the Stranger
The Five-Minute Marriage
Last Movement
Voices in an Empty House
Midnight Is a Place
A Cluster of Separate Sparks
The Embroidered Sunset
The Crystal Crow
Dark Interval
Beware of the Bouquet
The Fortune Hunters
The Silence of Herondale

Juvenile Books:

Give Yourself a Fright:
  Thirteen Tales of the Supernatural
The Teeth of the Gale Dido and Pa
The Stolen Lake
The Shadow Guests
A Touch of Chill and Other Tales
The Skin Spinners: Poems
Arabel and Mortimer
Not What You Expected
Bridle the Wind
Go Saddle the Sea
Arabel's Raven
Street: A Play for Children
The Mooncusser's Daughter:
  A Play for Children

The Green Flash and Other Tales
Winterthurn: A Children's Play
The Cuckoo Tree
Died on a Rainy Sunday
Night Fall
Smoke from Cromwell's Time and
  Other Stories
The Whispering Mountain
A Necklace of Raindrops
Armitage, Armitage Fly Away Home
Nightbirds on Nantucket
Black Hearts in Battersea
The Wolves of Willoughby Chase
The Kingdom and the Cave

BLACKGROUND

BLACKGROUND

Joan Aiken

Doubleday

New York   London   Toronto   Sydney   Auckland

PUBLISHED BY DOUBLEDAY

a division of Bantam Doubleday Dell Publishing Group, Inc.
666 Fifth Avenue, New York, New York 10103

DOUBLEDAY and the portrayal of an anchor with a dolphin
are trademarks of Doubleday, a division of Bantam
Doubleday Dell Publishing Group, Inc.

Library of Congress Cataloging-in-Publication Data

Aiken, Joan, 1924–
Blackground / Joan Aiken. — 1st ed. in the United States
of America.
p.   cm.
ISBN 0-385-26021-0
I. Title.
PR6051.I35B57   1989   88-30497
823'.914—dc19   CIP

Copyright © 1989 by Joan Aiken Enterprises, Ltd.
All Rights Reserved

BOOK DESIGN BY DOROTHY KLINE

Printed in the United States of America

FIRST EDITION IN THE UNITED STATES OF AMERICA, 1989

My thanks are due to the Thornton Endowment Program of Lynchburg College, Virginia, where, as Writer in Residence, I was able to complete and revise this novel, and particularly to Professor Richard Burke, my kind mentor, and Director of the Thornton Endowment Program during my visit.

BLACKGROUND

1

THIS is how it all came about. I will omit early struggles, a walk-on with a fringe group at the Edinburgh Festival, one song in a musical in Amsterdam, hind legs of Puss at Nottingham, and a mime part in Papp's Public Theatre, New York. Yet another nonspeaking part, which I gladly accepted, was that of a ghost, in a BBC TV ghost story. I had to play a few notes on a ghostly harp. For this I was chosen—believe it or not—because I actually can play a few notes on the harp; for three happy years I formed part of an amateur music ensemble and alternated on harp and guitar, with occasional brief but exhilarating sessions on drums. One of the men in that group subsequently rose to higher spheres in Pyramid Television and had become a casting director; by lucky chance he remembered my harping expertise and fetched me in for the spook play. I had to sit in a dim glow at the foot of a flight of stairs, dressed in shimmery green, pluck gracefully at the strings of this enormous silver harp, and turn my neck languidly to and fro. The neck movement was supposed to be *sinister,* also blind; "Think of a maggot, darling," Harald the director had instructed me, "a maggot or a blind hungry worm that scents food but can't see it, a worm twisting its head like a radar screen to pick up tiny clues of odour on the air." Ah, dear Harald Flanagan, that director, he was a broth of a boy for a mixed metaphor. So, blind maggot or radar scanner, I manipulated my head this way and that, after the manner of a tennis umpire, or an expectant daffodil. The ghost play was nothing, a winter trifle that got deservedly panned and was forgotten in a week, buried out of sight in the vast necropolis of television failures; but all my industrious neck-undulation lodged in some casting director's memory, and all of a sudden, six months later, to my utter astonishment I was summoned to audition for one of two plum roles in a thirteen-part serial. Nineteenth-century costume drama, masterpiece-theatre stuff. *Dodo and Rosy,* it was going to be called, tossing overboard the original book title, a place name that was imaginary, and not interesting anyway.

The part I tried out for was that of Rosy, the blond minx who, by selfishness, snobbery, and extravagance, utterly wrecks the life of her handsome, idealistic doctor husband. Oh, she's a real pig, that Rosy, a sweet, pretty, accomplished, soft-spoken, flint-hearted bitch of a girl. Her two primary characteristics, at first sight, are the long neck and a rose-petal complexion.

All the women of my family (that is my mother, and her four sisters, and me) have, or had, extra-long Russian necks and fair complexions. So there was the first hurdle passed. In point of fact, Rosy is supposed to be twenty, and I am thirty-five, so you would think this was an idiotic bit of casting; but I am always taken for ten years younger than my age, and nobody seemed to worry at all about that particular discrepancy.

"She'll have to get her teeth fixed and wear blue contact lenses," growled the female tycoon on the casting committee, scanning me as if I were a half-decorated dining alcove. It's a very queer, depriving sensation, that of being assessed, not as a person, but as a bit of property. At first it used to make me very dejected; I felt, as slaves must have felt, disidentified, depersonalised, wiped out. But nowadays I find the process quite liberating. After all, ho ho, inside this shell that they are busily creating, there I still am, Cat Conwil, fully aware of myself, them, and all else that's going on: the Girl in the Iron Mask. When somebody draws an outline all around you, and gives the command, "Don't stir beyond that point!" their outline defines you to yourself, in what may be a hitherto unsuspected way. Like being left alone in a locked room.

I didn't object to the blue contact lenses, though it was a bore learning to slot them in; for a spell at the start of shooting I continually held up the action and had upwards of thirty light technicians, dolly-pushers, camera-men, actors, and makeup girls on their knees, combing the studio floor for a dropped lens, which mostly proved to have worked its way around to the back of my eyeball. By and by I grew nimbler at slipping lenses in and out with a touch of the tongue for lubrication. Having my teeth fixed might be considered a really positive benefit, paid for moreover by Pyramid TV in their lavish lordliness. Before treatment my two front incisors had bowed towards each other like those of a beaver; *I* didn't dislike my own appearance, it made me look friendly and confiding, which can be an asset; but if you are an actress, closeness to the norm is likely to net you more parts, especially for commercials. One has to be realistic. Nobody is going to use beavers' teeth to advertise Supadent.

Being physically remodelled for Rosy was an advantage, too, when it came to working myself into the role. My hair, naturally dead straight and apricot jam colour, had to fade several shades paler; for hers, in the book, is described as being of infantine fairness, neither flaxen nor yellow. I was obliged, also, to gain a few pounds in weight, because her figure is described as nymphlike, which in nineteenth-century parlance meant curvy rather than skinny. So, by gradual degrees, I began to be enveloped by a wholly different personality from me, Cat; I tried to think about Rosy all the time, as much as I was able, her relations with her parents, brother, cousins, and neighbours in the dull provincial town where she lived, and where her forebears had always lived, and where her father, a third-generation manufacturer, was an alderman, about to become mayor. (When I say that the town was dull, I mean, of course, dull to Rosy; she longed for wider spheres.) She had been to a school for young ladies and learned to play the piano, surprisingly well, for she was clever at picking up other people's tricks of technique, and the harp, just a little—so my small accomplishment came in useful yet again; she had learned how to climb in and out of a carriage in a ladylike manner, and how to defer prettily in conversation to gentlemen and older people. *She knew nothing else at all.* Girls of that period and class didn't even learn to cook, or fill in a form, or change a light bulb, any of the basics that kids now get in their first year at secondary school. All she had to think about was herself, and what impression she made on men; so she had become a total narcissist.

I became quite fascinated by turning myself into Rosy— she formed such a sharp contrast to the way life has obliged me to develop. Due to various circumstances which I will enlarge on if necessary, I've had little education but needed :o be independent and resourceful about practical matters. Since the age of sixteen I've earned my own living and contributed to the support of others as well. So it felt like wonderful luxury to receive a lavish salary for playing the part of a girl who never did anything more active at home than pull a bell-rope and tell the maid to bring some more buttered toast, and who in conversation, always took care to adapt her manner to that of the person she was addressing. Oh yes, I can tell you, it was a whole lot of fun becoming Rosy—like taking a warm bath, tossing in cupfuls of bubble essence, so that the froth stands up in peaks and scrunches around you when you lie down.

Mind you, I had to learn several accomplishments that Rosy had acquired and I lacked; horse-riding was one. Day after day I trudged off to a School of Equitation just beside the Park, and, day after day, hobbled home stiff and sore with legs that felt like sticks of rhubarb ready to snap; for, later on in the script, when she has corralled her handsome doctor, wilful, selfish Rosy goes out riding with a military admirer, against her husband's orders, takes a toss off her mettlesome grey, and so has a miscarriage.

Accordingly I learned to ride, and sidesaddle at that. Also I had to learn tatting, since that was what young ladies mostly did in those days, while they were sitting about at home waiting for Mr. Right.

"Tatting?" said Masha, my mother. "You want to learn *tatting?* What in the world for? Yes, yes, of course I can teach you; it won't take any time at all. Just look in the top drawer of the little sewing table, right at the back, you'll find the tatting bobbin that your Aunt Tasha gave me."

The little rosewood sewing table had accompanied my mother everywhere, from flat to house, from, rectory to vicarage, all her married life. Grandmother Conwil gave it to her as a wedding present. It used to fascinate me as a child because it looked exactly the same back and front, but the drawers at the back were false ones. All through childhood my greatest pleasure was to rummage in those two shallow drawers, untidy them, tidy them up again, explore the contents of the round tin button box with a picture of a Turkish lady that had once held Turkish Delight, open the little dark blue leather wallet of embroidery tools, play with the scissors shaped like a bird, the bead-covered emery ball for derusting needles, and the tape measure made like a silk strawberry containing tape on a spring that zipped back when you let go

—until the day I pulled it too hard and it never went back again.

Perhaps the part played by this drawer in my early life was the cause of my subsequent obsessive passion for paper clips? All those small, shiny, efficient gadgets?

I found the tatting bobbin—an oval tortoiseshell tool, about the length of my thumb—and, sure enough, Masha taught me how to do simple tatting in half an hour. She chuckled as she did so.

"How very odd that you should need it for your job—considering how set against any form of needlework you were as a child."

Perfectly true. In those days I couldn't wait to get out into some profession where I would be on equal terms with men. None of your tatting or fancywork for me. Perhaps it was the result of Papa being a clergyman; the combination of father and God made me naturally disposed to assert my rights.

(Oddly enough, since the day Masha taught me, I have become quite keen on tatting, and find it first-rate as an accompaniment to feeling out a part, to any creative thought, or just for reducing tension. I must say the *product* is hard to dispose of: yards and yards of skimpy lace, the kind used at the beginning of this century for edging table mats and nightdress collars. But sometimes one's friends will accept it for trimming lingerie.)

Masha was a little pale and breathless by the end of the tatting lesson. She had been, at that time, in bed for five months of her terminal illness, and of course had been walking about with it, getting on with her life and duties, for God knows how long before that. I noticed her check her breathing once or twice and press a hand against her back.

"Are you in pain?" I asked with dread, for I knew she was approaching the point when pills were not going to be enough, when injections would have to be administered. How can one summon up the courage to give an injection to one's own mother? Trained for two years as a nurse, I possessed the technical ability. It was courage I lacked.

But no, no, she said, she was not in pain, just the merest trifling rheumatic twinge.

Masha's dogged lifelong heroism, her stoic disregard of pain, adverse circumstances, or any inconvenience to herself, her total self-sacrifice and generosity to others, may be among the contributory causes which make me such a contemptible coward and hypochondriac. Just to imagine, to attempt to grasp what she went through during her illness is enough to make me break out in cold perspiration, turn dizzy, almost keel over. As I write I can feel my hip and spine begin to ache.

"Anyway," she went on comfortably, "now you know how to tat. Such a useful accomplishment! I'm so pleased there's still something left that I can teach you."

And she chuckled again with satisfaction, with a kind of triumph. I too, even amid my unhappiness and worry, felt a smug complacency that I had been able to give her this pleasure. How incredibly selfish, how egotistical we are when dealing with our parents. Why, why did I ask her so little, ever, about herself, about how she felt, what she thought? On this occasion we discussed the part of Rosy, and Masha did enjoy that, she always liked to get her teeth into an abstract topic. She had been to Cambridge, but had to give up teaching during Papa's change of life. The novel from which the TV serial had been taken was in her bookshelf, she said, and told me to get it out, a well-thumbed classic two-volume Everyman edition; hopefully she asked if I would not like to borrow it, longing to be allowed to do me that service as well. But I declined her offer since I had already bought a paperback copy for myself (brought out in anticipation of the TV publicity); shortly after that I made an opportunity to take my leave. They were *drainingly* exhausting, those visits; one had to be so cheerful, so careful, so carefree, so false;

assuming a hope and confidence that were wholly without foundation.

Rosy, I'm sure, in such circumstances would have made out far better than I ever could. Falsity wouldn't have troubled her, not a whit; she never noticed the difference between falsity and reality. *She* would not have become tired and frantic; she could have stayed all day, smiling and serene, because it was the proper thing to do.

Now, long after, I wonder why, why in the world during that period did I never, never level with my mother? Why didn't I say, Look, I know—*you* must know too—that you are dying. What do you think about this, what do you feel about it, do you want to discuss it, what do you have to say about it? We're both intelligent, it's important, we love each other, you are my mother, I'm your only daughter, why can't we be honest with one another about this?

I get a hole in my heart now, thinking back to those dissembling interviews. My only relief comes from the recurrent notion that perhaps it was Masha who created the climate for them and forced the pretence on us both. She was a strong individual; perhaps she knew what was best for her? Or did she think it best for me? Perhaps honesty is a luxury that one ceases to wish for during the approach to death?

"I must go," I repeated, and she said wistfully, "Must you? Really? Can't you stay just a little longer?"

She had never been a demonstrative parent, after one had outgrown the small-child stage of falling and hurting oneself and needing to be hugged to make the hurt better. I think she missed that stage. She said to me once, sadly, "Children grow up so fast. The time has flashed by before one realises." And in her last illness she liked to hold one's hand, as one sat by the bed and chatted; from that clasp it was hard, often very hard, to disengage oneself.

"Tell me about Fitz," she said now quickly. "You haven't

told me anything yet about Fitz. Is he enjoying Harvard still?"

Unfortunately his last letter had been read to her on my previous visit; Fitz is not a lavish correspondent, though his infrequent letters, when they do come, make marvellous reading. "I'm writing to you from a dungeon," he wrote to Masha once, and she was delighted. I resolved to telephone him that night and urge him to write to her without delay. I knew it would fret her too much if he phoned her; the terrifying extravagance of a transatlantic call would quite paralyse her powers of verbal communication.

"Well, never mind," she said. "Read me his last letter again. I shall enjoy that just as much as a new one."

The deep and loving bond between Masha and Fitz made them seem almost of the same generation; their rapport, of love and intellect both, put them closer to each other than to me. I have never been jealous of this; how could I?

As a matter of fact I have often felt fairly complacent about having brought them together.

Alas, I had left his previous letter back at my flat in Notting Hill, and so I said yet again that I must go, and managed to detach the hand she had been clasping.

"You had better keep the tatting hook," she said. "They are probably hard to come by. And I doubt if I'll be using it again. Last year I began to get a little arthritis in my right forearm; that was why I stopped doing it. But I don't imagine you'll do enough to give yourself arthritis." And she chuckled again.

I said I would like to keep the hook very much. "How old were you when Aunt Tasha gave it to you?"

"Oh, twelve or thirteen. It was a Christmas stocking present."

There were five of the Conwil sisters—Tasha, Dolly, Mig, Minka, and my mother. Tasha and Dolly, the two eldest, never married, but lived together. They were one-quarter

Russian, three-quarters Welsh. Great Granny Conwil's maiden name had been Ousspensky. Masha had been the youngest and was the last to survive.

"You will come again soon—won't you?" She had managed to reclaim my hand, clasping it tightly. "Tomorrow?"

"Well—we have a rehearsal at twelve. I'll try. But this part really does take up a good deal of my time."

"It's *absolutely lovely* that you've got it," she said with warmth and pride. "I'm so very, very glad about it."

Indeed she was. I knew she'd be boasting with innocent vanity about it to the nurses. But just the same, there was a note of wistfulness, of disappointment in her voice, that my time for her was now so limited. And I daresay I made the TV serial an excuse to come less often than I might have, why conceal the fact? Because how many hours of each day can one spend sitting by somebody's bed in despairing grief? The anguish begins to leave its mark and one's work deteriorates.

Nervous, at bay, I glanced round her little private room. Would she have been happier in a hospital, in a public ward? Where there was company?

She'd enjoy the general goings-on, but I knew that, basically, privacy was as essential to her as fresh air. The room was tiny, just space for bed, chair, her own sewing table and bookshelf (Yeats, Donne, Plato), but from her window she could see the pleasant garden, a paved walk, lavender hedge, and the graceful majestic droop of a big ilex; light from the declining sun shone kindly on a section of old brick wall. No rays came into the twilit room at this hour, but the sun woke her before breakfast, and that, she said, was what she liked best. And the window, despite the efforts of cleaners, nurses, matron, doctors and visitors, stood wide open all day. Like Rosy in one respect, my mother possessed a will of iron when it came to getting her own way.

"Well—supposing you can't come tomorrow—you will on Friday?"

Of course, of course I'd come on Friday, I said, and stooped and kissed her cold soft downy cheek. Friday would be her birthday and I had devoted much fruitless thought to the choice of a suitable gift. What can be offered to somebody on the threshold of death? In the end I bought her a shawl, but was denied the chance of presenting it, for she died on the Thursday night.

People very often do die just before their birthdays, I have learned since then.

After that, for weeks and months I went around in two kinds of anguish, one deep, one trivial. There had been something else I had intended to say, to ask her, on that final visit. *What could it have been?* I tormented myself by the thought of her twilit figure, my final view of her in the shadowy room, leaning back with resignation on her piled pillows —but nevertheless craning her neck round at a desperately uncomfortable angle in order to get the last, the very last glimpse of me as I went away.

Before that, while still able to sit up in a chair, she had always insisted on moving that chair to the window, before one left, in order to look out and wave as one walked across the garden to the gate. Her eyes, through the glass, were like the hands of shipwrecked sailors, extended beseechingly out of the water.

"WOULD you like me to come back for the funeral?" Fitz said at once when I telephoned him to tell him of Masha's death. "I can get on a standby flight tonight?"

"No, no, love, what would be the point? Just to hear a few words said in some revolting crematorium building? Masha would be appalled at such extravagance and waste of your time. I'll see you when you come back at the end of May." I tried to keep my tone firm and brisk. May seemed light years away. "It would be a sin to interrupt your work, just when you've got started. And I'm all right. Really I am. Busy with this part." He knew about the part, from my letters.

"Well, thank heaven for that, at least," he said. "But you're sure you're okay?" He still sounded doubtful, anxious, loving. Anyone lucky enough to have a Fitz in their life ought to thank heaven on annual barefoot pilgrimage to Compostella. What have I done to deserve him? I sometimes wonder. Well—Masha gave him to me.

"Will there be someone to keep you company at the funeral?"

Papa had died last year, and the four elder Conwil sisters before that. I could not think of any relations. But hundreds of people had loved Masha—unfortunately, many of them were poor, ill, or elderly, and might find it impossible to get to the ceremony.

"There'll be plenty of people," I said. "And I'm going to take her ashes to Dorset and scatter them in the garden at Yetford, where the squills grew, under the big cedar. She'd like to be in that place. It was her favourite."

"Yes it was," he agreed. "She always talked about it. You don't think the Dickinsons will mind? Worry that her ghost will haunt them?"

"He's a vicar, he shouldn't entertain such idle superstitions. Besides," I said, "anyone ought to be *pleased* to be haunted by Masha's ghost." I wiped a tear from my right cheek and tried to laugh but it came out shaky.

"Well, okay old Cat; if you're really sure," said Fitz. "I wish you could get away and come over here."

"I wish I could too. This part—"

"Yeah, yeah, yeah. Well I hope they're paying you a hell of a lot."

"It's not peanuts. And there will be more, if they do repeats and sell it overseas."

"Good. When I come back we'll buy a Peugeot and go gliding round Europe in it."

"That'll be terrific—"

"Are you eating enough food and stuff?"

"Oh God yes; I have to, for—"

"I know, I know, the part, the part. Well, take care—"

"You too," I said, choking.

"I *must* go now," he said. "Lecture."

"I'll look forward to that Peugeot ride—" I called, but he had hung up.

The next time I saw Fitz, I was married. To James Tybold, Lord Fortuneswell.

IN the first three episodes Rosy, as an unmarried daughter at home, wears her hair demurely arranged, mid-nineteenth-century-provincial-young-lady style, pulled straight back or with coiled plaits at the front and small cluster of ringlets at the rear. No problem, I could do it myself, though they sometimes used to tidy up my ringlets a bit in the makeup room.

But, in the latter half of the story, Rosy has nabbled her doctor and is leading the life of a successful married woman and leader of small-town fashion, wearing exquisitely fitted diaphanous blue dresses and elaborate hairstyles. For these I was despatched to Maitre Jules Paschal in Brook Street who himself personally cut, shaped, washed, set, dried, combed, did this, did that, and then with a triumphant flourish displayed the result of his activities. A cold rigor came over me as my incredulous eyes met the glass.

"I don't look like *that!*"

"*Now* you do, Madame," corrected Maitre Jules, worshippingly surveying the rococo machicolations of my new hairstyle.

"But it's atrocious! It's intolerable! I can't go around like that! I look exactly like a lemon meringue pie!"

"Now, Madame," he chided in his phoney Franglais, "it is very beautiful, *au contraire,* very becoming. Madame does not look in the very least like a lemon meringue pie but, quite the reverse, most stylish, ravishingly chic, *absolument comme il faut.*"

"Even at the studio I can't believe they'll like it," I muttered, poking at the cendré-fair contortions, resolving to get my head under a shower at the very first opportunity and eliminate all those bouncy silvery curlicues. I felt like an Oxford Street store, decorated for Christmas.

"They will rave about it," pronounced Maitre Jules, and he was right, of course. Worse, I was obliged to live with this hideous embellishment through five episodes. Several times I rebelliously did try to wash it away under the shower, but I might as well have tried to wash away a Henry Moore statue; Maitre Paschal's work was equally impervious to water and shampoo, returning with lively, steely resilience to the shape in which he had cast it.

I suppose spies and criminals become inured to living incognito, wearing always an appearance, an identity that isn't their own. Perhaps at last, after years in disguise, you lose track of your original shape and aspect altogether; or it ceases to have any significance for you. We live in a fluid universe and we are, I suppose, about seventy per cent our own creations: likenesses, images that we have contrived from our basic bodies with the help of paint and dye and woven materials; just collages, really.

The trouble was that I had been accustomed to my own invented image, felt comfortable in it and approved it; walking around all the time in disguise like this I found really disconcerting. Encountering, in bar mirrors, in shop windows, in my own bathroom glass in Notting Hill, the image of this fantastic stranger, my first response, every time, was to mistake it for some third party and search again in startled dismay for my own lost reflexion. Over and over again it was like the shock of that dire moment in Schloss Dracula where poor visiting Jonathan observes for the first time that his courtly if peculiar host has no reflexion in the glass. I felt that my true self had been spirited away and some opulent extra-terrestrial alien left in substitute. That feeling was repeatedly confirmed when friends failed to recognise me in the street, or colleagues in the offices of Pyramid TV. Even if I greeted them, people were slow to respond.

"Good *God,* what have you done to yourself, Cat, I didn't know it was you!"

Doubtful, embarrassed appraisals, conveying uncertainty as to whether I expected admiration or sympathy.

"I had to do this for Rosy; it's not what I would have wished myself."

"Oh I see, that explains it then. What an amazing change in your appearance, I'd hardly have thought it possible," they would respond nervously, as if looking for fangs to protrude from the corners of my mouth.

I have two natural dimples which normally I take pains to suppress. I have always thought there is something repul-sively cute about dimples, they are emphatically not my cast of mannerism. But Rosy was much given to dimpling. She rarely smiled; first, because the frightful creature had not the vestige of a sense of humour, and secondly because, endowed with such a hugely inflated sense of her own value, she found none of her companions worth a smile, certainly not her poor wretched husband once she had him stapled down. "The lovely curves of her face looked good-tempered enough without smiling," it says about her. *Ugh!* As if she charged for her smiles by the second. So, in civil life, I practised winding my head about on my long neck and just faintly displaying my dimples at people, males mostly. It certainly was an eye-opener to discover how different were the reactions to this technique from those evoked by my normal behaviour. And the new hairstyle in itself brought a whole series of unsought, unwonted encounters with strangers. Men came up and spoke to me in trains and buses, asked if they had seen me on telly, offered in pubs to buy me drinks; I was both fascinated and alarmed by this alter ego that I had acquired willy-nilly, and began, in a bemused, nervous, superstitious way, to wonder whether in time Rosy would take me over entirely. Plato says something of this kind, Masha once told me.

If Masha had still been alive . . . But she wasn't.

At the start of the part I had been objective about Rosy; just worked hard at getting under her skin. Then I began to loathe her, because I knew her so well, because she was so destructively successful. And then last of all, I grew to feel sorry for her because, poor shallow egotist, she was never satisfied, like the Fisherman's Wife, always craved what she hadn't got, and messed up the life of a decent man in the process. By that time I had grown fond of her again, as one might of a fallible but accustomed friend.

There were many reasons for the obsessional fervour with which I threw myself into the part. It was my first big chance. I had never done anything on such a scale before, and found it an exciting challenge. Further, I was buoyed up by the other players, all much better known, more experienced, more professional than I. It was like a tennis match against first-class players; one's own game can't help improving.

I became specially friendly with two others in the cast: the first was Nol Domingo, the actor who played Will, a kind of secondary hero in the complicated plot. He was gay, which made him comfortably easy to get along with, handsome in a Latin style, quick-witted, great fun off the set, and a stunningly good performer on it. He'd done a lot of stage work, National Theatre, Shaw and Shakespeare, and this was his third or fourth big TV role. He taught me a tremendous lot about acting, in the scenes where he had to flirt with and then furiously reject me. Another of my mentors was Sophie Pitt, a middle-aged actress with a good minor role as an aristocratic, snobbish, sharp-tongued clergyman's wife; she had a splendid ravaged tragedy-queen's appearance, just right for the part, and, by her excellent unselfish acting and shrewd good nature, made herself greatly valued during the weeks of rehearsal. She possessed a gift for pulling the group together, making a homogenous unit from a randomly assorted gang of people who met at odd intervals and intermittently. The plot structure of *Rosy and Dodo* is built from a leisurely novel about class-conscious Victorian provincial society, where the County never mixed with Trade, or Trade with Professional, or Professional with County, except when called in for advisory purposes; which meant that for quite a while the action was carried forward by separate groups who did not begin to intermingle until three quarters of the way through the story. Only one figure, that of my husband the doctor, well born but not well off, mixed freely with all three groups and formed a link between them. He, my husband, was played by a rather moody taciturn character called Mike Fourways. Mike was a capable actor, our scenes together went well enough, but off the set I felt I knew him not at all and found him unapproachable; the only person he talked to was the middle-aged actor who had the part of Dodo's husband. The most distinguished member of our group, he had played Hamlet in every major city of the world including Khatmandu.

So I hurled myself into the identity of Rosy, wrote to Fitz, cheerful letters, not too often, and took pains not to let him gather any idea that I missed him acutely.

Shooting the serial took longer than expected, partly because of the electricians' strike, partly because of the seasons. Winter, spring and summer all had to be displayed in the outdoor sequences. Because of the strike we lost a chunk of summer and had to wait till next year to replace the missing scenes. Several different country locations were needed, a farm, a village church, houses ranging from stately to humble. For these purposes Lord Fortuneswell—a recently created peer, who sat near the apex on the board of Pyramid TV, was active in the Arts Council and, besides that, owned a small but successful publishing house—had helpfully lent us his manor in Dorset.

By rights, the exteriors should have been shot in the midlands, but no one looks a free manor house in the teeth, and the style of Knoyle Court, non-committal Queen Anne, could have been found anywhere and would do well enough. The thirty-acre estate provided a church, a hamlet with almshouses, and a couple of farms, all in Fortuneswell's gift. The gardens of Knoyle Court, with lofty yew hedges, paved walks, and terraces, were well suited to our needs. I found them gloomy myself, but I suppose it would take a brave spirit to chop down dozens of two-hundred-year-old ancestral yew trees. Lord Fortuneswell himself was not in residence, which made for greater comfort and freedom. He had left for the Antipodes to look into the possibility of buying a newspaper chain; he was one of those busy-bee tycoons, I gathered, always hunting for new ways to add to their millions.

"What's he like?" I asked Sophie Pitt. She had met him because *My Cue,* her volume of theatrical memoirs, had been published by Obelisk Press, his publishing firm.

Sophie drew in her chin, a trick she has, and looked thoughtfully down her long nose and high-boned, high-coloured cheeks.

"Very unassuming," she said slowly. "Seeing him for the first time you'd never guess he was a millionaire. Rather fanatical he looks—a fanatical country squire. You'd expect him to be mad keen on preserving the lives of badgers or protecting Small Blue butterflies. Or at least," added Sophie, who is nobody's fool, "that's the impression he wants to create. Corduroy suit, open-necked shirt, desert boots; he looks thirty-two, really I believe he's older, but still the Young Wonder Boy on the Pyramid board. When you look again you notice that the cord he's wearing is of superb quality and his boots are handmade. He looks as if he spent his days planting rare orchid bulbs."

"And? How does he spend his days?"

"Making more money," said Sophie. "Still, I expect you'd like him. You couldn't help it."

Fitz would see through him at a glance, I thought. Fitz has very strong views about millionaires.

Knoyle Court seemed pleasant enough: not ostentatiously stuffed with Chippendale and Romneys, just comfortable country-house furniture and harmless nineteenth-century watercolours, many of them painted by ladies of the family. I gathered that he, the owner, spent next to no time there; he had a penthouse in Battersea, a chalet in Switzerland, a palazzo in Florence, and a yacht. The Dorset house had been left him by a friend, one of those unconsidered legacies that happen to millionaires. If I were bequeathed a manor in Dorset the whole pattern of my life would be changed to embrace it, but by him it passed almost ignored. And yet it was a handsome house, with some character. I could easily have become fond of it. Only twenty miles, too, from Yetford, where I had passed the latter portion of my childhood. One morning, when they were shooting Dodo's scenes and I was not required, I borrowed Sophie's mini and made a sad little pilgrimage to the big nineteenth-century vicarage where we had lived, and said another good-bye to my mother's ashes.

Coming back I took a detour through Dorchester and called in at the Ludwell Hospital to inquire after old friends and enemies. But seventeen years had passed, the place was changed out of all recognition, and the only face I knew was that of Kerne, the porter. Hospital staff ebb and flow with hectic speed because the work is so taxing; even Sister Coverdale, my old bugbear, had gone, elevated to be Matron at a big modern hospital in Bournemouth, Kerne told me.

"Hundreds of hospital cases in Bournemouth because all the old trouts move there when their husbands retire or die, so there's plenty fancy illnesses," he told me with relish.

"Sister Coverdale will be in her element." How easily I could remember the voice of exasperation broken free of all restraint in which she had said to me, "Smith, you wouldn't make a nurse if you stayed in this hospital till the year two thousand. I honestly can't imagine what you should take up as a career; all I can tell you is that nursing is the last thing you should ever have attempted."

That was because I fought against the rigid rules enforced in the kids' ward. Sick children must be firmly disciplined, Sister Coverdale said, or their treatment can't be carried out properly. Maybe she was right. Children's wards are where young trainee nurses are broken in, because if you can stand it, you can take anything. But it turned out that I could not take it. I was constantly in a rage over what seemed to me inhumanity and stupid, thick-skinned inflexibility; either that or I was passing out cold on the floor.

"Oh God: Smith's fainted again," I was continually hearing as I came to on the pale green composition tiles among chromium legs and rubber wheels. Smith was the name I had adopted then, Mars-Smith being too much of a mouthful for the hospital staff. But Cathy Smith is a hopeless name for the theatre, you might as well call yourself Miss Blank Blank; besides, there were half a dozen others on the Equity roster when I applied, so I reverted, for stage purposes, to Masha's maiden name, and called myself Cat Conwil.

Oddly enough, I haven't fainted since those days.

Though glad to escape in most ways, I felt sorry and ashamed at being defeated by the demands of nursing. As a discipline, it interested me. Passing the exams was no problem. I guessed that Papa would have been disappointed in my failure, but he was off in his own realms by then, out of human touch. First, there had been the embarrassing incident in Yetford church. At the moment when he should have begun preaching one of his solipsistic sermons he began, instead, slowly and fumblingly removing his clerical regalia. Then, before the alarmed and startled eyes of his small congregation, he removed shirt, trousers, and the expensive thermofibron undervest that Masha made sure he always wore. Then, off came the thick socks and full-length thermofibron underpants. Then—but why go on? It was too disgusting and upsetting, for the congregation at least. Masha, I'm happy to say, took it in her philosophical stride. "What *does* it matter what people think?" was one of her maxims— But she did hate having to leave the big peaceful roomy vicarage at Yetford and the patch of blue squills under the cedar tree. They moved into a dismal little residence on the outskirts of Reading, funded in part by some trust for the support of ailing indigent clergy, and in part by me. Papa never noticed. By that time he was living on an imaginary desert island. "It is very inconsiderate of you," he would say crossly, "to summon me at this moment when I was contemplating the immensity of the Ocean." Sometimes the island appeared to be Bermuda, sometimes Iona. Masha chuckled about it, but I felt that this bizarre self-created liberation of his came particularly hard on her. She had always passionately longed to travel, to see Delphi, Rome, Santiago, but in the days when he would have been well enough, he was too busy to get away, and later their straitened means made travel out of the question.

Masha longed for wilderness. Brought up among Welsh mountains, she craved the Rockies, the Andes, the Urals, the Himalayas. One of the postcards she kept stuck up in the knife rack in the pantry was a painting by the nineteenth-century American, Bierstadt (Tasha had brought it back from a New York ILO conference): a view of a mountain, monumental, majestic, tree- and snow-clad. *"Oh,"* I can remember my mother sighing, "do you suppose that place *still exists?"*

I knew what she meant. Things change so fast now. You go back to a place, it has been razed, gutted, and high-rise monuments erected over its grave. One has a feeling of total insecurity, that this might happen to any loved thing: suppose, for example, that you picked up *Hamlet* and found that it had been completely re-written, as the city of Worcester has been disembowelled and rebuilt—that the original play had been lost forever? What a nightmare.

"Oh," breathed Masha wistfully, "if I had a car, and could drive, I'd get into it and drive away, on and on, and never stop . . ."

I think that was the only rebellious remark I ever heard her make.

I knew, though it was below the level of communication, that she was deeply disappointed when Papa gave up medicine and went into the church. For she hated waste, above all things. I'd had a sort of cockeyed notion that my becoming a nurse might redress this balance again. (Though whether it is better in the eye of God to drive a Bentley and take a pleat in somebody's cortex every other day, or preach to five rheumatic old ladies every Sunday in a damp village church, who can say?) Anyway after my second hospital fiasco I moved to London, took various jobs in department stores, found that earning a living is no problem if you are single-minded about it, which I was, because of sending money to Masha; and then by degrees I shifted into theatre circles. I discovered that I could make extra money by modelling at art schools, a friend at the Slade recommended me for a TV commercial, and I began attending night classes in acting. Oddly, my main driving force was Masha. Stout by now (on a poor diet of stodge, the best bits of meat always for Papa), solid, weathered, round-faced as a babushka, with a peasant's craggy, landscaped features, my mother would have seemed the very last person to nurture hopeless longings for a stage career. Yet she had been an active member of the university dramatic society at Cambridge, and gave talks on the Drama at women's institutes—talks which ought to have been way above the heads of her hearers but were presented with such lively humour that villagers flocked to them.

I was her fulfilment, her safety valve. She made no secret of her delight when I began making appearances on TV, even if it was only to press a tube of Molarbrite denture cleaner into the hand of my sceptical husband. Masha, utterly unassuming herself, was consumed with fiery ambition for me and longed for my name in lights on Shaftesbury Avenue. I tried to persuade her to transfer these aspirations to Fitz—but, though she loved him so deeply, it was hard for her to identify with the urge to write a treatise on the structuralist elements in Heidegger.

These and other thoughts of Masha made me sorrowful as I drove back towards Knoyle Court from Dorchester. I would be glad, I thought, when we finished location shooting and returned to the clatter and sociability of studio work in London. The emptiness and silence of the country remind one too forcibly of loss and loneliness, the haunting green landscape—and the landscape of Dorset *is* particularly haunting, the comma-like curves of those sharp little hills are set at improbable uptilted angles like the waves and volcanoes of Hokusai, the land looks as if it has been deliberately rumpled up by some almighty inspired fist on one of His more inventive days—all this ravishing countryside made me feel humble and sad.

A sharp clatter of gunfire broke out as I turned the car southeastwards towards Knoyle, reminding me that one reason for the landscape's idyllic emptiness lay in the presence of the Army, who had somehow got their clutches on vast acreages of ridge-land just north of the coast.

ROAD CLOSED TO CIVILIAN TRAFFIC, proclaimed

several signs on minor roads to my left as I drove seawards, and other signs, even more forceful, said KEEP OUT! UNEXPLODED SHELLS. Wildlife, they said, throve in these army-occupied regions; birds, badgers and wildflowers multiplied and proliferated. So perhaps it was of no importance that humans were not allowed there to strew broken glass, plastic, filthy paper, rusty cans, weekend cottages and trailers along the coastline; people have wrought all the havoc they can elsewhere, one should be thankful to the Department of Defence for sparing this area from their destructive presence. Armoured personnel carriers and target practice were things that foxes and primroses could come to terms with, as they could not with Homo Domesticus.

Steering away from the KEEP OUT signs, I bore westwards again, avoiding the road to Caundle Quay. Such a charming name, but I had been there once, and once was amply enough. The dismal desolation of Caundle Quay entirely justified any claims made by the Department of Defence that their use of the Dorset countryside was far more desirable than that of H. domesticus.

Caundle Quay ought to have been a coastal hamlet of seven houses and a pub, set snugly steplike down the zigzag windings of a brook which had carved itself a steep stairway through the folded cliffs to the sea. But thirty years ago a speculator acquired half a dozen fields at the top of the village and bought himself permission to put four hundred trailer caravans into them. The brook was now choked with filth from April to October; the grass and rocks by the sea's edge were grimier and more trampled than the pavements of Oxford Street; even in winter a squalid indestructible legacy of plastic, rubber, and dirty nylon rags festooned the brambles and hazel bushes for half a mile round the site.

I had gone there, long ago, with Fitz and Masha, thinking that the place looked inviting on the map; but it made her so sad and him so disgusted that the very name on the signpost now made me press my foot down on the accelerator.

How strange, how frightening it is that, for so many thousands upon thousands of years, people had lived in Dorset, in Iron Age and Bronze Age hamlets, had done remarkably little harm, dug a bit of metal out of the ground, made a few weapons, killed a few of each other, herded cattle, tilled fields, piled up earthworks, fought a few battles, but not to excess; the balance of man in his surroundings remained stable, even when the Romans arrived, even when Hadrian attacked Maiden Castle and broke open its defences. Even in the last two thousand years, slowly urbanising man made little difference to the green curvy landscape; it is only twentieth-century man, Homo moriturus, Homo in articulo mortis, who in his dying frenzy has done such terrible damage.

Why has it happened? What cancerous death wish made us multiply so fast, so wildly, made us begin inventing and creating at such a hectic pace, expanding, colonising, consuming, covering the ground with our dwellings and our detritus?

Thinking these glum thoughts, longing for the comfortable matter-of-factness that Masha would bring to the subject, or the calm logic of Fitz, I recalled that I had on me, as a kind of talisman, his last letter to Masha. I had phoned him in Cambridge, Mass. and begged him to write to her; he had complied but the letter arrived too late. I bore it as a luck-bringer, a link with them both.

"Beloved Masha," he had written in his clear beautiful hand, "I am writing to you from a bench in Washington Square, having hitched a ride to New York for the weekend. What am I doing in Washington Square (which still looks like the place Henry James knew, though it is not)? I am watching men with wrinkled faces play chess on stone tables. What else is going on? So much that it would take a four-hour documentary film to record it consecutively—and then all the open endings would have to be left out. Two huge fat police armed with huge fat guns are cruising in a huge slow-moving car, watching everybody. A desperate penniless drug user is roaming hysterically about, pleading 'Smoke? Smoke?' No one pays any attention. Drug peddlers in blue jeans, leather jackets and black glasses are ignoring him, standing in a loose, sinister group looking for custom. A man who might be Russian with a shock of pale grey hair and bushy beard sits under the stone Washington Arch playing a slow mazurka on a piano of which the case is missing. How did he manhandle the piano to that spot? What will happen if it begins to rain? A small crowd politely listen to him. He can't be heard except near at hand for, in the middle of the square, two different rock groups with amplifiers are kicking up a terrific racket. East of them, roller skaters are operating on a clear paved space, bobbing, bouncing, and wheeling exhibitionistically. A man in white leather kneebreeches is particularly expert. The skaters zip past each other as if they must collide, missing by inches, like water beetles on a pond; perhaps they wear bow-waves of air that act as buffers. A fat man in red breeches and jacket is balance-walking along a railing with a lot of bounce and waggle and arm-waving to conceal the fact that he is really very skilful. Dogs are everywhere and so are their turds; you would hate that aspect of New York, Masha dear, but you'd love the children who are completely fearless and candid, leaping intrepidly off the swings and climbing-frames, calling each other in clear uninhibited tones, very different from the quenched English children you so much deplore. Some are on skateboards. They are as stylish as the adults. The black ones are so beautiful they make one feel God made a mistake inventing the white races. A spotty young white man in a pink velvet shirt just strolled past me; he looked sixteen and he was saying earnestly to his girl-friend who looked fourteen, 'It's a strange thing, but my *father* gets on much better with my *son* than my *mother* does with my *daughter,*' and she was nodding sympathetically and comprehendingly. Shabby moth-eaten squirrels are shooting about, up and down trees and across the grass (which has an artificial crumpled neatness like a green doormat); some of the squirrels are black. They have hostile, mean expressions; you would not want to meet them at a disadvantage, they might hold you up to ransom. A sad black man just passed me, he was saying to nobody, 'It's *disgusting!* But never mind!' I think of the village of Yetford where we lived for what seemed half my life; more has taken place in this square, in half an hour, then happened in Yetford in twelve years. I wonder if the actual texture of life varies from one century to another? What do you think, Masha? Does time go at a different pace? Has it accelerated recently? If you were here I'd skip the discussion forum on German nineteenth-century philosophy and we'd have dinner on top of the 104-story World Trade Center and look at the view. I know you like a good view."

To read this letter in greater comfort I had parked my borrowed car in a wide gateway which led to a recently cut stubble field. The stubble was a mild ginger colour, interseamed with some fragile creeping green weed. In the middle of the field was a small dip, relic perhaps of an ancient burial barrow. To avoid observation from the road, I laid myself down in this dip. I was wearing, as it happened, a ginger-and-green dappled raincoat (for the weather, as usual in the south of England in August, was damp and misty), and so snuggled into the dip with an agreeable feeling of protective coloration.

Peacefully reading Fitz's letter to Masha, I fell peacefully asleep.

I was woken by a growing roar of sound so shatteringly loud that I thought I must be dreaming about Washington Square, and that the police had opened fire on the drug pushers. My eyes flew open. All they could see was sky. Instinctively I shrank lower in my burrow. At that moment the whole sky above me blackened, a tremendous gale of wind whipped the sheets of the letter from my hands, and the noise intensified to a level far beyond what was tolerable.

Before I could make any sense of these events, they were over. The sound diminished, slightly, the sky cleared again. A helicopter landed, with rotors gradually slowing into visibility, about twenty feet away from me. It opened its hatch, put down a doorstep, and somebody got out.

By this time I had sprung to my feet. I remember once sleeping on the cliffs near Yetford and waking to find an adder coiled asleep beside me; I shot from horizontal to vertical with about the same degree of precipitance as on that occasion.

A furious voice accosted me: "Of all the *idiotic* places to lie down! What do you think you're *doing?* I might have *killed* you! Lying slap in the middle of a field like that!"

With equal fury I retorted: "I'm idiotic? What about *you?* Couldn't you *see* me?" with shaking hands trying to retie the green scarf I had knotted over Rosy's hair.

"No I could not!"

"Why land *here,* anyway?"

"Why not?"

"And you made me lose a letter which was of particular importance—look—"

The rotor blades had not only whirled away the pages of my letter but shredded them; they were now blowing away over the distant bank which gave, I knew, on to cliff and sea.

My voice shook with rage, fright, and general upset; I really hated losing that letter.

"Serve you right," said he unsympathetically, "for choosing such a daft place to read it."

His voice, clipped into a fashionable upper-crust executive crispness, retained in the vowels just a smidgen of north-country flavour.

Turning, he glanced after the disappearing fragments of my letter. He was, I judged, something over six feet tall, dark-haired; he wore a sheepskin jacket and flying boots. Seeing the letter was gone beyond recall, he turned again to glare at me. I glared right back; we were thoroughly displeased with one another.

The first thing I noticed was his eyes. Anybody would notice them first, because of their size and unbelievable blueness. Wide-set, stony, huge, round as owls' eyes, they blazed at me like two circular holes drilled right through his head and out to the blue sky beyond. (For it had become blue while I slept.) I have never, on any other person, seen such an intensity of colour; they were luminous, incandescent, ferocious. Did they look slightly mad? Or just wholly detached? One imagines that successful religious leaders must stare about them with such fanatical dispassion. Above the eyes rose a high forehead crowned with a crop of thick dark hair. His ears were large, well shaped and delicate; the mouth—wide, full, but sharply indented at the corners—was compressed, as if he wanted to rearrange the line by pulling in the upper lip and flattening the lower. Perhaps it might show a trace of weakness if he did not take it firmly in hand? His eyebrows were thick and level, his nose jutted out formidably from a thin face with sharp-angled jawline.

Looking back at the eyes again I discovered they were deep-set under triangular eyelids. He wore sideburns, a current affectation which looked silly on the forward-thrusting determination of the face. The whiskers, I noticed, were faintly grizzled, though he seemed young, early thirties I'd guess . . .

"Anyway," he said, "what's a letter? You can always have it replaced. People always keep copies of letters."

He spoke with impatience; in his world people always did keep copies of letters. It had not occurred to him that there might be lost tribes or regions where this necessary precaution was omitted.

I shrugged. The letter was gone; I must accept that loss along with the rest; no use to argue. Putting aside my grief for later, I wondered who this bossy stranger might be? A head boy from Pyramid no doubt—judging by his manner and mode of arrival. Had he come to tell us that further funding for *Dodo and Rosy* had been withdrawn?

But he, meanwhile, was studying me.

"We know each other," he said abruptly. "We've met before—" now beginning to go through the usual Rosy routine.

"No we haven't," I snapped. "I haven't *been* anywhere before. I come out of a book."

It seemed unlikely that he had read it. Most unwilling to prolong this conversation, I stooped and picked up the paper clip that had fallen from Fitz's letter, put it into my purse, then walked swiftly back to my car, observing that a grey chauffeur-driven Rolls had now pulled in beside it.

"Sorry if I gave you a fright," I called over my shoulder, and then lost sight of him as I backed the mini and drove off down the lane. He had called something after me which I ignored. If I did not make haste I was going to be late for rehearsal. I took the quick route, in by the back drive of Knoyle Court, which led to a stable yard, kitchen regions, and the big servants' hall which we were using for a greenroom. I had to change into a riding habit.

We rehearsed and then shot the scene in which Rosy is thrown from her horse; that completed the outdoor sequences involving me. Dodo finding her elderly husband dead in the summerhouse had been done last winter. Now all that remained was a bit of indoor studio work for which we would return to town. So, as this was the last shooting day at Knoyle Court, we held a party that evening for the cast and technicians. Various other people were there as well: Randolph Grove, the director, the permanent staff of Knoyle Court and some tenants of the estate who had lent houses or gardens, a journalist who was doing a feature about the project for a Sunday colour supplement, and a couple of photographers who had come down with him to take pictures.

One of these, Joel Redmond, I had known from ten years back when, equally poor as church mice, both attending classes at the Polytechnic, he in photography, I in voice production, we went down in a lift together; he noticed a *Lamentations* record under my arm, made some remark about it, and so we got acquainted and took to having coffee together when we came from our respective classes, and then to attending Early Music concerts together in draughty churches; it was a while before he found out that the record I carried had not been for myself but a gift for Fitz. The acknowledgment to each other that we had only a limited tolerance for early music and draughty churches took our friendship forward a long step to the comfortable basis on which it had remained ever since. Joel was a highly gifted photographer; crowned heads and world-famous opera stars competed for his attentions these days; but he remained the same friendly unshaved, moth-nibbled-looking character that he had been when I first met him, with shrewd gargoyle face, tiny bright eyes like a fieldmouse, receding dark hair and skinny extremities. He was a boon to any party, as he could be very funny, had an agreeable singing voice, and a gift for jazz improvisation on the piano.

Joel had not seen me since my transformation into Rosy and was both appalled and fascinated by the change.

"Darling! God in heaven! How could they *do* it to you? I must say, it makes you look rather marvellous, in a disgusting way—like Blackpool Rock—hard and shiny and sickeningly sweet all through. Must be quite liberating?"

"Oh, it is," I assured him. "Now I'm used to the change I'm really enjoying it—like riding along on an elephant, you know, you can flatten anything that gets in the way. It's a winner for getting attention in crowded stores and bars."

"What you've always needed, sweetheart. Haven't I been telling you for years that you should take a course in Personal Aggressiveness? Now perhaps you'll shed some of that puritanical humility that has stood you in bad stead for so long. I'm going to take lots and lots of pictures of you and see they get published *everywhere*. Then people will forget you ever looked different."

He seemed genuinely delighted at my good luck.

"But what would be the point of that? When I'm going to change back into me?"

"Ah, don't do that yet, acushla," he said. "Stick with it a bit longer. Like maybe for ever."

And for the rest of the evening Joel devoted a conspicuous amount of attention to me, handing me ceremoniously in and out of the dining room where the buffet was laid out, as if I were Anna Karenina, flirting with me, engaging in a lot of Regency flourishes, presently demanding that I have my property harp fetched from the housekeeper's room and accompany him in improvised duets and songs.

I demurred a bit, but Randolph Grove had no objections. "The harp's insured to the hilt," he said, "and we've finished all the harp-playing scenes anyway, you can take it apart string by string if you want to, my dear."

So the harp was dollied in from the room where we had shot Rosy's family home sequences, and Joel and I improvised a music-hall waltz based on the minuet and trio from a Haydn symphony:

"When the bluebells were blooming in gay Bloomsbury Square
Oh how happy we were to eat our sandwiches there . . .
With the pigeons cooing
And the sparrows chirping
We were happy as the day is long

There was song
In the air!
Oh, when the bluebells were blooming . . ." etc.

We had everybody in the room dancing after eight bars.

It was a good party, and managed to assuage, for a little, the aching cavity of sadness that I carry at all times inside me.

"Just relax, will ya?" Joel muttered, his hands flashing over the keys of the servants' hall upright Bechstein piano. "Pretend the world is a happy place, can you not? You might just as well. It isn't going to make a jot of difference, in the end."

"I daresay you're right, Joel."

"Of course I'm right, you outrageous beauty." And he spread his hands and kissed his fingertips in histrionic ecstasy. Joel is Jewish-Irish. *Both* lost tribes, he says.

At this moment Randolph Grove tapped me on the shoulder. Naturally I had noticed him across the room, half an hour earlier, in conversation with my blue-eyed acquaintance of the morning, and assumed I'd been right in my guess that the latter was some high-up executive from Pyramid; now this was confirmed when Randolph said,

"Joel, Cat: Lord Fortuneswell would like to meet you both. He's come down to attend to some local business at Knoyle and spend the night here; very disappointed to find he's just too late for the shooting."

Grove spoke in that plummy tone which people adopt when they reveal their familiarity with some well-known person; Joel and I both reacted with the exaggerated ease and calm of manner which other people assume in these circumstances, just to show they aren't impressed.

Joel of course really *wasn't* impressed; TV personalities and millionaire peers were a trifle in his life.

"I remember taking your picture five years ago when you started up the Wessex Trust," he remarked kindly. "How's it coming along? What was the main project? To rescue some vandalised bit of coast?"

"Caundle Quay, yes," Lord Fortuneswell replied, equally flat in tone, as if the subject bored him; but I was interested and pricked up my ears.

"Caundle Quay? The cove where there's that frightful caravan site?"

"Trailer park, honey pie," said Joel, playing chopsticks with one hand and the Moonlight Sonata with the other. "You must march with the times. We all speak American now."

But Fortuneswell turned the searchlight blue eyes on me. Not an amp or a watt of their intensity had abated since the morning; amid the come-and-go of the party they shone like cobalt explosions.

"You haven't been to Caundle Quay then?"

Evidently we were to forget our little spat and begin on a new footing. That was okay by me; I hate bearing grudges.

"Not for eight or nine years and never again," I said. "The most depressing place in the world. Nothing would drag me back."

He smiled, which did nothing to abate the intensity of the blue stare, just added a kind of rictus.

"Oh, then you're in for a big surprise," he said. "Would you care to go over there tomorrow morning with me?"

I could feel Grove, beside me, register this like the click of a geiger counter.

Remembering that I was Rosy, not Cat (I was even wearing one of Rosy's dresses), I didn't bother about explanations or thanks, just wound my head about on my long neck a bit, dropped my eyelids over the blue lenses, flashed a perfunctory dimple, and drawled,

"Kind of you, but I can't, I fear; we all have to be back in the Battersea studio tomorrow by ten-thirty," and rippled an arpeggio on the harp strings.

"Come on, Joel, Cat! Play us another tune!" someone shouted.

The blue stare narrowed. Fortuneswell was not accustomed to having his invitations declined. Joel jumped up from the piano.

"Somebody else's turn to play! I'm thirsty. Come along, Catarina, let's top up. Can I get a drink for you?" he asked with offhand politeness to Lord Fortuneswell.

But Randolph had already disappeared in the direction of the bar and, by the time we reached it, was holding four glasses of champagne. Parties at Knoyle Court, when graced by the presence of the owner, were conducted with style.

Randolph then took pains to be excessively, laboriously civil about the beauties and amenities of the house and estate, and how well it had served us on our location shooting. I could see that these civilities, obviously produced as a hint to Joel and me to mind our manners, cut no ice with Fortuneswell, who, turning his back on Grove in a dismissive and snubbing manner, said to me,

"When can you come down again to look over Caundle Quay?"

"Well, not for a while," I told him, meaning, Never. I had no wish to revisit the place which would be printed over with the images of Masha and Fitz and our lost (nonexistent) halcyon time. "What's there to see, anyway? Can't you just describe it *now?*" tilting my head away from him at a Rosy angle.

"Don't you know about it, Cat? Don't you ever read the papers?"

That was Randolph, anxious, unsnubbable, doing his best to play man-of-the-world, by assigning to me the role of brainless beautiful birdwit.

As a matter of fact I do read the papers for half an hour every morning, over my coffee, but it is true that the story of

Caundle Quay I had managed to miss. Perhaps it happened while I was doing the Boston mime.

"I bought the site and turned it into a Greek village," curtly observed his lordship.

"A Greek *village?* What a very *odd* thing to do. Why did you do that?" I lisped. "You mean, like Portmeirion—only Greek? How peculiar."

"Why did I do it? Because it was absolutely disgusting the way it was. Filthy. Squalid. Unsanitary. Verminous. An eyesore."

"But why Greek? Why not just Dorset?" Absently, I removed a paper clip from the bar.

"Because I knew a Greek architect and some Greek builders who were interested in the scheme. Because I had visited a Greek island, Castelorizo, where they had derelict villages to give away. The inhabitants had all migrated to the mainland. So I bought one, lock, stock and barrel, and transferred it to Caundle."

"A truly heroic conception," said Randolph Grove, working terribly hard at it.

"Did the Greek village fit the site?" I asked. "And what did you do with the indigenous inhabitants at Caundle? There must have been *some?* Those trailers weren't all inhabited by summer tenants. Didn't they mind? Like the Palestinians?"

"Ninety percent of the caravans were used by summer visitors," Fortuneswell answered coldly. "For the rest, I found alternative accommodation. I can assure you that nobody suffered."

"Oh *naturally* not," I told him on the breath of a polite ironic yawn.

Baiting him was the sort of game I hadn't played for a long time and I was enjoying myself. I caught a sympathetic gleam in Joel's eye, but he shook his head at me and remarked,

"It's remarkable how well the Greek architecture fits into the Dorset landscape—the walls and the steps and the white-washed cottages—"

"Oh, you've been there, Joel, have you?"

"Took a batch of pictures for *Country Life*. They're using them in April, time for Orthodox Easter."

"There's a church too, then? Byzantine?"

"Oh yes," chipped in Randolph, "and Lord Fortuneswell even imported a Greek priest, didn't you, Ty, Father Athanasius, is it?"

"How very thorough, sir," said Joel.

"Do call me Ty, everyone does," commanded our host, a shaft evidently aimed at Grove, and he fetched up a repeat order of Moët with one snap of the fingers. I could see that even in my role as Rosy he left me laps behind when it came to obtaining bar service.

Then, turning to me, he went on as if the other two were not there. "I did of course try to persuade the Greek inhabitants to come with the village. But they had their hearts set on Rhodes and weren't interested in Dorset country life. The priest wanted to stay with his church, though."

"Is it finished? When did all this happen? Who lives there now?"

Really I couldn't help being interested. If only Masha were still alive! She'd be absolutely pumping him with questions. So would Fitz. Already, of course, I was planning my letter to him.

"It's almost complete now," said Lord Fortuneswell, or Ty, as he had asked us to call him. James Tybold, I remembered his name was. Child of some north-country magnate? Who had made good and migrated to warmer climes? The son James had shrewdly and cannily deployed a chunk of inherited money—from electronics? Computers? Pinball games?—and used the resulting accretion of wealth to lever himself a peerage from the last government but two. By doing something benevolent for the arts, was it? Perhaps the Caundle Quay affair had earned his good-conduct stripe?

"Who lives there?" I asked again. "Dispossessed peasantry from the land the Army has taken? It's too bad you can't get that back as well."

"Most of the houses are still empty." Fortuneswell ignored my remark about the Army. "What I plan is to let accommodation at peppercorn rents to young artists, or people who need peace and quiet to get on with some project."

Not a particularly original idea, and (I thought) probably one of those schemes doomed to failure from their inception. On paper it looked good, but the artists would fail to pay their peppercorn rents, would quarrel with one another, and probably leave the place as squalid as the caravan dwellers had done. But it would doubtless put its originator in line for a Nobel Prize, or something of the kind, and I said politely that it sounded quite, quite brilliant, a truly capital notion, what a lucky set of artists they would be. Who selected them? I wondered, and added idly,

"I just hope there isn't some old lady banished from her caravan who lays a hoodoo on the whole enterprise"—and what put such an idea into my head, who can tell? A touch of telepathy perhaps; if there is such a thing as telepathy it must work in a relevant way just *sometimes.* "Remember that North Sea Gas town they built on a Shetland island, and it turned out that some evicted monks had laid a fearful hex on the place a few centuries earlier, and they had endless trouble with the rigs and all the machinery. In the end they had to fetch in an exorcist."

"*I* heard of a terrific curse only the other day," said Joel, cheerfully following on my lead. "That actress Polly Lasceles who ran off with somebody's husband—"

"Nat ODell the singer—"

"Right, and so his wife Kitty ODell sent Polly one of

those boxes of five thousand printed labels, Polly Lasceles, c/o Nat ODell, 15 Powdermaker Mansions."

"So what's wrong with that? A kind thought surely?"

"She'd put a curse on the labels. Five thousand of them! Kitty only stayed with Nat a week in Powdermaker Mansions, and then they quarrelled and he kicked her out. Never used a single label."

"What a good idea. I must remember that," I said, thinking that just at present I didn't have anybody who needed cursing. Perhaps, long ago, I should have laid a curse on Papa? Or perhaps somebody *had,* and that was why he was the way he was? Curses must have unpredictable ripple effects, extending far beyond the immediate consequences.

Joel and I began swapping recollections of other notable curses and suggestions for effective new ones, laughing heartily at our frivolous ideas: at least Joel laughed heartily and I practised my Rosy dimple. A frigidity next to me conveyed that Lord Fortuneswell did not find the curse theme at all entertaining; he could have given Queen Victoria two rooks and still beaten her.

Randolph Grove was hopping from foot to foot and trying to lead the conversation elsewhere, but no one was paying him any heed.

However, at this moment we were joined by Zoë Grandison, the actress who played the part of Dodo. Dodo, in the story, is an earnest girl, very carefully brought up and educated, so wholly focussed on the pursuit of Good with a capital *G* that she continually makes an ass of herself. But of course you can't help liking her, because she means so well. In the end, even horrible selfish Rosy comes to value Dodo's goodness, and performs her one disinterested action of the book—but that doesn't make Rosy reform *herself,* oh dear, no.

Zoë Grandison's looks were just right for Dodo, nobody needed to do any transforming work on her in the studio.

She had huge myopic grey eyes, a pale heart-shaped face, and a cloud of glossy, dusky hair so long that she could sit on it. She washed the hair every day and in normal life it hung loose, so that as she walked it brushed her beautifully shaped little rump, which was generally encased in skintight jeans. I have seen susceptible males literally totter as Zoë strolled past them; she exuded an aura of sex powerful as garlic bread. Of course for the part of Dodo the sex bit was sub-dued; Zoë was an instinctively good actress who played from her id, not from her brain, and made Dodo into a dumb, ardent and touching cluck, always up to her neck in philan-thropic aspirations, and without the least idea of the powerful effect she has on others, notably the opposite sex. The choice of Zoë for that part was a shrewd bit of casting.

Randolph Grove hastily introduced Zoë to Lord For-tuneswell, with the air of a ringmaster tossing a propitiating and delicious gateau to a tetchy tiger.

But, strangely enough, our host did not seem to be propi-tiated, though Zoë batted her eyelids at him, smiled her faint smile, and looked down at her feet. It was a good smile, just a voluptuous curve of the lip; I wished I could have used it for Rosy but it wouldn't have done; Rosy is too selfish to be voluptuous. Joel had been right: she's peppermint rock candy all through, with the name Rosy printed on each layer.

Tiepolo would have gone for the soft mass of feathery hair impinging on Zoë's hard tight little curve of buttock. It possessed aesthetic besides sexual charm; but Fortuneswell seemed unaffected. Maybe he's gay? I thought, but that didn't seem likely, in view of the ravenous looks he was giv-ing *me*. Should I let him know that I am not a natural blonde?

Falling off a horse half a dozen times, even when carefully stage-managed, is not really a good preparation for a party, and after half an hour or so the various aches and bruises I had acquired during the morning's shooting began to make themselves felt. Breaking off an innocuous conversation about Fellini with Rosy's sublime disregard of other people's wishes, I said,

"Joel, my angel, if I have to be at the studio by ten-thirty tomorrow morning, I think we should be on our way." He had offered to drive me back to town. "I've a lot of things to do at home—my Hoya needs watering."

"That Hoya!" said Joel. "Hasn't it smashed its way into the flat above yet?"

"I wish it had. Then the Craddocks could water it."

Masha had given me a single Hoya leaf years ago. At first it grew slowly, a leaf a year, but then went into mathematical progression and would soon be into logarithms. My one-room flat was a jungle.

Fortuneswell seemed strongly displeased at our opting out, and made various alternative suggestions, such as that he should take me back in the helicopter tomorrow or lend me his Rolls and chauffeur later in the night, but all these I parried with Rosy's social imperviousness. I didn't at all want to miss the ride with Joel, my comfortable friend. So we said good-bye and slid away from the happy throng.

"You really scalped him," observed Joel, guiding his Porsche through the misty Dorset lanes. Joel may be moth-eaten and unshaven himself, but he goes for comfort and high performance in cars and cameras.

"Yes. I wonder why? Perhaps I remind him of his dear old mum."

Joel sniffed. But later, when I came to know Ty better, I wondered if there had not been an element of truth in this idle observation. If so, no tender feelings came into the connection; quite the reverse.

"My love, you could be Lady Fortuneswell if you play your cards carefully."

Joel's high-pitched imitation of the harpy mother in a current TV serial didn't fool me; he seemed to mean it.

"Isn't there a Lady F. already?"

"No, and never has been. And no, he's not gay; I'd know. Just been too concentrated on making his way, no time for fooling around."

"Well I haven't the least wish to be Lady F."

"Wedded to your career?" he said with light mockery.

I considered. I am not really wedded to the stage; having turned to it because it proved to be a way in which I could earn my living, I continued in the profession out of inertia. And, of course, it was fun; exciting occasionally; one met varied and lively people; but was that all I wanted for the rest of my life?

The truth is, I don't expect the rest of my life to last for very long. That, indeed, is why all the following events came about.

Besides, I had no education or training for anything else.

"Married to James Tybold, you'd be in clover," Joel observed dispassionately. "He's really loaded. Inherited one fortune from his dad, made another from some gadget, and then he was left a whole chunk to do good with by Whatshisname."

"Whatshisname?"

"It'll come to me in a moment. Founder of the pharmaceutical firm who made Accelerin and Ovaroids—*he* was loaded too. I daresay he had a guilty conscience because one of his products was taken off the market pretty smartly—it made women grow a third breast or something—that was probably why he left the money to James Tybold to do good with. If you married him *you* could have fun doing good too."

"Doing good has a disputed boundary with interference."

"Don't do good then," he said placidly. "Enjoy yourself for a change. What would you do if you could choose?"

At once I had a mental picture of the blue squills under the big cedar. I'd poke bulbs into the earth, I thought. Plant avenues. Build stone walls and train creepers over them. Lay out formal gardens furry with lavender and catmint, pounced with pinks and roses. Give back something of what we have taken and destroyed.

"Why are you so set on marrying me to Fortuneswell?" I said, without mentioning this thought. "Why can't I go on as I am?"

"I worry about you," was Joel's unexpected reply. "Specially just now. Got the notion that you're heading for a fall."

In a moment's wild temptation I considered telling Joel about the racking chest pains, the intermittent numbness in my right leg and arm, the forehead twitch, the mysterious ache in my neck and jaw . . . As a matter of fact, I thought, skipping the follow-up, his worries were unfounded; I'd hardly have *time* to do anything stupid.

Anyway, mightn't marrying Fortuneswell be that? A thoroughly disagreeable man, I had thought him, with all the Yuppie vices and no virtues. (Of course it was true he could afford to send me to the best clinics and consultants; but then, they say that you really get better treatment on the Health service. But I don't *want* to be cobbled up like an old sock, obliged to pretend gratitude for care that I'd prefer to do without. An overdose is quicker and tidier. But then, but then, what about Fitz . . . ?)

These profitless thoughts revolved in me as we sped on towards London.

I never confide my innermost terrors to anybody. Shame, I suppose, inhibits me. I lost the habit of confidentiality at the age of six or so, when even the self-centred child I was could see that Masha's daily worries burdened her too much without my adding to them.

I can remember the occasion: I was afflicted with a griping pain in my abdomen, probably due to overindulgence in greengages; we lived then in a little north-country rectory with one overburdened tree.

"Masha, I've got rather a bad pain."

"Oh, Katya, *have* you?" Her voice conveyed that this was the last straw. She was encamped outside Papa's locked study door, behind which he had for three days been wrestling with his soul in a mixture of prayer and hunger strike aimed, ostensibly, at grabbing the attention of God.

"Edred, my dear. Don't you think it's time you came out and had something to eat?"

"My pain's *really* bad, Masha," I repeated, clenched with urgency.

"Well, you know where the soda mints are, in the medicine cupboard. Suck two. And take your temperature—have you got a headache?" She laid a preoccupied hand on my forehead. "It seems cool enough. I wonder—they couldn't possibly be period pains? No, you are much too young for that . . . Edred, I do really think it is time you took a few spoonfuls of soup."

Slowly I crept upstairs to the medicine cupboard. "And try putting a hot water bottle on your stomach," Masha called after me absently . . .

In due course my pains abated. Pains mostly do. Either that or you die. And next time they recurred I knew better than to bother Masha; I found my own remedies. Studying to be a nurse was one. Even if that misfired, I found out a useful amount about the things that can *cause* pains; enough to supply me with symptoms for life.

Masha told me after Papa's death that only then did she feel at liberty to do much worrying about anybody else; he was a full-time job.

Oh, what a waste!

"How lucky it is that women have experience in looking after children," she said. "Or they'd never have the patience to look after men."

It seemed to me there was a fallacy there. Didn't the men come first? But she went on,

"Men are a much harder job, because you have to cope with their helplessness, but at the same time do that without embarrassing them by drawing attention to it. Because if the illusion that they are stronger and more efficient than women is taken away, they truly have nothing left, poor dears . . . The really *important* thing," she said, fixing me with her firm grey eye, "the really *important,* thing is not to let them feel guilty. Because once they do that, they've properly got you over a barrel. They'll expect you to feel sorry for them *and* sympathise with the pangs of guilt that assail them for neglecting you—or whatever it is they haven't done."

I didn't ask if Masha had studied other specimens of the male sex besides Papa, or whether he was her Everyman. When young she had been beautiful: photographs show her round-faced, eager, with a cloud of dark hair loosely piled in a chignon, longer than Zoë's, probably, when it was down, and great eyes sparkling with hope and enthusiasm. I daresay she was a bit like Dodo. And, like Dodo, she had to go and marry Papa.

Thank heaven she never had to worry about Fitz. They were in total harmony from the very first moment.

And if there were any worrying factors in *my* life, I kept them from her. It was the very least I could do.

JOEL dropped me at my flat, and next day he came round to the Pyramid studios and took reams of pictures of me which got into magazines, and, in a mild way, I became a celebrity. I don't know how long the celebrity side would have lasted under its own steam, because meanwhile James Tybold began courting me intensively. He telephoned three, four times a day, took me to lunch at the Ritz, and to first nights, openings, and private views; he sent me bouquets and potted plants and Liberty scarves and liqueur chocolates, and when I laughed at these conventional gifts he asked what I really wanted and I said a cheetah kitten and a bicycle. When he instantly produced the bicycle (handmade with fifteen gears, more suitable for the Andes than London; how Masha would have loved it) I quickly cancelled the request for the kitten because I couldn't think where it would fit in my one-room flat or lifestyle.

Being wooed was fun, I must admit. Never in my life had I been the focus of such attention and spoiling. Can you wonder that I enjoyed becoming the object of someone else's wholehearted, obsessive pursuit and admiration? And the prospect of enjoying this fun, this pampering, for life? Unlimited light and heat forever, never another worry about gas bills, phone bills; no more need to trudge to sales or buy clothes that don't fit and alter them; no more stingy anxieties about how to scrape through Christmas without ruinous expenditure? Never again look at the right-hand side of the menu?

Is it so surprising that in the end I said yes?

2

PEOPLE tended to think that Pat Limbourne and Elspeth
Morgan must be lesbians, but this was not the case. They had
simply known each other all their lives, and after Elspeth
retired from teaching, and Pat, having risen as high in jour-
nalism as a female could aspire to, had flung out of her job in
disgust and taken to freelance work, the two decided to set
up house together. Elspeth was a born spinster; cordially rel-
ished the company of the male sex but never had the least
wish to cohabit with one of them. At seventy she had so many
occupations and interests that the farewell to the school over
which she had presided for the last twenty years passed without the slightest twinge of regret: she corresponded with
learned societies, kept hens and goats, wove, gardened,
carpentered, made pots, lectured on these matters, dashed off
rather capable watercolours, and was proficient in karate and
archery. Her friend Pat, ten years younger, had once dipped
into matrimony for a short, harassed period, but her tongue
was too acerbic and her nature too masterful to render the
experiment anything but disastrous. After the divorce, various brief involvements proved sufficient; she preferred to re-

tain the males that she knew as friends, not lovers. By this means their inefficiency, dilatoriness, inability to reach decisions, laziness, volatility, messy habits, unpunctuality, and infinite range of psychosomatic infirmities need not be her responsibility.

As she once said to Elspeth: "Observant, intelligent men with a sense of humour are *so rare* that, if you come across one, the only thing to do is to cherish him like an exotic orchid; it would be asking too much to expect him to be capable or deedy; and I haven't time."

Elspeth merely nodded in reply; she was not given to garrulity, particularly when her hands were occupied.

Both ladies had adventurous, impulsive temperaments and greatly enjoyed a change. They dealt together harmoniously; a mutual fondness and strong respect outweighed the intermittent bursts of exasperation which the habits of each called out, from time to time, in the other. Elspeth was able to forgive Pat's slapdash untidiness, and Pat, Elspeth's enraging way of abandoning a day's dishes unwashed in the kitchen while she occupied herself outside, separating bulbs or sorting pea-sticks. Both had travelled widely and held down responsible jobs, both were capable administrators and enjoyed transactions with other people. After they set up house together Pat continued her freelance activities and sporadic forays into public affairs; it was on one of these that she ran across Lord Fortuneswell when both, due to previous connections, were involved in setting up a Dorset Youth Theatre trust. No particular liking was involved, but suave young tycoon and middle-aged sharp-witted woman acknowledged in one another an affinity, a kindred spark; thereafter they maintained a pattern of intermittent contact; Pat Limbourne directed the more intelligent of her TV and newspaper friends to Fortuneswell for interviews, and proposed him for several public and charitable positions; he put various opportunities in her way and, when he was looking around for administrators to run his Caundle Quay project, recalled Pat and her elderly friend.

They would be the ideal pair, he recognised, to live in a prototype house, function as caretakers and godmothers for the community, and present an image of good sense, domesticity and sobriety to combat any notion that Caundle Quay might degenerate into a nest of hippies and dropouts. No one who tasted Miss Morgan's brown bread, observed her flower beds full of huge peonies, or encountered Pat Limbourne's shrewd raking stare could entertain such a notion for more than an instant.

No scruple about uprooting two elderly ladies and entirely changing their way of life would impede Fortuneswell; he proposed the scheme to Pat, meeting her at a library opening; her imagination instantly kindled at the prospect of becoming pioneer inhabitant of a Dorset Creek village (pioneer, that is, apart from Father Athanasios, already installed) and, in the space of a ten-minute conversation, the whole arrangement was set in train. Pat's decisions were always made in this way.

"We are growing tired of Twickenham," she said. "Elspeth needs a shake-up now she's sold her school. And the neighbours are beginning to grumble about the goats. I lived in Dorset as a child—glad to go back there. Still have friends."

Elspeth received the news of their imminent departure from the house where she had lived for thirty years with total calm; she organised transport for the goats—"They will have a much better diet in Dorset"—transferred her favourite garden plants to pots for the move and, when she learned that the house they were to occupy was already supplied with traditional Greek furnishings, made arrangements to have her own rather good Victorian pieces despatched into store.

"We should have little Shuna come and live with us, don't you think?" she suggested to Pat. Shuna was a kind of adopted great-niece, orphan of a disaster-bent daughter of friends who had come to an untimely end.

"Why not, good idea," agreed Pat. "Caundle will be much better for her than that boarding school—she can run around in the fresh air and help with the goats. Glifonis, I mean; must try to remember to call it that."

With minimal fuss the two ladies transplanted themselves, Pat's only stipulation being that she must have a darkroom with a sink. An outbuilding was adapted for this purpose, seven-year-old Shuna was removed from her convent school and, until there should be a nucleus of other incomers' children large enough to justify a school bus to Dorchester, she learned her lessons with Elspeth who, of course, was amply qualified for the task. Shuna, a solitary, self-sufficient little creature, throve in the unusual atmosphere of Caundle/Glifonis, spent hours silently observing the operations of the Greek builders and could already have passed an examination in traditional Greek construction techniques; she explored the whole terrain of the village, such empty houses as were built and awaiting occupancy, and the neighbouring coastline; formed an acquaintance with Father Athanasios and his dim, richly scented, gorgeously decorated church; found her way down to the pebbly, fossil-studded beach, flew her kite, and talked to herself continuously.

"Is it quite all right for that child to talk to herself so much?" reflected Pat one evening, pulling off her gum boots before sitting down to a late cold supper. Neither of the ladies could be bothered to waste time on elaborate cookery. They lived on corned beef, cold potatoes and lettuce from the garden. Elspeth made a few loaves and a batch of scones from time to time.

"She doesn't talk to herself, but to the Toe tribe," corrected Elspeth, transferring the mud-clotted boots to the porch. Dorset and the Greek builders jointly provided an unlimited supply of red gluey clay, but a cobbled and marble-stepped main street was under construction. "Shuna's conversation is perfectly grammatical and rational; I don't see any cause to correct the habit. Besides, it keeps her in practice for the day when real companions arrive."

"Who are these Toes?"

"A large clan. Professor McToe, Archdeacon Toe, Colonel Toe, Sir Jasper Toe, Lady Emily Toe and their four children: Mercy, Percy, Chris and Bliss."

"I see." Pat reflected for a moment, then said, "No wonder the nuns were glad to see the back of her. Does she need a new calculator?"

"I got her one in Dorchester today. She is a thoroughly well-behaved, sensible child," Elspeth countered calmly.

"Well, it's a good thing Fortuneswell won't allow houses in Glifonis to have TV sets; she may have a chance of remaining so."

A FEW days later Lord Fortuneswell arrived on one of his periodic visits of inspection, landing by helicopter at the top of the combe through which the main thoroughfare of the village wound its zigzag course.

Carefully picking his steps, he crossed the builders' operational area studded with lumps of raw cement and piles of sand (the plot scheduled to be occupied, at a later date, by the village hall) and walked down to Number 2, Glifonis, the cottage occupied by the two friends and their adopted child.

Already, thanks to Elspeth's gardening expertise, the small paved forecourt in front of the house dazzled with pots of geraniums, begonias and some late lilies; a thriving young fig tree and a healthy vine were trained up a trellis. Underwear on the clothesline added a touch of Greek domesticity.

Elspeth Morgan owned several worn but good oriental rugs, and these she had brought with her since they were compatible with the Greek furnishings; two of them had been laid to air in the forecourt, and a child sat on one of them, making a careful intricate pattern of pebbles and tiny scraps of paper which she had laid in groups among the triangular birdlike shapes of the woven pattern. She was addressing her arrangements in a low, precise, authoritative tone.

"So, Colonel Toe, you will lead the attack through the Azure Gap. Your troops are arrayed behind you— On your toes, all of you. And toe the line," she added in a louder voice. "You must watch out for dragons—they are unfortunately numerous just there. Professor McToe, your camp is here, on the island. You can only escape by boat across the lake. Archdeacon Toe, you and the doctor must remain with the women and children. You had better hide underneath those hooks—they are great rocks, which may fall down on you if you shout. Sir Jasper, you must ride your faithful steed through the rocky mountain pass, here, to summon help from Gold Kingy—you have to pass dreadful dangers on your way, winged lions and three-tailed eagles. All around the edge of the lake are the armies of Black Marby. They have bows and spears and crossbows and rockets full of soap—oh, *look* what you have done!" she broke off to exclaim, admonishingly, to Lord Fortuneswell, who, as he ducked under the clothesline, had destroyed a large part of her dispositions by walking on them. He stopped, vaguely aware of the child's disapproval, though not of its cause.

"Can you tell me if Miss Limbourne is in, or Miss Morgan?"

Wholly unused to children, he did not welcome her presence; she had not yet arrived on his previous visits. He addressed her in a cold, constrained tone, being doubtful if she were of an age to reply rationally. She seemed too small, he thought distastefully—almost miniature in her proportions— a puny little creature with hair braided up on top of her head and a round face whose neatly defined features and large dark grey eyes surveyed the visitor with dispassion.

"They have gone down to the harbour; they will be back very soon," was her reply, delivered in a clear, self-possessed tone.

"I see. Then I had better go down and find them."

"You may stay here if you like."

"No, I'm in a hurry."

He had not the least intention of remaining to make conversation with the child. But as he turned to retrace his steps —destroying yet more of her battle deployments—she asked him:

"Have you ever been to a funeral?"

"Er—yes, I suppose so; yes, I have. Why?"

"How many people were there? As well as the dead person?"

"I—I imagine about a dozen. Do—"

"When do they put the dead person in the box?"

"I don't know. I didn't see," he said shortly. "Why don't you play with your toys and stop asking questions."

"You have made a *dreadful* mess of Black Marby's army. I shall have to arrange it all over again."

She looked at him, frowning, obviously waiting for an apology. Since none would have been forthcoming, it was lucky that the voices of Pat and Elspeth were heard at this moment, as the two friends climbed the footway.

"A sand beach would be more in keeping, I'd say—"

"But you have to be realistic, Bets—"

Pat's voice was clear and authoritative, Elspeth's clear and resonant. It was plain from whom the child had acquired her precision of diction. The two women greeted Lord Fortuneswell cheerfully and invited him in for coffee, but from this he excused himself, explaining that he had to be in Dorchester by eleven for a meeting of the Planning Committee. He hated impromptu hospitality.

"I just called to ask if you would keep an eye out for the dredger, which is due to arrive from Poole today; when it comes, could you phone me at this number? It should be here by now. You have to keep these fellows up to the mark."

He wrote on a card which he gave Pat. As yet the two friends possessed the only telephone in the settlement.

"Certainly." Pat was brisk. "No trouble, we'll be here all day. The rest of the marble slabs have arrived, you'll be glad to know, and Vassily is going to lay them tomorrow. After that, access to the harbour will be much easier."

"Yes, well, about time, too—" He was on his way back up the hill already, quick and absorbed in other matters; but he turned to give them the smile that was their due.

He flicks it on like a torch, thought Elspeth with detachment, moving off to test for dryness the tea cloths which she had laid along the cypress hedge.

"Who was that man, Aunt Elspeth?" inquired the child, occupied in careful rearrangement of her pebbles and scraps of paper.

"That was Lord Fortuneswell, who owns this land."

"The houses too?"

"Yes."

"He is a very careless person," said the child coldly. "He should not have kicked over my armies and never said he was sorry."

"He probably didn't notice what he had done. He's a very busy businessman with a lot of things on his mind."

"Just the same, he should have said he was sorry. Do businessmen have worse manners than ordinary people? And when I asked him if he had been to a funeral, he couldn't tell me when they put the dead person in the box."

"Very likely he didn't know. Grown-ups don't always know everything."

Miss Morgan paused a moment, however, thoughtfully, hugging the bundle of clean dry washing as she surveyed her ward over the top of it. Then she said, "Come along in. It's time for your glass of milk and your computer lesson."

Negotiations were already under way regarding Shuna's admission, when she should have reached age twelve, to an Oxford women's college; her mathematics were already well in advance of the sixth-form standard at the local school.

"YOUR friend seems to be coming down the hill again," observed Elspeth ten minutes later, glancing up the steep bank that formed their garden boundary, to the road above. "He must have forgotten something."

"Unlike him," commented Pat, skimming cream from a pan of goats' milk just inside the front door.

"Hullo—I'm back again; sorry to trouble you." Fortuneswell's annoyed twitch of smile conveyed that he was not sorry, and took it for granted that nothing he might ask would be less than a fitting tribute to him.

"What can we do?" inquired Pat with brisk goodwill.

"Some fool has dumped a whole mountain of rubble at the top of the hill. I can't get past it to my helicopter. May I use your phone?"

He was already making for it. "Asses!" remarked Pat with good-humoured vigour. "They're always doing things like that. They never think."

She clomped off to put on a kettle. By the time Fortuneswell had expostulated, listened, expostulated again, and finally crashed down the receiver, old Elspeth, her crumpled face full of benevolence, was proffering a small round silver tray which contained a cup of Nescafe, black as tar, and two homemade scones on a plate accompanied by a large lump of butter, a dollop of gooey strawberry jam, and a huge clot of thick butter-coloured cream. *"All* made on the premises," she chirped, beaming up at his thunderous countenance. "We're planning to serve teas, once the tourists find Glifonis—How soon can they shift the rubble?"

"Not for an *hour!* The man's round on the other side of the headland—oh—thank you—I don't—as a rule—" He glanced at the scones with disfavour.

"I know—I know—it ought to be ouzo and tsatsiki," soothed Elspeth, easily reading his thought—though what he really had in mind was Bath Olivers and Clicquot, "but sit down, do, and relax; it's all you *can* do."

"I suppose so." With a very ill grace he sat, sipped his coffee and made little effort to conceal his shudder.

"Since you have to wait, perhaps you'd care to go through the list of people who have applied for houses?" Pat suggested, pulling a typewritten sheet from a toppling pile of books and papers.

"Oh, I'm quite sure anybody vetted by you will be perfectly—"

"But still I think it would be best if you were at least familiar with the names."

"Oh—very well."

He was having hideous trouble with the newly baked scones, which were intensely fragile and crumbly, while the butter, straight from the monumental refrigerator, was hard as ivory. Elspeth watched his struggles indulgently. "If I'd only known you'd be here, I would have taken the butter out to warm up twenty minutes ago. All the equipment that you installed in these cottages is really *first-class,* Lord Fortuneswell," she assured him. "Every appliance quite the best of its kind."

"Good," he snapped, wrapping a lump of butter in crumbs and jam.

"You've forgotten the cream," remarked Shuna, gravely observant of his difficulties.

"It can go in my coffee."

"There's hardly room."

"Why aren't you having some?" he demanded in exasperation, trying to deflect her attention.

"It isn't my lunchtime," explained the child. "Also I'm not allowed cream. It makes me bilious."

Conscious that their unwilling guest's irritation was rising high, Pat began reading aloud the list of names.

"Llewellyn Pool and his wife and son."

"The architect? Shouldn't have thought he'd need to apply for a—"

"He's working on the V & A project, he wanted peace and quiet," Pat said quickly.

"Oh well—in that case. He's a first-rate architect, I believe. But wasn't there something about the son. How old's that boy?"

"Seventeen. He's got a place at Cambridge," added Pat with a frowning glance at Elspeth, who had opened her mouth to speak. "A brilliant boy, I understand."

"Very well. Just so long as there's no—"

"No eggs, no meat, no cheese, no coconut oil," remarked the child Shuna to herself in a quiet, distinct tone. She pressed a button of her calculator and surveyed the result.

"Hush, Shuna, we are talking business," Pat reproved her mildly. Looking at the list, she added, "Then there is Laurence Noble."

"The composer." Pat nodded. "He won't bring a whole troop of shrill boyfriends with him?"

"Only a dog, I understand."

"No dogs. Tell him I won't have dogs here."

Pat shrugged and made a note, remarking as she did so, "He's writing a life of Liszt and composing a sea elegy."

"Very well. Who else?"

"A couple called Goadby from the midlands. Their child died in an accident, they want piece and quiet to recover from the tragedy."

"Sounds all right. Next?"

"Sophie Pitt, the actress."

"Oh yes, I met her while they were shooting that thing at Knoyle. Wants to study a part, is that it?"

"Yes, she says now she's growing older she finds it hard to memorise unless she is off on her own."

"Okay. Next?"

"Chicot and Laura."

"The singers? Definitely *no.*"

Elspeth opened her mouth, but Pat frowned, shaking her head. Fortuneswell went on, "I *will not* have anybody here who has been *in any way* connected with drug abuse. Is that understood?"

"Can't say I blame you," Pat remarked, methodically crossing out the names.

"It *was* a *long* time ago. I believe they are quite reformed characters now—busy helping youngsters to resist the habit," Elspeth observed in a gentle tone, neither pleading nor extenuating.

"Just the same, no! There must be plenty of other applicants."

"Oh, plenty."

"If there's any problem with the preliminary screening, just get on to my office; they can provide all the research necessary." Fortuneswell glanced again, impatiently, out of the window. "Who is *that?*" he demanded testily.

A man was walking up the hill that crossed the window on a diagonal. As he walked he swept the paving from side to side with a birch broom.

"That?" Pat glanced out. "Oh, that's Odd Tom. He helps the Greeks. If it were not for Odd Tom, no cleaning would get done around here; at first they sent three men with a vacuum. Odd Tom can do in one day what took them a week."

Fortuneswell was not interested. "They *must* have shifted that pile at the top of the hill by now. I'll be on my way—"

"You should see our Greek pavement," Pat said.

He made a movement of wild impatience, but Elspeth chirped, "Yes, yes, show him the Greek pavement!" so, with visible lack of enthusiasm, he followed Pat to a side entrance. This opened on a small walled courtyard. Its floor, in faithful imitation of Greek village tradition, had been inlaid with black and white pebbles the size of walnuts, set in a conventional pattern of dolphins and wave crests. The wall enclosing the yard, cut into the steep hillside, contained a flight of steps which led up to a terraced garden, already planted with vegetables, a shed and another wall, topped with a cypress hedge bordering the zigzag main street.

Even Fortuneswell, eager to be elsewhere, could not help admiring the pavement.

"That really is charming. Excellent work."

"The pebbles come from Chesil Bank," Pat told him.

"Who did it? One of the Greeks?"

"As a matter of fact, no. It was Odd Tom, the man you saw before. We showed him a photograph and he soon picked up the idea. Our niece Shuna helped him."

"Odd Tom is a *splendid* character," added Elspeth, who had hobbled out by this time, accompanied by little Shuna, but Fortuneswell was already striding up the half-completed marble causeway without waiting to hear more.

"He's rather abrupt, isn't he," remarked Elspeth, looking after him. As usual, there was neither approval nor condemnation in her tone.

"Oh well. I'm sure he's never had to live with burst pipes, or clinkered boilers, or cars that won't start," said Pat. "People of his kind expect to get through life at a faster rate than we do. A heap of rubble in his path is probably something that hasn't happened to him in twenty years."

"Yes; and such people are likelier to die of high blood

pressure or heart disease in their late fifties than we are," observed Elspeth, who was seventy-five.

"Here's Odd Tom," said Shuna. "He just missed meeting the Lord."

"I daresay he passed him on the road."

Odd Tom came drifting down the marble steps like a sheet of waste paper. He had a curious sidelong gait, light, uncertain, without apparent purpose, tacking a little from side to side, but in the end steering himself towards some dimly proposed goal. Taking no notice of the ladies, who lingered in the sunshine on the front step of their house, he veered sideways and entered the small yard that he had paved, passing through the wicket gate at the right of the house. In the yard he stood meditative, feet apart, staring down at his work, with no discernible expression on his face. Odd Tom's mouth hung slightly open, as a rule, showing a slit of dark, for he had no teeth. His narrow little face was covered by white and gray stubble, which never seemed to grow any longer. A flat navy blue cap sat on his balding head; if removed it revealed a fringe of downy white hair at the back, above a brown seamed neck. He wore a dingy white turtlenecked sweater, the collar drawn up under his chin as high as it would reach; the inner edge of this collar was black with grime. No one knew where Odd Tom lived. In a barrel on Poole Harbour, somebody had suggested. Over the white sweater hung a greasy, ragged black windcheater; his thin old grey trousers were frayed at the ankle and his grimy white sneakers had holes in their toes. He exuded a strong and salty smell, like bacon or smoked fish. This smell was one of the things that little Shuna had first liked about him.

"Where's Arkwright?" she asked him now, and he nodded briefly backward. A gigantic tabby cat was picking its way with majestic care across the mudpatch which would one day be the front garden of Number 3, Glifonis.

"Did you see the lord?" Shuna asked Tom. "That man who just left? He was Lord Fortuneswell."

"Eye aw i' " replied Odd Tom. "Eh ee aw ouee." Due to the lack of teeth, his conversation was incomprehensible to most people, but Shuna understood him perfectly. She had helped him for hours over the paving of the court, and they talked all the time as they worked. It was she who had discovered the cat's name. "It was because his wife was called Jenny," she explained to Pat and Elspeth.

Odd Tom's wife had died, whether recently or long ago nobody was certain. He had drifted into the busy ants' nest of Glifonis one day, observed the work being carried out, and edged himself in little by little. He was not on the regular payroll but the Greeks had taken a fancy to him and paid him to run errands and perform bits of drudgery. His battered old bicycle lived up in the car park or down on the harbour. The cat Arkwright travelled perched in a fish basket at the back. All Odd Tom's tasks were performed with great care and diligence.

"Can you oil my garden tools for me, Tom?" Elspeth said to him now. "They get rusty so quickly in this damp sea air. I'll pay you a pound for the job, and I've made you a lardy-cake."

"Eye oo a' " replied Tom, and went up the steps to the toolshed, which contained a complete record of the friends' careers in sporting and outdoor equipment, from ice hockey to archery, from golf to rock climbing. Pat had been ladies' golf champion in Hampshire when younger, Elspeth had half a dozen silver cups for longbow and crossbow shooting; they were both early members of the Ladies' Alpine Club.

"Come along, Shuna," said Elspeth. "Back to your computer."

But Shuna said, "I've finished all those problems. You'll have to set me some more." And she added to herself, in a tone of temperate judgment, "That lord is rather bad. Even Black Marby wouldn't trust him."

Odd Tom, settling to his task on the ledge of land outside the toolshed, looked up the track that Fortuneswell had taken, and spat.

3

THE first few days of our honeymoon Ty and I spent rechristening each other and talking about our mothers. Or anyway, about his mother.

Venice in February? What folly! The climate is like an aspirin sucked slowly; harsh enough to make you shudder. The damp eats into you; you feel like an etching under construction. There is fog even inside the coffee cups; you want to rub your eyeballs every few minutes as if they were windscreens, the cats wear their fur in spikes, the pigeons huddle in crannies of masonry. Night falls immediately after lunch and the lights are so dim that you can't see across the narrowest alley. Silence too, everywhere; I had thought fog was supposed to carry sounds, but this is not so in Venice, where it acts as an insulator, like Styrofoam. If you set light to that fog, it would give off black, dense smoke.

All this suited Ty and me excellently well; we were, perhaps, somewhat ashamed of our precipitate wedding, we spent our days in bed, ignoring the cultural aspects of the city we had come to, and crept out only in late evening to dine in some tiny gourmet's retreat among a few baggy-eyed millionaires and their popsies; they made us feel wonderfully respectable, being married, which neither of us had been before.

At night we lay in one another's arms in the almost palpable dark, listening to the faint clang of distant bells, or to the wail of a boat feeling its way in from the Adriatic. Sometimes you could hear the wan water of Venice doing whatever it does. Lapping with low sounds by the shore. Sometimes nothing but the sound of torrential rain.

The faint candlepower lights, the murky dim air, the swirling layers of sea fog—all these things helped us maintain our mystery for each other. For we were still complete strangers. Our courtship had been conducted so swiftly, and most of it in public, that we had not the least notion of one another's real essence. We had seen nothing of each other's private lives. I had been ashamed to invite Ty back to my tiny room with the scrambling Hoya, the shell boxes marked "A Present from Ramsgate" and thin ancient rugs and posters on the walls and miscellaneous enamelware and books stacked on planks with bricks in between; while Ty, obviously, had so many domiciles that none could be said to represent his inner being. A rather formidable factotum called Parkson looked after all these dwellings, went on ahead and saw to necessities such as clean sheets and supplies of champagne, fresh coffee, and smoked salmon (Parkson was even here in Venice but keeping a low profile); a lifestyle such as mine, in which sheets were changed only every few weeks, when one had time to get to the laundrette, was evidently outside Ty's experience.

We groped around Venice like a couple of ghosts with invisible faces, touching only in bed, and then with our eyes shut.

Looking back, the astonishing thing seems to be that we did not collide sooner; dozens, perhaps hundreds of times we must have brushed past within a hair's breadth of each other, like bats in a cave. If we had spent the time anywhere else but in Venice—in Paris, for example, with its unsparing grey light and sharp outlines, or Manhattan, windy and angular—the showdown must have come far sooner.

Anyhow. On the first morning, Ty said, "I can't call you Cat. That's not a name—it's a theatrical label. You must have a real name—what is it?"

"You saw it. On our wedding certificate. It's Catherine."

"I never read forms unless Ponsonby tells me to," he said impatiently.

Ponsonby was another factotum: a lawyer who followed around with a briefcase full of agreements.

For a moment this struck me as odd—Ty's whole financial empire must be entirely strapped together by forms—but then I realised that, like Sherlock Holmes banishing from his mind bits of unnecessary information about the solar system, my new husband was obliged to concentrate on essentials, and limit his form perusal to the absolutely basic ones, terms finally arrived at after negotiations between colossal interests. Judged on such a scale, our marriage certificate would scarcely rate higher than a bus ticket.

"I shall call you Cathy," he presently announced.

Cathy? I didn't care for that. Masha's sisters, my aunts, had called me Cathy, I wanted no reminder of that lost incarnation. And other associations—Heathcliff, Thrushcross Grange—were on the gloomy side. But still, the way Ty said it—slowly, lingeringly, possessively—had power to run a prickle down my back.

"For that matter"—I was not fighting the prickle, merely prolonging the exquisite anticipatory pause—"for that matter, *I'm* not mad about Ty, which sounds like one of those pithy, manly, jocular epithets that men clap on each other in pubs and clubs—'known to his intimates as Cal, Mo, Tig'—I think I shall call you Jas."

It was like poking a finger into the mountainside and

starting off an avalanche. At first he said nothing. His face went totally blank. But in the silence that lay between us—we were on the Accademia Bridge just then, as it happened, looking down at a vaporetto swishing in through the gloom towards the landing place—in that silence, audible even over the chug of the boat, I could hear whole huge fragments of his personality detaching themselves, moving about as in continental drift; gulfs opened in solid land, opposing sides of straits clashed together.

"What is it?" I asked quickly, with an instinctive sense that if I didn't leap across at once to that receding shore I'd never be able to cross the widening gap at all. "Don't you want to be called Jas?"

"Let's not go into it here," he said, looking around, as if the entire staff of Pyramid Diffusion and all the shareholders of Fortuneswell Holdings and Obelisk Press were gathered about us on the high and empty bridge. "Come along, it's cold, it's wet, let's go back to the hotel."

Our hotel, not large, was so luxurious that it seemed almost a sin to step outside it. Byron probably stayed there, and the Sitwells, and Frank Lloyd Wright. Among the current guests we seemed the only pair who were not minor royalty, but we saw little of the other inmates, only occasionally encountering them by the creaking gold-and-velvet-lined *ascensore.* We all, naturally, breakfasted in our suites, where champagne was served with the orange juice as a matter of course, and little flasks of grappa nightly appeared on the bedside table, left by the chambermaid when she frilled out one's nightdress into a decorative garland. (Thank heaven Joel, good friend Joel, had for a wedding present sent me from Paris, where he was taking pictures of Mme. Chirac, six outrageously exquisite Campanillana nightdresses, Chinese silk and Valenciennes, so that, if the rest of my wardrobe was hopelessly inadequate, at least in the nightwear department I was properly equipped and able, if I had ever encountered her, to look the chambermaid in the eye. In fact I never wore them.)

Now, Ty practically hurled me onto the bed, which, of course, was ducal in size. Our lovemaking had a decided element of hostility about it. We flew at one another like wild beasts. But liberating, oh yes. *A l'outrance,* no quarter. It does, as they say, take you out of yourself. I used to think of those deathbed reports, on record from people who have been fetched back at the last gasp, at the moment of dissolution, how they say they have found themselves detached, hovering six feet above the bed around which doctors, nurses, and relatives frantically work to avert the dying process; well, in just that way, many and many a time did I seem to be hovering, disjoined and abstracted, several feet above the enseamèd couch where Ty and I fought and grappled. I wonder if he felt that too? So many areas of his nature were sealed up in watertight compartments that it seemed not improbable. But that was one question I never asked him. Among the many.

After midnight, when we were lying, spent and tranquil, listening to the rain falling like a whole skyful of gravel into the canal outside, I returned, with some rashness, to my original point: "Why mustn't I call you Jas?"

So then he told me the story of his childhood. Or some of it.

"My parents were horrible people. I can't remember a time when I didn't despise them."

"Why? Who were they? What did they do?"

His father, it seemed, had been that Brighton police chief responsible for the tracking down and ultimate arrest of the woman who came to be known, in the late forties by the tabloid press, as Acid Annie, because of the things she did to her six husbands. So far no harm, though one can see that having a policeman for a father must impose all kinds of extra strain. Like having a clergyman. But then Tybold senior had retired, and sold his memoirs to those same tabloid newspapers for an enormous sum. There was a certain amount of outcry at this from the more serious press, and from people who were personally involved in his reminiscences, but it seemed that legally he could not be stopped. James, by now at prep school, began to notice the adverse reactions of his teachers and schoolmates; later on, at a minor public school, it was a great deal worse.

"Tybold is not a common name, do you see; they always made the connection. I was treated like a plague dog. That was when I decided to get myself a title, so as to cover up the name with another."

"It didn't occur to you just to change your name?"

"That would have been cowardly."

Well, one had to respect him.

"Where was your father, meanwhile?"

"Oh, he had long since gone off with Mother to live in a tax dodgers' haven: Jersey at first, then they moved to Malta."

"You never told him how you minded what he had done?"

"Tell my father? You must be joking. Anyway, it was done, he had declared himself: a heartless profiteer who made a pile out of other people's guilt and misery; who contradicted all that his career as a cop had seemed to represent. Police are supposed to be our guardians, aren't they? He had demonstrated his cynical disbelief in all that."

"What was he like? Your father?"

I knew Ty's parents had died some time back, killed in a motor accident, driving on Italian mountains.

"Like?" Ty looked bleak. "Soap-faced. Sanctimonious. He was a horrible man. I loathed him. *And* my mother. Unlike our neighbours in Jersey, who at least made no pretence about the fact that they were there to get the most out of their money and have a good time, Dad and Mother seemed permanently angry and guilty. Mean as hell, too. Stingy. My father had a queer habit of always looking on both sides of a pound note before handing it away, as if it might have cheated him by being worth ten pounds on the underside. He'd spend ten minutes selecting the cheapest item on a menu, and then ten more, inching his way through the bill to make sure not a penny had been added. And they were disgustingly righteous. Evangelical. On at me, all the time, about right and wrong, good and evil. Yet Dad despised the government—whichever party was in power, Labour or Tory, it made not the least difference to him—he detested any form of authority, automatically assumed it to be corrupt. He despised and mistrusted all laws, all justice, read a crooked motive into any piece of behaviour. My mother was exactly the same, they were perfectly matched. And they both disbelieved, flatly, as a matter of course, in anything they were told or read."

"How dismal." And how odd, I thought, that Ty had turned out so different from his progenitors. Simple, I was, at that period. But a honeymoon is not an ideal time for balanced judgment.

"You think I'm making this up," he said angrily, "that I'm exaggerating, that such a pair couldn't exist. You ought to have met them! You wouldn't have a single thought in common with either of them. You'd have nothing—simply nothing—to say to each other. For a start, they totally disapproved of acting, films, plays, they never read fiction. Dad didn't read books at all, ever—only the newspapers. He thought books were frivolous luxuries, and misleading, at that. Mother read biographies of well-known people. 'I only like facts,' she used to say. 'Don't fancy made-up stuff.' They made me learn the Bible—from age four on—I had to learn and recite it, ten verses a day. Do you know how many verses there are in the Book of Genesis? One thousand, three hundred and thirty-two. At one time I could say them all. By age twelve I could recite the whole of the Old Testament, including Joel, Habakkuk and Zechariah."

"Must have been good for your prose style. And your memorising capacity. Terribly useful, too, when you can't get to sleep."

"Oh, *don't* always look on the bright side," he said furiously. "Father used to beat me with a slipper when I forgot, or made a mistake."

"How did you *survive?*" I asked, riven by pity.

"Then, when I got to boarding school"—the avalanche was really pouring down the hillside now—"when I got to school (it wasn't a good school) I had far less pocket money than the others in my form, though Father was probably richer than any of the other parents. He'd invested his newspaper payments shrewdly in an electronics firm, and then he bought a chain of shops, Asteroid Radio, you've probably seen them, there's one in every High Street now. I didn't know he was rich, of course. They told *me* there was no cash to throw around, Father had retired and was living on his pension, and I must on no account be extravagant at school. Christ, I didn't dare even take a bun or glass of milk at breaktime . . . And if I asked for extra lessons, music, art, tennis coaching, it was always 'No, how can your father possibly afford that?' I longed for drawing lessons, they did have quite a good art master at Morecambe, but it was extra, Father wouldn't think of it."

I'd noticed Ty glancing askance at small drawings I had made, in a pocket sketchpad, of people and buildings in Venice; now I understood why that irked him and resolved to do no more. Or at least not in his presence.

"Lies, of course, my parents regarded as a direct message from the devil. If I was caught in a lie, I was savagely punished."

"How?"

"No pocket money for a month. Mouth washed out with

soap. Made to mow the grass in front of the house with a placard that said LIAR in big letters on my back."

"Suppose it happened to be winter?"

"How do you mean?"

"No grass to cut."

"Then I just had to walk up and down," he said impatiently.

"I could see why they had such an abhorrence of lying," he went on after a few minutes' frowning inspection of the past, "because they were both so completely unimaginative that lies, invention, would have been an impossibility for them. Mother didn't even really like the parables in the New Testament. It was her opinion that Christ would have done better to stick to plain facts—though of course she didn't put it in so many words. The ability to make things up terrified her. *Naturally* I had no storybooks. Even going to the public library was suspect."

"Did you have any friends?" I said, aghast at this story.

Only then—astonishingly for the first time—did it occur to me to wonder whether Ty had any friends *now,* now that he was grown up—was he part of any group, did he have confidantes, boon companions? Our relationship had been so sudden, and so exclusive, we had dropped so completely from our own worlds into a kind of no-man's-land, that I had formed no picture of the kind of people who might be his associates.

All that, I supposed, must be faced on our return to real life. Not just yet.

"I did have *one* friend—a boy called Lyndhurst. He used to help me with my English compositions, which I found impossibly hard. Naturally I'd not the least notion of how to set about them. In return I helped him with his maths."

"What was he like, Lyndhurst?"

"A marvellous liar. That was what I admired about him. At the flick of an eyelash he could bring out the most amaz-

ing, plausible stories—plausible just because they were so
wild, one would never believe they had been invented on the
spur of the moment. 'What were you doing out of bounds,
Lyndhurst?' 'Well, sir, we saw this truck drive past and it
went over a bump and a tombstone bounced out and fell in
the road; the driver didn't realise, he drove on, and there was
this tombstone with an inscription "To darling Mum and
Dad," we thought someone would be waiting for it.' I was
never allowed—of course—to have friends visit, but
Lyndhurst's parents spent a holiday in Jersey one summer,
they met Dad at the golf club and brought their son to our
house, and at first Mother *believed* all the things he told her,
she listened with her eyes starting out—"

"Then what happened?"

"Oh, Dad played golf with Lyndhurst senior and discovered that none of the stories were true. All hell broke loose,
naturally, I was forbidden to see him again. I went on being
friends with him at school—they couldn't control that—but
their attitude to Lyndhurst really slammed down the guillo-
tine on any possibility of my having a decent relationship
with my parents."

"Where is Lyndhurst now? Are you still friends?"

"He was killed. In a potholing accident a year later," said
Ty shortly. "Trapped down in a black hole hundreds of yards
underground. He was there for two days and drowned by a
flash flood before they could get him out. Mother said it was
God's judgment on him."

"How *horrible.*"

"I have nightmares, sometimes, about his death. If I let
out a yell in the night, you might kindly wake me."

"Well of course," I said, wrung with pity and the inability
to convey it.

I was beginning now to understand the reasons for Ty's
urgent interest in and contributions to the arts—his publishing company, his dealings with television, even the new

Greek village caper in Dorset, which I privately thought rather silly. Wholly uncreative himself—I had already found that out—locked in a prison constructed by his parents, he could only participate at one remove. It was a riposte against Dad and Mother—the generous donations to such useless activities as dancing, painting, music.

Was that the basis of *my* attraction for him, I wondered—my bits of random facility, the fact that I felt free to sing, to act and model, to paint and make patchwork quilts? I found such an idea rather depressing. To be somebody's vicarious bit of God, to be appropriated as a share in the mystery and productiveness of the universe—no, no, this is not what I want at all. Well, then, why *do* I want to be loved? Not for wit, looks, charm, intellect or cookery, which moth and rust can corrupt and custom stale—I want to suit somebody and fit them like an old glove, endeared through decades of habit.

You may say—and rightly—that this should all have been thought through before I married Ty. So it should. Our lives are lived much too fast. Don't you get this feeling? That we are all so close to the edge, the final brink of nevermore, that taking time for deliberation seems a waste of the few precious moments yet remaining? Better have *some* experience before Lights Out.

"But what," I said, harking back with probably irritating persistence—still, I really did want to know—"what has all this got to do with your not wanting me to call you Jas?"

So then, by degrees, I got the rest of the story. It came out so rustily, I wondered if he had ever told it to anybody before.

His parents always addressed him as Jim, which he hated. It seemed, he said, a typical example of their parsimony—the shortest, meanest possible version of his name, chosen not from fondness as a pet name but for economy's sake. One of the most boring names in the English language, he said, suitable only for trade union officials or slaves on Mississippi plantations— So he had rechristened himself Jas. Jas, in his imagination, was the astute one, the clever one, the one who had the adventures and thought of the witty answers; while Jim was indoors cleaning the shoes and getting ten verses of Chronicles by heart, carefree Jas was out climbing cliffs and swimming in wild waters; while Jim cut the grass with a LIAR placard across his shoulders, Jas would be freewheeling over the island of Jersey on his bicycle, accosting girls with a tongue full of blarney, going into pubs and making all kinds of amazing friends. While Jim silently, sullenly obeyed orders, Jas created mayhem and havoc, twitched the tablecloth off the table scattering roast beef and yorkshire pudding on the carpet, told his parents where they got off, and administered a dose of arsenic to his mother's hideous asthmatic pug dogs, Ming and Chang.

Naturally he never did any of those things. At home he submitted to the name of Jim, at school he was Tybold. It was like shifting from one cage to another, he said, each of them the sort in which you can neither sit, stand nor lie down.

After school, then what? He had gone to an accounting college—again dutifully submitting to parental decision. "And as a matter of fact," he said, "though I loathed it, I'm bound to say that it came in extremely useful. I learned how to organise, how to look round the financial scene and see which bits are bright and which are dark. It's a bit like studying a painting—a painting which is continually changing. No, I don't regret that accounting course."

"Where did you take it?"

"Manchester. Father's forebears had come from the North—my great-grandfather was a weaver, brought up in a weaver's cottage with nine siblings; he became an itinerant preacher . . . Dad thought it would be good for me to return to those parts—from which *he* had skived off to more comfortable quarters. So to Manchester I went. At least it was a long way from Jersey."

The other students at the business college had been a mixed lot—different ages, different backgrounds—again, much more interesting than the boys at his mediocre public school. Two of them—Ponsonby, a law student, and Mirthes, his accountant—had remained close associates ever since.

"Meanwhile what about Jas and Jim? Were they still coexisting inside you?"

"Oh yes. But Jas seldom saw the light of day. Money was still scanty—I was kept on a niggardly allowance and even that was reduced if my results didn't give satisfaction—I lived with an aunt and uncle, vegetarian Seventh-Day Adventists, on a diet of lentils and carrots and bread and margarine, which is not conducive to escapades."

I made a mental note to keep those items out of any cookery I might be called upon to do in future.

But would I, in fact, be called on to cook? Or would I merely preside as a gracious hostess at meals conjured out of Harrods and Fortnum's by Parkson, or tossed up by catering firms? Sometimes my lack of briefing about our future existence gave me a numb ache at the pit of my stomach. Sometimes the accustomed stabbing pain in my chest aggravated to such a degree that I thought how ironic it would be if the first post-marital collation organised by Parkson were to be my funeral baked meats.

Ty went on telling me about life as Jas and Jim.

On the eve of his final examination at business school came the news of his parents' simultaneous death while holiday driving in the Italian Alps.

"Father was a horrible driver—timid but blustering; he had probably exasperated some Italian by always nudging into the middle of the road when the guy tried to overtake, and when he finally pulled out it was fatally too late, and three cars went over the edge on the mountain road."

"How did the news affect you?"

"I went on and did my exams. Did well, too! Then the lid

shot off. I felt ecstatically, unbelievably released. I hadn't been seeing them much—they were living in Malta by that time—but just their presence in the world—my world—was like a swarm of locusts on the horizon coming my way—it's impossible to give you any notion of their devastating power to deplete and damage. Dad's mean suspicions, his vile attribution of the lowest possible motive to *every*body—even the *Queen*—for every act—and Mother's thin-lipped, utterly humourless conviction that God was sitting up on the picture rail counting every lump of sugar one dropped in one's teacup—to be rid of that gave me a euphoric feeling of freedom and joy. I'd never, for instance, been able to have sex with anybody before without terrible incapacitations of guilt—Mother would tramp into my mind at the most inopportune moments, there was absolutely nothing Jas could do about that—"

"A sort of female Holy Ghost?"

"More like all three Eumenides rolled into one."

Not only, after the death of his parents, was Ty liberated morally and mentally, but, he was also dumbfounded to discover, in worldly terms he was now extremely rich. His father had left him over eight hundred thousand. "And before inflation, too, when the pound was worth something."

"You had never guessed he was so well off?"

"Hadn't a notion. How could I? His lifestyle never suggested it. In Jersey he drove a rusty old Morris Minor. Mother had a woman in once a week and did the rest of the work herself. I cleaned the boots and cut the grass. They never ate out—except tea—or went to the theatre. Golf was Dad's one indulgence—and that only so that he could make useful acquaintances. I don't think he enjoyed it."

I couldn't help thinking about Masha, how she adored life. Even when Edred was at his gloomiest, sunk almost totally into a swamp of himself and God, floating slowly round the bend into that frozen tundra of outer space where he ended up—even then, Masha found endless delight in shapes, colours, sunshine, birdsong. Thrift she loved, turning a handful of gloomy leftover food—two cold wizened baked potatoes, a hunk of mouldy cheese, a soggy tomato, a cupful of sour milk—into a tasty and inviting dish; scents of leaves and flowers she loved. Looking at things, household objects, and thinking how they would fit into a picture, she loved. She used to exasperate Edred by pointing out beauties to him: "Do look at those geese flying over, Edred, look at the reflections in that puddle!" "Yes, yes," he would say crossly, trudging on without turning his head. Looking at pictures themselves she adored—those postcards all over the house. Doing jobs properly, she loved, Her standards were high. She was, in fact, fairly hard to help in small ways about the house, unless you realised this. "Thank you, that's *lovely,*" she would say, absently, or with what seemed genuine appreciation of your intention, if not performance. She never criticised help that was spontaneously offered. But then, half an hour later, you would observe her quietly putting right what you had done. And you'd realise that the work you had thought sufficiently well carried out had, in fact, been half finished, careless, unplanned. *Slipshod* was her worst adjective of condemnation. "I can't bear things done stupidly or messily," I have heard her say a thousand times, unwrapping the paper from round a block of butter so as to cut off a neat cube, instead of scooping it out from inside the paper as some people do . . .

I wondered what Masha would have made of Ty.

Would I have married him if she had still been around?

"What are you smiling at?" he asked, pulling me against him.

We had got up, eaten a small-hours' snack of grapes and champagne, and were back in bed, with the rain lashing into the canal outside.

I could hardly say, "Thinking how lucky I am to have had a mother like Masha instead of your horrible parents." Besides, what is luck? If I'd had a mother like Mrs. Tybold, I should now be a millionaire, instead of married to one.

"Thinking how different you are from your parents."

"When I first knew you," he said, "I didn't believe you *could* smile."

He spoke with the comfortable security of long acquaintance—yet it was only a few months since we had first met.

"You sound as if we had known each other for years," I said, crossing my fingers to avert the evil eye.

"I'd seen you on TV. Before I met you. In that terrible ghost play. And in rushes of *Rosy and Dodo*—before we met in that field. You always looked—" He searched for a word. "Not toffee-nosed, exactly. Indifferent? As if nothing were worth your notice. It was a shock, at the party, to find that you could laugh."

Fooling with Joel, I remembered. Perhaps not a pleasant shock? Did Ty not wish me to laugh? Humour isn't one of my more highly developed faculties, I'll admit—there hasn't been much time for it. But still, with Fitz, with Masha, with Joel, with various women friends, I have on occasion been reduced to rib-aching, joyful helpless abandonment; this had yet to happen with Ty. We had, of course, acquired various bits of private lovers' nonsense; but his sense of humour was a region as yet mainly unexplored. (I had, though, made the rather daunting discovery that he was given to practical jokes, short-sheeting beds, shoes full of bath salts, locking one in the loo. Well, what could you expect? They probably did it to him at school. I hoped to wean him to more civilised ways in course of time.)

We drifted off to sleep, lulled by the sound of the rain's continual plashing. No wonder I began to dream of some dangerous Dorset beach, where the tide was rising fast, threatening to wash our piles of clothes away, while Fitz and Masha, heedless, deaf to my shouts of warning, continued to swim far out on the horizon, in deep water.

I was greatly relieved to be woken from this dream by Ty, who gave a loud gasp and called, *"Grab* him! Grab hold of him! Pull him back—quick!"* He had his hands round my throat, half throttling me.

"Stop that, you fool! Lay off me!" I choked, not wholly conscious yet—and fought him off so violently that we both rolled from the bed to the floor. Fully awake at last, we pantingly apologised to one another and I did my best to straighten out the tangle of silk sheets and featherweight blankets.

"Were you dreaming about your friend, you poor thing?" I asked, massaging my windpipe.

Ty merely grunted—his apologies had been a good deal less effusive than mine—and readdressed himself to sleep, hoisting the blankets round him so that I had far less than my share. Fleetingly I wondered if his relationship with Lyndhurst had been a homosexual one—who, these days, after all, or indeed at any period, has not some such episode in his past? No business of mine, perhaps, but if we were to make a going concern of our relationship, all these stray bits of the pattern would have to be slotted in.

Next morning Ty's taciturnity could be explained by the fact that my fist or elbow must have connected quite powerfully during our brief but fierce tussle—he had a lurid black eye.

This did strike me as funny and I couldn't help laughing.

"Well, everyone must have guessed that we are a honeymoon couple—it's just more evidence of my wifely passion! Of course the Italians would think it more natural if *I* had the shiner—shall I make myself one with eye paint? Or carry my arm in a sling?"

Later I was to remember this ill-timed facetiousness. Ty was not at all amused. He was, I'd already noticed, more than a touch narcissistic about his quite impressive good looks. Why not? Women turned to gaze at him in the street—specially the discerning Venetian ladies. He received admiring glances under lashes from pretty chambermaids and waitresses, who went out of their way to encounter him in halls and passages. All his wardrobe was most carefully chosen with luxurious thick textures: bloomy expensive wool, rich sombre silk ties, superfine tailored shirts—sheepskin, camel hair, vicuna, yak. Part of my appeal for him, I had regretfully begun to admit to myself, was because together we made a handsome couple; I, still masquerading in my Rosy disguise due to the fact that, when we returned from Venice, there would be a few last interior scenes to be shot, and my final confrontation with Dodo. While we were in Venice they were getting on with the many parts involving other characters. Ty's position as a member of the board meant that everyone at Pyramid had fallen over backwards to facilitate the arrangements for our honeymoon: it had been excellent publicity for the programme. MILLIONAIRE TV EXECUTIVE WEDS STAR FROM OWN SERIAL was fine tabloid stuff.

Fitz had been a little disapproving; even American papers carried the story, so he had known about it before my letter reached him. (Somehow I couldn't bring myself to break the news by telephone.)

He, however, had phoned me from Harvard.

"Are you sure this isn't all a bit hasty? You know I'd be the last person to question any of your actions—?"

Fitz rarely questions anybody's action. His mental motions are so far removed from most people's daily life that tolerance *has* to be an inbuilt part of him. I think it's not that he wouldn't presume to judge, but that he sees no occasion for judgment.

"No, it isn't hasty, it's a good thing," I assured him. "I'm having fun, set your mind at rest. For the first time in my life, I'm being pampered. And I enjoy every minute of it. Also, Ty has promised that I can do a lot of interesting and useful things with some of his money."

I detailed a few: opening an art gallery in Deptford, financing a couple of theatre groups run by friends of whom I thought highly, buying a bit of land for a nature reserve—

Fitz admitted cautiously that the programme seemed most interesting and worthwhile. "Though you do sound a bit like Dorothea Brooke with her endless cottages! I always imagined them as the most awful council houses. But you're really happy, old Cat? You're sure I hadn't better come to the wedding?"

No, I said, on the whole better not. I was truly concerned about not taking Fitz away from his intensive year's work. I did want him to be free of me. And, secondly, I hadn't got around to telling Ty about him yet. Just before our headlong wedding had not felt like the right moment. Up to this point in our honeymoon the right moment still had not arrived. Fitz, I feared, might think this rather laggardly of me, but he'd not consider it of signal importance. Other people are *not* of great importance to him—unless they are likely to come out with a new philosophical concept.

Other people are of crucial importance to me, and that is why I waited for a really suitable occasion before telling Ty about Fitz.

Ty disconcerted me by flatly refusing to go out and walk around the streets of Venice with a black eye. He turned a deaf ear to all my persuasions.

"You could wear a black patch and look like Moshe Dayan. Or I could disguise it with pearly makeup. Or I could buy you a sombrero—I've seen lots of Italian men wearing hats with wide brims—you could wear it pulled down over a silk scarf."

"I never wear a hat. And a patch would look affected. And makeup wouldn't work."

"Oh, it would, I assure you."

"Well I don't want to mess about. The eye is too sore."

"Poor dear, it is a shame," I said, though feeling privately that he was making rather a fuss over a trifle. That morning, for instance, he had retreated into the bathroom and left me to deal with the arrival of breakfast; did he intend to remain in purdah, seeing nobody, not even waiter or chambermaid, until the bruise abated?

"Going out would take your mind off it," I suggested hopefully.

"What do you want to go out *for?*"

"Not *for* anything. We could ride around in a gondola."

"It's raining."

It had been raining for the last five days; hitherto that had not deterred us. We had gone in and out like birds, regardless of the weather. In many ways, we had hardly been conscious of our whereabouts. Now, all at once I felt imprisoned by the luxurious, overheated, untidy room, and realised for the first time that I had no reading matter. I longed to find a bookshop and buy a paperback, no matter what. But manners restrained me. I did not wish to suggest dissatisfaction with Ty's company.

"Come back to bed," he said, yawning. "Last night was too fidgety. Champagne after three is a mistake. Gives you dreams . . . God, that was a ghastly dream about the cave. I thought he was going to pull me right down into it."

"Meanwhile you nearly garrotted *me,*" I said, climbing in beside him. "Look at the bruises on my neck."

"You'll have to wear one of those high lace collars," he said, turning to the financial page of the *Herald Tribune.* "Anyway we shan't be going out tonight."

Then he made some phone calls, to Ponsonby and Mirthes, and the architect Rupert Vassiliaides, who was masterminding the Greek village in Dorset.

"Yes; and tell them that I want the harbour completely dredged out. They can use what they scoop out from the harbour to put on the beach; why not? And proper sand on top of that. Very well, then. And a breakwater built around.

No, I know that can't all be done this winter, but there must be a mole. You must work out costs. It has to be a viable harbour. *Planning permission?* Oh, very well then. Tell him to get on with it. There is? That's civil of them. Say thanks, will you? Oh well; I'm not sure about that. We'll see. Yes; thanks; quite. Yes I will. Right. Good-bye."

A long way from poor downtrodden little Jim who had to clean the shoes and cut the grass, I thought, as he replaced the receiver.

"Vass asks to have his respects sent to you."

I had met Vassiliaides at the Knoyle party: a tall, lanky lantern-faced man who looked more English than Greek; a gifted and valuable architect, Joel had told me. Joel! Momentarily I felt homesick for his undemanding, easy company.

"Rupert says," Ty went on, "that the weather in Dorset is perfect, mild and sunny. Says we ought to go and finish our honeymoon there."

"At Knoyle?" I tried to keep the eagerness from my voice. Venice had been Ty's plan, and up to now it had been wonderful, yes it had. But the thought of the plunging, swooping green Dorset countryside—and the beach down below, and Yetford only thirty miles away—and there was a splendid nineteenth-century library at the Manor, I had browsed through its titles a couple of times while waiting for the lighting experts to get their wattage right—and we could take walks—

Ty quelled these hopes by saying, "Not at Knoyle, no. That's let to a seminar on ecology and enimonics."

"Enimonics?"

"Not a clue. Ponsonby arranged it. Anyway we can't stay at Knoyle, but Rupert said one of the finished houses at Glifonis had been permanently set aside for Lord and Lady Fortuneswell on their visits of inspection."

"How charming of them."

I had not become used to being Lady Fortuneswell yet,

and probably never would. Of course, in Venice one was continually addressed as miladi, or la Contessa, or signora, and one took little notice, knowing it meant nothing; but to be called *my lady* by English voices—that would be strange indeed! Would Masha approve? Or be scandalized? Titles meant nothing to her. She had once given a frightful scolding —in Edred's surgical days—to a visiting European royalty who offered a bonbon to a crying little girl in a children's ward.

"How *could* you do such an irresponsible thing?" she shouted at him, pouncing to whisk the sweet out of harm's way and nearly precipitating an international incident. Papa had thought it was a great nuisance. No, my being Lady Fortuneswell would cut no ice with her.

"Do you think it would be fun to go and stay in this Greek house?" I suggested, keeping my voice so uninflected that it seemed to come out of my ears.

"Are you *mad?* In *midwinter?*"

He returned to his financial reading, and I took a short nap.

When I woke, it was because he was prodding me to open the door and admit lunch while he beat another tactical retreat to the bathroom. Lunch over—a rather drunken lunch, to celebrate the rain, and Ty's black eye, and a certain shift in our relations that we both, I think, sensed the possibility of but were not able to express, either to ourselves or to each other, or take any measures to avert—after lunch we returned to lovemaking; like sports addicts, we were bent on refining our technique to the uttermost edge . . . And if we were beginning to regard each other a thought warily, our bodies at least were friends. They found nothing amiss with our relationship and hung together like two old drunken boon companions.

"I'm going to call you James," I announced into one of those peaceful blank pauses that occur from time to time in bed, negative time; like negative space between the more important shapes in pictures, space which is itself equally important and must be taken into account; negative time probably adds months if not years onto one's life expectancy. "James is a good name, I don't know why it didn't occur to me before. Sonorous, well connected with saints, and with literature; and it has a sober domestic sound too. 'I must ask James,' I can hear myself saying, about all kinds of minor issues."

"God, what a relief to get *that* settled," he mumbled with his face in my neck.

We began biting each other like professional sharks.

"You can buy videotapes of this sort of thing," I suggested. "It might save a lot of trouble."

"Oh, hush . . ."

"Do you like what I'm doing?"

"Hush . . ." And he added, "You are the fulfilment of all my dreams."

This should have charmed me but it didn't. It sounded too like a line from a bad novel. He went on: "Go to sleep, now, while I do this . . ."

I didn't want to go to sleep. But in the end, both of us did.

Next day, Ty's eye had gone from black to green, a livid, iridescent green, shading out of olive into dead spinach. Still he refused to go out. So the hotel produced chess and mahjongg and, at my request, *Paradise Lost* and Shakespeare's sonnets. Ty never seemed to have done much reading for pleasure; if he was going to begin now, I reckoned he might as well begin at the top. So we lay in bed arguing about Milton's God and his behaviour to Adam. I had always considered this perfectly outrageous, and expected that Ty, in the light of his attitude to his own father, would do so too, but to my surprise he took the opposing, authoritarian line.

"Adam had to accept the conditions that were laid down

for him. Raphael had told him quite plainly what they were. You can't survive, or make any success of your environment, unless you accept your limitations."

"But why did God have to *be* so arbitrary and tyrannical? Why *have* a Tree of Knowledge in the first place? Or, if it was there, why forbid Adam to eat the fruit?"

"Because, once he had, Adam would be as great as his creator."

"What's wrong with that?"

"You need to have a hierarchy," pronounced Ty, "or society falls apart."

"But anyway, he did eat it, and he *didn't* become as great as his creator—how do you account for that?"

"Don't ask *me!* God somehow managed to shuffle things, I suppose."

"Characteristically! To suit himself! I wonder what would have happened," I pondered, "if, in Book Nine, Adam hadn't eaten the fruit; he only seems to have eaten it out of British decency, because his wife had done for herself and he felt obliged to back her up—not because he *wanted* to know about good and evil. Suppose Eve had been the only one to eat it? She might have been better off on her own."

"And what would Adam have done then?"

"Gone back to his first wife."

"It doesn't say anything about *her* in this book."

"No, but I read about her somewhere else. Her name was Lilith; and after he left her she turned into a vampire and tried to put a curse on his subsequent relationships. As you'd expect of a first wife. And, I suppose, succeeded."

"I've had enough literature," said Ty suddenly. "Pour me another glass of grappa. And come here . . ."

"Tell me some more about Jas and Jim," I suggested, procrastinating. "Did Jas never, never get out? Not even for half an hour?"

"What makes you ask that?" His tone was sharp. He

looked at me as if he had discovered me with a bloodstained skeleton in my hand.

"I don't know. Thinking about Adam and Satan, I suppose. Eve and Lilith. Our other aspects. Surely you can't always have been so dismally irreproachable?"

"Well, there was once . . ." He refilled his own glass and topped up mine, then rolled over and lay brooding, chin on fists. "There's a zoo in Jersey, run by that naturalist fellow, and I got a job there in my teens, cleaning out cages, things like that. My parents, for once, approved. Good healthy money-earning activity . . . I was paid five pounds a week and I had to give the money straight to my father."

"Good God, James! In your *teens?*"

"I know, I know, you think I must have been retarded or mad, not to rebel. But when you are in a prison situation, your whole personality becomes so shrunk and reduced that rebellion doesn't occur to you as a possibility."

"Yes. I suppose that must be true. Look at the examples in history. So what happened?"

"One Saturday I'd just been paid and I was holding my five-pound note, and I stopped for a moment outside the chimpanzee cage—he was a big untidy beast called Jerry, quite a friend of mine, I used to take him apples from our tree. And he reached out calmly through the bars, and removed my five-pound note and swallowed it, before I could stop him. When I told the story to my parents—I thought it was quite funny myself—they simply didn't believe me, thought this was like one of Lyndhurst's inventions, my sneaky way of hanging on to the cash and blaming a poor dumb animal that couldn't speak up for itself. So I got a thrashing, besides hell in various other ways."

"But why in the *world* didn't you tell someone at the zoo —your boss—get him to speak up for you—there must have been other people who saw what had happened?" I was choked with indignation on his behalf.

"Well—I didn't. It was a Saturday. I was given assorted penalties. I forget what. Dad and Mother went off, he to play golf and she to sit with her knitting in the sunroom of the golf club. One of my jobs at home was to kill weeds with a flamethrower, a blowtorch that Father kept for burning down groundsel and stuff on the drive. Mother had sets and sets of cherished ornamental table mats that she practically never used—because we hardly ever had guests to meals—with deep borders of real lace. Two or three times a summer she'd wash them and put them out in the sun to bleach. Using the blowtorch—with a fearful, terrified satisfaction—I burned the lot."

"Heavens! What happened?"

"Oddly enough, she never found out. Or not that I had done it. There was next to no ash left, and a breeze blew away what there was . . . And I suppose it just didn't occur to them that I would do such a thing. Mother was convinced that gypsies must have come by and stolen her precious doilies. And that satisfied Jas, for the time at least."

"He never got loose again?"

"Well; there was one other time. But that was years later, quite a different kind of thing."

"Tell me about it."

He tipped more liquor into our glasses, carelessly, spilling a trail across the sheets—which were remarkably sticky and creased already.

I loved the feeling of unconcern about that. Somebody else would remake our bed with clean sheets this evening. Someone else would do the laundry . . . "Tell me about it," I repeated, rolling over on the puddle of grappa and propping myself comfortably against his shoulder.

"The religion in my family goes a long way back on both sides," he said. "Hedge preachers—deacons—Methodists—Baptists. Cantankerous, argumentative bastards. There was a money-making streak, too. They were a canny lot. The piling up of property never seems to have interfered with their religious views—or vice versa. Until it came to me—maybe the split had slowly been growing wider and wider until it became total."

"I'm not sure that I'm with you, but go on."

"When I was a kid, the girls wouldn't look at me. For one thing, I was terrified of them. For another, I was a mess. I was continually biting my nails, and my fingers; for years they were always ragged and bloody and tattered. Couldn't leave scabs alone—anything like that. I used to worry at myself as if I was a goddamn bone. If there was anything wrong with me, I made it more so by picking and scratching."

"Self-mortification."

"Uh-huh. I used to get scabs on my head, and pulled quite large tufts of hair out, getting them off. And then they'd come back, only bigger. So I had bald patches. The hair came out in handfuls. And I had ghastly pimples and spots, some on my face, some on my knees, that I couldn't resist squeezing . . . I was a total mess. *You* wouldn't have taken a second look at me," he said with triumph. " 'Leave yourself alone!' Mother used to screech at me, but I never did. Pulling myself to pieces was my hobby. You simply cannot imagine what a moth-eaten, unhealthy, rat-nibbled little monster I was in those days."

"When did all that change?"

I did indeed find it difficult to imagine him as he must have been. He was so sleek now, so smooth, prosperous and impressive in appearance. Just at present the black eye slightly impaired this high-quality image, but in a way I was glad of that, because a little imperfection gave him more reality; he was wilder, more natural. Even a black eye could not detract from his stunning good looks. (During the days of courtship, when my influence was at its strongest, I had persuaded him to shave off those side-whiskers.) Intermittently I still felt that it was a privilege to be in bed with him, here, in one of Venice's most expensive hotels, listening to the rain belting down outside.

"Oh, when my parents died," he said, as if this were the most natural consequence. "Then I went to a hypnotist. My spots and chilblains began to clear up at once, I made better headway with the girls. The first one, up in Manchester, she was at the university reading economics. She was pretty wild . . ." His voice trailed away as if he rather wished he had not mentioned her.

It must have taken a fairly wild girl, I reckoned, to breach the defences of poor Jim as he was then, with his history of spots and chilblains, that upbringing of poverty and obedience, his mother's ghost looming over him like the three Eumenides rolled into one.

"Her name?"

"I don't remember." Plainly he did, but never mind. "She'd been smoking pot for a couple of terms and then she went on to acid. I tried it, one night at her place. Awful gloomy dark bedsit she had in Eccles Gardens."

"What happened?"

"I didn't enjoy it much. Other people have told me what wonderful visions they had, how they felt the whole world opened out like a flower, all that sort of thing. Nothing of the kind happened to me."

"What did happen? Was it bad? Frightening?"

"N—no," he said slowly. "But not good, either. I was outside of myself. Have you ever had that experience?"

"Once or twice." And more recently than you might guess, my friend, I thought. But he went on without waiting for amplification.

"I could actually see the two of me—Jas and Jim. Me. Myself. Saw them separate, but overlapping—the kind of double image you get when your eyes go out of focus. When they do that, you can push the two images together or let them slide farther apart. Well—I can remember pushing and pushing, but my two images *wouldn't* come back together. On the contrary, they kept moving farther away from each other. At the same time I had the most ghastly, helpless feeling, as if my feet were on two separate ice floes that were drifting apart."

"What happened then?"

"I heard a voice say, 'Well, that's the last you'll see of *me,*' and then I suppose I passed out. I woke feeling terrible, with a headache like an iron cuff around the back of my skull, which I could tell was going to get much, *much* worse and last for about two days. Which it did. And, as well, that sensation of one's mind racing out of gear—do you know?—images dashing past, you can't stop them, exhausting, frantic, you can't get your breath, you can't stop the procession, they rush on and on. Sometimes I think that death will be like that, the period just before death, revving up to an utterly unbearable climax—"

For some reason, just then, Fitz came into my mind, a childhood memory. We had found a hedgehog, apparently dead in the middle of the lawn at Yetford. He lifted it up gently on a spade, to move it to a more seemly resting place. And, at that, it suddenly stretched, yawned, rolled on its back, exposing the softer, defenceless underpart of a hedgehog that normally one never sees. Just pale fur. There seemed something totally relaxed, confiding, about that leisurely, tranquil yawn, uncurling its little pink hands; and, at the peak of the yawn, it died.

"Oh!" exclaimed Fitz in simple wonder. "Oh—is *that* what dying is like?"

That single moment, I feel certain, divested him forever of any dread or apprehension about death.

I was glad, in a way, that he had been out of England when Masha died, for one of the nurses had told me that she died in terrible, unbearable pain; much better let him keep his image of the peaceful hedgehog.

"Did the headache really last two days?"

"Yes. So I never tried acid again. Once was plenty."

"And which of them was it that you'd seen the last of, Jas or Jim?"

"I assumed it was Jas." He sounded surprised, as if the other alternative had never occurred to him. "And in fact I never—never thought of him anymore—till you came out with the name on the bridge."

"Stirring up sunken wrecks that ought to be left alone. Muddy ponds of memory— What about the girl?"

"What girl?" He had rolled over towards me and started on a slow but arousing process of delicate nibbles, touches, and movements, a formula that had proved highly satisfactory in the past and almost certainly would again.

"The girl who took the acid? What became of her? The one who read economics?"

"Oh," he answered vaguely, "I lost sight of her after that. She was rather a hopeless girl . . ."

He picked up my hands, which had been resting on his thorax, and studied them. My hands are not beautiful. One of my worse features. Small, thin, worn, roughened and reddened from years of immersion in water, wringing out cloths in hospitals, then dishwashing in Greek restaurants, then scene-painting and hauling on ropes; I have to put a lot of whitener on them for the screen, specially for a part like Rosy.

"Why do you wear that crummy little jet ring?" Ty asked censoriously. "It looks like something picked up at a flea market."

Almost certainly it had been. Fitz had given it to me for my birthday, ages ago. I always wore it. Ty had never noticed it before.

"I'll get you a black diamond," he said. "You can't go about in *that.*"

Ty had shown approval of my thoroughgoing enjoyment

of luxury, though I had honestly told him that I didn't in the least object to privation or discomfort. He said it was good that opposing forces were reconciled in me. That I seemed well balanced. But it did seem to irritate him when he came across traces of my humble past. He wanted them expunged. He expected me to be Rosy through and through.

"Well," I said, mildly belligerent, "before you I spent most of my life at flea markets."

"Hush—"

Later on, after our usual highly successful conclusion, as we lay spent and reflective among the grape seeds and splashes of grappa, I announced, still rather combatively, feeling it was time this got said,

"You haven't asked me about *my* past life. About *my* horrible father. Or my mother."

"I know more than you think." His tone was indulgent, a little bored.

"What *can* you mean?"

"It was I who wangled you that part as Rosy. You'd never have got it otherwise."

"*What?*"

"When they were casting. I remembered the play that Flanagan directed. I remembered you. So when Randolph wanted someone to play the part of Rosy, I suggested you. I had to throw my weight about quite a bit." He chuckled. "Grove was horrified— Of course he changed his mind later, agreed that it had been a really inspired choice."

I felt as if I had swallowed a frozen cucumber, whole.

"But I hardly spoke two lines in that ghost play—and I looked absolutely different—how—"

"Oh, I know. But I could see what your potential might be, with a bit of grooming and retouching. I must admit, though," he added generously, "that even my conception fell short of the mark."

I was speechless with outrage; and just as well, really.

I could have murdered him.

My lovely part, my lovely triumph, and here he was, taking all the credit.

But I'd show him, I'd—

Luckily, just after that point, I toppled into a canyon of sleep.

NEXT day Ty's black eye had faded to a delicate, greenish grey, like the outside of a hardboiled egg yolk. Mah-jongg and *Paradise Lost* had long begun to pall, and the foggy rain, the rainy fog, still hung in a mussel-coloured murk through the streets of Venice. So at long last he consented to buy a hat and take the air. He looked terrific in the hat: Goya would have painted him in a grey cloak swirling and two hounds straining at the leash and a range of Castilian mountains in the distance.

We hired a gondola and rode about in the brume, through the quiet canals behind the Zattere, listening to the drip of sweeps and the gondoliers' doleful cries. *"Premi!"* and *"Stali!"* they are supposed to shout, according as to whether they intend to pass on the right or on the left, but in nine cases out of ten it sounds like the first few bars of *"Voi che sapete."* Palazzi everywhere were boarded up against possible flooding, boatmen shrouded in oilskins, walkers wore shawls and fur hats.

Ty had the intention of buying me a watch; he thought nothing of the hard-wearing nurse's watch that I had worn since the age of fifteen. "Good for timing eggs, or taking temperatures, perhaps, but not the kind of thing you can wear now, where anybody might see you," was his comment.

So we presently uncoiled ourselves from the gondola's waterproof wrappings, stepped ashore and went, not to one of the flashy arcade jewellers' shops near the Rialto or San

Marco, but to an almost sinisterly small, exclusive and remote little establishment in a narrow alley, where we had to be received by appointment, and two doors were unlocked for us by a bowing majordomo who ushered us through to an inner room, curtained and carpeted in grey velvet, with pale grey velvet armchairs and not a jewel to be seen. I never feel comfortable in that kind of boutique; vulgarly commonplace, I fear, in my tastes, I prefer a straightforward emporium, where the goods are laid out on display, and you may wander at will and see what's to be had without committing yourself.

Right away I felt myself growing prickly and nervous.

However, a beautiful whiskery expert, grey-haired to match the carpet, with brilliant black eyes—he looked like a compromise between Albert Einstein and a prawn—was already giving a big hello to Ty, who, it seemed, had made other purchases there.

Who for? I wondered, and fleetingly wished that, previous to me, Ty had conducted a long liaison with some gorgeous Bird of Paradise, had garlanded her with diamonds and scattered rubies under her feet. For I was beginning to feel my position a shade invidious; to sense the existence of a curious vacuum in his past. Just where, with most people, you begin to be aware of layers, geological series, events built into strata in their makeup, giving a sense of solidarity, one incident leading to another, things, people in definite order, with Ty this was not the case. There appeared to be a kind of echo chamber within him. When you tapped, all you got back was a hollow ring, no feel of solidarity at all.

Where had he been, who had been his friends or lovers for all those years after he left off biting his nails and picking off his scabs, after he inherited his father's fortune, quit the accounting school, and went into business on his own?

Two or three glittering, spindly little baubles were brought out. They were merely samples—this was made clear; I gathered that I was to have a watch built for me, specially adapted to my personality.

The trouble was that I'm not all that keen on gold and diamonds.

I didn't like any of them. They were all too small, with peevish tiny faces, oblong or heart-shaped; one was digital, others had gems or art-deco hieroglyphics instead of proper numbers. I didn't care for a watch masquerading as a bracelet; I want a watch to tell the time, simply.

"I'm afraid these don't look right on my wrist," I said. "I need something plainer."

"But Signora la Contessa has such beautiful hands," lamented Einstein Prawn. He must have been pretty desperate to bring out such a whopper. *"Eccolo!* They set off my gems to perfection."

"You are behaving like Jane Eyre, insisting on being married in grey bombazine," said Ty to me coldly.

Aha! So there was one book he had read. Unless, of course, he saw the movie.

With guilt and shame I agreed that he was right; I was being a nuisance and a killjoy.

"Wait, wait a little moment—I will show you—wait—"

Signor Seal hastened away to an inner repository from which he came back with a whole tray of watches, each one clasped around the wrist of a grey velvet hand.

The effect was highly surreal—not to say macabre—a forest of grey jewelled hands all reaching up, Dali's comment on Buchenwald, perhaps.

"Oh, *how* extraordinary!" I was fascinated. "Aren't they exactly like enormous grey crocuses."

I longed for Joel to see them, to take a picture of them, or a pair of my friends, Mad and Dom, who put together very original TV plays and would, I felt sure, be able to use those hands for a launching point into some complex, bizarre, dramatic and significant tangle.

I was turning to James, trying to express a little of this, to assure him that if I lacked subtlety in my taste for watches, at least I could appreciate the unexpected existential experiences he was able to offer so lavishly—but I stopped in dismay, for his complexion had gone as grey as the velvet hands; he looked mortally ill, with a sick, disgusted expression, as if his thoughts were too awful to be borne; he shivered, kept swallowing, and had come out in a fine pearly sweat.

"James! What *is* it? Do you feel bad?"

"Mal di stomaco? Il Conte soffre di influenza, raffreddore, forse," sadly suggested Signor Seal. "The signor should at once lie down, take a little brandy—at this season, in Venice, such afflictions are common. *Le posso offrire qualcosa? No?"*

Speechless, James shook his head, and we left in haste amid copious regrets and profuse thanks and numerous polite promises to return very soon, tomorrow maybe, certainly within the week.

By good luck it was not more than a ten-minute walk back to our hotel, but I seriously wondered if James would be able to make it, for he looked so deathly. If only there were sedan chairs in Venice nowadays! However, he curtly threw off my suggestions of calling for help, and presently we were back in our luxurious rooms (which unseen hands had tidied and made presentable during our absence) and I was able to administer a slug of brandy and request the chambermaid to produce a hot water bottle *(la borsa d'acqua calda)* which to my amazement she did, quite speedily. James seemed chilled to the bone and lay retching miserably and shivering; then, after the rigor passed off, he began to complain of an unbearable headache.

"Have an aspirin? Codeine? Paracetamol?"

"No. It's one of my migraines," he muttered. "It'll last at least twenty-four hours—there's nothing to be done about it."

I was appalled. "But that's dreadful! Can't I get a doctor?"

"No, no, he'd be no help at all. You'll find some pills in my sponge bag—feverfew—they are the only thing that works and they don't help much."

He swallowed a handful, curled into a fetal position, and clamped his eyes shut. His forehead was corrugated with pain.

I felt hideously helpless and inadequate. Had it been my obstinacy, my difficult and thankless behaviour over his proffered gift that had brought on this sudden seizure? Up to that moment he had seemed perfectly normal.

Were these migraines of frequent occurrence in his life?

"Can't I massage your scalp? I'm quite good at that. Or make you a tisane?"

"Just leave me alone," he snarled. "Will you? I have to sleep it off. Can you dim the light? It hurts my eyes. And make sure no one disturbs me."

Since I saw no value in sitting for an incalculable number of hours in a darkened hotel room, I tiptoed out, hung the DO NOT DISTURB sign outside, and impressed forcibly on the desk that no calls, none, were to be put through to Signor Il Conte; messages were to be taken and given to me; he was on no account to be woken.

"*Si senti poco bene.*"

"*Ah! Il povero—*"

They were full of sympathy, commiseration, suggestions for doctors, hospitals, masseurs, even acupuncturists, but, politely declining all these offers, I found a Penguin copy of *Vanity Fair* in the hotel boutique and decided that I might as well eat an early dinner in the dining room.

I was not dressed for dinner, but I didn't wish to go back and run the risk of disturbing James if, by chance, he had managed to escape from his pain into sleep. In order to shop for wristwatches I had put on a charcoal grey wool dress, short-sleeved and cowl-necked; let the marchesas and principessas look down their noses at it if they must. To me it seemed suitable enough for a solitary dinner. In fact, at such an early hour, very few other people were in the dining room.

I had rather expected a diminution in the attention of the headwaiter when I appeared solo without Il Milord Inglese, but my Rosy persona was still earning dividends, it seemed, and he escorted me to a perfectly respectable table and solicitously tendered a two-foot menu and wine list to match. It occurred to me, as I threaded my way through their complexities, that this was the first time since marrying Ty that I had reverted to the status of solitary female fending for herself; it had been amazingly restful to sink into the role of Little Woman and let Ty take care of the ordering, which he did with maximum efficiency; his appearance and manner brought waiters, porters, taxi drivers and gondolieri flocking like pigeons to corn; but, I wondered for the first time, did I really want this kind of attention for the rest of my life? Just at present, yes; luxury made, there was no denying, a wonderful holiday. Just at present; but in perpetuity?

I hadn't settled the argument, was still meditatively sipping my Orvieto and nibbling my saltimbocca when the receptionist came threading his way between the tables.

"A telephone call from England for Signor il Conte; will Signora la Contessa take it here?"

I said I would, and the phone was brought to my table.

The caller turned out to be Ponsonby, Ty's man of business. When I explained that Ty was afflicted with a bad migraine and at present quite unable to come to the telephone, he expressed deep sympathy.

"Poor old Ty; I know those turns of his. I know: all he can do is sleep it off. What rotten bad luck. Wonder what brought it on." Tactfully, he did not pursue that thread, for surely on a man's honeymoon he should not be laid low with a psychosomatic complaint, but went on, "I have a piece of news, though, which, if he's at all in a state to hear it, may be able to cheer him up. That's why I'm calling."

"Oh, what is it? Can you tell me? Can I tell him?"

"Certainly; but don't breathe a word about it anywhere else; it is still under wraps, absolutely between ourselves. So you will maintain *total* discretion, won't you?"

"Of course." I didn't trouble to add that, in any case, I had no acquaintance in Venice, no confidante to whom I could betray Ty's secret; I simply said, "I won't breathe a word to a soul."

"Well: I had a whisper along the pipeline that Ty has been shortlisted for the Companions of Roland. Which, in fact, is tantamount to saying that he'll be elected; 99 percent of the preliminary checking must have been done already."

"Companions of—?"

"Roland."

"I'm sorry: you'll think me terribly ignorant, but I've never heard of them."

"You're not unique—many people haven't." He sounded indulgent. "It's a European organisation—keeps a very low profile. But I know that being invited to join has been Ty's secret ambition for years; I believe he'd rather that than win the Nobel Peace Prize."

"My goodness! Well, that's wonderful. What a splendid piece of news. I'll tell him the very minute he wakes up— You say he's been shortlisted. When will he be let know for certain?"

"Next month, they hold the annual elections. He knows all that. Give him my very best congratulations."

"You're quite sure they won't be premature?"

"Oh no. I can't think of anything that could cause a hitch in the proceedings at this stage. It's just formalities from here on."

Armed with this piece of information I finished my dinner

and tiptoed back to our suite, where I found Ty in a state of half-sleep, half-wake, miserably shifting from side to side and grunting with agony at each movement.

"James? Can you hear me?"

"Umh? What's that?" he muttered irritably.

He seemed conscious enough to take in the information, so I related it, slowly and carefully, adding Ponsonby's message of congratulation. A silence followed my announcement; I wondered if he had taken in what I said.

Presently he mumbled, "What was that? Did you tell me something, or did I imagine it?"

I repeated the message word for word, adding, "I'm terribly glad for you, love. Ponsonby said you'd be pleased about it."

"Of course I'm pleased. What do you think? Can you get me a glass of water and some more of those feverfew pills."

His voice sounded firmer, and when he had swallowed the pills I suggested a cup of tea. After considering for a moment he agreed, and when it had been brought and he had drunk it, a more normal tinge of colour returned to his face. He was able to lean back on heaped pillows; the crease of pain in his forehead gradually cleared and his hands relaxed. He looked less deathly.

I said with caution, "Tell me about these Companions of Roland? What in the world are they? I never heard of them."

"It's a European organisation. Goes a long way back—to Byzantium. Connected with the Crusades originally, I believe."

"Like Knights of St. John?"

He nodded and winced. "It's a kind of high-class Rotary now."

He spoke lightly, but this was to conceal, I could see, his enormous pleasure. He was deeply, deeply impressed by the news I had brought; plainly this accolade meant something hugely important to him.

"Twice a year they hold meetings," he said. "In Rome and Paris. All kinds of people belong—government officials and scientists and writers and priests—the Pope is one—and industrialists. You can't apply, you have to wait to be invited. It's a great honour."

"But that's marvellous," I said warmly. "How terrific that you get news of it now! And Ponsonby said it was pretty well a foregone conclusion that you'd be elected."

"Yes, once you are nominated you are virtually in." Ty's tone was absent. "They do a tremendously thorough scrutiny of your life to make sure you qualify—it's a very strait-laced setup. I believe divorce or litigation in your past gets you blackballed; or bankruptcy; maybe even having your driving licence suspended."

"Oh well, it's lucky you have a nice respectable wife," I told him cheerfully, and as soon as I'd said it a faint, the very faintest of chills passed through me. Had Ty's marriage provided the final seal of respectability rendering him eligible for this honour? Could there possibly have been any thought of this consideration when he proposed to me?

"Do you know," he said, "I believe I could eat something light—perhaps an omelette. And some fruit. Can you call Room Service?"

From that moment on, his recovery was swift. In fact, as he later said himself, in grateful wonder, he had never come out of a migraine so fast.

It seemed slow enough to me, I said. By now it was eleven-thirty at night; the headache had hit him between two and three in the afternoon. Eight hours of excruciating pain seemed no light thing to me. But he assured me that one of his really bad attacks could last five times as long.

"When it's over, though, I always come out fighting fit. That isn't really a compensation but it seems so at the time. Ready for anything. Bursting with energy."

In proof of which he began kissing me, and it was true, he

did seem newly charged with vitality. We lay entwined, very happily, and I asked what special privileges or titles would accrue to him as a Knight of Armorica. "Will you be Sir James, as well as Lord Fortuneswell? Do you get to wear a purple garter? Or one of those terrific crosses with ribbons and diamonds? Is there a ceremony? Shall I be allowed to come and watch it? Do you keep vigil all night before, in a haunted chapel?"

Ty was not accustomed to this kind of foolery; I had discovered on previous occasions that it tended to disgruntle him (can you disgruntle transitively?) but just now he was so lit up that nothing could have diminished his euphoria. He was even able to reply in kind.

"Certainly I have to keep vigil; and you have to kneel down behind me as well, stark naked apart from a wreath of ivy round your neck. And the ceremony takes place next day under the Arc de Triomphe."

It turned out that in fact he knew next to nothing about the procedure; the Companions of Roland keep their profile so low that it is practically underground.

His complete and joyful recovery was a huge relief. Ty as I first knew him, with his healthy outdoor appearance, thick upspringing hair and commanding ways, had seemed such an epitome of life and vigour that I had assumed this was the whole picture (how happily would I turn over the task of looking after me and my inventory of ills to this capable stranger. Little did he know what he had taken on). So it had been with a sense of dismay and letdown that I learned he had an Achilles' heel of his own. I did my best to feel kindly and forgiving towards him, though, as the beggar-maid must have felt when she learned that King Cophetua held his throne in the teeth of several other claimants and a strong Republican party.

Our lovemaking that night reached unexampled heights of excellence. It carried a kind of wild gaiety, happy absurdity—we would break off from whatever we were doing to put crazy questions to each other, address one another by extempore names—"Might I inquire, Sir Conrad, where you have concealed the cruet? Could I trouble you to be so kind as to pass the ketchup if I'm not robbing you?" "Why, for you, liebste Frau Buergomeister, it will be an honour, but can you untie the octopus?" "Did you remember, Your Grace, to wind the grandfather clock and take off your galoshes?"

It makes me sad, very sad, now, to remember that night. Sad and faintly queasy; lovers' jokes are not for repetition. Not even for remembering.

"You are wonderful—wonderful—wonderful," he mumbled at one point.

Words, what do they really mean? Not a thing.

Wonderful, I? I was an image in his mind; it suited him that I should be wonderful.

And all the time the Venetian rain pitching down outside like a black forest growing backwards into the ground.

"Do you like this?" he said. "What I'm doing? Do you like it?"

And I said, "Yes, it's entirely, extravagantly perfect; just make me a promise—will you—that you'll do it again—in precisely the same way—every night for the next twenty-five years—"

"You don't think that might be a little repetitious?"

"Oh no. Just promise."

"I promise," he said. "Or may the Chichevache swallow me whole."

The Chichevache rang a faint, ominous bell in my mind but I had no leisure to attend to its message just then. Later, however, I asked,

"What in the world is the Chichevache?"

"Our weekly cleaning woman in Jersey used to swear by her. She is a skinny cow-horned monster who dines only on virtuous wives, and so she spends her whole life in a state of starvation and bad temper . . ."

His explanation touched no echo, then, in my memory, but I went on puzzling about it vaguely while we refreshed ourselves with a little Pol Roger.

Then suddenly—fifteen minutes later—it all came back to me, the entire occasion, in one complete scenario—scents returned, sounds, colours I'd forgotten for seventeen years came hurtling back—and I stammered out dizzily:

"Why—why, I *remember* you!—I've met you before—oh, not to speak to—years ago at Ludwell Hospital—but you had a beard in those days, didn't you? It would have been seventeen years ago. It *was* you—wasn't it? You were making some promise to the dying old man—what was his name?—the darling old man—"

Only then did I notice his face.

And slowly began to realise that I had burst our bubble.

"You were a *nurse?*" he said slowly, "at Ludwell Hospital? But why? You must have been idiotically young? Why did your family allow it? Didn't they want you to have a proper education?"

He seemed to ask these questions, not because he wanted answers, but to give himself time. Time for what?

"Why be a nurse at—what—sixteen?"

"Seventeen. It was a training scheme."

"But why not university first?"

I wasn't about to go into Papa's change of life, or the years of money spent on crazy Uncle Laurence in his expensive bin. That, I feared, might alienate Ty's sympathy even further. I knew he didn't like illness or oddness. And he was looking at me in a very chilling way.

"But why didn't I remember your name? It was Nurse Smith—but she was killed in a road accident."

I felt a queer shock. "How in the world did you come to know that?"

He bent his frowning gaze on me; it had come back from miles and years away.

"Oh—I heard—everyone said—old Ossy had been fond of Nurse Smith. But when I inquired—thinking—some re-membrance—I heard she was dead."

Odd; very odd. I noticed, but did not raise the discrep-ancy. Poor Celia Smith, a devoted, dedicated girl, my abso-lute antithesis, had not been killed on the A30 with a boy-friend until more than a year after the old man's death.

Why should Ty have been asking for her so long after-wards? Why not right away? That was when you gave people remembrances.

"But *you*," he said, slightly shaking his head, with the movement that wriggles a blade into a crack, *"You* were working at the Ludwell then? For how long afterwards?"

"Oh, not long. A few months."

"Why did you leave?"

Tell him about Fitz? Or not?

Fortunately—perhaps—at that moment the phone rang. A cable for milord. Perhaps urgent. Should it be brought to the room/read aloud/left in milord's pigeonhole till morning?

Read it, read it, he said. It was the provisional acceptance from the Companions of Roland.

After that, out of sheer alarm, I went to sleep almost at once.

I heard Ty get up later in the night and, I thought, rum-mage in my top drawer. Was he looking for paracetamol? I tried to rouse myself but fell back into a troubled dream of crying children and fallen trees. In the morning I forgot the impression and noticed without registering that the articles in the drawer were disturbed and that my passport lay on top; weeks later I realised that he must have been studying it.

LATE that day, returning from a shopping excursion—suddenly I had felt the need to get away from Ty and go off on my own, do something disconnected from him, buy an extravagant, foolish present for Joel or Fitz—I ran into a chambermaid, my favourite, the very pretty, kittenish one with a bloom on her cheek like the pollen on a tiger lily. The cheek was not blooming now, though; it was scarlet. She was walking along the corridor, heaving with suppressed sobs, holding her hand to it.

When she saw me she stopped, gasped, spun on her heel and scurried away down a service stair.

Vaguely puzzled and disturbed, I went on to our suite, where Ty was writing letters. Telling people his news, I supposed. A tray of coffee stood on the marble table.

"Was the chambermaid in here?" it suddenly occurred to me to ask.

"What chambermaid?"

"I met her—she seemed to be upset about something."

"I don't know what you are talking about."

Ty shrugged and returned to his writing.

NEXT day the rain continued. And now Venice was in flood: St. Mark's Square had become a great lake with, on the edges, slippery wooden duckboards for pedestrians.

"Perhaps we should go back to England?" I suggested, for Ty's mood today was beginning to alarm me; he seemed utterly remote, cocooned in his own calculations, like a cat collecting spit necessary for washing, with no time to devote to casual exchanges.

"Back? Oh—yes—very well—if you want to," he replied vaguely.

"Well—shall I tell Parkson to organise flights?"

"If you want," he repeated in the same tone; I wondered if he had really heard me at all.

Later that morning a call was put through to us from a

Principessa di Montefiori, an acquaintance of Ty's in Venice whom I had heard him describe as a prize nitwitted bitch, an American film magnate's widow now remarried to an Italian, whom he had been at pains to keep in ignorance of our presence here. Now she had discovered it—from the jeweller, I gathered—and was inviting us to lunch. Rather to my dismay and greatly to my astonishment, I heard Ty accept. Yet perhaps a lunch with strangers might help to dissipate this queer unpleasant mist that seemed to have descended between us, veiling us from each other?

I would far have preferred to stay in our cosy hotel, not go out in the wet and face a crowd of unknown Venetians, but I doggedly donned some trousseau items, thinking, This is married life. The rough with the smooth, etc.

For some obscure reason I remembered an occasion, years earlier, when Fitz told me that, at the time when he started searching so acrimoniously for God, Papa had become impotent. But which had been the cause, Fitz wondered, and which the effect?

"How in the world do you know that?" I had demanded. Not that I doubted Fitz; the story seemed wholly probable; it was his knowing it that surprised me.

"Masha told me."

"Masha told *you?* Why?" I was still deeply astonished.

"Reckon she just wanted to talk about it to somebody. It had been a dreadful blow to her at the time. Physically *and* mentally. Old Masha was quite a girl in her youth, I bet," Fitz added in his pondering way.

I said, in a cantankerous tone, "But why should she tell you when she never told me?" I had to swallow jealousy, which rose in me bitter as bile. The loss of Masha, the loss of Fitz: *they* had each other, but I was cast out into the world on my own to sink or swim. And the fact that I knew this was an unfair judgment made it no easier to bear.

Fitz answered with calm reasonableness, "Probably she

knew that I'd sympathise with the poor old shard. It would only have increased *your* prejudice against him. And it's easier to tell some things to a man."

"Hah!"

Fitz gave me two impatient affectionate little taps, very fast. "Come on, out of it, old Cat. You know what I mean. There were plenty of other things she told you, not me."

That was perfectly true.

Fitz is tall and slight. He has dark hair and his eyes are beautiful—deep grey and very wide-set—Tartar eyes perhaps, though they do not slant. He does look Russian. And his mouth is always curved in a half smile, up at the corners, even when he is quite serious. His clothes invariably appear neat and clean on him, even when they are not.

Thoughts of Fitz, buried in his work at Harvard, comforted me as we stepped out into the wet glacial Venetian weather. One thing Venice, like the Kingdom of Heaven, does is reduce rich and poor to the same level. All are pedestrians. (By good fortune the Principessa's palazzo was not far from our hotel). Thoughts of Fitz, though, I suppose also made me careless; I slipped on the duckboard, which was like frosted grease. Ty grabbed me but that only helped to unbalance me still further, and I fell heavily.

"Watch out!" someone shouted, and a woman let out a high, piercing cry.

I lay where I was, feeling sorry for myself. I had heard my wrist crack as I fell on it—what a thing to happen on one's honeymoon! And my left leg was doubled underneath me in a very awkward position. Also, the Grand Canal was only a couple of inches from my cheek, which lay pillowed uncomfortably on icy, greasy stone; the canal water looked exactly the colour of ratatouille, never my favourite dish. So I lay where I was until kind, careful hands picked me up.

To my utter astonishment, two of the hands turned out to belong to my friend Joel; he was being aided by a couple of gondolieri, for whose services, in such weather, there was little other demand.

"Joel! What in the world are you doing in Venice?"

"Came here to take pictures of Posy wearing a Mancini coat," he said, nodding at the girl who had cried out at my downfall. "You and she know each other, don't you?"

I nodded without enthusiasm. She was Posy Winchester, a debby model girl who did small parts and some TV commercials. I had never liked her much, but now she was certainly being very solicitous, exclaiming in her languid nasal croak,

"Poor darling, you *did* come a purler! What a shame! Just *look* at your stockings! And your poor *fur.* How did you come to *slip,* I wonder?"

I wasn't concerned about my stockings or my poor fur, but about my wrist and my ankle, both of which felt as if they had suffered serious damage. Also I was aware of Ty, quietly furious, just behind my shoulder; if there was one thing he hated, as I had already discovered, it was public mishap and fuss. First his black eye and now this! It seemed our honeymoon was doomed to grotesque disaster.

The gondolieri made a chair of their hands and carried me back to the hotel. There a doctor was swiftly at hand to tell me that I had broken my wrist and badly sprained the ankle. During my trip to the hospital for X rays, setting, and plastering, Ty was not in evidence; all this misfortune had been too much for him, evidently. I wondered if he had gone off to the Principessa's luncheon. But Joel and Posy kindly accompanied me to the x-ray unit, and I was glad to have him at hand though I could have done without *her* cooing and lamenting. Afterwards they saw me back to the hotel and Joel ordered soup for me from Room Service; I didn't want it, feeling rather sick from pain, but he made me swallow it down. "Helps you to sleep," he said sensibly. I knew this was to be true. I have a built-in sleep factor that takes over when I am ill or injured, and on this occasion I fairly soon began to droop and drowse.

"That's the way," said Joel kindly, and settled a pillow under my plastered arm. "Just lie back now, and as soon as you're sleeping we'll leave you alone."

I lay back and their voices, softly murmuring at the other end of the big lavish bedroom, dwindled into a vague blur.

Joel's did, at least. Posy, with that trick of italicizing every other word, came through here and there.

". . . *only* married her for pub*licity* reasons, of *course*," pronounced her carrying whine. "*Any*body could see that. Vida says she knows for a *fact* that's why he *did* it . . . wouldn't give it six *months,* myself . . . darling Ty such a *rover*—as we *all* know . . ."

"Shut up, Posy," said Joel. "Don't be a raven."

Bird of ill omen, I thought. That's just what she is, with her fuzzy golliwog hair and black malicious eyes; and then I did fall asleep, and when I woke was not sure if I had really heard their voices or imagined them, since it was just the kind of remark that Posy could be expected to make.

Also when I woke up, Ty was there, politely inquiring how I did, but still, as I was acutely aware, separated from me by that curious imponderable screen of misty distance. He had, he told me, revised our arrangements, in view of my accident; he must fly back to London tonight because of details connected with his forthcoming investiture; but the doctor had forbidden me to travel for several days yet.

"You won't feel too abandoned, I hope, as your friends are here," he observed, and I realised from his tone that he probably disliked Joel very much.

"Posy's no friend of mine," I muttered.

"But Joel Redmond is in love with you, which compensates. I'm sure he will take very good care of you," Ty said, in a gentle measured way.

I stared at him.

"Ty, what total nonsense! Joel and I have known each other forever. Besides, to the best of my knowledge he's gay."

"You are wrong," said Ty dogmatically. "He is in love with you. I know things like that which you seem blind to. I would not," he added, "have been so taken with you myself if it weren't for another man being after you."

It took me a minute to assimilate this; then I replied, "You deceived yourself. In order to jack up my value, you deceived yourself. And you are entirely wrong about Joel."

He gave me look of naked hostility, then shrugged, smiled and said, "Have it your own way. What difference does it make? I must call Parkson to pack for me— Here, swallow these pills. The doctor left them—said you were to have them when you woke." And he passed me a little gilt-edged saucer of tablets, a whole handful of different ones, some white, some red, some round, some torpedo-shaped.

"Better have a glass of Mouton to wash them down," said Ty, and poured it. Then he rang for Parkson and went away to his dressing room. I, however, drank the wine and dumped the pills down the loo. I have a complete antipathy to pills, perhaps dating back to the huge horrible codliver-oil capsules Masha forced me to swallow when I was a child; or, more probably, from my experiences as a student nurse, obliged to make poor old characters in the geriatric ward gulp down fistfuls of tablets which, I knew full well, were intended only to keep them quiet, not to cure them of anything. Consequently I will never swallow a pill, though my life depended on it. It is, I suppose, yet another manifestation of my terrible neurosis—which, I see, it is now incumbent upon me to describe.

I am a hypochondriac. I *know* that I am one, I am heartily ashamed of myself and feel a fool, but there is absolutely no way in which I can rid myself of the shaming weakness. I own a big leather-bound book, a dictionary of symptoms, left over from my nursing career, and it is my bible. For whole days I have limped around utterly certain that I am dying of progressive bone disease; or that the spots in front of my eyes are signs of advanced glaucoma; or that my stiff neck and difficulty in swallowing are due to cancer of the throat. My knee, my shoulder, my palate, my ear, my inability to sit still for very long, to breathe cigarette smoke, to drink milk, are all warning signs of terminal diseases. I can mock myself out of the more farfetched afflictions, such as Cheesewasher's lung or pulpy kidney, or Kuru (suffered only by cannibals in New Guinea), but cancer of the stomach I *know* I have, and shall presently die of; how else could my symptoms reproduce so identically those of Masha? Of course I am not going to go to a doctor; what would be the point of that? His ineffectual remedies and messing about would only prolong the grisly process as it did in her case; I intend to keep silent until the very last moment or (preferably) beyond, so that my loved ones need not endure the protracted agony and horror that we went through with Masha.

That is why—I must acknowledge—I married Ty with a certain feeling of guilty deceit and irresponsibility. This did seem a major factor among the things about me of which he was ignorant, and I did acknowledge to myself that he might be getting rather a poor deal. But—on the other hand—I did fend him off as long as I could. In the end, since he seemed so extremely keen on acquiring me, I thought, Hell! Why not? I shall be given a bit of fun and comfort and luxury, welcome indeed after a life confined to hard work and short commons; Ty wins the blonde prize he apparently wants, and will soon have the distinction of being a stricken widower mourning his youthful bride. Everyone will feel extremely sorry for him and he can have his pick of any number of sympathetic girls. It seemed quite a fair bargain, ailing though I was. (This valetudinarian streak is horribly important in my life. As will be seen again).

But now that a mysterious rift had opened between Ty and me, I found it hard to make plans. I didn't know what Ty was thinking. Could he really have taken such a violent dislike to me (for that is how it seemed) simply on account of this odd little discovery, that we had met once before, momentarily, eighteen or so years ago? I had been sixteen or seventeen, enduring misery and drudgery at Ludwell—an unimportant and despised bottom cog in the hospital hierarchy. But the old dying businessman, accommodated in superior quarters in a side ward, had taken a fancy to me, always cracked a joke, had a kindly word as I polished his bedside locker or carried away his wash-water. Seasmith, he used to call me, on account of my name badge, C. SMITH, encased in plastic on my starched bib: "And how is my jokey little Seasmith today?" he would inquire fondly as I wheeled in all the paraphernalia. He had had a successful heart bypass operation some years earlier and was now due for another. The general opinion, not transmitted to him of course, was that this time the chance of success was far lower; only one in five. And so it proved.

He was a nice old man. To me anyway. What was his name?

"The accustomed sight of death." Where does that line come from? Sometimes—often—I regret my lost education; I wish I had read English literature properly, instead of by random gulps, read Plato and Catullus, knew the meaning of names like Goethe and Heidegger, Masha, even in her years of agony, had masses of mental resources to fall back on, and made good use of them; she was reading *The Golden Bowl* on the day she died in hideous pain.

What *was* that old man's name? I see him lying dead, the colour of grey wax, with his eyes closed, the folds in his cheeks gone rigid, like a frosted rutted path. His eyebrows—extraordinary eyebrows—thrust out in front, sharp as snails' horns, in white points, three quarters of an inch ahead of his face. And the eyes, in deep triangular sockets below, sparkled when he was alive with shrewdness and acquisitiveness. He had been a tough old character in his day; got a knighthood for some crafty piece of dealing—connected with building? with educational supplies? with North Sea Gas? What *was* his name?

Here comes my jokey little Seasmith.

Jokey I certainly wasn't, except in his room. The matron only tolerated my presence in the hospital because of Papa's bygone reputation, the Sisters rated me lower than an intestinal worm; the mere sight of me caused charge nurses to narrow their eyes and tighten their mouths. I felt frozen—outcast—an object of disgust, utterly without value. Yet one molecule of me knew that was not quite true, because on what I earned depended the welfare of the people at home. Papa by now was drifting out of reach. That thought, like a small central core of warmth, kept me alive.

Here comes my jokey little Seasmith.

He had huge strong-knuckled hands. The game of bowls had been his hobby; "like Francis Drake," he told me grandly. I could imagine those massive hands grasping the polished heavy sphere.

On the day of his operation I took the old man a big bunch of primroses and a good-luck card. (In those bygone days, primroses grew plentifully on the banks of every road—in Dorset, at least; farmers weren't so free then with their weed-killer sprays.) In a bowl on the locker by his bed they breathed out their delicate mysterious fragrance. "Thank you, my dear. I expect they'll bring me luck. They take me back to my days as a young 'un. All over Jersey, they grew. You could smell 'em like nutmeg as you walked along the road."

He'd come from the Channel Islands originally; that was why he used that curious expression, "may the Chichevache get you."

I wish I could remember his name. It has lodged halfway up my brain, like a snippet of apple peel in the throat.

I have him connected with a portrait—the card I took him, a man in grey, skating, with his arms folded. It was one of Masha's pictures, which she stuck up all over the house, wherever they could please her eye as she worked. (Once, in the Louvre, I burst out crying at the sight of a still life, by Cézanne I think it was, all blue and green with some oranges and a triangle of crumpled tea towel hanging down. That took me, straight as a dagger, back to Masha.) I begged the skater postcard from her, when I went home on my free afternoon, and gave it to the old boy. There was something of his calm dignity about this poker-faced character gliding along the ice in a black hat against a wintry background. "Don't you think it looks just like you, Sir Ostin?" I said to him. He chuckled. "Never did learn to skate. Not much ice in Jersey. Nice picture, though. Kind of you to bring it. I like a picture that tells you something. My daughter, now, Lilias, she's all for this *conceptural* stuff—putting a pink bedroom chair in the middle of a hazel copse. Stuff and nonsense! This, I like. Leave it there against the water glass. I'll think about that old boy slipping along, while they are putting me under. What's the painter's name?" He turned over the card. "Raeburn. Rhymes with mine. Never heard of him, but he's good."

"You'll look after Lilias, won't you, Jimmy?" he asked, when the transfusions hadn't helped, and it was plain that he was going fast. *"Marry her—look after her—see she doesn't come to grief?"*

"Of course I will, sir. You needn't have asked," responded that other character, that far-away, long-ago person whom I now know to have been Ty. But how different he was then! With a heavy black moustache, his thick black hair brushed sideways and covered with Brylcreem, his face (what one could see of it behind the moustache) young, unformed, not yet settled into the lines of authority and decision it has since acquired. The only familiar details were the huge, unusual ears and handsome curved nose. "Of *course* I'll look after her," he repeated.

"I'm leaving the money to you, not to her. Leaving it to her would be like throwing it in the sea." The old man moved fretfully. "You'll have to dish it out to her in small quantities—stop it getting into the hands of some ghastly guru, make sure she doesn't spend it on dope. It's a big responsibility."

"It's a lot of money," said Ty respectfully. Yes, his voice had not changed. It was the same; lighter, younger, but his all right. I had slipped in to perform some menial task.

"Good lad. You'll do it, I know." And then the old man had used that odd phrase.

I slipped out again; I was so lowly a bit of furniture, Ty had probably never noticed my presence. He must have had a lot on his mind. This was a charged moment for him. Making a promise to a dying person. How many of us have to do such a thing? Poor Dodo does in the TV serial—but luckily her grisly old husband dies before finally exacting it.

Had Ty kept the promise?

That day had been important in my life, not only because of the old man's death, but because later on I met for the first time Andrei Baradin, a young homesick Russian doctor, over in England on a six-month course. His grandfather was a farfetched cousin of Masha's mother, and so he telephoned the rectory, and Masha told him that I worked in the hospital and would give him directions how to find his way to Yetford. Family-minded Masha was enchanted, of course, at the chance to meet a new relation, however distant. She became very fond of him. He used to go out there as often as he could. He loved Masha. Yetford was like a second home to him, he said.

And I fell in love with him.

FOR two days after Ty had gone to England I stayed in my room. I felt fairly shattered. In part, because I was getting quite severe pain from my wrist and ankle; but mostly because of Ty.

I had not, I thought, nourished unreasonable expectations of our union. I am basically cagey and pessimistic about relationships, having been rejected so unequivocally, once and for all, by Papa. But then, Ty's pursuit of me had been so violently obsessional, he had appeared to put such a huge value on me, that, lulled into a false sense of security, I had been taken off guard. After all, we had seemed to get along so well together during those early weeks of courtship. One tiny childish fragment of my mind still wistfully suggested that perhaps we would do so again, perhaps this severance was just a temporary thing, he had been excited and preoccupied over the acceptance by the Companions of Roland, he was not good at responding or being supportive to other people's illness—why should he be, he never had to deal with such a situation before? Matters would right themselves, surely, when I got back to London?

But the rest of me knew this was total delusion. I had in some way given him a mortal shock, and his view of me had changed so much that quite possibly he wished never to set eyes on me again. And—observed yet another part of me, the down-to-earth puritanical part which comes from Masha's Welsh ancestry—you really have no right to complain about that, for your motives in marrying him were impure and self-centred; you thought that life as Lady Fortuneswell would be a cushy billet, that you would be looked after for the rest of your days. However few.

Hah!

So what has happened just serves you gladly, as Mrs. Eppy used to say.

AFTER a couple of days Randolph Grove called me from London.

Joel was still in Venice. Taking a few pictures of S. Giacometto was his ostensible reason, but concern for me was, I thought, the real one. He had been round to the hotel each day, leaving books, tapes, and a headset, but since I was rather low-spirited and in pain, had not stayed long either time. On the day when Randolph called, he had gone off to Torcello, leaving word that he would drop in that evening.

"Cat? Is that you?" said Randolph in London. "I really hate to disturb you on your honeymoon, but something very unfortunate and distressing has happened."

It was instructive to observe the changes in people's manner towards me since I had become Lady Fortuneswell. Some, like Joel, were completely unaffected; but Randolph's tone today was the one of plummy devotion that he used with Ty.

"I'm sorry, *very* sorry to have to tear you away from your good time," he went on—plainly he had not heard of my accident, or Ty's departure—"but we're going to have to reshoot all the scenes with Jerry Faber—"

"Oh *no!*" I said, aghast, "don't tell me—"

"Yes," he said, "yes, I'm afraid so. He died this week. And some of his scenes were still outstanding—"

"Oh, how dreadful. How *dreadful.*"

Jerry Faber was a youngish actor who specialised in old-man parts. In our serial he had the role of Peter Featherstone, a foxy old character who, at death's door, takes delight in plaguing all his hopeful, greedy relatives by not letting them know who is going to inherit his fortune. They come daily, camp in his house, clamour their claims, and get nowhere. It makes very good television. And the old man's favourite nephew, one of the story's heroes, nearly has his life ruined through dependance on expectations which come to nothing because—in a very striking scene—one of the heroines will not burn a Last Will and Testament at the dying old man's request.

The really grim irony of Jerry Faber's taking the part was that he himself was close to death. From AIDS. He knew it, everyone else knew it too, but this didn't affect his resolve to keep on working as long as he possibly could. He was a very fine actor and, as he said, acting was the only thing that he enjoyed about his life these days—so why not keep on doing it?

He had been happy and triumphant because everyone agreed that he was playing Featherstone's part exceptionally well. "It will do as my memorial," he said to me once. But he spoke too soon, poor wretch. All those scenes of his would now have to go into limbo. Like him.

"Oh, *poor* Jerry," I said again. "I'm so very, very sorry."

I was, too. We had all loved Jerry, who never whined or repined but was, on the contrary, cheerful and gallant about his prospects, even contriving to crack jokes, really funny ones. Everybody in the group would miss him. The accustomed face of death, I thought. Here it is again. After somebody you have been fond of dies, what have you left? Only the world.

On my own account I felt a selfish dismay, because how in heaven's name could my particular scene with Featherstone be remade, lumbered as I now was with a wrist and ankle both in bandages and the wrist in a plaster cast? Fortunately there was only one scene, but that an important one. I had to call at his house, arriving on horseback with my brother, take off my hat and veil, sing a couple of ballads to the old man, and then hang around, thus contriving to be seen for the first time by the handsome new young doctor whom, sight un-seen, I have already laid my plans to marry. It had been one of my favourite scenes in the whole serial; I had given it my very best, and felt uncertain, just now, that I would be able to repeat that best.

I explained my plight to Randolph Grove, who listened with equal dismay.

"Oh well," he said at length, "We'll have to fudge it somehow. Separate shots—head only with you and we'll splice in bits from the first batch. Shawn Kyle is taking over the part. We'll do some tailoring, we'll manage somehow. But I'd like you to come back to Knoyle for a few days. Just to *be* there. We need extra footage—the accountants are grumbling—to justify the use of Knoyle again. Anyway, if Ty is already back in England I feel better about asking you."

No apologies for making me travel in my damaged state, I thought crossly. But then, Randolph never did consider other people's convenience. And in fact I'd be glad enough to leave Venice; this hotel was getting me down; though I'd just as soon have stayed away from Knoyle.

"The nuisance of it is," said Randolph's voice, "that we can't use the Manor itself. The house has been let for some damned ecologists' conference. You probably know about that."

"But we shan't need the Manor itself, shall we?" I suggested. "The Featherstone scenes were all shot at one of the farms on the estate."

"Yes, that is true. We'll have to lodge the team in the Trust House at Weymouth. Rig up a greenroom in a tent or something," he said fretfully, and went on to more details which he would never have bothered to share with me before I was Lady Fortuneswell. "So when can you come back, Cat? Tonight? And down to Dorset tomorrow? Good, I'll see you. Call me as soon as you arrive." And he rang off.

I summoned Parkson, who had been left behind (with a fairly ill grace) by my husband, to take care of my practical needs, and told him to get me a London flight, pack my things, and organise a wheelchair. How easily, I thought, we acquire the habits of wealth. But I had better prepare to abandon them again.

Joel returned from Torcello and I told him the news. He was shocked and saddened but not surprised by Jerry's death.

"Poor devil, I could see it in his face," he said. "That last evening at Knoyle. But what about you, Katya? Are you really fit to travel?"

"Oh yes," I said. "I'll be glad to go. Parkson's doing all the organising."

Joel stuck out his bottom jaw, as he does when worried.

"What's the plan? Are you going to Ty's Battersea place?"

"No," I told him (for this had been arranged in the course of the day), "Ty isn't there anyway, he's in Paris." (Going through preliminary processes for the Companions of Roland, he was, but I didn't tell Joel that.) "No, what I'm going to do is make my way straight down to Knoyle; Parkson will drive me in the Rolls."

"Where will you stay?"

"Ty has a house—remember? One of the houses at Caundle Quay has been permanently dedicated to his use. So I'm going to put up there. It will," I added a trifle doubtfully, "it will be fun."

"*Fun?*" Joel exploded with rage. "*Fun?* Who set up this crazy plan? Caundle Quay? How will you get up and down the hill?"

"I'm becoming quite expert on my crutches. Anyway,

Ty's house is near the top, I'm told. Someone can push me in my wheelchair. It will all work out," I said.

"But what will you *eat?* Suppose you need a doctor?"

"For heaven's sake, Joel! All that can be arranged!"

"It *can* be," he growled, "but will it, that's what I'd like to know?"

Joel wasn't able to get a seat on the same plane as me, so I flew back in lonely first-class comfort, with my crutches propped in the closet where they hang the garment bags. And at Gatwick, efficient Parkson had arranged to have the Rolls waiting, in which he swiftly drove me down to Dorset.

So that was how I arrived for the second time at Caundle Quay.

4

"OLGA Laszlo moves into Number 6 today," Pat Limbourne said to her friend. "Can you put the basics into the house, and generally make her welcome? I have to go into Dorchester for the story-prize ceremony. *Terrible* stories . . . never mind. It keeps them out of betting shops."

She gathered up a large untidy pile of handwritten manuscripts from among the flowerpots, garden bast, coffee cups and photographic equipment on the kitchen table.

But Elspeth, engaged in taking off gum boots, sat back on the doorstep nursing one aged knobby foot, and gazed upwards in something as close to consternation as her amiable, crumpled face would permit.

"*Olga Laszlo?* You never told me *she* was coming here?"

"Didn't know myself," Pat said shortly. "Ty's office passed on the glad news yesterday evening. She'd applied direct, and it seems her father was a friend or professional associate of old Leyburn—ran his advertising—knew him from way back—and she's engaged on some design work for the Dorchester theatre—on the face of it she seems perfectly eligible—I suppose they thought so in the office—"

"Oh *dear,*" said Elspeth, slowly pulling off the other gum boot. Her face was all creased sideways in a frowning grin of distress and perplexity. "That girl is such a disruptive influence, poor thing. One can't exactly blame her, I suppose, after having been a refugee in childhood and so forth—"

"Other people have been refugees and survived to lead normal lives. Anyway, let's hope she won't be here for long. If it is just for one specific job she won't have any reason to stay on afterwards."

"She *is* very talented—or so people say—" Elspeth shuffled her buniony feet into espadrilles and stood up by cautious degrees. Then, through the window, she caught sight of little Shuna. Odd Tom was busy in the yard, training the grape vine, with great delicacy fastening its long and floppy fronds to lengths of wire which he had nailed across the courtyard wall. Little Shuna was handing him strips of rag for this purpose. Also, apparently to encourage the vine to bear fruit, she was embellishing it with fruits of her own construction, small round typewriter-ribbon tins, enamelled in red and hung on strings.

She was making some comment about this to Odd Tom, who responded with an eager flow of reply, waving his hands, mouthing vigorously, nodding his head up and down.

"Odd Tom is teaching Shuna sympathetic magic," observed Elspeth, who had taken a degree in anthropology back in the thirties.

"He has a local reputation as a healer—did you know that? Mrs. Monkton at the post office told me." Pat whisked a comb through her short brown hair and briefly glanced into a pocket mirror. Her forthright, uncompromising countenance bore a fairly close resemblance to that of Oliver Cromwell.

"Oh, dear heavens—I've just thought of something else about Olga—" Elspeth began.

"I must go, Bets, I'll be late. Well—what?"

"Do you suppose Olga could have any idea—about—"

Elspeth nodded her snowy head in the direction of the child outside the window.

"Shouldn't think so. Seems quite unlikely. Why should she? Nobody knew."

But Pat was frowning too.

"That would be *absolutely* undesirable— You know what Olga's like—full of half-baked psychological theories. No discretion whatsoever."

"And picks up gossip like black velvet picks up dust. And Satan's own passion for meddling. Specially with children."

"Well, it's because she lost her own two," Elspeth went on distressfully. "Which makes her even more inclined—"

"That was her own stupid fault."

"Of course, though she'd never admit it. But she does take a devouring interest in other people's—"

"Don't I know. Feels she's that much more qualified to sort out their problems. Well," said Pat, exchanging her grubby cardigan for a tweed jacket, "We'll just have to be as tight as clams. Invent some story, Bets—you're good at that."

Elspeth suddenly grinned an eldritch grin.

"We'll have to hope for the best. What time does she arrive?"

"Dunno. After lunch. See you by and by."

Pat gathered up her manuscripts and went out, waving to Tom and the child as she passed, then climbing briskly up the steep marble-stepped street towards the car park at the top.

Elspeth presently announced to the two workers in the courtyard that it was lunchtime. The child came in; Odd Tom remained outside. He had become accustomed to solitude and preferred it. Elspeth took him out an apple dumpling, a tomato and a bottle of stout, which he accepted with a nod of thanks, putting them beside the crisps and cheese he had brought with him.

"His diet is all wrong," Elspeth lamented, going back indoors.

"But he is healthy," objected Shuna. "Quite as healthy as you."

"He seems healthy now; but if he got ill he wouldn't have any resistance. What have you got there, my love?" she asked, noticing, as she sat down to her own hastily assembled meal, that the child was studying a thick packet of greasy newspaper cuttings. They were yellow and ravelled with age or usage. Elspeth's first instinct was to snatch the unhealthy-looking wad away from the child.

"It's about Tom's wife. He was telling me. It's very sad."

"What happened to her?" Elspeth asked with interest.

"She got sick. Like you said Tom might. And then, while she was in hospital, people came and took their home away."

"Took it away?"

"Yes, took it right away. When they got back, it was gone. Tom had been staying in the town where the hospital was. Poole, I think. When they got back, there was just a patch of earth, all bare and muddy."

"My heavens!"

"It was horrible," Shuna said seriously.

"Was their home a tent or caravan?"

"A mobile home, Tom called it. It was *really nice* inside, he said—they had a green and gold stove, and a fitted carpet, and Jenny had made the curtains. And all their things. His collection of matchboxes. They never saw it again. They couldn't find out where it had been taken. She got ill again, and he hadn't the time."

"But that's *dreadful.*" Elspeth frowned in anger and pity. Reaching across, she took a cutting and read the headline PENSIONERS LOSE FIGHT TO SAVE MOBILE HOME. "I wonder if they got proper legal aid? I suppose the council must have had some kind of a case—I must try and talk to Tom about it. (Only I do find it so hard to understand what he says). I wonder if he'd let us help him get some teeth."

"His were in the mobile home, he says. Now he's got

used to doing without them and reckons they were just a nuisance. He only wore them for company occasions.''

"What happened to his wife?''

"She took another bad turn—finding their home gone like that. And went back into the hospital and died. Then Tom went and lived on a traffic circle.''

"A *traffic circle?*''

"On the Dorchester bypass. As a—what do people do when they want to show they haven't been treated properly?''

"Protest.''

"Yes, a protest. He lived in a tent on the traffic circle. But the police made him leave. Then he found Arkwright somewhere, wandering about. Arkwright had been their cat when they had their home. He was real pleased to meet up with old Arkwright again, he said. Hadn't reckoned on such a bit of luck. So he and Arkwright lived in an old APV till the soldiers found them and threw them out.''

"What is an APV?''

"I don't know,'' said Shuna.

"Some sort of army vehicle, I suppose.''

"He said the soldiers would have let him stay, he wasn't doing no harm, but the Major said he was to go.''

"Where does he live now?'' asked Elspeth, studying the rest of the clippings, which were almost illegible from grease and wear.

"He will never tell. Mum's the word, he says.''

"You can't really blame him . . . I wonder if Lord Fortuneswell would give him a cottage in Glifonis . . .'' Elspeth's voice faded as she considered the improbability of this. Odd Tom was not at all the kind of occupant Lord Fortuneswell had in mind for his chic Greek cottages.

"A whole house?'' Shuna's expression was sceptical. "I don't think Tom would want a whole house. He wouldn't

mind a nice railway carriage, he says, if British Rail was offering any. Or an old Wessex bus, pensioned off."

"How long ago did all this happen? There aren't dates on
any of these."

"I don't know. Quite a long time, I should think— Why
are you putting in your hearing aid? Is somebody coming?"

"Yes, later on this afternoon."

Elspeth had recently taken to a small inconspicuous hearing device which sat snugly in her ear. Impatient of all gadgets, she had adopted it with the greatest reluctance and still
wore it infrequently. Pat and the child had clear voices to
which she was well accustomed, so at home she rarely troubled to use the aid. But in the presence of strangers she found
it an advantage. Olga Laszlo, she remembered, had an extremely soft, confidential voice, delivered in a rapid breathless murmur.

"Who is coming?" inquired Shuna, watching with technical interest as a tiny yellow protective shield was peeled from
the pinhead-sized battery, which was then deftly slotted into
the moulded pink plastic device, itself little bigger than a
kidney bean.

"A lady called Olga Laszlo. She's working on a job at the
Dorchester theatre. She'll be very busy and she won't be here
long," Elspeth answered rather repressively.

"What kind of a job?"

"Designing scenery."

Shuna's eyes lit with interest, but Elspeth said, "Now,
that's enough chat. It's time for your afternoon rest. And
after that I've set you ten Latin exercises and a bit of parsing.
When those are finished you can draw a picture—anything
you like—then practise your piano pieces for twenty minutes,
then you can go out and help Tom some more."

"Can I first give him back his pieces of newspaper?"

"Yes, of course."

Looking after the child as she ran out, Elspeth heaved a

deep habitual sigh, of care and responsibility. Then, briskly, she addressed herself to compiling a list of the supplies that would be needed to make Olga Laszlo's house fit for occupation.

A delivery van plied weekly from the Dorchester supermarkets, and would bring out most household necessities if instructed beforehand; accordingly, pencil in hand, Elspeth went to the telephone. Just as she got there, it rang.

"Number 2, Glifonis?" Elspeth announced.

"Oh—hullo—Miss Morgan, is that you? Lord Fortuneswell's office here. We have another new neighbour for you— can you take delivery?"

"Of course! The more the merrier. Glifonis is really filling up—that's so nice. With such interesting people, too! Who is coming now?"

"The new Lady Fortuneswell—Cat Conwil the actress."

"Now, that really *is* interesting— But I thought they were still on their honeymoon?" inquired Elspeth, who knew everything in the news from an addictive reading of *The Independent* every night.

"Lord Fortuneswell has had to fly over to Paris on business and she has to come down to Dorset because they are obliged to reshoot some of that TV serial they were working on at Knoyle. And she can't stay in the Manor because of the conference being held there. So can you see that Lord Fortuneswell's own house—Number 1, is it?—will be ready for occupation?"

"Certainly, I'll be glad to. No problem!" Elspeth chirped. "I'll get Mrs. Monkton just to run over and give it a polish. And make sure the heat is on."

ON her way back later from this errand, Elspeth saw, with a slight lowering of the spirits, that Olga Laszlo had arrived and was picking her way cautiously down the wide-spaced marble steps, rendered slippery and hazardous by a sea mist. Olga's raincoated figure bore a cautious, deferential air, depressingly familiar to Elspeth—as if the new arrival were, in advance, apologising for her presence, knew that she could be received only on sufferance, and hated to give everybody the acute trouble she knew she must be causing.

"Good afternoon!" called Miss Morgan cordially. "Your little house is all ready for you! Just come on down this way. We can get your luggage later. Or one of the Greeks will carry it down for you. They are such nice, obliging men."

"Oh," sighed Olga. "Thank you. But I have nothing—just a little knapsack."

She gave Elspeth a wan smile; it conveyed that her entire worldly goods were packed into the little knapsack.

"Very good, then you can get it yourself," said Elspeth comfortably, not about to take any nonsense. She knew that Olga made a handsome living from her theatrical designs.

Olga Laszlo was handsome in a haggard, hollow-cheeked, hollow-eyed fashion, but made the worst of herself—on purpose, Elspeth thought tartly. Her dark hair, revealed as she pulled off the dirty brown wool scarf, was unkempt, rough, and could obviously do with a good wash. Her sallow skin was equally rough. Looks as if she never ate an orange in her life, surmised Elspeth. And then she carries herself so badly! —with her head poked forward, and her spine slouched, like an old woman. Which she certainly is not, thought Elspeth; I doubt if she is a day over thirty-four. And just look at those teeth! Not bad teeth, but does she *ever* brush them? A chain-smoker too. And she once had two little girls. What a terrible mother she must have been to the poor children; really, from their point of view, it's probably a mercy that she lost the custody.

But then Elspeth's kinder nature reproved her for these judgments. All children should be with their own mothers—

especially girls; the girls probably loved Olga just as dearly as if she had been Mrs. Beeton and Niobe rolled into one. No doubt she loved them too. It's not to be wondered at that she has let herself go.

None of these ruminations were reflected in Elspeth's face or voice as she opened the solid wooden door (painted a deep chocolate brown) saying, cheerfully, "Here you are, then! Number 6, Glifonis. It's all yours. Front room here, in the front—kitchen behind—bathroom to the left—bedroom at the back. All as Greek as can be—except that in Greece the bathroom would be on the other side of the courtyard. But in view of the English climate and to economize on space—which is very limited in this little crack of land—the bathroom has been fitted inside the house."

"But it is charming—perfectly charming!" Olga's low, breathless voice combined a touch of her father's Hungarian accent with an English upper-class intonation acquired from a very superior boarding school (where she had been maintained by the kind offices of friends). The result was often unintentionally patronising; as now. Elspeth bristled a little, then laughed at herself.

"Groceries in here—towels—extra blankets—I'm afraid there's no room for a work-desk, but I got them to put you in an extra-large kitchen table—"

"Oh, you are so *kind,*" sighed Olga. Her gaze rested on the table with a hint of disparagement. "Could there be an easel as well, I wonder? And is there a telephone?"

"No, I'm afraid none of the houses has a phone yet," said Elspeth, passing over the easel, "except for ours, Number 2 (British Telecom, you know how they are)—but you are welcome to come and use our phone at any time," she added untruthfully.

"Oh—but I wouldn't—that is such an imposition—isn't there a call box? Can't something be done to hurry British Telecom? Perhaps if Ty himself were to get on to them?"

"I think he's off in Paris at the moment," Miss Morgan said restrainedly.

"Oh—well—then I suppose I must be *resigned.* Could I possibly come and use it *now?* I do have so many arrangements to make—"

And five minutes later she was up at Number 2 holding a series of prolonged conversations over the telephone, which stood on the kitchen windowsill. Elspeth at first did her best to ignore these, pottering in and out with cuttings in jam jars, and bowls of washing hung out in the damp air to get damper; but, despite herself, she could not avoid hearing a good deal of them.

"Darling Tig, yes, I'll be in tomorrow with *some* of the drawings—I'm afraid I've only done four or *five,* there were so many other pressing commitments—time? Yes, darling, of course there will be time—yes, it's a *funny* little house—primitive to a degree—but still, beggars as you know cannot be *choosers . . ."* "Dearest Swit—I had to leave London in a rush—but I'll be in touch *very soon*—could you be a *dove* and collect a packet of transparencies for me from Nonpareil and *post* them down to me here express registered—yes, I'm in the back of beyond in *Dorset*—they've put me in a funny little Greek villa—and, Swit, could you be a first-class *angel* and go round to Lexham Gardens and see if there's an *electric* bill and if so could you be another dove and *pay* it—as well as anything else that looks at all ominous? I'll refund you as *soon* as they pay me down here—oh, not *bad,* yes, Swit, *do* you happen to know if Mars Timlo's show is still on at the Walden? If *so,* I wonder if you'd be a real *honey* and go round and perhaps get a few trans*par*encies made—could you?"

Elspeth began to be sorry for the unknown Swit and to feel that he/she was being made to pay quite dearly for all those terms of endearment.

"How about a cup of tea or coffee?" she inquired presently, when Olga was between calls—coffee being her own unvarying habit around three-thirty of an afternoon.

"Oh, wonderful, yes, thank you," Olga replied inattentively, and was off into another round of one-sided conversations. When presented with a cup of Elspeth's inky instant coffee she took one sip, grimaced, and pushed the cup a short distance away along the windowsill. The accompanying scone she ignored.

Elspeth acknowledged this piece of behaviour with a slight nod to herself, eyebrows raised, as if marking squares on an imaginary form.

"*Right,* dearest Gretl, then I'll be hearing from you very soon," concluded Olga, and finally replaced the receiver giving Elspeth, as she did so, a mournful smile. "Everything takes so *long* to ar*range,* don't you find? But now I'll slip away and leave you in peace."

Shuna, lessons completed, had been spending the afternoon down with the Greeks on the harbour front, watching them erect a boat shed. At this moment, pink, damp, and slightly spangled with sawdust, she returned for her tea.

"*Aha!*" exclaimed Olga, her eyes lighting up as if someone had pressed a switch marked "Main Beam," when the child came through the door. "And whom have we *here?*"

"This is Shuna," said Elspeth shortly. "Shuna lives with us at present. Shuna, this is Mrs. Pendennis."

"Oh, good heavens *no,* not any *more,* don't call me that, I beg you! I went back to Miss Laszlo long, long ago. But in any case I hope you will call me Olga! And will you be my little friend and show me all over the village? I expect you know every nook and *cranny* of the place, don't you?" Olga said, fixing little Shuna with that headlamp gaze.

Elspeth longed to say, "Shuna has her lessons to get on with," but with an effort kept silent. Shuna replied matter-of-factly, "Yes, I will, but it's not at all complicated. Just a street down to the bottom. And won't you be very busy? Aunt Elspeth said so, with your work at the theatre."

"Yes, of course I shall, but I always have time to make a new *friend.*"

Olga divided equally between them the slightly tragic smile which suggested that she had hardly a friend in the world, and that friends in her estimate were valued above front-row seats in the auditorium of heaven. On the evidence of her recent telephone conversations this hardly seemed the case.

" 'Bye—" she breathed, gave a conspiratorial wink at the child, and left, pulling on her brown scarf.

Shuna sat down, without comment, to her tea.

5

I was spared any need for sensations of sorrowful memory on
our late arrival at Caundle Quay, for the night was pitch-dark,
and rain, sluicing over the windscreen of the Rolls, was swept
off it in great opaque swathes by the wipers; nothing could be
seen at all.

"They don't seem to go in for lavish street lighting
around here," I remarked, when our headlights finally lo-
cated a sign that said GLIFONIS—RESIDENTS' PARKING
ONLY, and Parkson pulled to a halt beneath it. There
weren't many other cars to be seen in the largish dark space
—two or three, perhaps.

Parkson made no answer to my remark. He had not been
at all enthusiastic about this assignment and had made no
secret of the fact that he considered his duty was to Lord
Fortuneswell, not to me. Being obliged to grope around a
steep, muddy village in the dark, in a downpour, was going
to be the last straw for him, I could see.

"You'd better stay there while I go to the house and un-
lock it," he said. "Then I'll carry down the luggage and stuff.

Then I'll unfold your wheelchair and take you down." He picked a hamper off the back seat.

I made no demur to this proposal, in view of the utter absence of welcoming committee, curtseying peasants, smiling tenantry prepared to carry me on their shoulders to my abode. It was, after all, eleven o'clock on a very nasty evening. Not a light showed; the inhabitants of Glifonis were all abed.

Accordingly I waited in the car, feeling sorry for Parkson, who was presently going to have to drive back to London, so as to catch an early morning flight to Paris.

After several minutes a small light sprang out, downhill, past a corner of road. More time passed; then Parkson returned, without comment took my bags from the boot, and vanished again into the rainy dark.

This time I had a lengthier wait. There were two food hampers, besides my luggage; he was probably unpacking them.

By and by he materialised again, got out the wheelchair, which had travelled in the back of the car, and set it up. Then, still in silence, he helped me from the front seat. This was an awkward process. I have played scenes with actors whom I disliked, or who disliked me; the physical contact is always hard to handle.

He had a good deal of difficulty pushing the wheelchair over the soft surface of the car park, a mixture of mud and builders' rubble; I heard him grunt. Next we came to a sloping paved way which presented its own problems; twice he slipped and muttered something under his breath. "Take it easy, Parkson," I said, wondering if we were both going to hurtle all the way down to the harbour foot.

"It's this—marble," he muttered. Then he jolted the chair down a step. Not having expected this, I let out a yelp as the bump jarred my ankle and wrist. Parkson made no apology. "Take it easy," I said again. "How many more of these steps are there?'' He pretended he hadn't heard and strode on. There were five or six steps, I found, spaced at perhaps twelve-foot intervals. Though I tried to relax, and clutched the chair arm with my good hand, each step found me unprepared and wrenched my injured joints. Also, the icy downpour was working its way through my raincoat and no doubt beginning to soak the plaster on my wrist. Still it must be much worse for Parkson, who had been out in it, now, for over twenty minutes.

Soon he turned aside from the paved track and hauled the chair, backwards, up some more steps towards a lighted doorway.

"Here you are, then," he said curtly, adding, "Lucky the chair goes through the door," in a morose tone, as if that amount of luck was wholly undeserved, in his opinion, by anybody idiotic enough to have thought up such a plan as this.

I blinked in the dazzle of light, which was not in fact particularly bright, but seemed so after the inky darkness outside. We were in a plain little front room with a tiled floor and the minimum of Spartan simplicity in its furnishings: small couch by the door, a table, two chairs.

"Kitchen's through there," said Parkson with a nod. "I put your stores in the fridge. Right? Bathroom to the left, bedroom behind. Okay?"

He made motions of imminent departure.

"Wait, wait a minute," I said hastily. "Won't—won't you have a cup of tea—or something—before you drive all the way back?"

He shook his head. "No time. I have to be on my way."

"Hey, but—wait just a minute!" He turned, impatiently, already halfway through the door. "This chair—how exactly does it work?"

The chair, compact, elaborate and heavy, was electrical and capable of self-propulsion. No doubt it would serve me well, though not, I feared, in Glifonis, which seemed to be all steps. But I had met the chair for the first time two hours ago at Gatwick Airport.

"Controls on the armrest," said Parkson with patience. "Here, see? Switch on. That lever's forward motion." I tried the switch and shot with startling speed across the room.

"Wow!"

"Other lever is backward," said Parkson. "That's your steering handle for the wheels. That's neutral. Brake here. Okay?" And then he really was gone, without a good-bye, obviously feeling that he had done his duty and more than his duty by me.

I took ten minutes or so getting the measure of the wheel-chair. Useful preparation for disability in later life, I thought wryly, as I did my best to control and forestall its wayward dashes; both of us receiving several sharpish knocks in the process. (It was a lucky thing, quite providential really, that the little house was so sparsely furnished.) By and by I managed the delicate passage through the doorway into the kitchen, which proved to be about the same size as the front room, and was equipped with a refrigerator the size of St. Paul's, an electric cooker spacious as a rugby field, a lot of empty shelves, a capacious sink, a counter, and a stool. A plate, knife, fork, spoon, bowl, cup and saucer had been hastily ranged along the counter. A new kettle and saucepan stood on the cooker. A glass French door by the sink led out to some kind of yard or terrace.

Feeling a strong need for alcohol, I looked in a drawer below the counter for a corkscrew. The drawer was empty. But fortunately, I remembered, there had been some bottles of champagne in those hampers lugged to the house by Parkson. They must now be in the fridge. I manoeuvred myself over to its door and, after a number of tries, managed to work the chair into a position from which the door could be opened and the bottle removed. This struggle brought back painful recollections of my equitation lessons for the part of Rosy. A lot of lesson time had been devoted to the business of opening and closing field gates while astride of a horse; people who ride horses are very preoccupied by gates. The wheelchair was quite as stupid and uncooperative as any horse, and much more volatile. Having at last successfully extracted a bottle of Veuve du Boulanger, I accidentally jolted the Forward lever with my elbow while shutting the fridge door, shot precipitately across the kitchen, in panic pressed the Backward level, and nearly smashed myself and the bottle against the sink. The fizz, by the time I poured it, was almost pure gas, but welcome just the same; hours seemed to have passed since my last meal on the plane. Hours *had* passed. It was now after midnight, definitely time for bed. But would I be able to sleep? Ankle and wrist now ached in deep, sharp throbs. I drank another glass of champagne, then, having become a little more adept, edged the wheelchair with exquisite care into the bedroom which, Spartan as the other rooms, contained a low flat bed, Grecian-style, on a platform railed off by a low wooden balustrade. There was also one chair, and a clothes closet. My crutches had been left leaning against the rail. On the bed, curled in a ball, was a large wet tabby cat, which raised its head upon my entry, and howled at me.

"Good God," I said, startled, "Where did you come from?"

A foolish question. Outside was where it had plainly come from, judging by the condition of its sodden fur, which stood out in spikes of wet.

"Okay, okay, puss, keep your fur on, I'm not going to throw you out in this deluge. I wouldn't put a dog out in such a downpour—certainly not a cat."

I am fond of cats. Don't keep one, because, where would it live? But Masha always had some cat—most of those rectories were mouse- and rat-infested; the cat was there for strictly utilitarian reasons and simply addressed as "you cat," but it was well fed and had a place on the hearth beside Masha, who would occasionally rub its ears.

This tabby stood up hastily (leaving a damp muddy hollow lined with hairs on the white coverlet), as if unsure of its welcome; so I found a towel and rubbed some of the wet off its fur. That established better relations between us. Into the single saucer I then poured some long-life milk, which was accepted.

After that, doing my best to ignore the steady painful throb from wrist and ankle, I levered myself out of the wheelchair, up the platform step, and hoisted myself, still dressed, onto the bed. Undressing, washing, all that must wait for daylight. Just now, I had had all I could take.

After three minutes I felt a thud beside me on the bed. The cat had arrived, and proceeded to use me as a backrest, propping itself against me and washing vigorously.

"*Stop* that!" I snarled. "Can't you just go to sleep?"

To my surprise, it complied. Outside, the rain continued to fall, pattering steadily on the roof. If it were not raining, I wondered, would it be possible to hear the sea? Which must be quite close?

I've always longed for a house near enough to the beach so that one could lie and listen to the sound of waves; Masha had the same longing. But all our rectories were inland.

Presently, despite pain and the heavy bulk of damp cat propped against me, I slept.

I was woken, sometime further on into the night, by the cat's anguished and raucous howling.

"Oh, do shut up!" I muttered, and then, as it continued to howl even louder and more steadily, "What *is* it? Do you want to go out?"

Plainly, it did. The howling went on and on. "Oh damn, damn," I said, realising also that I was afflicted by a stuffed-up nose. This condition, even when it is one nostril only, invariably wakes me up at dead of night, engulfing me in dark awful thoughts about face cancer, mastoid, and meningitis. Both nostrils have to be completely clear before I am able to go back to sleep; sometimes I am obliged to sit cross-legged for hours, rotating my head and massaging my sinus cavities, before the problem abates. (Perhaps fortunately, this condition had not troubled me in Venice.) At present both nostrils were blocked and I was breathing through my mouth like a landed fish; I switched on the bedside lamp, wondering miserably where Parkson had dumped my essential small travel bag which contains inhalant, Vitamin C tablets, wintergreen ointment, Vicks, antiseptic cream, Vitamin E cream, ear drops, nose drops, Alka Seltzer, gauze, Band-Aids—but why go on?

I could not see the small travel bag. I could hardly see the bedside lamp. I couldn't see the cat. But its howling was louder than ever. The room seemed to be packed full of thick, fawn-coloured smoke, which was steadily darkening in colour. As if, I thought vaguely, the fog of Venice had been packed and despatched after me . . .

Plainly this was quite an emergency. The cat evidently thought so. It wanted out. Out, indeed, seemed essential for both of us.

Gingerly I slid off the bed onto my good foot, worked my way down the steps, grasping the rail, and reached for my crutches. This seemed no time for the niceties of the wheelchair. One crutch had been fitted with a strap so that I could use my elbow for support instead of the broken wrist. Blundering, lurching, doing my best not to breathe, I made for the sound of the cat's clamour, assuming that was where the front door must be—I really could see nothing and had quite lost my sense of direction. The howls grew louder, the smoke thicker. I was in the front room by now—I could tell because at one point I banged into the table. Then my shin caught against the low couch which, I recalled, stood just to the left of the front door as you entered. This wall in front of me, then—I felt it with my good hand—must, if I groped along it to the left, contain the door.

It is difficult to grope when you have only one functioning hand, are supported by crutches, and have a frantic cat interweaving itself continually between the crutches and your legs. "Okay, okay," I muttered, "just keep calm, the door handle's got to be here somewhere."

At last I found the knob and turned, pulled, but the door wouldn't open. Had I locked it? I could not recall taking such a prudent measure, but my last waking minutes had been veiled in a mist of champagne. Perhaps I had. Sliding my fingertips over the surface of the door I found a keyhole, but there was no key in it. Damn again!

Could the key have fallen out onto the floor? Could I have knocked it out myself, during my gropings?

I tried to search on the floor, dropped a crutch, had a hard time retrieving it, got a frightful lungful of smoke—which seemed to be issuing from the couch—and beat a hurried retreat into the kitchen, or where I thought the kitchen had to be, hoping the smoke in that room might be thinner. And by the sink there was a back door, I remembered.

I put up a prayer to St. Catherine, my patron saint, goddess of fireworks, that the back door would be unlocked.

Saint Catherine must be out of town, on holiday. The glass door was immovable, shut, locked, and no key in the keyhole.

By now the cat was becoming desperate. Its howls had taken on that hollow, coyote ring that cats only give out when engaged in combat, or when they feel the human race has really let them down.

I was becoming fairly desperate myself, running out of

options. It is not a moment I care to remember. I tried thwacking the back door with a crutch, but, supported on one foot only, was unable to muster up sufficient force to break it. The glass was plainly very strong, double-thick, burglarproof.

Well, chum, I thought, you are continually expecting death, and here it damn well is. What did H. James say? Here it is at last, the distinguished thing. As if it were some kind of superior family pet. Not a bit the way you had anticipated. Quite a joke on you, really.

I felt cross, though. I'd really wanted to finish the Rosy and Dodo serial, and hear public reactions to it. My best part! And, I thought, how aghast poor Randolph Grove would be at yet another of his cast being snatched away untimely.

The cat's yelling distressed me very much. Why should *it* have to perish, poor beast, just because it took shelter from the rain? I felt responsible for its welfare. I should have steeled myself and put it out at bedtime.

Then I recollected the wheelchair and its mad turn of speed. Its weight. Its solidity.

"Mind now, cat!" (The cat had followed me. It relied on me to get it out of this predicament.)

I remembered seeing a tea towel, neatly folded, on the counter, by the plate and cup.

The towel was still there, just where it had been before, which cheered me a good deal. (My mind was still groping, perplexedly, after those keys. Where could they have got to? *Both* of them? Was there some other reason why the doors would not open? Were they simply new, stiff? Or bolted, latched in some unexpected way? There had certainly been a front door key. Could Parkson have absentmindedly gone off with it?)

Meanwhile I wetted and wrapped the tea towel over my face as best, without only one functioning hand, I could, and hoisted myself back towards the bedroom, keeping eyes closed because the smoke stung and burned them, doing my best to breathe as little as possible.

Abandoning my faithful crutches, putting myself in the wheelchair—which I had left parked by the rail—was hard to do. Morally hard, I mean. Suppose the chair wouldn't work, refused to start, suppose I couldn't steer it through the smoke into the kitchen?

As I had feared, nudging the chair through the doorway was indeed frightful. I was nervous, my hands shook. I kept catching the door jamb and bruising my fingers. Once I gave my ankle an almighty wrench, as the chair somehow got caught cornerways and swung round. But finally, mercifully, I was through. Now—as I recalled—there should be a straight run from one door to the other across the room.

Watch out, cat, I thought. Mind out of the way.

The cat had fallen silent. I hoped he was still alive. The smoke was so dense in here now, as well, that my own head was beginning to swim; I knew I had no time to waste.

Turning the chair, so that its back and mine faced the glass door, I set the lever to Reverse, and pulled the handle back as far as it would go.

The result was like the Crack of Doom. That chair had superb acceleration; it seemed as if, by the time we reached the door, we were travelling at takeoff speed. The glass door totally disintegrated under the impact. I and the chair hurtled out through the gap into cold, fresh air, travelled onward for what felt like three or four feet, and came up against what I thought was a box hedge. (It proved to be close-planted cupressos.)

The rain had ended and, by the light of a small sickle moon, I could see the back of my house. It was square and white; a vine had been trained up beside the kitchen window; through the shattered glass door, thick black smoke was pouring.

I wondered what I was supposed to do now. Summon the

fire brigade? But how? Where were the other inhabitants of Glifonis?

I was not obliged to reach any decision about these matters, for a couple of neighbours, roused (how could they not be?) by the almighty crash, almost immediately made their appearance.

Voices could be heard round the corner of the house, so I steered my chair in that direction. Marvellous piece of mechanism: breaking the door had not impaired its action at all. It had probably cost a fortune, and was worth every penny. Moving easily over wet marble-slabbed pavement, I glided like the Queen of Sheba around to the front of the house, and there encountered two female figures with tousled hair and outer garments hastily donned over nightwear.

"Good heavens? What *happened?*" said the larger of these, while the smaller one cried, "Lady Fortuneswell? My dear, is that you? Are you all right? What is the matter?"

She was a little gnomelike woman, with a shock of thistledown hair, which gleamed in the moonshine. Her face contained more creases than a dried fig. She was squinting now, with distress and amazement; she looked like a cracker just about to be pulled.

"Yes, I'm quite all right," I said, "but I think my house is on fire."

"Believe you're right," said the other woman concisely. "Better call the brigade."

She turned back the way they had come, but came face to face with another neighbour now climbing my front steps. This was a bulky man, quite bald, wearing overalls under an aged and baggy cardigan. His face appeared impressive, like that of a Roman emperor, until one noticed the weak, petulant mouth.

"What is it, what in the world is the *matter?*" he said querulously. "I was just walking about, enjoying the cessation of the rain, relishing the silence and the sounds of the night—when—all of a sudden—this truly atrocious crash—"

"Lady Fortuneswell's house is on fire," explained the larger of the two women. To me she added, "I'm Pat Limbourne. This is Elspeth Morgan. We live at Number 2. And this is Laurence Noble, from Number 4."

"How do you do," I said. Laurence Noble, I recalled, was a composer. He had written a piece called "Ebb-Tide Variations"—something like that—which Joel thought poorly of. We had heard it at a lunchtime concert in Smith Square.

"I'm going to call the fire brigade," said the woman called Pat Limbourne.

An expression of distaste crossed Laurence Noble's face.

"Is that *really* necessary? They make such a noise! The fire does not appear to have established much of a hold, as yet. Can we not deal with it ourselves?"

He climbed the steps to my front door and tried it.

"It's locked," I said. "That's the trouble. I couldn't get out that way. Couldn't find the key. And the back door was locked too. That was why I had to break it."

They looked puzzled, as well they might.

I said, "The smoke seemed to be coming from a couch—from a sofa in the front room. If—I suppose, if we could break that front window—and throw some water in—there don't seem to be any flames yet—"

"If it *does* break into flame it'll really blaze," said Pat Limbourne doubtfully. "I really do think—"

She glanced downhill towards the house across the road; theirs, I supposed.

"All the more reason to do something quickly," Mr. Noble pronounced with unexpected decision. "The firemen would probably take about forty minutes to get here."

He glanced about. In the empty patch uphill from my house was a builders' tank and pile of rough tools, shovels and plasterers' trowels. The tank, filled by the recent storm, was brimming with water. Noble filled a pail with water from the tank and picked up a heavy shovel.

"Stand back," he ordered authoritatively. The two ladies did so. I was in no position to move, so stayed where I was in my chair. Mr. Noble briskly approached the front window and smashed it with his shovel. Out poured a coil of black smoke. Through the pane he had broken out he dashed his pailful of water, then hastily stepped aside. More and much messier smoke, laden with bits of papery ash, gushed out, but no flame. Pat Limbourne was instantly at hand, offering another pail of water. Even tiny old Miss Morgan appeared keen to play her part in the bucket gang, but I said to her,

"Won't you please stay with me? I really think they seem to be getting it under control."

"Oh, but how can it ever have *started?*" she cried distressfully. "Could you have dropped a cigarette end? A match?"

"I don't smoke. I only got here two or three hours ago." In the moonlight my watch said two-thirty.

"We did mean to sit up and welcome you—but I'm afraid we keep early hours"—she grimaced apologetically—"when ten o'clock came, we thought perhaps you had deferred your arrival—*I* know! We have a spare key! We have keys to all the houses—I will just run and get it."

By the time she returned with the key, the other two, taking turns to toss pails of water through the front window, seemed fairly confident that the fire was under control, if not out. Noble unlocked the front door, opened it, put his head in with caution, and shone a powerful torch which he pulled from an overall pocket.

"The couch is certainly just about burned up," he came back to report. "Nothing left but a black mess. Made from that repellant plastic foam, I don't doubt. Curious how it smoulders and smoulders before it begins to burn."

"But the smoke is deadly," said Miss Limbourne. "You

were very lucky to wake up in time—it could easily have asphyxiated you."

"The cat woke me. Howling."

"You have a cat?" They looked around.

"It seemed to come with the house? A big tabby."

"Oh, Arkwright."

"It was so wet, I let it sleep on my bed. And its yelling woke me."

"Saved your life," said little Miss Morgan, nodding.

"I hope it got out all right."

"Oh, Arkwright can take care of himself. He's got plenty of lives saved up. But come now, you poor thing, you had better spend the rest of the night in *our* house. Yours is still full of smoke."

Laurence Noble had been back, prospecting carefully with his torch inside my front room. He now emerged with a bright silver key.

"This was on the floor, right along in the left-hand corner. Must have got knocked out of the door, evidently. By your wheelchair, perhaps. I don't suppose you'd ever have found it."

"No, never," I said, thinking of trying to find my crutch on the floor. "I'm so grateful to you all . . . Do you think the house is safe to be left? It would be dreadful if the fire broke out again. Defective wiring, could it have been?"

"Miss Limbourne," said Mr. Noble, "perhaps you'd help me lift the piece of furniture out of doors? It is not at all heavy."

Between them they carried out a charred skeletal object which could hardly have been recognised as the neat little couch I dimly recalled from my arrival.

"Why are you all bandaged up?" Miss Morgan asked me, studying my plight with sympathetic curiosity.

"Oh—I had a fall in Venice. I wouldn't have come down

here in this state if I didn't have to—but we have to reshoot some scenes—"

"Are you by yourself? Nobody to look after you?"

She seemed very scandalized.

"You see—my husband had to go off to Paris—"

The other two came down the steps, brushing soot from their hands.

"I do not believe there is any further risk," pronounced Mr. Noble.

I looked at him with a good deal of respect. He had really been very efficient.

"So I will say good night to you ladies," he added with a little bow, and ambled off down the hill.

"Come along," said Miss Morgan. "Pat will push your chair. It's only four steps down to our house. You can have my bed and I'll sleep on the sofa—and let's hope *that* doesn't burn up in the night."

6

WHEN I woke, I could sense at once that the hour was late. And by the time I had stiffly rolled myself along to the ladies' bathroom, combed my hair and made some sort of elementary toilet, it was later still.

I felt low: by no means at my best. Too many things seemed to be going wrong with my life. I don't suffer from the common superstitions that actors affect—ladders and birds and quotations from *Macbeth;* but I do have a strong feeling that there are currents, wavelengths, forces blowing and roaring away out there, alongside our narrow bubble of human life; run counter to those, and you are in trouble. Just now I certainly seemed out of synch with my destiny; and I wondered rather gloomily what next it had in store for me.

The house was silent. My two kind hostesses must have gone out, considerately, leaving me to sleep off the effects of my adventure. It was now 11 A.M., and I rolled myself in the direction of the kitchen (their house was on the same plan as mine but with an upstairs) hoping they might have left a pot of coffee keeping warm—or at least a jar of instant and a kettle.

Then, as I reached the hither side of the kitchen door, I heard a voice. It seemed to be talking to itself; it must be telephoning.

"Darling Mervyn," said this voice, "could you be a *saint* and do something for me? Go round and get the key of my place from Swit—who must be in bed, ill, or something, that line is *continually* busy—and go to Lexham Gardens for me and see if there's a bill from Tagus, and if there is, *pay* it— and *pacify* Nefertiti Press and say I'll *soon* be in touch—can you do that?—You have? Oh, but that can wait—you know they never worry about that sort of thing—"

The voice was familiar to me, most depressingly so; and when I laboriously manoeuvred my wheelchair round the door jamb and into the sunny kitchen, my gloomiest apprehensions were confirmed. At the phone, just finishing her talk and replacing the receiver, was the person who, above all others, filled me with dejection, dislike and horrible guilt feelings.

I hate the thought of breaking up a marriage. I have had lovers—some—but they were never married people. Human relations are so delicate, vulnerable, easily unbalanced—a fact of which I was even more forcibly aware, just at present, than I had ever been—that I think being instrumental in smashing one of those fragile frameworks must be one of the major sins, one of the most destructive and wicked human acts—I recall that agonising story of the Queen accidentally sitting down upon the thousand-piece bird-bone fan that some aged islander had just presented to her. "Oh, I'm so *very* sorry—I do hope that you can make me another?" "Well, Ma'am, I can start . . ."

But once I, myself, did become involved in such a deed. At that time Olga Laszlo was married, had been married eight years or so to a barrister (he has since become a judge, Creighton Pendennis), and they had two dear little girls. He loved her besottedly. But *she* had fallen in love, she was conducting an undercover romance, a wild, whirlwind romantic passion (or so it then seemed to me) with an actor. What was his name? No matter. He had a lead part in a play where I had a walk-on. Olga was a friend of the woman who had done the sets. She became friendly with me. I was very impressed by her romantic devotion for her lover. To me the pair seemed enwreathed in glamour, Romeo, Tristan, Juliet, Isolde, all rolled into one bewitching scenario. What did I know of her husband and children? Nothing at all. So I gave her free use of my primitive garret, just around the corner from the theatre, very convenient; they used to meet there, and finally they decided she must leave her boring husband, run away from him, with the children, and set up house with this other fellow. Axel Grift, that was what he called himself; I wonder what's become of him? You never hear his name anymore.

So, it was arranged, they were going to meet at my place one Saturday, she with the children, and go off to France or somewhere together. But somebody must have blown the gaff—friend? neighbour? servant?—and suddenly there's her husband at my flat, bursting in the door like an avenging angel, breathing outrage, fury, hatred and disgust. Axel hadn't even turned up yet, Olga was there alone with her bags and the kids. Screams, shouts, tears and denunciations. He has a waiting car, whisks the kids away—poor little devils, not knowing what's hit them—and that's the last Olga sees of them for years. And years. With his legal connections, she had as much chance of custody as a butter-pat in Vesuvius. She and Axel got married, of course, after the divorce, and she proceeded to make life miserable for *his* child, a sad little boy called Peter, who was promptly bundled off to boarding school because Olga, you see, *couldn't take to him.* Was still too anguished about her own lost darlings. Last I heard of Peter, he had dropped out of college and was on heroin; of course that might have happened anyway. And Axel and Olga didn't stay together very long; things, one way and another, just didn't work out for them.

This sad and cautionary tale was one of the reasons why I have always taken great pains to steer clear of married persons. And why, also, I had not tried to keep in touch with Olga; I found the sight of her—haggard, tragic, perpetually contriving to give the impression that it was all *somebody else's fault*—too painful a reminder of my own silly gullibility when younger, and of the far-reaching harm it had led to. Maybe, if I had not allowed Olga to meet her lover in my attic, the affair would have fizzled out for lack of occasion, and those three children could have grown up with their own parents. Children should be with their own parents, I think.

Or at least (putting it more realistically) I need feel less responsibility in the matter of Olga's ruined life.

So I greeted her rather soberly. But she gave me a great big hello, widening her large haunted dark eyes with apparent delight.

"Isn't this such fun? Darling Cat—here we are together again after so *long!* But, you poor dear, what a time you've been having!"

"Getting married, you mean?" I said, deliberately misunderstanding.

She gave her humourless laugh, like a hopelessly blocked drain.

"Well, that too, of course—darling, congratu*la*tions!—I'm so excited for you—but I meant all these fatalities, breaking your poor leg and then nearly getting burned alive—"

"Yes, quite a run of bad luck, wasn't it," I said, occupied in a search for Nescafe among the amazing clutter on the counter—washing dishes was a chore plainly left by the ladies at Number 2 until every dish and utensil had been used at least twice—"I only hope it isn't contagious," finding a steaming kettle on the hob (bless them) and filling a mug.

"Contagious, darling?"

"Like Typhoid Mary. Anyway, how are *you,* Olga? What are you doing down here?"

She told me about her job at the Dorchester theatre. In professional matters she was both intelligent and capable. But I knew plenty of directors who would have nothing to do with her because of her inability to finish work on time. It was clever—highly ingenious—and always weeks late.

Then: "Fancy you being married to old Ty," she said. A reminiscent, melancholy smile played around her mouth; she could, I gathered, if she chose, tell me a thing or two about old Ty. As I asked no question, obstinately sipped at my coffee: "He's *hard,* you know," she said. "Can be heartless. Has a crazy streak. I know a girl—once knew a girl—he treated *very* heartlessly. He's not one to be relied on. But then—" she widened her great dark eyes at me again—"you are such a practical, self-reliant little person, aren't you, Cat? You can look after yourself so well. So perhaps you will be the very *thing* for darling Ty."

"Would you like some of this coffee, Olga?" I asked neutrally. "And do you think you ought to be telling me all these things about darling Ty? After all, I've been married to him less than a month."

"But, my angel, everyone knows you're on the point of separation already? Why would Ty go haring off to Paris in the middle of your honeymoon? After knocking you down in the middle of the Piazza San Marco? Why, even Joel—who never gossips—said he saw that happen—"

Luckily—just as I was about to explode—a child came in by the back door and studied me with interest.

I was not sure what age she might be—having had so few dealings with children, really—eight or nine, maybe. She was a neat, complete little character, hair done in tidy plaits on top of her head, face rather plain but with bright intelligent eyes and remarkable eyebrows which gave it force.

"You must be Lady Fortuneswell," she said to me. Her

voice was clear and her articulation beautifully precise; she could get a TV part in a twinkling, I thought, if she had a pushy, stagestruck mother; that plain little face would make up very well for the small screen.

But she looked as if she had brains; too intelligent to be an actress, perhaps?

"Yes, I'm Lady Fortuneswell. And you are—?"

"This is Shuna," Olga said proprietorially. "Shuna is my great *friend,* aren't you, darling?" She put her arm through that of the child, who said, "Yes," in a noncommittal way. I noticed that her eyes were fixed thoughtfully on the toes of my right foot, which extended out of the strapping. They looked rather grimy. Grime from Venice, from the plane journey, and honest Dorset soot.

"Won't they get cold?" she asked.

"Yes, they do, rather. Nobody thinks of that."

"You need a thing like a tea-cosy."

"So I do."

"I expect I could make you one— Does that chair move by itself?"

"Yes, like this—see—"

I demonstrated. While I was doing so, Miss Limbourne and Miss Morgan returned, full of bustle. "Ah, you found the kettle—that's right—"

"Well, I suppose I had better get off to my *job,"* said Olga, with a harassed smile.

Yes, you better had, at ten minutes to noon, I thought, as she fluttered her fingers at us all and left, wistfully.

"We have been as busy as bees," Miss Morgan told me, "setting your house to rights. Those good Greeks! One of them, Stavros, confessed that it *might* have been he who left a smouldering cigarette—they did find a stub near the front door—he was so dreadfully guilty and cast down about it—as well he might be—that we agreed to let the matter go no further! They have already replaced the broken panes; and

Mrs. Monkton is helping scrub and clean up. Pat is going to telephone for a replacement sofa and some more chinaware —I'm afraid you just had a scratch lot from our own supply—"

"It was so extremely kind of you—"

"So," said Miss Limbourne, "if you'd like to stay and have some lunch with us, we can promise that your own place will be fit for habitation afterwards—if you don't mind corned beef, that is."

"There are two huge hampers of food up at my house," I remembered. "Won't you share them with me? There's paté and game pie and all sorts of stuff—in jars and plastic packs, I don't suppose affected by the smoke—"

"Love to," said Pat Limbourne promptly. "Elspeth is supposed to do our provisioning, but her mind's always in the garden. Shuna, do you want to come up with me and bring back some goodies?"

"Is Shuna your niece?" I asked when the pair had gone off.

"No, her mother was the daughter of a friend. She's dead, poor young thing, and there really seemed to be *no one* to look after the child, so we took her in."

"How very lucky for her," I commented, thinking that an orphan might do a great deal worse than fall into the custody of this capable cheerful pair.

"Lucky for us!" Miss Morgan's face creased up fondly. "She's an excellent little person. More than a touch of genius too. No, I mean it" —as I must have looked a trifle sceptical —"her IQ is way above normal. But her family history was a sad one—I won't go into it—so Pat and I are very keen to see she doesn't get spoiled, or have her head turned by the wrong kind of attention. That's why"—Miss Morgan glanced briefly out of the window, then gave me a very shrewd look —"I'm not wild about her getting taken up by theatre people, such as Olga Laszlo, clever and well-meaning though she is. We brought Shuna down to Dorset because we thought country life would be just right for her—not too much excitement—"

"Yes, I perfectly understand. Judging on two minutes' acquaintance, I'd say you were doing a terrific job." I could indeed understand why Miss Morgan was not overenthusiastic about Olga's friendship for her chick; and was I being tactfully warned off too? "Will she go to school by and by?"

"Oh, she's down for Oxford already. Somerville and Balliol are both interested."

"Good heavens," I said faintly.

At this moment Miss Limbourne and the child returned, swinging a basket of food between them and carrying french loaves and bottles under their arms.

"Might I use your telephone?" I asked.

"Of course, my dear, it's for the convenience of anyone in the village."

"I ought to call my director and tell him I'm here."

"Randolph Grove?" said Pat Limbourne. "I'm sorry, I ought to have told you. There was a message from him. The team can't get down till Thursday next week—something in connection with a sequence they are shooting in the studio? —so, he said, they won't need you till then. You can give yourself a good rest, convalesce, take your time. And he sent his love."

"Thank you." I felt a little blank, as one always does, after rushing to an appointment, only to find that it has been postponed to the fairly distant future. Suddenly I had a vacant week—eight days really—what should I do with it? Go back to London? But to which domicile? My own place? Ty's penthouse? And where *was* Ty? Still in Paris? I assumed so. Would he get in touch? Would I ever see him again? Did Olga's hints have any foundation in fact? And where the devil did she get her information from?

Feeling suddenly very tired, when lunch was finished I

said I thought I had disrupted the ladies with my presence quite long enough, but was afraid I must ask for their assistance—or somebody else's—in returning to my house. Perhaps one of those helpful Greeks? (Their presence had been manifest outside all morning in the roadway, clanking up and down with barrowloads of mortar and marble, shouting vigorous Greek comments and directions from top to bottom of the hill.)

"Of course. Dmitri will take you," said Miss Limbourne. She stuck her head out of her front door and shouted, "Dmitri!"

"Kyria Limbourne!" A curly-black-bearded countenance appeared in the door about thirty seconds later.

"Can you wheel the Kyria Fortuneswell up to her house?"

"Sure, no problem." (He had evidently learned his English in New York.)

"And I'll help!" Little Shuna bounded to the door. She was plainly dying to study the mechanics of the chair.

"You are to come right back as soon as you have seen Lady Fortuneswell to her house," Miss Morgan told her firmly. "She needs a rest and so do you."

But, counterbalancing this admonition as we passed the open window, I heard Miss Morgan say to her friend, "Well, she seems a perfectly nice girl; not at all spoiled."

"I should hope not!" said Pat Limbourne.

Now, for the first time, as Dmitri dragged me backwards (but much more carefully and gently than Parkson had done) up the central roadway towards my house, I had a view of Caundle Quay, transmuted by my husband into Glifonis.

I was bound to admit that I would never have recognised the littered, rutted, squalid field, crawling with trailers as a sheepskin with maggots, messily curving down to the little combe at the bottom where the original hamlet nestled.

A certain amount of landscaping, I thought, had taken

place. The field itself had changed shape, the central area been flattened out, the sides made steeper. The stepped track wound precipitately down, zigzag, zigzag, between small white Greek houses with tiled roofs, angled irregularly among plots for vineyards and gardens, as they would be on a Mediterranean hillside. The result was charming. (Where had they found the roof tiles? Even in Greece they were now hard to come by.)

Down at the foot, I could see, from a glimpse of roofs and chimneys and mature trees, the original Dorset hamlet still remained. I was glad of that, for it had been pleasant in its own right; its forlornness had derived from the hideous squalor up above. Beyond lay the sea—today blue as a post-card, smiling under the benign sun. And yes: I thought I *could* hear a distant whisper as we paused outside my front door. I preferred to believe so, anyway. But in actuality there were plenty of other sounds to drown the noise of waves. Caundle Harbour had never been much to boast of, but now an impressive breakwater was in process of construction, curving around like an elbow. A dredger was at work, its great arm rising and falling as it scooped shingle from the seabed and dropped loads into a waiting drifter. Bulldozers plied back and forth along the completed section of sea wall. Motor dinghies hurried about.

As from another life, I remembered Ty's voice in Venice saying, "There has to be a viable harbour."

How strange, how very strange, that all this activity, all this change, all this (I must admit) very pleasing and imaginative creation, which had made something quite rare and special out of a wretched vulgar dump—all this was due to Ty, his vision, his force. Somehow, for the last few days, I had been denigrating him in my mind, underrating him because of his odd reaction to that small—not particularly crucial?—discovery about his past. Why had it seemed so important to him? He appeared really shattered at finding that I had been a witness to the event. So, he had made a promise and not kept it. Well, that was bad, but keeping a promise is not always simply possible. Circumstances alter. I wouldn't begin to make any judgments about that. But why such a startling change of aspect towards *me*? What had *I* done to deserve that?

Gazing down at Glifonis, the fruit of his imagination, of his drive, made me feel kindly again towards Ty, and wish that relations between us could still be mended.

Though, deep down inside me, I was certain they could not.

"Could you take me round to the back of the house, onto the terrace?" I asked Dmitri. "I'd like to see what the view is from there."

I was pleased to find that from my back porch you could look right down to the harbour; and I also noticed, what I had not last night, that if my chair had burst its way through that planted hedge of cupressos, it and I would have catapulted over a sharp drop, across the next bend of the causeway, straight onto the upper terrace of Miss Morgan and Miss Limbourne. I could see the dandelion head of the elder lady, pegging out washing, twelve feet below. While assimilating this fact, I heard a curious croak behind me, and turned to see a skinny, waiflike little elderly man vigorously beckoning the child Shuna. She ran and talked to him at the far end of my terrace, he waving his arms about a great deal, she shaking her head. He kept looking towards me, evidently asking some question.

"What does he want?" I called. "Anything I can do?" The little guy looked both piteous and urgent—very like the Ancient Mariner.

"It's Odd Tom," Shuna said.

"How are you, Tom?" I said. He jerked his head and mumbled something unintelligible.

"He wants to know where Lord Fortuneswell is."

Why in the world would he want to know that? I wondered. Had he some favour to ask? I explained rather slowly, wondering if he were mentally defective, that my husband was not with me, that to the best of my knowledge he was at present in Paris. The old man shook his head and went into another long stream of communication, all thrown away on me because of his lack of consonants. But Shuna seemed to understand him perfectly well.

"He was sure your husband was with you."

"He really isn't, I'm afraid. Tell him I'm sorry. Is there any message I can pass on?"

(Not, I feared, that Ty would take much interest in a message from this queer old derelict—unless it related in some way to the welfare of the Glifonis project?) However, Odd Tom shook his head, shrugging; his business could wait, it seemed.

The large cat, whose name I now knew to be Arkwright, made its appearance through my open kitchen door (the glass had been neatly replaced) and jumped with an accustomed air onto my lap.

"Oy! Mind my bad leg!" But I stroked him, pleased to see that he had survived the fire.

"He saved your life," Shuna stated. "By waking you with his howling. He saved you. Otherwise you would have been suffocated. Aunt Elspeth said so."

"Perfectly true. But also I saved *his* life. By smashing a way out for both of us."

"Yes," she said. "I hadn't thought of that. Arkwright, that ought to teach you not to go into other people's houses without leave—I wish I could have seen you come crashing through that glass door," Shuna added sadly.

"Well, I'm not going to do it again! Still, you can see me go back through it in the regular way, now, if you like—cat and all."

I demonstrated. But Arkwright, disliking the sudden movement, jumped off my knee and went to join the old man, who had wandered away down the steps, scratching the thin ruff of hair under his cap and talking to himself with an air of perplexity. Arkwright walked behind him.

"Does the cat belong to Odd Tom?"

"Oh yes— He says he was *sure* he saw your husband."

"Last night?" I asked, enlightened. Had the old man perhaps been hovering around when we arrived? "No, that wasn't my husband, it was Parkson, the man who drove me down. He's gone back to London."

"Do you have all you need?" inquired Shuna, after I had steered myself into the kitchen. Carefully restraining a smile —her tone was so adult and solicitous—I said thank you, yes, I was sure I had, thought of suggesting that she should drop in for an orange juice later, remembered Miss Morgan's gentle warning-off, and finished, "I can always send a Greek with a message. They seem to pass to and fro nonstop, like ants."

She flashed a grin—which showed dimples, much more attractive ones than Rosy's—and ran off.

The house had been vigorously cleaned, and no trace remained of last night's episode save a touch of damp here and there, new putty round the window and French door, and the sharp sour smell of sooty smoke, which takes days and days to disperse.

I wheeled myself through into the bedroom, left the chair, negotiated the step, and levered myself onto the bed. By now I was becoming quite expert at these antics, I thought dourly; rather depressing; I would much prefer not to find in myself such a blind instinctive talent for survival. Who wants to survive? Where's the percentage in doing so? I remembered a verse by a female poet with whom I used to feel I had some affinity, Ingrid Christ—*she* drove her car over a cliff though, poor thing; I wouldn't ever do that:

My cunning corpse, as I lie sleeping
Takes stubbornly the air I grieve
And thus with breath keeps warm the coffin
Which I would give my life to leave—

Lying on the bed (newly made with clean sheets and blankets), I felt very peaceful. Remembered I had omitted to shut the back door after I came in, but what did it matter? The day was warm—remarkably so for March; I would get up by and by and close it . . .

Just before I slept I had a dismaying playback of Olga Laszlo's last remark: "Everyone knows that you're on the point of separation already." Who was *everyone?* And was that true? Olga, I remembered from the days when we were friendly, had a fearsome talent for overdramatisation and exaggeration. Even when younger, even when I looked up to her and admired her, I had observed that. Now, for the first time, it occurred to me to wonder: did Olga feel any residual grudge, any bitterness towards me, for the part I had played in her own catastrophe? It would not be rational, exactly, but —I supposed—it would be no more than understandable if she did. There had been something spiteful, ill-wishing about that remark. Perhaps she envied my luck; grudged it? After all, compared with her, I must seem to be sitting pretty; a plum of a television part, *and* married to Pyramid's Lord Fauntleroy, as the *Mirror* called him.

I wished very strongly that Olga were not here in Dorset, and hoped that her stay might be a short one.

Little does she know, I thought gloomily, making an attempt to shift my creaking, aching right arm without putting any pressure on the point where the bones joined, little does she know what my real state is.

My back hurt, my neck ached, my throat was sore from smoke inhalation. My wrenched leg was numb in a particularly sinister way; perhaps it was beginning to gangrene and would have to be amputated.

Nonetheless, at last I did drift off to sleep.

I had slithered into unconsciousness with a piece of paper in my hand, a scrap of wrapping material from those that had been scattered on the bed. (It's a compulsive habit; I often do it; once I slept the whole night through clutching a paperback copy of John Gabriel Borckman, with my finger marking the page; I had awful dreams that night.)

I must throw this untidy scrap into the wastepaper basket, I thought idly, lying in bed, rubbing it between my fingers when I woke; only where is the wastepaper basket in this house? Have I seen one anywhere?

Too lazy to get up and search, I studied the rough scrap between my fingers as, for lack of other reading, one studies the message on a matchpack, or milk bottle. It was about the size of a matchpack, orange and black, the kind of thin, rough paper that firelighters and packets of candles come wrapped in. It must, I thought, be the torn end of a dye packet; the letters 'S DYE were printed across it. Somebody's Dye. A touch of orange powder came off on my finger when I rubbed the underside. Aha! Had not orange curtains hung at the windows of the house, Number 2, where I had lunched with the ladies? My own house had plain white cotton curtains; maybe the two ladies preferred a brighter colour, one that wouldn't show dirt so easily, and had dyed theirs?

Amused at my detective prowess, I studied the scrap again and noticed that the S had been carefully scratched out with black ink, and three extra letters added. No, two letters and a number. A U, an R, and a 2. Some game of little Shuna's? Or simply a counter code in the hardware shop where the dye had been bought?

It's time to get up, I thought lazily. Get up and do—what? What is there to do in this spare, bare little house? Not a scrap of writing paper does it contain, not a book, pencil, radio, picture, chalk, needle, thread, pot of paint, bottle of ink, tape, LP or compact disc. All I shall be able to do here is eat, sit, sleep, look at the sea. How restful! How very restful! And I continued to lie motionless on the hard flat bed, pleased that billows of heavy acrid smoke were not rolling over me, and aware, too, that I was more peacefully relaxed than I had been for many days, perhaps for many weeks.

Possibly because my mind was so empty, the enigmatic little scrap of paper continued to buzz its tiny message there, like a fly in a bell jar.

DYE U R 2. U R 2 DYE.

You are to die.

Certainly. So are we all, I thought, nodding mental agreement; and then the significance of the message suddenly punched me, and I sat bolt upright, ignoring the squawks from my injured joints.

The message was *not* a general statement to all mankind; it was addressed to *me*. Like a fortune cookie. *You are to die.*

Well, I know that of course. Have been preparing for it these many years. But not for somebody else to tell me so. In such a deliberate and enigmatic way.

Who could it have been?

Somebody wants me to die? Intends me to die? And then, a corollary sneaking into my mind by the back door: did somebody *plan* that event last night? I don't suppose I have ever been closer to death than I was then. It would have been easy for a person to lock the back door beforehand; then, after I had gone to bed, to open the front door with a spare key—there may be several, Miss Morgan had one, after all— tuck some slow-burning stuff into the couch, put the other key in a corner, where I would never find it once the fire was under way, where it would later look as if it had been accidentally knocked or kicked—then step quietly out again, relocking the front door. I was dead asleep, full of champagne, the rain was rattling down, the fridge in the kitchen makes as much noise as an electrical generating plant. CHUG, boom, boom, boom, boom, chug, chug; it was doing so now. When the noise died out it was quite a startling shock. And it soon began again. So much for my dream of lying in bed listening to the sigh of the sea . . .

The refrigerator cut out. And I heard a footstep.

This time I shot off the bed almost as fast as if I were in my normal state of health—wrenched my ankle—and let out a gasp of pain. My gasp was answered by somebody else's, and I heard a pitter-patter of soft-shod feet on the kitchen tiles. Little Shuna? Lurching on my crutches, I reached the kitchen in time to see the old man, Odd Tom, retreat hastily through the open back door onto the terrace, preceded by his cat Arkwright, who bounded ahead of him as if this were all a most enjoyable game.

"Hey!" I called sharply. "Did you want something?"

He was such a forlorn, dishevelled little specimen that I could not feel at all apprehensive about him; my main thought was that perhaps he hoped to pick up some tidbits in the kitchen for himself or his pet. To which they were both quite welcome.

But he threw me an anxious, harassed look, mumbling what seemed to be a denial, waving his hands about a great deal. If only I could understand him! It must be possible, for little Shuna seemed to find his speech perfectly comprehensible.

"Come back!" I called. "I don't mind your being here. You *or* Arkwright!" But he only mumbled some more, glancing agitatedly at my hand on the crutch; then took himself off at a quick shuffling pace, down the steps and out of sight.

I stepped back inside the house—dusk was falling by now —shut the door and this time locked it, observing that the key was correctly in the lock, and turned in the regular way, quite easily. I had been holding the little scrap of orange paper when I went to the door; I laid it thoughtfully on the kitchen draining board, under the soap container. Next I hopped to my wheelchair, rolled through the house on it, and checked the front door, which was shut and locked.

Then I settled soberly to asking myself if I had any enemies.

Someone who had wanted the part of Rosy? But, if so, why not dispose of me much sooner, before most of her scenes had been shot?

Someone who was jealous of my relations with Ty? But ditto, and why bother, now that it seemed to be on the skids? At this moment it did occur to me to wonder, though, in a nervous and embarrassed way, what my financial standing would be if Ty himself were to perish untimely, in a helicopter crash, say; he was greatly addicted to flitting about in helicopters. As his widow, would I be in line for his huge fortune? If so I would immediately and automatically renounce it; I didn't even have to think about that. Nobody knew that but me, though. Money had never been mentioned between Ty and me, beyond his automatically taking care of the bills and proposing to replace my flea-market jewellery.

That scene in the jeweller's shop. All those grey velvet hands wearing wristwatches. Ty had almost fainted. And— why had this never occurred to me before?—it was just after that curious little episode that Ty had come down with the frightful migraine—from which he had only been reprieved by news of the Companions of Roland citation . . . ?

There was a loud rat-tat at the front door. I almost jumped out of my skin, but presently opened the door to the homely and welcome countenance of Pat Limbourne, who bore a remarkable resemblance to the Lord Protector, warts and all. I wondered if anyone had ever told her so.

"Hullo! I just came up to ask if you'd like to come down

and take potluck with us. Potluck is what it will be," said Pat briskly. "One of Elspeth's watery stews."

"You are very kind," I said, and meant it. "But you've had enough of me for the day. And I've lots of stores here; I can eat salad and paté."

"I know that's true," said Pat, "so I won't press you. I expect you're still tired after all the excitement."

"Won't you stop a moment and have a glass of sherry? I'm afraid it's all I have—"

"Love to," she said promptly. "Can I get it?" Which she did without loss of time.

"Cheers," she said, filling with businesslike briskness the two glasses she had brought, passing me one, and raising hers. "Hope you'll soon be out of those bandages. Glifonis isn't the ideal refuge for a person in a wheelchair. But you'll find the Greeks very obliging—they'll wheel you anywhere you want. They're a good lot of men."

"They seem very good-natured. What about Odd Tom? Where does he fit in?"

"Oh, he's an inoffensive old body. Not an ounce of harm in him. Likes to wander about the place and make himself useful."

"You don't think"—I took a gulp of my sherry—"you don't think he could have started the fire here last night?"

"*Tom?* Good heavens no! He's a good old fellow— wouldn't hurt a fly." But she looked suddenly thoughtful. "What in the world gave you that idea?"

I tried to explain my thoughts about the keys. Pat shook her head.

"Doesn't seem much, to base such a suspicion on? Besides—why should someone want to burn you to death?" Her smile showed a sceptical scorn for my foolish ideas. "Much more likely to have been faulty wiring."

"I know—it does sound paranoid—which I don't think I am really. But I was thinking—suppose somebody assumed that my husband was here with me—I imagine *he* has picked up an enemy or two in the course of his career—" I did not mention Tom again. I guessed he was a protégé of the two ladies. Anyway, if Tom thought Ty was with me, others might too.

To prove my point, there came another rap on the front door. It opened and a voice called, "Anyone in? Ty?—are you at home?"

The head that came round was familiar to me—that of Vass, Rupert Vassiliaides, the architect.

"Oh!" he said, disappointed, seeing me and Pat. "Ty not here? I'd heard he was in these parts. I wanted to tell him we'd got planning permission for the two-tier breakwater—"

"Like Lyme Regis?" I said. "How splendid. No, Ty's not here at present, but I'm sure he'll be delighted. Come in anyway, and have a glass of sherry."

He was very willing, and came accompanied by a spruce young character with horn-rimmed glasses and a long neck and fair hair whom he introduced as "my assistant, Peter Hart-Crouch." Vass was a tall black-haired man who, though Greek, looked and sounded English. He and Pat evidently knew each other well. She poured sherry and Vass commiserated with me on my injuries. "But I'm sure Peter here will be happy to push you round the village." Not if I know it, said Peter's expression, plain as print. I took an instant dislike to him. He had a languid voice, rolled his neck about a great deal, and frequently referred to "Corb" in his discussion of what he called "orkitecture."

"We're tiring you, Lady Fortuneswell," said Pat fairly soon. "We'd better leave you in peace."

And they went, calling amiable good-nights, and leaving the place full of cigarette smoke from the two men. Paranoid I was, in truth; I scoured the room for stubs after they had gone. But, fortunately, found none.

Pat had kindly rinsed the glasses on her way out. "Don't let Shuna be a nuisance to you," she called from the kitchen.

"I'm sure she won't. She seems a most sensible little entity."

"I'll think some more about what you said."

I would really like to see more of little Shuna, I thought, after the door had slammed behind Pat, and I had locked it. Shuna seemed an interesting child. And I had had so few dealings with children. So few dealings with Fitz when he was a child. That was a permanent gap in my life. Perhaps in his too.

Papa, at the time when Andrei began visiting us, had been going through one of the more disagreeable phases of his retreat from reality. He felt the need to deal out blame; as if his inner discomforts, uncertainties, discords, could only be relieved by lamming into external groups—vegetarians, Christian Scientists, trade unionists, hunt-protest groups, zoo keepers, the police, the Social Democratic party. Almost any "they" would do as a target. He could be comfortable, it seemed, only when casting aspersions on a safely distant, arbitrarily designated body of hypothetical other people who were in no position to defend themselves. He had to have a scape-group; their actual identity was of secondary importance, his own need to condemn, primary. If a real person had walked up to Papa and announced, "I am a vegetarian hunt-protester," I'm sure he would have been quite nonplussed. Retired to his study with a vague nod and a wave of the hand, most likely.

His conversation by then consisted entirely of one-sided argument. He would pounce on any statement made, dispute it, enter into a whole campaign of rebuttal, but always, in the clinch, fall back on a general assertion of his own position.

"Oh, well, of course, I never watch television. It's total

rubbish. Never travel by car. Anybody who does is a fool. Fiction? I don't read it. Only second-class minds read fiction. I never leave the house on Saturdays. Too many hooligans about then. Giving presents? I never do. Gift-giving is a form of buying people's favour, that's all. I despise it. Christmas has become a disgusting commercial orgy. I prefer to ignore it." (So he did, greatly disconcerting his parishioners). "Dogs are filthy verminous monsters—they should all be exterminated."

Papa loved to contradict. Gently, courteously, whatever you had just said—even if it were to agree with a statement he had just made—he would refute you.

"No—no, I fear you haven't taken my point. You have failed to understand me. In fact, it was *just* the other way round . . ."

Masha bore with him kindly, tirelessly, never seeming to run out of patience or sympathy. She also bore with his continually recurring Doubts. These were not doubts of a religious nature, like Prendergast's, but doubts as to whether he had chosen the right course in giving up his professional career.

"Should I have left it all, Maria? Was it wrong of me? Was I abandoning my true duty?"

How many, many times have I heard her answer him: "Only you can be the judge of that, Edred." For she too, under that gentle manner, had a streak of ruthlessness. "Use your own intelligence. Decide for yourself," she would tell me, time and again, when I asked did she think it would rain, should I take a waterproof to school, would it be correct to go to the school party in flat heels and ankle socks?

Papa's Doubts were aggravated by the fact that he did not take at all kindly to our considerable poverty. He could never reconcile himself to thrifty habits, switching off lights, using only a small panful of hot water for washing, picking out the last bits of coal from the fire before going to bed. In grand absence of mind he forgot these measures, and being reminded about them always roused him to fury.

"I *would have remembered,* Maria! Please give me credit for *rudimentary* sense. I am not quite a fool, I hope!"

If she alluded to the fact that he had left the Rayburn cooker oven door open for two hours, rambling out into the garden to ruminate while the heat wasted itself, he would turn on her with haughty ferocity.

"It was just an accident. A single occurrence! *Anybody* might have such a mishap."

Later, however, he would be discovered at his study desk with grey bowed head resting on his forearm, suffused with self-pity. "Oh, I am a hopeless hopeless impediment to you. I should have left you, I truly believe. Gone into the wilderness on my own." Infinite intelligent, diplomatic sympathy, many cups of tea from Masha would be required before he was restored to normal equilibrium.

In my early teens it both puzzled and enraged me that Masha—calm, perceptive, shrewd Masha—should apply so much energy every time, such boundless patience and tact, to rebuild his ego. It did not, at that time, strike me that life on the whole was more comfortable when Papa's ego was in good fettle. Not comfortable; but more so.

I suppose my own intransigence was why, when it came to the crunch, Masha thought it best for me to go.

Once or twice I too had tried sympathising with Papa, following her line, thinking to accelerate the return to normality; but that proved a total mistake. Each time I did so he would turn on me with icy rage: "Catherine, please do not intrude yourself on what has nothing to do with you. God knows *you* are often careless and tiresome enough, giving your poor mother a great deal of unnecessary trouble."

He would watch sharply, with a jealous eye, to make sure that she did not render me too many services. "Surely the girl can mend that herself? It would be useful practice for her."

He himself continually put Masha to extra trouble over what seemed trifles to me, despite the fact that she was on her feet and working all day long while he sat in his study.

"My dear Maria, when you get rid of dead flowers from vases, could you kindly dispose of them a little farther from the house than that bramble patch beside the back entrance? Suppose one of our friends were to see them lying there? What kind of a slovenly impression would that make?"

One of Masha's pleasures was to have such garden flowers or wildflowers as were easily available in pots and jars about the house.

"People come to the front door, Edred, not the back."

"Well, *my* susceptibilities are offended," he said testily. "I do not care to see dank dead flowers flung among the brambles."

So she had to carry them all the way to the end of the garden.

Papa had a habit of looking sideways, quickly, during a conversation, as if the sight of his interlocutor aroused in him more irritation than he could bear.

Yet he *was* capable of performing kind acts; towards Masha at least; I can't remember his ever doing anything for me. But I can recall an occasion when she was stuck indoors with a severe cold and passionately wished to listen to a performance of Handel's *L'Allegro ed Il Penseroso* on the Third Programme. Masha had an irrational notion—most of her life was guided by such vehemently rational principles that it was charming and touching to find these pockets of unreason in her—that recorded music was apt to be stale, subject to decay, to have "gone off" in some odd way; if possible she preferred to hear music, in which she took intense delight, played by live players, preferably in her presence. How seldom she was granted this luxury . . . On the occasion when she had her bad cold the radio battery had expired, so Papa most uncharacteristically volunteered to walk down to the village shop through pouring rain to buy a new battery. He returned with the battery all right, but with somebody else's *Times* under his arm that he had picked up and read absently in the shop; his discovery of this fact, his consternation and agitation, his fruitless excursions back to the shop and then hither and thither about the village occupied the entire period of the broadcast. And of course he had the batteries in his pocket.

Masha had read English and Drama at Cambridge in the thirties; she took her master's, concentrating on Ibsen and learning Scandinavian languages. Russian she already knew, thanks to Great-aunt Elena. Much good all this did her. Well, the Ibsen may have helped, who knows? She met Papa at Cambridge, where he was studying medicine, and they were married almost at once. He was a solitary; his father, Sir Paul Mars-Smith, had been a Governor of some Pacific outpost; he and his wife died of tropical diseases, leaving two orphan sons to be reared by an uncle. And one of the sons was brain-damaged.

To help their finances while Papa went on training in London, Masha taught at the Wolsey Hospital School for Girls, and they lived in Islington very frugally. While he passed through the lengthy process that turns people into doctors, she became respected in her sphere. By the time Edred got his membership, she was in line for senior mistress at the Wolsey. By now World War II had happened and male teachers were being called up.

Edred, of course, escaped military service because of being in the medical profession—I wonder if he felt guilty about that, after the war? He could have volunteered for overseas medical jobs in the forces, but he never did; perhaps that is why he always became so angry and hostile, later on, if other men talked in his presence about their war experiences.

From being poor, they suddenly grew quite rich. He had made several new medical beginnings, but finally elected for brain surgery, specialising in some particular job, a minute, fiddling, skilful piece of unplugging and rewiring which, it turned out, he could perform far better than anybody else in the field. Even though it was wartime, people used to travel from other lands to watch him in action; several slow-motion films were made of his hands at their delicate work; he became a kind of surgical Menuhin. He exercised his skill on the brain of an aging Royal and, if he had been a grocer, would thereafter have been permitted to put "By Appointment" over his door. By then he was in great demand for senior statesmen and war leaders. The flat in Islington was soon exchanged for a house in Park Crescent. Edred acquired a number of wealthy and influential acquaintances—I do not use the term friends because he never seemed to value other people to that degree. He looked, to perfection, the part of a famous surgeon: in his photographs from that time he is a handsome figurehead, tall and arrogant in appearance, with sharp-cut features, deepset eyes, upright carriage and a fine straight mouth very much tucked in at the corners, so that deep grooves ran up and down his cheeks.

One day, as a child, I discovered by accident that I could draw his portrait by making a horizontal for a mouth, bracketing it by two verticals, then putting in two dots for eyes, rather close together. *"Look,* Masha, look—I've drawn Papa!"

She, for some reason, appeared distressed by the drawing and withstood all my demands to show him my achievement. "Later: Papa's very busy just now." And then, somehow, the piece of paper got lost. I drew it again, several times, but never with quite such success. It was a bitter disappointment that she would not show him the drawing; at that time I still craved his approval. Although he frightened me, and I would never venture into his presence by myself, I somehow hoped that Masha would act as mediator— But she, of course, suggested that I run outside and dig in my little flowerbed.

"It's a beautiful sunny day, what are you doing frowsting indoors?"

That was after the change in our lives, naturally.

Masha had had to abandon her teaching career because Edred needed her for entertaining; by this time he knew dozens of celebrities. So, in what time was left over, she took to translating from Russian. In the cracks between their social life she saw her four sisters, Dolly and Tasha, Mig and Minka. None of them lived in London at that time, so they sometimes spent the night at our house after attending public meetings.

Papa used to make slight, scathing remarks about them after they had gone.

Then what happened?

Joel asked me once—he is *absorbedly* drawn by other people's family histories—whether perhaps one of Edred's operations had gone wrong, slashing at the roots of his confidence? I couldn't answer Joel, I had no idea, and I could see that he thought this gap in my knowledge odd and disgraceful.

That was while Masha was still alive. So, the next time I went to visit, I put the question to her.

"What happened to Papa? Why *did* he stop being a surgeon? Did he lose the knack?"

I could imagine how terrifying such a failure might be. One day you begin serving all your balls into the net; or losing your balance on the high wire; or forgetting your lines, or typing all the words back to front. Your brain just declines to obey the orders sent to it. (Sometimes I think this is happening to me. I fall into odd gaps of consciousness; arrive in a room and don't know what message sent me there; lose, into an utter void, some commonplace familiar word that had been trembling on the tip of my tongue).— So, what can you do? No great matter if it is just your own self in question; you wait a while and try again. But if you are in the business of carving up *somebody else's brain?*

Maybe the sight of all those exposed brains had given Papa the horrors?

But no, Masha said, it wasn't like that. "He was just as clever as ever. And quick! His hands moved like lace-makers —the fingers flickered so fast you couldn't follow them. Surgical assistants had to be absolutely top-class to keep up with him—hand him the things he wanted."

"Did you often watch him at work?"

"Only once," she said drily. "I fainted dead away, which was a nuisance for the staff, so of course I didn't ask to watch again."

"Was Papa angry?"

"He never knew. I asked them not to tell him."

Her green-grey eyes came back from a distance and surveyed me reflectively. Was she wondering why I had never asked before?

"So was it very sudden—when he decided to stop?"

"The decision was sudden. But he'd been worrying about it for a couple of years. I'd had a stillborn baby five years before you—a boy, born with the cord round his neck."

She sounded thoughtful, detached.

How badly had she minded that, I wondered. I could not imagine Papa being much comfort.

"Was he upset?"

She bypassed my question and said, "He had begun reading a lot of books about God and science—men who explained how the nineteenth-century image of God was out of date, how the advance of scientific discovery need not interfere with people's religious beliefs. After about five years of this kind of reading, he began to feel quite strongly that he ought to devote the rest of his life to the business of coming to grips with God."

"Did he *believe* in God?"

"Not when we were first married," said Masha. "He was quite an atheist then." Her tone was dry, amused, reminiscent. She herself, I was well aware, had an untroubled, uncritical belief in the ultimate presence and benevolence of God; true, He seemed to have let things get into rather a muddle just at present in this world, but most of that was our own fault, doubtless He had other worlds to manage, and no doubt matters would sort themselves out in the end. I am quite sure she never discussed her beliefs with Papa; she had an immense sense of personal privacy. But they supplied the basis for her capacity to cope with adverse circumstances.

I have a memory from around that time. It was my third birthday. I had had a party, I don't know who came, children from the playgroup I attended. Papa had not been at home for it, he never participated in such affairs. I had gone to bed, before he came home, with my new kaleidoscope, and Kipling's *Just-So Stories*, both presents from Masha. I could not read yet, but she had read aloud the first story, and I looked at the pictures.

By and by I heard the front door slam, signaling that Papa had come home. Others shut the door gently, he with a bang that reverberated through the house. Creeping out of my bedroom, I looked down the stairwell. Would he come up and say good night to me, since it was my birthday?

He did not. Tiptoeing down one flight of stairs, I heard their voices from the sitting room, a long, back-and-forth, subdued exchange. I could catch no actual words, only a tone that was unfamiliar, and made me uneasy.

After a while, Masha's voice grew louder, as if she had moved; I heard her say, "I must go up to Katya for five minutes, her fingernails need cutting."

I just had time to dart upstairs again and scramble into bed before she appeared in my bedroom with the nail scissors.

"But you cut my nails this morning," I protested. "For the party."

"So I did."

That is my first memory of her inventing a pretext to have a private conversation with me: "I have to wash Katya's hair." "I must measure her for her new school blouses." "I have to go through her things for next term." They became frequent and recognisable.

At the age of three I hadn't yet become aware of Papa's disturbingly strong resentment of the rapport between Masha and me. He did not care to be excluded. Ignoring my presence, as he did for ninety per cent of the time, hardly ever addressing me directly, he had a paranoid sensitivity to all dialogue between Masha and me, he would grow silent, chill, and tense. If, crossing the hall, he heard us talking in the kitchen, while we hulled black currants or performed some of the day's tasks together, he would wander into the room and stand with a preoccupied expression, his eyes fixed on Masha.

"Er . . ." And there would ensue a long silence, through which she waited patiently, going on meanwhile with whatever work was in hand. At last he would come out with some trivial inquiry, or demand her assistance to sort his papers, type a letter for him, press the pocket flaps of his better jacket before a churchwardens' meeting. Quite plainly he feared and distrusted the river of communication that ran between us so freely.

When we had moved to tiny, cramped, clerical quarters these things of course became far more noticeable. By that time, anyway, I was older, and more observant.

On my third birthday night, dimly aware that some change was at hand, I clung to Masha—who, uncharacteristically, put an arm around me and held me close to her.

She said, "Did you enjoy your birthday?"

Yes, I told her, it had been lovely, and I loved my kaleidoscope best of all. "Look, there's a rainbow in it."

"Soon we're going to live in the country," said Masha. "Where you'll see real rainbows. And sheep and cows and haystacks and trees to climb. Won't that be fun?" Her tone did not quite ring true.

I was dubious. "Why are we going? What about my playgroup? Will there be toy shops?"

"You'll find new friends. And better things than toy shops. We're going because Papa has decided to stop being a doctor."

"What will he do instead?"

"He's going to be a clergyman and think a lot about God."

To me this seemed an odd step. God was there all the time, why bother to think about Him? But it was no use trying to follow the vagaries of grown-ups.

"You'll be very *good* in the country, won't you? And not bother Papa? Because he'll be at home all day, instead of going to the hospital, and our house will be very much smaller. But I know you will," said Masha. "You are always a good child."

To my surprise, I noticed a tear slide down her cheek. This is the sole occasion on which I can recall such a manifestation—except when her sisters died.

"Good night," she said then. "Go to sleep now," and firmly moved my book and toy to a distant chair before leaving my bedroom with the unused nail scissors still in her hand.

AFTER that, memory takes a leap. I have no recollection of the first rectory we occupied, after Papa had been ordained. It was in Newcastle, I know, and I have heard Masha speak of the frightful cold, the cockroaches and the roar of traffic by day and by night; but nothing comes back save dim pictures of a gritty little city garden with clipped dwarf box-hedges giving off that particularly repellant smell that box has—quintessence of acid dust.

I do remember that, after Masha's predictions of country life, Newcastle seemed a total letdown; but before long we moved again, to a grey stone village between a coalmine and a moor. Here the people addressed us in such a gluey, unfamiliar dialect that it took Masha and me a long time—weeks for her, months for me—before we could understand what they were saying; and I don't think Papa ever did communicate with his parishioners.

I'm sure he was a total washout as a clergyman. The main duties of priests, I suppose, are to help, instruct, comfort, and support their flock. I can't at the farthest stretch of my imagination see Papa doing any of those things. What he wanted, what he intended to do, was to carry on a dialogue with God; or to try to; the congregation might listen to his dissertations on this theme, if they chose; or otherwise manage as best they could.

It is hardly surprising that he changed parishes so often. Even as a famous and successful surgeon he had a reputation for extreme intractability; he left a trail of angry hospital management boards, alienated patients, obstinate fools of colleagues and crass subordinates. In his new vocation he fell foul of pigheaded vestry committees and idiotic local authorities, bigoted bishops and stubborn rural deans; between the ages of five and ten I can remember four moves in quick succession. Masha began to look weather-worn; her black hair became streaked with silver, her broad forehead acquired vertical creases; yet she was only fifty. We lost touch with her sisters. At first she used to take me to Sunday Matins. We both enjoyed singing hymns. And Masha attended with scrupulous care to Papa's soliloquies about the difficulty of getting up a dialogue with God. (He always seemed offended about this, prickly and disgruntled. Since he had gone to so much trouble to establish communication, why would not God make some suitable response?) Why, I wondered, since God it seemed did not choose to answer, why did Papa go on talking to Him? It seemed such a one-sided business. Why not, for a change, try talking to me? But the only remarks ever delivered to me by Papa were snubs.

"You know nothing about the subject, Catherine, so don't interrupt; it is very rude for a child to break into adult conversation." "Be quiet, Catherine, please; this is not your affair."

Masha's and my churchgoing stopped, because Papa announced that if we went to any of the services, we must attend them all. It did not do for the rector's wife to appear intermittently.

In that case, retorted Masha with her usual firmness, she feared we must stay away entirely. She was not prepared to pay lip service when the spirit did not move her, and, moreover, she had not the time to go twice every Sunday.

By now we were very hard up indeed. I discovered later that a huge amount of Edred's money had been disbursed on the support of his unfortunate brother in an expensive sanatorium in Switzerland. This brother, Reginald, died when I was eight or nine. What we lived on after that was Masha's savings from her teaching career and what she earned from translations.

Why did she not return to teaching? Because Edred needed, she felt, her constant support. I was at home also. She did nearly all the work of our various parsonages, besides gardening and cooking. She never made the least attempt to enlist Papa's help in these tasks; he sat in his study and wrestled with God while she fetched coal and logs, pumped, dug, chopped kindling, scrubbed floors, sawed wood, hammered nails, mended fuses, and painted walls. However small the house we occupied, Papa's study was always forbidden territory, never to be invaded by visitors or children. In several of our homes, the study was a room I never entered from first to last.

During these years we became cut off from my aunts. I don't know that Edred actually raised objections to their visits. I think Masha may have found it too difficult being a buffer between irreconcilable viewpoints, and stopped inviting them.

Besides, we were always in such inaccessible places.

At the time, when I was twelve, that we moved to Dorset, life had become a little easier. My two eldest aunts, Tasha and Dolly, were killed in a plane crash on their way to an ILO conference in the Philippines. They had left their money to each other and, if both died simultaneously, to Masha. She felt their loss deeply—though they had not met in years, they wrote letters every single week, all those sisters were devoted to each other—but they had been considerably older, both in their mid-sixties, so her mourning was more like that for parents than for siblings. And the money made a great difference; for the first time since Papa quit medicine, we could afford a couple of night-store heaters in our freezing rectory, and a woman who came twice a week to do the rough cleaning. (Why did not Dolly and Tasha give financial help during their lifetime? I'm sure they must have tried; Masha probably told them to give it to famine relief). So, when I was thirteen, we acquired Mrs. Eppy, a solid, resigned war widow with curly grey hair, a red face, and a biting tongue.

She admired Masha immensely.

"Oh, Mrs. Mars-Smith, *you do try,*" was her constant, wondering tribute—admiration tinged with a touch of irony.

What she thought of Papa was never expressed. But I noticed that he soon grew quite as sensitive to her communication with Masha as he was to mine and, when he heard their voices together for more than a minute or so, would emerge from his room to stand, clearing his throat and with lifted eyebrows, waiting for them to fall into attentive silence, or move elsewhere.

The Dorset rectory, though cold as any of its predecessors, was handsome, and the surrounding country had such bewitching unspoiled charm that even Papa, it seemed, was not wholly unaffected. Or perhaps he was getting through to God at last.

For a short time life seemed reasonably normal and happy.

7

"I like her," Elspeth said. "She seems responsible. Wouldn't you say? I wonder why in the world she married Fauntleroy?"

"Usual reasons, I suppose. Liked him. He's got a lot of charm."

"Hmm." Elspeth's expression was dubious. Leafing through a dahlia catalogue she remarked, "I was never so hundred-percent *for* him as you."

"I wouldn't go so far as to marry him! Even if he asked me."

"And if you didn't happen to be twice his age."

"But his heart is in the right place, Bets. Look at what he's done here. Think what a horrible squalid dump this area was before. And he's done a lot of good elsewhere—quite unobtrusively too—donations to charity, to the arts—"

"He can afford to."

"You're in a crabby mood this morning."

"*You* always think, because somebody's efficient at getting things done, that their heart is in the right place."

"Well," said Pat with conviction, "the world is so full of

fools—sitting on committees, loving the sound of their own voices, muddling about, procrastinating, frustrating everybody else—that, when you meet someone who sees what needs doing and damn well goes ahead and *does* it—how can you help liking them?"

"I don't know, *I* don't know," said Elspeth, "it seems to me very odd that he should let that girl come down here, on her own, in the state she's in, with no one to look after her, so very soon after they got married. Why, they were still on their honeymoon! No—say what you like, it's odd. And—I heard something rather queer and nasty about him—"

Olga Laszlo put her head round the door without knocking, inquired, "Darlings, can I use your phone?" and came right in.

"Of course. Help yourself." Pat's expression appeared a little less cordial than her voice. She put on her tweed jacket, said, "Anything needs to be bought in Dorchester, Bets?" to Elspeth, who shook her head, then walked rapidly out.

Elspeth, having written her order and put it in a stamped envelope, began sorting seed potatoes for planting. She had them in boxes all over the room, on chairs, tables, and the counter, among the permanent clutter of books, dishes, and piles of catalogues. As she examined them she unabashedly listened to Olga's conversation.

". . . Swit? *Could* you be a love and get my key back from Gretl—who must have had a *stroke* or something—and go round to Lexham Gardens and, if there's a phone bill, pay it—and see if some transparencies have come—those fools at Tagus must have sent them there for they haven't arrived *here* —what? Gretl's in *Paris*—? But—well then—well, see if *Mervyn* has the key, would you, there's a love? But do pay that phone bill, I'll let you have—yes, I'm not going to be here *very* long, only another week or so, I devoutly *hope*—Oh no, I'm not precisely starving but you know what it's like in the backwoods, nobody one can really talk to—"

Elspeth gave herself a small grim appreciative nod, working away at her potatoes. Olga's telephone conversations had become her daily pleasure.

Presently Shuna wandered in.

"I've finished Mr. Frisby's calculus work. And done the grammar lesson and learned 'Kubla Khan.' Shall I say it to you?"

"In a minute." Elspeth had one eye on Olga. "Can you first give this plateful of scraps to the birds? Put them right up on the top level of terracing at the back—so the birds won't have to come too close to the house."

"Then we shan't be able to see them very well."

"Yes, but more birds come and get the benefit."

Shuna returned from this errand just as Olga, winding up her final telephone conversation, replaced the receiver. She greeted the child with effervescent enthusiasm.

"Hallo my darling! How are you today? What's that you have there?"

"A map."

"Let me see? What map is this?"

Shuna handed over the sheet of paper. "It's a map of Fridayland," she explained.

"Fridayland, my angel? Where is that?"

"It's where the Toes live."

"But why Fridayland? Why not Thursdayland?"

"Fridayland is better. Friday's yellow, don't you see—a good, bright yellow; Thursday's only grey, like Tuesday. Thursdayland is a misty kind of place; *no* Toes would want to live there."

"And what do they do, these Toes, in Fridayland?"

"The usual sort of things," replied Shuna, in a tone of surprise. "The usual things that Toes do."

"Such as?"

"Building castles—fighting battles—playing in symphony orchestras—"

"This child's imagination is so *wonderful*—!" Olga burst out in a ferment of rapture. Shuna looked at her with a vaguely puzzled expression, taking back the map from Olga's unheeding hand. In one corner she wrote CAR PARK, as if this necessity had just occurred to her.

"Shuna," said Elspeth, "could you run up with this packet to Lady Fortuneswell? It's marked 'Pyramid TV,' so I expect she ought to have it right away. You can recite your 'Kubla Khan' to me when you get back. And just make sure Odd Tom's not being a trouble to her, will you? He does seem rather inclined to hang round her house—I'm not quite sure why."

"I think it's because Arkwright likes her," Shuna said, putting down her map and taking the envelope the postman had left.

Olga gazed after the child, obviously half inclined to accompany her. But, to Elspeth's relief, she decided to stay for a gossip.

"Was it *ever* known who her father was?"

"I really couldn't say." Elspeth's face and voice were both expressionless.

"What a dreadful, dreadful pity about her poor mother! What a shattering thing to happen! Such a waste! When she had been so *brilliant!* One can quite see where the child gets it—"

Elspeth opened her mouth to speak, then checked herself.

"The poor girl would have been so proud, so happy," Olga declared mournfully.

"No doubt." Elspeth was noncommittal. She began working over another box of potatoes.

"There was never any follow-up from those people? In that place where she had been?"

"Somebody seems to be at the front door," said Elspeth. "Could you open it? My fingers are all earthy."

The somebody proved to be Sophie Pitt. Elspeth greeted her with considerable warmth.

"Sophie, my dear! What can I do for you? Do you want the phone?"

Sophie, even with no makeup, grizzled dishevelled hair, and dirty jeans, never looked less than a duchess.

"No, not the phone," she said grandly. "I just came because I have finished learning my part, so I'm inviting the whole village to a soirée."

"A soirée!"

"This evening at six. I intend to tell everybody's fortune. And there will be punch."

"Telling *fortunes?* But how *won*derful!" breathed Olga. Her eyes shone. Her smile would have melted icebergs. Sophie, who rather disliked her, for no particular reason since they had hardly exchanged half a dozen words, overcame her reluctance and said graciously, "I hope you will be free to come?"

"I shall make a *point* of getting back from the theatre in *plenty* of time," promised Olga. "But now I had better get off to my work or they will be *won*dering what has be*come* of me. Staying here, engrossed in gossip! But you always have such interesting things to tell!"

With a chiding, reproving smile for Elspeth, she took her departure.

"Grubby little bitch," remarked Sophie, lighting a cigarette and helping herself, uninvited, to coffee.

8

As I may have mentioned before, I have a passion for paper clips, which I collect— That gives a wrong impression. I don't spend my days in stationers' buying box after box, like the man who had trunks full of pancakes under the bed. But I do like to pick them up, from the floors of concert halls, offices, trains, restaurants; from streets and pathways, from churches, elevators and escalators, from stages, studios, and art galleries. I have found paper clips in the Louvre, St. Paul's, and even the Parthenon. To pick up three in a day is a sign of good luck. That seldom happens. One is the norm, and two reasonably frequent. Sometimes, in seasons of scarcity, I will leave a clip lying for a while, confident that I can come back to it on a meagre day and refurbish my luck; so you can imagine my chagrin last October on planning to reclaim one, a reliable clip that I had noticed for weeks, lodged in a pavement crack just outside Broadcasting House, the front entrance, to get there and find it gone . . . Hair pins are quite as common as paper clips, but I've never had the *least* wish to pick *them* up. There is something sordid about a hair pin, something greasy and personal, whereas a paper clip is shining, symmetrical and extrinsic, a friend to man to whom it says . . . What do I do with my collection? They are housed in a small tin chest of drawers, once given me by Fitz; and the interesting (and wholesome) feature of my hobby is that the paper clips slide out of my keeping quite as quickly as they slide into it, on letters, on acting parts, recipes, copies of songs, I hardly know what; they come and go at an equal rate, there is a continual flow.

So it was really singular to find myself housed in a little dwelling that contained not a single paper clip, not one. In the course of orienting myself I went over Number 1 Glifonis pretty thoroughly, as you may imagine, but I did not really expect to find clips in drawers or cupboards and so was not unduly disappointed. This just was not paper clip territory. I tried to scold myself into common sense but did, in consequence, feel faintly anxious, ill at ease, unsettled. I was also (apart from my fractured wrist and wrenched ankle) feeling ominously healthy; the cancer symptoms in my spine and chest had temporarily abated, the spots before my eyes had reduced in density, and even a *very* alarming recent symptom, of what felt like broken-off eyelashes gouging holes into my left eyeball, all these had been alleviated in a way that did make me wonder if they were subsiding together before the advent of the *real* killer.

Anyway, apart from being a bad omen, the lack of paper clips about the house was a real nuisance. One needs paper clips for so many things. Why had not Ty thought to set up a village shop in Glifonis? Or at least a taverna? The poor Greeks had to travel five miles for a beer, over to Toller Asinorem. It was queer, I thought, that Ty, such a careful planner, had not anticipated this basic need.

I was pleased, therefore, when the child Shuna brought me a thick packet from Pyramid (which proved to be the extra scenes written in to *Rosy and Dodo* so as to satisfy the accountants about the need for returning to Knoyle) because

Randolph Grove's covering letter was fastened to the stapled text by a big, comely brass paper clip. And I was furious at the mocking malignity of Providence when, on my extracting the thick wad of paper from its envelope, the paper clip flipped off the top and spun away through the sunlit air, to fall somewhere on my terrace.

"Oh, damnation!"

"I'll find it!" said Shuna, and skipped off eagerly searching between the marble flagstones and along the edge of the cupressos hedge. The cat Arkwright accompanied her, thinking it was a game, pouncing on shadows.

But even Shuna's sharp young eyes failed to find the paper clip.

"Oh well. Never mind. Thanks very much. I'll manage without it. I just like to collect them."

"Tom used to collect matchboxes," she said. "He had nine hundred and three when their house was taken away. But after that, he said he couldn't pick up the interest to start again."

I had heard the story of Tom's house from Shuna, and wondered with a deep worry *where* the house had been; but that Shuna did not know.

"How are things going in Fridayland?"

"The rebellion has been put down. Marshall Toe is back in power."

"What happened to all the majors?" It was the majors who had organised the uprising in Fridayland, I knew, and, after their coup, had even run the country for a few weeks; I suspected that Shuna was secretly on their side, though she claimed total impartiality.

"Oh, they were all executed."

"Good heavens!"

"Marshal Toe said there was no place in Fridayland for people who could not be trusted." Shuna's face was perfectly calm, but I thought she sounded a little sad. She had written a poem about the colonels and the majors and Orpheus which appeared to show a fondness for the majors; it also, I thought, demonstrated a remarkable poetic gift in someone who was also deeply interested in the number of integers that could be crammed between one and one-point-five; an infinite number, she thought, and I saw no reason to doubt her.

"Well—perhaps the Marshal is right. But to execute them *all*— Couldn't he have deported them?"

"Where to?"

"I suppose, a penal colony. Thursdayland?"

"But then they'd just hate him from there until they were strong enough to make ships and come back like the Normans."

"I'm afraid you must be right."

"I'll think about it some more," she said, sounding like Pat.

Sophie Pitt arrived with a loaf of bread.

"Hallo, my loves; I've been baking." She put the bread on the table.

"Delicious, it smells."

"Good-bye, Cat. I have to go and say 'Kubla Khan' now." Shuna skipped away. Then she came back to say, "Aunt Elspeth told me to make sure Odd Tom wasn't being a trouble to you."

"No trouble at all. I *see* quite a bit of him, wandering around; he seems to be looking for something. But he never comes within talking distance."

"He wouldn't hurt you," Shuna assured me. "I think he left something by mistake in your house that he wants to pick up again. A note or something. But he's *very* kind." Off she went again.

"Funny little thing." Sophie looked after her. "She's a genius, they say."

"I shouldn't wonder," I said absently, thinking of Odd Tom. Had he left U R 2 DYE?

Sophie said, "I've come to invite you to my conversazione. I thought all we Glifonis incomers ought to get together. Tonight at six."

"Gracious. We'll be rather an ill-assorted group, I should think?"

"So much the more interesting." Sophie stubbed out her cigarette in a pot of geraniums; whatever the house lacked in furnishing it lavishly made up for in plant life—all Miss Morgan's work, I imagined.

"Who else will be there?"

"Zoë. She's coming to stay with me today."

"Oh, good. I like Zoë."

"And Miss Laszlo. I gather she's a friend of yours."

"I *know* her," I said cautiously. "I'm not sure that 'friend' quite covers it."

"And the Goadbys."

"The sad-looking fur-coated wife and grey-faced husband?"

"That's them. They lost their child in some tragedy, poor things. And old Laurence Noble—if he can tear himself away from 'Eine Kleine Neapmusik.' And the Pools."

"Don't know them."

"He's an architect. Friend of the Greek guy who designed the village. Elderly man. *Much* younger wife. Teenage son."

"Haven't seen any of them."

"Well you don't get about much, do you? They are in the house at the bottom. The husband and son stay indoors all the time. Wife and guest walk along the cliffs."

"What a lot you know, Sophie."

"I keep my eyes open," she said darkly. "I like to know what's going on. That's how I get good parts. I'm always just outside the casting-room door."

"It's a lucky talent."

She had a part exactly suited to her in *Rosy and Dodo*—a shrewd County parson's wife, managing to a halfpenny on her husband's scanty stipend, keeping all the parish in order. Masha would have enjoyed her performance very much, I thought.

"Okay, so I'll hope to see you at six. Shall I send old Laurence to wheel you down the steps?"

"No, I can manage, thank you. I'm getting reasonably agile on my crutches. Or I'll ask a Greek."

LATER in the day, however, I went to see old Laurence Noble on my own account.

I had tried first at the house of the Ladies (I could not help thinking of them as the Ladies of Glifonis, like the Ladies of Llangollen) but they were out. It would be hopeless hunting among the clutter in their kitchen; anyway Olga Laszlo was on the telephone to the unlucky Swit, and made big eyes at me but did not stop talking. I had not the least wish to become further involved with her and made haste out of there, and across the road to Mr. Noble's house. I could see him through his front window, wandering about, hands behind back like Beethoven, so I tapped with diffidence on the door.

He did not appear to recognise me at all when he came to open it; stared, frowning, through narrow eye-slits.

"Hallo, Mr. Noble; I'm your neighbour from up the road. You saved my house from burning the other night."

"Oh?" he said vaguely, "Yes? yes?" waiting for me to go away.

"I'm so sorry to trouble you—the ladies were out—I wondered if you had such a thing as a paper clip?"

"A *paper clip?*"

"It's my part that I'm trying to learn, you see—I'm an actress—" as he continued to look forbiddingly blank and unreceptive. "It was stapled together, and the staple has come out—there were so many pages—you know how staples do come out—"

"I'm afraid I haven't the least idea what you are talking about," he said pettishly.

"—and all the pages fly about; I've been sitting out on the terrace in this lovely warm sun; but the breeze—"

"I can't help you."

"Or even a pin?" I suggested desperately. "Would you have a pin, perhaps? Or a safety pin?"

"A pin?" His voice suggested that I spoke an unfamiliar language. "A pin . . . No." He began to close the door.

"Oh. Well, I'm sorry to have given you so much trouble." My sarcasm was wasted. The door clicked shut.

I looked down the hill. There were perhaps fifteen feet of gentle slope and one step before the next pair of houses, set diagonally on either side of the causeway. Was it, were they, worth the effort? But the day was sunny, the view inspiriting, a large vista, over the roofs of the lower houses to the cove, where the dredger went about its business and workmen clambered and scurried over the growing breakwater—and the blue, bounding sea beyond; I went on down.

At the first house, Number 4, the grey-faced husband— Mr. Goadby presumably—opened the door.

"Mr. Goadby? Good morning. I'm your neighbour from up the hill—Cat Conwil—come to ask a favour?"

No smile; his face seemed set in permanent folds of sadness. But he said, "What can I do for you?" in a flattish Midland accent, with reasonable goodwill.

"Would you have such a thing as a paper clip in your house?"

"Nay, lass, I'm afraid not; we've no papers, d'ye see, that need clipping."

"Or a pin? Perhaps—your wife—?"

"My wife is resting joost at present, lass, I'd as leave not disturb her."

"Oh well, then, never mind," I said apologetically, sorry not so much for disturbing them as for the cloud of misery that seemed to fill the house, palpable as the smoke in mine the other night. "Forgive me for bothering you. I—I hope I'll see you tonight at Miss Pitt's party."

"Oh, ay. I'm not sure if the wife will feel up to it." But his expression showed just a glimmer of response.

I hopped across the road to Number 5, the house diagonally opposite. What was the name here? Pool, that was it. "Mrs. Pool?" I said to the sharp little face in the doorway. "I'm your neighbor from up the hill—Cat Conwil—how do you do?"

"How do you do?" she responded with a trace of French accent and a look of what seemed unmixed dislike and suspicion. Hey, pal, what did I ever do to you? I wondered, and then remembered my Rosy capapace. Perhaps she took me for a predatory blonde. This theory was reinforced when over her shoulder came another face: not her husband, plainly, for he was much older, Sophie had said; this was a handsome, insolent-looking character of twenty-five or so, younger than Mrs. Pool, who might be my own age. He was very bronzed, as from Southern suns, and rested his chin on her clavicle in a proprietorial way.

"Hey? Were you in a battle?" he inquired in a fake American accent as he studied my crutches and bandages.

Wife and guest walk along the cliff, Sophie had said. Here, evidently, was guest.

"No, I just fell . . . Would you have such a thing as a paper clip in your house that I could borrow, do you think?"

"No, I am quite quite certain we haven't," she said without even pausing to think about it. "So sorry. Come Tad. We were just going out," she said to me, walking past.

"Jeremy might have one," Tad suggested. He turned his head and bawled, "Hey, Jeremy! You got a paper clip?"

"What?" demanded a bored reluctant voice from the rear of the house.

"Come here a minute."

A boy appeared—a tall, terribly thin boy, about eighteen perhaps. His arms were like sticks.

"What?" he said again, yawning.

"You got a paper clip anywhere among your stuff?"

"No," snarled Jeremy, and retreated faster than he had come. He had barely glanced at me. "Hurry up, Tad," called Mrs. Pool from yards down the hill.

"Sorry, mate," said Tad to me with a conspiratorial wink, and followed her. His accent was—what? Rhodesian perhaps? The vowels, under the phoney American surface, were short and clipped.

A little discomfited, I turned back up the hill, feeling that my morning was going to waste.

I turned too fast for prudence, lost my balance, incautiously put weight on the hurt foot, and sat down fast, swearing and sweating. Fortunately there was a lump of rock by the roadside; I was able to lurch to it and use it for a perch.

Now, I thought, I look a proper fool. And it's all my own stupid fault. I should have used a clothes peg to clip the pages. But probably there are no clothes pegs in the house either. I'll have to wait here until one of the Greeks comes along.

The first person to come along was the cat, Arkwright, who greeted me with great goodwill and sat down by me as if this had been a planned assignation. Perhaps it had. I daresay cats can foretell the future.

After another while, Odd Tom came slippering up the hill in his holey sneakers, with his weathered Adam's apple working around double-time inside the grimy white roll-neck collar. When he saw me he stopped and gave a little chirping croak of dismay and commiseration, which was followed by a long, incomprehensible lecture. He grew excited and waved his hands. I smiled apologetically and spread *my* hands out.

"——— ———?" said Tom. I shook my head.

"——— ———?" he said again. I made motions of noncomprehension.

Suddenly impatient, he stooped down by me and took hold of my bandaged foot. I flinched a bit, nervously, but with a cross jerk of his head he intimated that I was to keep still and not mess about.

The experience of his hands on my ankle came as a total surprise. His grip was firm, yet delicate; everything that his grubby, shabby appearance was not. He felt the joint and seemed to be listening to it, with his head on one side, like a person tuning an instrument; very, very carefully and minutely he moved it about. After a few minutes of this it seemed to me that the pain was not quite so severe.

"——— ——— ——— ——— ——— ———?" said Tom. About to shake my head helplessly, I suddenly realised that he had said, "How long ago did you do this?"

"Seven days ago," I said.

He nodded, and went back to his manipulation. A couple of the Greeks walked by and nodded as if this were an entirely familiar situation.

"He soon make it well, you see!" one of them called back over his shoulder.

After five minutes or so, Tom stood up (he had been kneeling to work on my ankle), passed me my crutches, and gave me an instruction, which I realised meant, "Stand up now, carefully, and try it."

I did so. He nodded.

"Now you can walk up to your house," he intimated.

"Using the foot?"

He shook his head vigorously. "No, no. Use the crutches."

With extreme care, I winched myself up the hill, Odd

Tom shuffling observantly by my side, sometimes taking my arm in a firm grip if he thought I was at risk.

"Sit on the front steps," he ordered, so I sat on the steps and he gave the foot another working-over.

"It feels better now," I said. Tom nodded as if this were no news to him.

"Now go on up the steps."

I hoisted myself up.

"Now wait there."

Arkwright shot past us at speed and entered the house as Tom opened the front door. Tom went in and reappeared with a chair, onto which I gratefully subsided. And then he worked over my foot for the third time.

"Tomorrow—you'll be walking on it," he said. "Let it rest for now."

His speech was perfectly intelligible really. All it lacked was consonants.

"Tom, I can't thank you enough. What can I—? Let me pay you something."

"No, no," he said. "Glass o' beer if you've got one."

"Would wine do?"

"Okay." He wandered about the terrace inspecting the plants in pots that stood around. From one of the pots he retrieved my brass paper clip and laid it on the kitchen windowsill. I brought him the glass of wine, which he drank.

"Work on your hand tomorrow, too," he said. Then he snapped his fingers. Arkwright came briskly out of the house, and the two went off together.

After a while I hobbled inside, leaving the chair and empty glass on the terrace. Shuna or somebody else could bring them in by and by. I felt, all of a sudden, extremely sleepy, and had to lie down for a nap.

The last thing that came to me before sleeping was a vision of that angry, unhappy young face, antagonistic to the whole world, Jeremy Pool. Thank God, thank God, I thought, Fitz never looked like that.

SOPHIE Pitt's party, later that day, proved highly characteristic. She had mixed up a great bowl of punch, which tasted mildly delicious at first, and then later caused your legs to float away from under you. Sophie was quite a drinker herself —she had the drinker's high colour and absent eye; but she never touched liquor, she had told me, when actually engaged on a part. So at the moment she confined herself to tomato juice and watched with technical interest as the punch undid the reservations of her guests. She had exchanged her usual dirty jeans for a blue-grey caftan and looked like the Sibyl of Cumae, garlanded in a wreath of cigarette smoke.

The only food offered at her conversazione consisted of thin crispbread wafers spread with cream cheese, upon which she had carefully dotted fragments of red pepper or small black lumps of caviar, thus turning the biscuits into facsimiles of playing cards. King, Queen, Jack were denoted by strips of red paprika cut into the letters *K, Q* and *J.* These edible cards were laid out on a big wooden spindle dish, like a lazy susan, in the middle of her circular table, and she herself kept it in motion by every now and then giving the central spindle a twirl.

Then, wandering witchlike among the group of guests, she would suddenly pounce.

"Cat—reach out your hand and take the nearest biscuit. Oh dear, dear, the eight of clubs; hmmm; let's see; you'd better take another."

"The eight of clubs, Sophie, what does that mean?"

"Someone close to you is angry about something. Take another. That person is *very* angry. The two of spades—oh, goodness me, you'd better have another drink."

"Are things really going against me, Sophie?"

"Not for long, love, let's hope." She gave me her large, vague scrutiny, patted my shoulder, muttering, "I'm quite sure it's not *your* fault," and grabbed the arm of Mr. Neighbour—what was his name? Goady, Goadby, that's it.

"Mr. Goadby—take a biscuit!"

Mechanically, the grey-faced man did so, and stood clutching it as if he were not certain of its purpose.

"*Very* good!" Sophie beamed at him. "The ace of spades! That should mean a long-sought ambition is about to be fulfilled for you!"

"Ambition? Eh, well"—he looked startled—"I reckon I'm too old to have ambition anymore, you know—"

"Well," she assured him, "something you really want is going to happen, and very soon. Now, have you met our new neighbour, Lady Fortuneswell—?"

"Ay, I have—" he was answering, and then broke off abruptly, staring at me. His biscuit broke off too, and the larger part fell to the floor. "Never mind, it's only tiles," Sophie murmured, scooped it up, and moved away to drop it in the sink (the party was drifting back and forth between her front parlour and kitchen, drinks being in the former, food in the latter). Mr. Goadby stepped hastily away from me, and I saw him speak to a largish, blondish woman in a handsome fur coat, who directed at me from watery blue eyes a remarkably hostile stare.

I seem to be picking up enemies faster than friends, I thought, and sighed. Rosy's persona, wrapped around me like sticky tape, was becoming desperately tiresome. The end of the TV serial could not come too soon so far as I was concerned.

I saw Zoë Grandison beyond the Goadbys and went over to say hello to her. She had been talking to the Pools' guest, who was devouring her with his gaze as a hungry hyena contemplates a bone (Zoë with her immense cloud of dark hair hanging down over pale skintight corduroys would be enough to tempt any hyena, even a vegetarian one), but she detached herself and hurried over to me.

"Hey, love? What did you do to your poor foot? I was going to suggest we do some walks together." Zoë is a passionate walker; she told me once that in East Sheen, where she lives, she gets up at 5 A.M. all through summer, so that she can explore the gardens of her neighbours on the way to Richmond Park. "I go through them all, hopping over fences; nobody's about at that hour, do you see? Not even the police. And you can find out such a lot about people, from their gardens."

"Oh, I wrenched it in Venice. But it's getting better fast. Maybe we can walk in a day or two."

"I understand there are beautiful paths along the cliffs."

"Isn't it mostly army land? Civilians not allowed?"

"Oh, I don't take any notice of *that,*" she said. "I've found some already." And then, nodding towards the Pools' guest, who was still casting lecherous looks at her across the room, "What a little tick! How in hell did he ever crawl into this classy environment?"

"Along with the Pools."

"Their resident toad. Well I'm sorry for Mr. Pool. Can I come and see your house, Cat?"

"Yes, do. Come to breakfast tomorrow."

"Love to! Shall I get you another of these knockout drops?"

I shook my head, and she wandered away to refill her own glass.

"Do you know what the two of spades signifies in Sophie's book?" I asked Miss Morgan, who was conducting a lively business chat with a tall spare grey-haired man: "You've got to get the fall, you see, the best drainage system in the world isn't going to work unless you've got the fall—"

She broke off, beamed at me comfortably, and said, "I

don't suppose you've met Llewellyn yet, have you? Llewellyn, this is Cat, Lady Fortuneswell. The two of spades, my love—I'm not quite sure. I think it might mean that you are innocently under a cloud—"

"Oh, well; just so long as I'm innocent—"

"Can I get you another drink?" said Lewellyn Pool.

"Goodness, no, thank you, my legs will only just hold me up as it is."

He got drinks for himself and Miss Morgan who, I suspected, could drink anybody here under the table, and we talked about the geology of Dorset. In digging out the foundations of Glifonis, he told me, a few fossils had been unearthed, not so many as there were farther along the coast, but enough so the Department of the Environment had shown an inclination to hold up the whole project until a commission of inquiry could decide if it would be worth excavating the area, geologically.

"My goodness!" I could imagine Ty's rage at such a check to his plans. "So what happened?"

"Oh, they decided it wasn't worth it. Maybe some palm was lightly greased? They couldn't spare the cash or time, it was quietly shelved. But there are fossils—if you go looking on the shore beyond where they are building the mole." He glanced apologetically at my crutches and said, "Well, not an activity I can recommend to you, just at present—"

Olga, who had drifted up during this conversation, listened with blazing eyes.

"Fossils! But how wonderful! I *adore* fossils! What kind?"

"Ammonites? Can I refill your drink?" said Mr. Pool politely.

He did so, then removed himself; I received the impression that he wasn't wild about Olga.

"Poor sad man," she murmured, glancing after him. "His son is on heroin, did you know? And the wife having it off with that dreadful dummy from voodooland—"

Taking few pains to disguise my disapproval of these art-less revelations within earshot of the persons concerned, I asked how her work at the Dorchester theatre was proceeding. To my surprise, she gave me a malicious grin; a really nasty grin. From her look, I thought she must have imbibed a good many glasses of Sophie's brew. "Oh, it goes not too badly; today, I had quite a good day's work. And you, my darling—?" Like the Bolter, she pronounced it *dullink*—"how are you making out, down here in your solitude? Quite a change, no, from lying in the lap of luxury in Venice?"

"I think you *sit* in the lap of luxury, rather than lie in it?"

Irrelevantly, I had a sudden heartwarming recollection of Masha teaching me, at age five or so, to core an apple, saying with exquisite tact, "I *think* you'd find, if you hold the apple like *this,* and the corer like *this,* it might be easier . . ."

The affectionate smile with which I recalled this incident apparently infuriated Olga beyond all bounds, for, to my utter astonishment and dismay, she suddenly burst into a whispered, hissing diatribe, cataloguing all my odious attributes: "think yourself so superior to everybody else," "never lift a finger to help others"; and my past sins: "wrecked my marriage, just from the pure love of *meddling.* Do you know how old my children are now, my daughters? Sixteen and seventeen! And they have hardly spent three nights with me since —since—since then! They don't *wish* to see me! Two superior English young ladies! I am not enough out of the top drawer for them! They are too *busy* for me—going to that grand finishing school, getting ready to be presented—why should they bother with tiresome, foreign old Olga?"

She thrust her sallow face furiously into mine.

"I'm sorry, Olga," I said stupidly. "I didn't realise you felt like that. Blamed me so much. But, then—it seemed to me—at that time—"

"Oh, what do we know, when we are in the thick of a passion? But you were then my *friend*—you should have advised me better. Sometimes," she said ferociously, "sometimes I am almost sure that it was you who told Cal Pendennis that I was planning to leave him! For, who else *could* it have been?"

"Oh, come *on*, Olga!" I said, sick with disgust and pity, "why in the world would I do a thing like that?"

"Olga, my dear—take a biscuit," said Sophie, materialising at her shoulder.

Automatically Olga did so, never removing her eyes from my face.

"The three of diamonds," I said. "What does that mean, Sophie?"

"It must be something in connection with your work, Olga." Sophie looked a little perturbed. "Are you perhaps meeting any opposition in your plans at the theatre?"

"Always—always!" Olga made a large gesture with her glass, then quickly swallowed the rest of its contents. "I never yet worked on any job where I did not encounter the opposition of fools." Like Papa, I thought. "It is lucky, so lucky, that I have good *friends* to cheer me up." And she gave me a sudden vigorous embrace, nearly unbalancing me. "Good friends, good, good friends like my darling Cat. Hmm?" She grinned at me sidelong, catlike, and munched up the three of diamonds in one bite.

I told Sophie that I believed I had better be going.

"It has been a lovely party, but crutches aren't the best support for parties—"

"Oh, my dear, you should have sat down—"

"Yes, but then I'd never have been able to get up again."

As I worked my way towards the door, I noticed Pat Limbourne just arriving. "Only this minute got back from Dorchester," I heard her say, and something about Arts Council awards. Her eye fell on me and a look passed over her face that I was unable to analyse—troubled, harassed, disapproving, perhaps?

Oh hell, I thought. Let's get out of here—but it's going to be hard work toiling back up the hill . . .

To my surprise, I found small, birdlike Miss Morgan at my elbow.

"I'm going too," she chirped. "We never like to leave Shuna for too long on her own—not that she isn't perfectly sensible—and it was so stuffy in there—such a lot of people still smoke, though you'd think they'd know better—"

In a businesslike way she removed my left-hand crutch and took my arm, supporting me with a remarkably strong grip, unexpected in somebody of her size.

"It's all the karate lessons," she explained simply. "And archery: that strengthens one's biceps. And, of course, gardening; I spend so much time out of doors."

I said how very grateful I was; and then told her about Odd Tom's ministrations.

"Isn't he a wonderful little man?" she exclaimed, delighted. "I did hope that he would—but he has to like you first, otherwise he wouldn't lift a finger. He'll probably have you walking in a day or two."

"That's what he said." I hesitated, wondering whether to ask if Odd Tom bore a grudge against my husband. In the end I decided not to.

Miss Morgan saw me to my door, and through it. "If I were you I'd go to bed very soon."

"Thank you, I shall."

I lay down on my bed, fully clothed. I felt exhausted, but sleep was far off. There had been too many crosscurrents at Sophie's party, after my days of solitude. Faces, voices, surged through my consciousness in a clattering, glittering cataract. No way could I bring the flow to a stop, or even slow it down. I tried reciting poetry, of which I have a goodly store, old stage parts, dates of English kings, but stuck at Henry V, 1413. Then I tried another expedient, which sometimes helps when I am suffering from overstimulation. I took my mind for a walk around the rooms and gardens of Yetford Rectory.

It was not a beautiful house, nor even a particularly comfortable one. The rooms were too high and too cold. But it had much character, and there was plenty of space in which we could spread out. And Masha loved the garden, because of the great cedar tree, and the shrubbery, and the stone bench . . . I loved it too. The cedar was the first tree I managed to climb—then the walnut, the wild cherry, the great willow, the oak, the copper beech—you had to cheat on the copper beech and throw a clothesline over the lowest branch, for otherwise there was no possible means of getting up its huge smooth trunk.

If I were offered a day to live again out of the whole of my life, I would choose a summer afternoon at Yetford.

Even if it meant having the rest of what followed over again?

No, no, not that. Not on any account. One life, once over, is quite enough.

Thinking about Yetford brought me unawares up to the day, the worst in my life, I suppose, when I had to tell Masha that I was pregnant.

She took the news like a stern general—in her habitual way; instantly began to plan, ignoring the past, concentrating on the future. She had never been given to postmortems. Andrei was back in Russia, there was no earthly use in telling him; if, indeed, it would even be possible to get in touch with him.

"You'll go on working as long as you can, of course."

"Of course."

"And Papa need not be told until a good deal later—I'm afraid he will be very upset—"

Papa by then had retired more and more into that exclusive male club which he shared with God. Occasionally he would wander into the kitchen and say, "Can you tell the staff to serve my lunch in the study?" What staff he had in mind we never knew. Perhaps, Fitz once suggested, much later, it was an allusion to the Twenty-third Psalm: "Thy rod and thy staff they comfort me." In the fullness of time, Fitz became wonderful at managing Papa, could conduct him like a string quartet. But that was years later. At first there were troubles, terrible, terrible troubles.

I can see now what I could not then, that a part of Masha must have been overjoyed at my news. So much of her life must have seemed a complete waste, a write-off—except in some mystical balance sheet which she entirely accepted but which the rest of us have to take on trust. Now, though, she had a second chance to be really *useful,* to employ her neglected powers. None of this, I am sure, showed in her face (which, as she aged, took on more and more of the aspect of a rocky landscape in a dry mountain region).

Her sheer surprise was hard to bear: "But, I taught you ethics? I thought that would be sufficient to keep you out of trouble." A deep, deep sigh. "I suppose I *have* been too preoccupied with Edred . . ."

Childbirth itself was neither here nor there. All I remember of it is the woman in the next bed. "Allah, Allah, Allah," she was murmuring, accent on the last syllable, a LA, a LA, a LA, as if giving birth and the name of God were both the very last word in style.

And Fitz's first year was a time of calm. It was when he began to run about, and develop, and have a will of his own, and come into conflict with Papa, that all hell broke loose.

That day, that excruciating day, when Masha said to me, "Katya, I really don't think you had better come home anymore." (I was still working at one of the hospitals then.) "It's too painful for all of us," Masha said.

"Not—?"

"Not come home, anymore," she repeated. "Not until

Fitz is a whole lot bigger. It is too hard on him. Too hard on Papa. Too hard on you." Of herself she did not speak.

Was it because Papa had cut her off from her sisters? Was that why she separated Fitz from me?

I can remember—it is printed on my ear forever, forever —his desperate, frantic heartbroken cry: "Mammy—Mammy —Mammy!" as she held him in and shut the front door and I raced off down the drive, blind with tears.

Nothing, ever again, can be as bad as that.

Such wounds cannot be healed. I feel it ache to this day. And Fitz? He seems completely stable. Masha undoubtedly brought him up much better than I would have.

Joel strongly disagrees about this.

"You mean she just let you *go*—off into the world by yourself at the age of sixteen—"

"Seventeen by then I think—"

"Just like that, after one terrible trauma—"

"The burned child, Masha thought; and she was quite right."

"That was barbarous. It was uncivilised."

"Well, but Masha wasn't exactly civilised—though she had such exquisite manners. She was Welsh and Russian—"

"I'm Irish and Jewish," Joel said. "I wouldn't behave like that."

"You *are* civilised, Joel. Masha was tribal. She was a matriarch. She thought in terms of the family."

"You were her family, damn it."

"But I'd introduced Fitz—the next generation. So now it was my job to get on and provide for him. She undertook to rear him—which she did perfectly; she managed to do that as well as take care of Papa, who was her primary job, she reckoned, the one she'd undertaken for life."

"I can't see why? When he was such a hopeless old stick? Didn't he *ever* do anything at all useful?"

Casting my mind back, I could think of no such occurrence. His contribution, at any time of crisis, was to stand awkwardly in the way, saying, "What shall we do? What do you think should be done, Maria?"

The surgery, his skill in the operating room, was a one-off, a single talent; it had left him, like the dew of the morning, like Wordsworth's early genius. What remained was only a shell.

"No," I said slowly, "he didn't . . ."

"Well, then—"

"But, you see, she looked on Edred as a wounded eagle. No, more than that. After all, he *had* once been the most brilliant surgeon in London, maybe in the world. He had given it up—of his own choice—"

"More fool him," said unsympathetic Joel.

"That's not the point! He had given it up to go and look for God. If there was one thing Masha had, it was a respect for other people's integrity—"

"Integrity! That old catchword! Godsakes!"

"For all she knew, Edred was on the point of some great discovery—something far finer than all his surgical wizardry. She respected his choice—as she did mine when I told her I couldn't be a nurse any longer and got myself a job selling stockings at D. H. Evans. And she did look after Fitz, she made him what he is—"

"But why, why, when the old boy went senile, had his stroke or whatever—when she could *see* he wasn't going to get wherever it was he wanted—"

"But she couldn't see that! Don't you understand? For all she knew, he was *there* already—at Shangri-la! Wherever he was going. Everyone knows that saints are difficult and impossible. For all she knew, he was one. He had to be given the benefit of the doubt. She gave everyone that benefit."

"Except you."

"She knew I'd make out. I was like her. Her great

strength was that she always accepted what happened, never asked the reason why—"

"She shouldn't have!"

"Well that wasn't her way. She just got on with the next option. Like an ant, like a termite. Somewhere once I read an essay on the necessity and senselessness of all human activity. Necessity, okay; senselessness I deny. Masha's activities were no more senseless than those of a coral insect; she had to be, she had to do."

And I have to be and do, I thought.

"Yet she was educated," said Joel wonderingly.

"Sure she was educated. What has that to say to anything?"

"Education teaches you to argue and make an outcry."

Perhaps that's why I don't do much of that, I thought. Because of having no education after age fifteen, except what I could pick up in snatches.

"Well," I said, "if so, Masha had jettisoned that aspect of her education. All she kept were the mental stores that saw her through bad times. That was why *The Idiot* was almost her favourite novel. Endlessly she—she chewed the cud of all she had once learned."

"Very indigestible."

"Maybe. But the result was that she survived. And was a huge help to other people. In those villages—where Papa was such a hopeless rector—people depended on her. They used to come to her with problems. She was an appreciator. People need that. There aren't enough of them."

Just the same, I wondered, had the frustration within her, the knowledge that she might have had a career in public affairs, that she never made proper use of her abilities—had that caused the cancer? This was no new thought. It had come to me many times. I don't think she missed the Buck House parties, the fame, the income. But she did always keep her beautiful Liberty dresses. After she died, I found them folded carefully away, unfaded, in tissue paper, with moth-balls. She must have been too fat to wear them for the last thirty years. A cheap diet is very fattening. She had never offered those dresses to me. But they would not have suited my lifestyle either.

Just before I slept I thought again about Olga's furious accusation: "Sometimes I'm almost sure that it was you who told Cal Pendennis I was planning to leave him." Now *that* was *really* paranoid, I thought. Why in the world should Olga think that—when I had been her aide, her confidante, her heart-and-soul partisan?

Was it because she knew herself to be capable of such a betrayal?

I woke, later, with a start. Somebody was calling me—over and over, persistently: "Lady Fortuneswell, Lady Fortuneswell!" And then, "Cat! Cat Conwil!" At last I was obliged to acknowledge that the voice was real, and I hoisted myself heavily off the bed, and crutched myself slowly to the front door.

The caller was Pat Limbourne.

"I'm terribly sorry," she said, taking in my dishevelled appearance. "Were you asleep? It's not very late really—but, I suppose—"

"Never mind," I said yawning. "What time is it?"

"Quarter to ten. Elspeth was for not disturbing you, but he sounded so urgent—"

"Who?" I yawned again. My sleep had been short but heavy. I felt like a block of concrete.

"Your husband. On the phone."

"Oh! Good heavens!" I swayed, and grabbed for the splaying crutches.

"It's all right. Don't panic. I said I'd fetch you, and he

said he'd call back in ten minutes. Would you like me to push you in your wheelchair?"

"No, no, I'm fine now, thank you. It was just the surprise of being woken— Where is he?"

"In Dorchester."

"Dorchester?"

"At the Close Hotel. He did say he'd tried to call earlier," explained Pat, helping me down the steps. "I suppose we were all at Sophie's party. I happened to know, actually, that he was in Dorchester, because I'd seen him this morning at a Wessex Arts meeting. And—" She stopped while she guided me solicitously over a stretch of slippery marble pavement; the fine day had turned to a night of soft rain. The sea's murmur could be heard very clearly. I paid it little heed however; I was startled to death over the fact that Ty was so close, in Dorchester—had actually got in touch!

What did he want? Were all my wild imaginings quite wide of the mark? Were we about to resume our marital relationship? I have to confess that my heart went pit-a-pat. I felt a crazy, feverish curiosity at the prospect of seeing Ty again. As if he were a stranger with whom I was in love. Women used to dream romantic dreams about Hitler, I've been told. In the Middle Ages I suppose they dreamed the same kind of dreams about the Devil. A mixture of wild attraction and fear.

Well, that was how I felt about Ty just then.

PAT and I talked no more on our way to the Ladies' house; the causeway was greasy with rain and mud, demanding attention even from a person with two good feet.

When we reached the house, we found Miss Morgan fidgeting about the kitchen; it could not be said that she was tidying it, as she simply moved things from one place to another. She and Pat exchanged a significant look. Up to this moment I had assumed their mutual sympathy and agreement to be total, but now, I perceived, they were at odds; some question had driven a breach between them.

Nervous in the strained silence, I asked if I might use their bathroom.

"You know where it is, go ahead," Miss Morgan said.

Returning, I heard her mutter urgently, "I don't care what you say, she *ought* to be told."

"It's gossip," Pat Limbourne replied curtly. "Trifling, spiteful—"

"Well, I'll risk it. I'm not ashamed!" And, as I hobbled back into the kitchen—so warm, cluttered, lived-in, with its piles of school textbooks and half-mended jerseys, compared to the austerity of my house—Elspeth announced to me, "Pat saw your husband in Dorchester earlier today, lunching with Olga Laszlo."

I was a little surprised, but said, "Oh, really? Something to do with the theatre, I imagine. He's on the board, isn't he? And she's known him for a long time." ("Fancy you being married to old Ty," I recalled, from the other morning.) I added, "Queer that she didn't mention it this evening at Sophie's. But she was in rather a twitchy mood."

"Tipsy, not twitchy," said Elspeth. "When Olga's taken a drink or two she has a tongue like a puff adder. Really nasty."

"Oh well," I said, "she won't remember a thing about it tomorrow. It'll be all hugs and kisses and best friends again. I've known Olga quite a few years too, remember."

"That's not what concerns us." Elspeth took her hearing aid out of her ear, scowled at it, and slipped it back in again: a process with which I was becoming familiar, denoting perturbation of mind. "The thing is, Pat says, when she saw them at lunch, she could see that Olga was in the same kind of state then."

Pat's face bore the expression of someone biting on a rancid hazelnut.

I said, "Ty had been giving her too much to drink, you mean?"

"Yes, and she was all worked up—excitable—ready for mischief."

The phone rang.

"Well," I said, levering myself towards it, "I don't really think there is much mischief she can make between me and Ty."

All possible harm has been done already, I thought, picking up the receiver, as the Ladies tactfully removed themselves to the other room.

"Hello?"

"Is that you?" said my husband's voice.

How very odd it was to hear him over the telephone, sounding so familiar. The last time we spoke like this, I thought, had been before our wedding, making arrangements for it. How much younger we had both been then.

(When he was wooing me so pertinaciously, we used to talk on the telephone for hours, sometimes; he would call me from Athens, Islamabad, Melbourne—wherever he happened to be.)

"Yes, it's me. Where are you?" I said, and felt at once that I had begun on a false note.

"At the Close Hotel in Dorchester. I have to see you," he said coldly.

"Well—I'm here! And I think *you* are rather more mobile than *I* am at the moment. Having no car at present. And still being in plaster, on crutches."

"Oh. Your foot," he said slowly, as if he had entirely forgotten about that, and must now rethink his arrangements.

"Why don't you come out to Glifonis? It's looking very pretty. You were quite right about it—it's a charming little place."

The falsity in my voice dismayed me. Yet all I did was try for the note that used to come naturally.

"No!" he retorted with some violence. "It's too shut-in down there. I was going to suggest a walk. If it weren't for your foot—Well, there's a piece of conceptual art that I want you to see."

"Conceptual art?"

This was totally unexpected. Since when had Ty interested himself in conceptual art?

"But if—your foot—I suppose that rules out doing it on foot," he muttered to himself. He was, I thought, well on the way to being drunk; though I had never known Ty much affected by alcohol.

"Yes! Conceptual art!" he suddenly announced belligerently. "You had some highfalutin idea, you were talking about it once—conceptual art, all over the South Downs—like the Stone Age, you said—"

"Why, yes." Now, with embarrassment, I vaguely remembered. "So I did. That was in Venice—the time when we had the big argument about colour charts—and you said a sixty-year-old woman couldn't possibly assimilate a new idea—and I said why not; and we were arguing about the *Dejeuner sur l'Herbe* and whether that gesture of her hand under her chin is meant to be erotic, and you got so cross—"

"Oh be quiet!" shouted Ty furiously, as if I were pulling short hairs out of his neck with tweezers. Then he added in quite another voice, cold, vindictive, measured, deadly, "Why did you tell that little loose-tongued bitch, Olga Laszlo, about the Companions of Roland possibility?"

"Olga Laszlo?" I was startled almost out of my skin. "I never did! I wouldn't dream of doing such a thing."

"I did think at least I could trust your discretion," he went on with intense bitterness.

"I never told her."

"She said you did."

"She told you a lie, then. Which wouldn't be the first," I added.

There was a long, charged silence. Then: "How else could she know?"

"Don't ask *me!*"

"*Oh—!*" It was a cry of exasperation that he let out, almost of anguish, as if he were beset on every side. Without thinking, I said,

"Have you got one of your migraines coming on?" and then could have bitten out my tongue. The last thing, just then, that he needed was sympathy from me, a reminder that I knew about his weakness. Wary, defensive, vulnerable Ty.

"I have to see you," he announced. "I'll pick you up at the Glifonis car park tomorrow morning. Half past eight."

"Too early. Make it nine."

I didn't want him to see me come clambering up the slope, and I would need at least a half hour for that.

"All right."

The receiver clanged down at his end before I could say good night.

Very gently, I replaced my own mouthpiece, with a deep feeling of sadness and loss. I suppose I never do realise how much I love people, until I have lost them.

. . . It's no use remembering Andrei, and I never do. All that area has been railed, screened, concreted off, like Chernobyl, with tons and tons of barricade. A leakage from the other side would be too dangerous, too painful, too disruptive. As Masha taught me, I go on, I don't look back. Most people, after all, have had a first love, most know the totality of that experience. For me, Andrei was Family, but Family translated into something strong, male, intelligent, and full of love; everything that Papa was not. God knows what *I* represented for *him:* western freedom, unlimited creativity, frivolity, perhaps. Little Katushka, he used to call me. No, no, I'm not going into all that. Let it lie, under the stone.

Fitz has never asked me about his father. Not once. Masha must either have laid some tremendous prohibition on the subject, once and for all, or else given him sufficient of a story to satisfy him. Fitz, in any case, occupies himself with wider matters . . .

9

NEXT day I woke very early; in fact it can hardly be said that
I went to sleep at all. For most of the night I had thrashed
about, my thoughts leaping from Ty to Olga and back again.
For how in the world had she come to know that Ty had been
shortlisted for the Companions of Roland? It was true, Olga
had so many connections, all over Europe, that this was just
the kind of information she might be expected to pick up;
confidentiality meant nothing to her, she paid for one well-
kept secret with another, and then either made practical use
of them as barter, or scattered them abroad at random, as the
fancy and the mood took her. In her hands Ty's secret was
about as safe as a pot of gelignite in a spin dryer; I wondered
unhappily whether the fact that it had percolated as far as
Olga would already have lost Ty his chance of final acceptance? He would be wondering the same thing. No wonder
he had sounded so enraged.

Would he have calmed down by 9 A.M.? Would he accept
my assurance that I had no connection with the leak? Our
relationship had been so short-lived that I could come to no
decision on this point. Even if he had trusted me before the

disclosure that I was Nurse Smith, the need for total realignment after that revelation might easily mean that he no longer did so. I knew that my own attitude to him had changed radically since I assimilated the news that he was Jimmy-who-made-the-promise about the old man's daughter; Jimmy who made the promise and hadn't kept it. (At least I assume he never kept the promise, for where is she now?) Of course he may have had excellent reasons, the very strongest reasons for not doing so. Maybe she is dead.

I was out of bed by six, making a pot of extra-strong coffee. The day was sunny but frosty; masses of wild daffodils planted over the slopes of Glifonis (as she had told me) by Elspeth Morgan, were going to wait another day or two before opening fully. The ice-blue sea gleamed like a hard stone.

To my great surprise, as I clomped cautiously about in the kitchen, I heard a tap at the back door and, turning, saw the figure of Odd Tom through the glass door, bristly and grimy as usual. He never seemed to shave, but the bristles never grew any longer. I opened and asked him in.

"Hello, Tom. You're an early bird."

"Do your foot now. Hand, too," he said, nodding.

"Take off the cast, do you mean?" I asked with some apprehension. He nodded again.

"Time, now. Only get weak if that cast stays on."

"Would you like a cup of coffee?"

The twitch that I now understood to be a grin passed over his face.

"Wouldn't say no. But that cast's coming off first."

He removed it expeditiously with a sharp kitchen knife. (During the last few days the equipment in my kitchen had been much augmented, thanks to the practical good sense of the Ladies of Glifonis.)

My wrist ached without the cast, felt draughty and vulnerable, but Odd Tom worked on it, as he had on the ankle, testing, listening, testing again, until it had the warm flexibility of a healthy joint. "Not much wrong there now," he pronounced, tapping it, and then started in on the ankle. "Have you hiking up to Bulbarrow before breakfast in a day or two," he boasted.

"Well I'm supposed to take a walk with my husband after breakfast this morning, as a matter of fact," I told him. "But on the cliffs near here, I think, not Bulbarrow."

"Your husband? Lord Fortuneswell?" Odd Tom sat back on his heels; he seemed considerably jolted by this information. He stared at me, mumbling his jaw and frowning. "Thought you was supposed to be parted?"

"Oh no." I couldn't help being a bit nettled that our marital affairs were, apparently, such common currency. "But he's very busy and had things to do in Paris and London, and I had to be down here for the TV job—"

"Don't you go walking with him," said Odd Tom. Then, for some reason, his former incomprehensibility returned in full measure; he poured out a vehement stream of syllables and I could hardly catch one word in fifty. But the gist was clear: it would be a great piece of folly to undertake any excursion with Ty.

"But I have to, Tom; I said I would. You were married, weren't you? To—to Jenny. You know how important it is to keep a promise to the person—"

We looked at one another, sad and baffled.

"Crutches anyhow—mind you take your crutches along," he said.

"So he won't expect me to be too agile? I'd have taken them anyway; I wouldn't trust myself without them yet . . . though I do feel amazingly better, thanks to you."

Who can I tell about Odd Tom? I was thinking. There must be dozens of people in the acting profession who would pay lavishly for his services. He could make a modest fortune in a few months—

As he blew on his cup of coffee I suddenly remembered that I had invited Zoë for breakfast.

"Would it be a great nuisance, Tom, to take a message down to Miss Grandison's house?"

No skin off his nose, he assured me, so I scribbled a note: "Have to see Ty this morning, can you make it lunch instead of breakfast?"

Tom then insisted on escorting me up to the car park and left me seated on the low stone parapet that surrounded it. As he shuffled off down the hill again, he cast many anxious glances back at me, until he had disappeared round the bend. Queer, good little man. I'd make sure, somehow, that he didn't have to go on living in a barrel on Poole Harbour (if that was where, indeed, he lived). I wondered if he looked on Ty as a kind of Antichrist? An idea had been growing in my mind over the last few days, from stray remarks he had let drop, that Tom had lived here before, in the former times of the trailer park, that it was to the old Caundle Quay that he had made that return with Jenny, only to discover that their home had gone. If Tom understood that Ty had been the motive force behind that dispossession, what must his feelings be towards my husband? I thought of the corner from the orange paper packet, U R 2 DYE. By now I felt fairly sure that Tom had left it in my kitchen. (From which, in a day or so, it had vanished, in the way such things do.) Had it been meant, not for me, but for Ty? And what about the fire that nearly killed me? The passage of time had somewhat dulled my first paranoid suspicions about that, since there were no further episodes; I had fallen into the Ladies' belief that it must have been accident, arising from defective wiring and carefree Greek builders. But now I wondered, had the fire been intended for Ty?

All these suspicions went very much against my natural instincts. I liked Odd Tom; and not only because he was mending my ankle and wrist; he seemed genuinely honest, guileless and kindhearted; I did not want to believe him capable of such acts.

The sound of a motor broke my musings and I looked up to see Ty arrive with a screech of brakes. That brought to mind the first descent he had made on me from the helicopter. His expression as he sprang out (not from the conspicuous Rolls but from a sturdy mud-splashed estate wagon) was just about as unconciliating as on the former occasion. He came striding across the open spaces of the car park like an angry hero on his way to chop off a monster's head. Ty had a queer stride—leaning back, very characteristic; perhaps from all those hours of walking up and down the lawn with the LIAR placard on his back.

"Hello. Why don't you come down to the house and have a cup of coffee?" I suggested, and added mildly, "It's really a nice little house."

I had become attached to it, as you do when you escape death in a place. Arkwright and Tom, the two odd familiars, endeared it to me also. And the visits of little Shuna. Perhaps, I thought foolishly, I ought to settle down here and become the village witch. Glifonis would be a friendly place in which to end one's days.

Ty's expression, like the bow-wave of the QEII, cast such notions aside.

"No," he said. "Come on, get in the car, hurry up. I haven't much time. And I want—I want—to show you this thing."

"In that case, would you like to bring the car a bit closer?"

I wondered why he had left it so far away; at the top extremity of the car park. Then realised that there it would not be visible from the houses down below. But plainly he was going to make no superfluous gesture on my behalf. His eyes blazed with hostility. And he glanced sharply about him

—as he had on the Accademia bridge—peopling the empty space with eavesdroppers.

"Oh well," I sighed. "Never mind," resignedly, and made a great thing of crutching myself uphill to the estate wagon, amusing myself by putting Ty in the wrong. Rosy would have appreciated this performance, I thought.

Ignoring all that, Ty strode past me, flung open the car door, and took my crutches—grabbed them, rather. Still exaggerating my infirmity, I laboriously edged myself onto the front seat. He tossed the crutches in the back, making no inquiry as to my injuries. I had taken the precaution of rebandaging my foot, and had put a strapping on my wrist for support, so they looked much as they had before.

After shutting the door on me, Ty went round and got in on his own side. Then, suddenly, volcanically, he demanded,

"Why didn't you tell me that you had a son?"

I felt the jolt as, I'm told, you do when you've been shot: shock, not pain.

"I would have told you. By and by. I meant to, in due course. I wasn't keeping him from you. It—it just didn't seem relevant."

"Relevant? What *would* be relevant, for God's sake?"

"I'd have told you," I repeated. "I didn't have any plan to keep him dark. *You* were so engaged," I added with chill mildness, modelling myself as hard as I could on Rosy, "you were so busy telling me about your own past (though leaving out a few items yourself) that you didn't really give me a great deal of chance to tell you *my* story."

By way of answer he switched on the ignition and slammed the car into gear.

The jerk with which we started would have been agony for me only a couple days ago. I thought of Parkson, sadistically bumping me down from step to step. The wheelchair hadn't really proved much use in Glifonis, I decided, and then retracted that, remembering its signal utility as a battering ram.

"Where is your son now?" Ty asked in a dry voice.

"At Harvard. He's a philosopher. He's twenty. I suppose Olga Laszlo told you about him?" Ty did not answer. I added, "Anybody might have. It's no secret. After all, nearly everybody has a son at Harvard."

Ignoring these foolish words, he drove along the road that led inland, then soon turned eastwards along a small third-class lane with high banks.

During the ten minutes while Tom and I slowly climbed steep Glifonis hill, and while I waited in the car park, the day had been quietly deteriorating. A filmy, insidious veil had crept across the sun, and the temperature had dropped sharply; as Ty drove eastwards and ascended a ridge, all the landscape on either side simply slipped out of sight. We were engulfed in a cold floating mist which seemed insubstantial but completely screened off the view.

A pity, really. This must, in better weather, be an exhilarating little road, so high up that the prospect on either side ought to be spectacular. Soutwards, on our right, sloping pastures ran down, doubtless to the cliffs and a view of the Channel; north and left, a steeper-seeming fall of land, outlined by the scruffy shapes of gorse and whin bushes, dropped into a grassy valley, bounded on its northern side, a mile away, by yet another furzy ridge. All this land, I had learned from the big map on the Ladies' kitchen wall, was War Department territory, untrodden by foot of civilian man. Great Bustards throve on these ridges, and other species long extinct in areas frequented by H. Sap.

"Is it all right for us to be here?" I said. "Aren't we in a no-go area?"

"Oh, I'm allowed," Ty replied. "I drive this way all the time. I got permission from Major General Dickinson. It's much the quickest way from Glifonis to Knoyle."

"What do the red flags mean?"

"Just a warning to the public to keep off."

The road ran over a lip of land and veered northwards, dropping into the valley. Now we might truly have been in Shangri-la; nothing but vague dark brown lumps, which were bushes, could occasionally be seen at the road's edge, and the pearly mist floating around us in all directions.

Ty said, "Did you tell your son about *me?*" snapping off the words like icicles.

"I told him that I was getting married, yes. And who to. Of course he knew who you were."

"What was his reaction?"

"Pleased, naturally."

Had Fitz been pleased, though, I wondered. Not really. Anxious, solicitous. I added, "Relieved to have the responsibility taken off his hands."

"Responsibility?" What a dry, cold voice. It might have been Papa speaking. Don't interrupt, Catherine. This is none of your business.

Had life with Masha turned him into what he was?

Of course it must have. We all affect each other all the time. This needs to be thought about. But not just at this present juncture. I said,

"Well—now he's free to live his own life. Doesn't have to concern himself about me anymore. Tiresome old Mum."

With a catch in my throat I remembered that lighthearted plan: We'll get a Porsche and drive all over Europe. I went on, "He'll almost certainly stay in America. Philosophers do much better over there." And then, in order to strike the ball out of my court, "Have you heard anymore about the Companions of Roland? When the—when the ceremony takes place?"

He did not answer. He swerved his car off the road onto a flat grassy space among cobwebbed gorse bushes, and cut the engine. The silence was, suddenly, formidable. We could hear nothing at all but the gargling, rising voices of curlews; normally a sound that I love, but just now they seemed inexpressibly mournful.

After a minute, Ty said, "Can you imagine how I *felt?* When I found that you had been keeping such a thing from me?" He lit a cigarette, which surprised me greatly; I had never seen him smoke before. His hands shook badly.

I thought he was pressing the moral advantage for more than it was worth. His voice sounded less hurt than censorious.

"Oh, Ty. For heaven's *sake!*" Fighting hard—because, of course, I did feel guilty—I retorted, "What about all that *you* kept from *me?*"

"Like what? I didn't have any children hidden in the background."

"What about that girl?"

"What girl?"

"The old man's daughter. Old Leyburn." I had finally recalled his name. "Sir Ostin. The one you promised to look after. What happened to *her?*"

"Oh. She died. A long time ago." He added, rather pompously, "Naturally—if she hadn't—I'd still be supporting her."

In his voice I caught suddenly what must have been the tones of his mother—cold, prim, inflexible. I suppose, I thought forlornly, it was a terrible, terrible piece of folly to marry the son of such a hateful pair; I can see that now; but then, how was I to know? He hadn't told me about them *then.*

"Ty, I'm very sorry. I *ought to* have told you about Fitz. Well, of course I ought. I can see that now. But, in a way, he was so cut out of my life for so long—my mother looked after him right through his childhood, all I did was provide for his support; and now he is completely self-sufficient and independent; as I said before, it just didn't seem relevant to you and me, to us; we were," I said sadly, "we were having such fun."

Fun. The word lay between us like a candy wrapper. Ty looked as if he had never heard it in his life. Olga really is a prize mischief-making bitch, I thought, and wondered why, at this precise juncture, she had deemed it necessary to tell Ty my story. Just because he happened to be there? Because she happened to encounter him in Dorchester? Just idly for her own amusement?

"Does it really matter so much to you, Ty?"

"Suppose I wanted a son myself?" he said furiously.

The one doesn't preclude the other, it seemed to me.

"*Do* you want a son, Ty? I'd have thought—having had such unhappy relations with your own parents—that would be the last thing you'd—"

"But suppose I did!"

Good heavens, here we are, I thought amazedly, up against the old original barricade. You'd think it would have been totally demolished, eroded away, by now, but no: he really wanted me to have been a virgin. He really wanted to have been the First Man in my life, upper case and gothic ornamental capitals. Because I was Rosy, and Rosy must be a virgin? Because he had made me into Rosy? Or had made Rosy out of me?

Never once did he ask about Fitz's father. So might Joseph, I thought, have preserved a baneful silence; not out of tact, but from bitter, bitter pride.

"Ty, I'm really sorry. I never dreamed, in all honesty, that it would mean so much to you. In fact I never thought my former life would be of particular *interest* to you—"

"You must have an odd notion of what would interest me."

"Well," I said in a practical tone, "do you now believe that our marriage has been a total mistake? Do you want a divorce? Because the whole relationship has been a—a misapprehension? If that's what you want, feel free! It *was* a kind of fairy tale, I suppose . . ."

Everybody ought to have a drama-school training. Voice control is really essential for scenes like these.

To my surprise, Ty did not immediately respond to this suggestion. "Divorce? I hadn't thought—perhaps. Oh, I don't know. *I don't know!* It's just the feeling I can't trust you! That I'll never again be sure what's going on behind that front of yours—"

Enough of this, I thought. We aren't getting anywhere. And it's too painful. You landed me in the mess, Fair Rosamond, you get me out now. With chill, mild dignity, I suggested, "All this commination is a bit of a waste of time and energy, don't you think? You feel that you can't trust me. Well; there are—there are aspects of you which came as a considerable surprise to *me*"—he gave me a daggerlike glance and opened his mouth to speak, but I went right on— "so I can see it's no manner of use our trying to live together any longer, having got off on the wrong foot like this. Why don't we have a cooling-off period—like trade unions—say, a month or so—and then talk about it again?"

What I had in mind was his Companions of Roland nomination. If we could get him safely over that hurdle, still respectably married to me—then, I hoped, tensions might ease all round. If the Roland nomination was still on. Which of course I couldn't ask.

After a silence he said, "Very well." His voice was rough, oddly pitched.

Trying for a lighter note, I went on, "Where's this piece of conceptual art you spoke of? Or was that just a—a figment?"—and then wished I had not used that particular word, one that we had tossed back and forth, with various silly connotations, in Venice.

"No, no," he said, still in that rough, exasperated way— as if it were a hideously unfair imposition to be obliged even to carry on a civil dialogue with me. "No—I'll show you. It's along here—we have to drive a bit farther—"

He glanced at his watch, then flung the half-smoked cigarette out of the car window.

I said, "Are you pressed for time? Do you have to get back for a meeting, or something? Because, because frankly —just now—I can take conceptual art or leave it alone. Besides, in this mist, there won't be much point, I'd have—"

"The mist won't matter," he snapped. "Make it more impressive." And then he added, putting the car into gear, "After all, you did say that you had always wanted to see Carnac."

So I had. At the very first party, the one where Randolph had introduced Joel and me to Ty, when we had all been so lighthearted, the talk had turned to Carnac. "Oh, I really, really long to see that place," I had lisped, and Ty instantly replied, "Then why don't we go? I'll fly you over in the helicopter tomorrow," to which I, all Rosy at that point, had replied languidly, "Sweet of you, but I have to be back in London tomorrow. Another time, perhaps."

I always *have* wanted to see Carnac. Photographs make it seem so much more mysterious than Stonehenge; or, at least, it looks the way Stonehenge must have been before government got its death-dealing hands on the area.

Ty swept the car on along the little road, through denser and denser mist.

"Ty, really I don't think this is much use—"

"No, no," he said impatiently, "the mist is bound to clear, I tell you, it often does, very suddenly. *Just have a little patience,* will you? Can't you wait a few minutes, even?"

Again he pulled off the road, on to a furrowed, rutted piece of land which looked as if giant pigs had been rooting in it for truffles.

"You wait there a moment while I look about," he told me, and, jumping nimbly out of the car, vanished in the brume. I waited, peering through the silvery dimness and thinking unhappy thoughts. Shouldn't I also, at this point, have revealed to Ty that my expectation of life really didn't seem very long?

That the ache in my back was now gripping and wrenching like a red-hot vice? That the pain in my throat and jaw had grown so severe that I envisaged myself, in a year's time, like Freud, always having to turn my left profile to the camera . . . ? If only Ty were prepared to wait nine months or so, I thought; a widower is *so* much more respectable than a divorced man.

Ty had taken off with him, rather unexpectedly, a folding canvas chair which he extracted from the boot. He now returned without it and said, "Yes, this is the right place. Come along. I'll give you a hand."

With swift efficiency he helped me from the car and then, firmly gripping my arm, began to lead me through the mist, over the rough ground.

"Wait—wait!" I said, hopping. "My crutches!"

"Oh, come on, it's only a couple of yards. The crutches would be no use on this soft stuff anyway. Here, I'll carry you."

To my utter amazement he picked me up and strode forward at great speed. I had never thought Ty particularly strong. Tough, yes, stringy, agile—but now he seemed endowed with prodigious energy and vigour. I had gasped, the breath quite jerked out of me as he whisked me up, and gasped again when he dumped me with equal suddenness on the canvas chair, which he had established beside some large vague shape. A barn? A huge rock? Then its bouquet reached me—a sweet, comforting reminder from childhood—the warm pepperiness of rather musty hay. Or straw.

"Good heavens! What a rampart," I said faintly.

"Wait there a minute and you'll begin to see several

more. They are all set along here in a huge curve—like something the Druids might have laid out—"

Ty glanced again, jerkily, at his wrist, and gave a sharp, annoyed exclamation.

"Damn!"

"What's up?"

"My watch. It's gone—"

"Came undone, perhaps, when you picked me up. You had it on before, I'm certain. What a nuisance—"

"Or"—he frowned—"when I threw my cigarette out of the car window. I believe I remember feeling it loosen. No, don't move"—as I began to hoist myself out of the chair—"you stay there and wait for the mist to clear. I'll have a hunt. I'll be back soon—"

He began moving off in the direction of the car, scanning the rough ground as he went. "You stay there!" he called back again. In a moment he had become just a vague shape in the mist; then he was gone, out of sight. A moment later I heard the sound of the engine; it revved, grew louder, soon died away.

For a few moments I sat in a kind of dreamy limbo. The respite from Ty's company—so jagged, furious, discordant—was wonderfully refreshing. I snuffed up the wet, fresh, hay-scented, sea-scented air in deep draughts. How different, I thought, Ty was from Andrei. Two random memories came into my mind: Andrei weeping after we had been to see *Dr. Zhivago.* In the street, he wept unashamedly. *"All* I want," he said, "is for everyone in the world just to have enough to eat." He was simple, he was a Russian, this seemed to him a simple aim. And I remembered how he used to be able to hypnotise cats, he had a gift for this; he would sing them a little Russian air and they would lie on their backs, paws in air, totally relaxed . . . I have never seen this done by any other person.

By degrees—as one tends to when suddenly abandoned

in an unfamiliar spot—I began to feel very dislocated. Who am I? Where is this? Do I really exist? Is there such a person as Cat Conwil? And, if so, am I she?

A curlew bubbled his questioning call somewhere to my left; otherwise, the silence was profound.

Into my peaceful emptiness of mind, by pinpoint stages, worry began to creep.

First I thought: Will Ty ever be able to find this spot again? Next, I thought, does he actually *intend* to come back? Is this his notion of a joke? (Remembering that horseplay in Venice and the time he locked me in the bathroom and refused to let me out unless I promised . . . well, never mind that.)

The watch had certainly been missing from his wrist, but he could have taken it off himself the first time he left the car.

But what would be the point? To give me an opportunity to repent my malfeasances towards him?

Instead of those, for some reason I had a piercing memory of how I once took a fancy to apply for a landscape-gardening job. I phoned Masha (who was by now living in the dismal little house outside Reading) and asked her for some plans of imaginary gardens that I had once drawn for her. "Do you still have them, Masha?" I asked with that confidence we have in our parents' being able to produce anything at a moment's notice. "Well," she said in a troubled way, "I'm not quite sure. They may be in a drawer, or a parcel . . . Things got packed up in the move—and put away—" "I'd be very grateful if you could find them," I said. "They'd be really useful. I'll come out tomorrow—shall I?—maybe you will have come across them by then."

When I drove out next day to the little house in Grosvenor Crescent I noticed that she was looking very unwell—face all drawn, a terrible colour, hair lank and lifeless. "Masha, what *is* it? Are you ill?" "Oh, I just had one of my little turns, you know—acidosis, indigestion, what Papa used to call collywobbles. It's nothing." Which, I later deduced, meant spending most of the night in the bathroom with wrenching pains and diarrhoea. "But I found your drawings!" she announced with triumph. "I had been so worried that I might have lost them in the move." And she handed me the yellowed little bunch of papers held by a rusty paper clip.

I was *smitten* with guilt, I can tell you. My careless, unthinking demand had put her to all this trouble and, I was sure, brought on the attack of gripes. If I hadn't carelessly mislaid my own drawings, I need never have troubled her . . .

I never did apply for that garden job.

Now my thoughts reverted to Ty. Did he think that if I were left out here long enough, I'd die of exposure? Like the Babes in the Wood? Or get lost and fall over the cliff? That seemed too preposterous. Just the same—supposing this were the Arctic—I could imagine him *capable* of such an act. He had a calm ruthlessness of purpose. I had seen him elbow his way to the front of queues; he was always the first passenger onto planes or trains. I had seen him narrowly miss a woman with a stroller and hand-led child on a pedestrian crossing, and had been distressed because he seemed to show no sign of compunction or guilt afterwards. I had seen him, at a party, when presented with a book that he had no intention of reading, slide it swiftly out of sight between the cushions of a sofa, the very instant the donor had moved away; he knew, to a nicety, what he meant to do and what he had no intention of doing.

What had he intended when he left me here?

I am given to sudden acute attacks of disquiet about my mind. Suppose, one day, it stops behaving rationally? Even now I suffer from terrifying blanks when its processes, for no apparent reason, go on strike, fail to produce the word I want, the instruction for what I am supposed to do next. I walk into a room and stand there clueless . . .

Perhaps this will be the moment when it chooses to go on permanent vacation? Perhaps they will find me here, weeks hence, witless, wandering on Egdon Heath like Mad Maggie?

I called, "Ty?" hopefully into the void. "Ty? Are you there?" knowing full well with my saner sector that he couldn't be within earshot, for I had heard no sound of the returning motor. Just the same, the sound of my own voice cheered me, and I called again, "Ty? Halloo-oo?"

To my surprise and great joy, a voice did answer: "Yoo-hoo! Halloo!"

I let out a couple more enthusiastic shouts and presently a figure became dimly discernible, wavering through the silvery fog. Not Ty: much shorter, and a completely different, more undulating, motion. When it came closer I saw to my astonishment that it was Zoë Grandison, sensibly dressed for walking, in cords and shaggy sweater with her cloud of hair tucked inside a woolly cap.

"So this is where you've got to!" she said. "Where's the big chief?"

"Zoë! How in the world did you get here?"

"Oh," she said, "I've been to this place before. Did he bring you in his car? It's not half so far as you'd think, coming by road; there's a footpath that cuts the distance by at least three miles. But just the same I think you had better get moving. Where is he?"

"He lost his watch and went off to look for it."

"Humph," said Zoë. "Cutting it a bit fine, wasn't he?"

"Cutting it fine? How do you mean?"

"Target practice, my honey. Come along—let's get the hell out of here. Where are your crutches?"

"Oh damn. They're still in the car."

Zoë had a stout ash-stick. She passed it to me. "I carry it

because of dogs," she explained. "So many people nowadays have them in the country. And nasty brutes! But if they see a stick they treat you with respect." Eschewing further comment she took my arm and obliged me to move, irregularly but at fair speed, over the rough pitted ground. There's a Scottish word, *hirpling,* that describes our progress well. Soon we came to a path, narrow as a rabbit track but plainly used by *somebody,* which made, with a purposeful directness, up a steepish bit of slope, diagonally in the direction of the sea. We saw two more of the huge straw castles, which were constructed, I saw when we passed beside one of them, from those immense circular bundles like giant Swiss rolls that farmers leave lying about in stubble fields.

"Top of the ridge," said Zoë cheerfully when we had left the stack behind us. "How are you holding out, love?"

"Okay." I didn't enlarge on that.

The walk was definitely more than my ankle, even after Odd Tom's ministration, was ready for; I had no energy to spare for comment or question. Knowing Zoë to be a deeply practical person (her general appearance of a walking sex symbol was quite delusive), I had straightway grasped the fact that there was need for speed. Her expression was calm, but the grip on my arm spoke volumes. So I hurried, as best I could, and kept questions for later.

Now the track widened but, from my viewpoint, became much more difficult. Descending the cliff on a steep slant, it degenerated into a sandy, tussocky slither, shaley underfoot, and such handholds as there were, limited to furze and low-growing brambles.

"Would it be easier for you to sit down and slide?" asked Zoë.

"No it wouldn't," I croaked, sweating, though the day was cold.

She went ahead, walking sideways and supporting me by a firm grip on my forearm.

"Do take care! If you go over backwards—"

"I'm just fine," she said. "I've been along this path several times. And I do a lot of yoga."

She did walk with a beautiful elastic smoothness and balance.

When we reached the foot of the cliff she said, "Okay to sit down along there, I should think," and I dropped, with infinite relief, onto a pile of the dry seaweed and dirty sand which always accumulates at the tops of beaches. Ten yards away from us the sea—high tide—scrunched and scuffled on sand that had already been washed clean.

"Just turned," said Zoë. "Luckily for us. It won't come any higher. But that means that Dos and Stav won't be able to get along this way with the beach buggy for half an hour."

"But why—?"

"Listen!" she said. And then I heard what she meant: a resounding crump up above us, behind the height of the cliff. The gulls shrieked affrontedly and rose in a swarm, circling over our heads. Below us the ground vibrated, and a few fragments of earth and rock fell on the shore a hundred yards away. Two minutes later there came another crump, and then another; twenty or so altogether at regular intervals.

"Tuesday, ten-thirty," said Zoë, looking at her watch. "Long-range firing practice. Every week."

I remembered Ty looking at his watch; before, in the car. Before he had lost it.

"What ammunition do they use?" I asked, feeling a little queasy.

"Oh, nothing very lethal! It's what they call 'anti-personnel mines,' " she said. "They are made of compressed peat. It's queer—isn't it—that if you call human beings personnel, it becomes perfectly all right to shoot at them with slabs of compressed peat."

"What would the compressed peat do to you?"

"Well I don't imagine it would do you any *good*. It's fired from quite a long way off, remember."

"So those straw things are really targets?"

"That's the idea," said Zoë. "Of course they weren't expecting *you* to be sitting in among them."

We both stayed silent for a while after that. The sea murmured to itself, gradually withdrawing; the waves folded and unfolded their lace-white ruffles on the grey sand. Like Masha's tatting.

"Why would Ty want to kill you?" Zoë finally said. "Is he mad?"

"I suppose he must be." I thought of Jas and Jim. Which of them had planned this, Jas or Jim?

"It seems so pointless."

"The thing is, I didn't turn out as he planned."

"You don't *kill* someone for that."

But Ty apparently did.

"What gave you—how did you happen to come looking for me?"

"Odd Tom brought down your note. And he seemed in a tremendous worry about you. Sophie was there too, but neither of us could properly understand what he was saying. Only he kept waving his arms and pointing along the cliff—"

"It was extremely kind of you," I said, "to come looking for me. You took a big risk yourself."

"I knew the timing," she said. "And the scene. I'd been along here before."

Another silence settled around us. I felt abysmally embarrassed; quite as drowned in guilt and shame as if I'd been caught stealing some old lady's life savings. The way people feel, possibly, upon release from kidnapping or hijacking. After a while I managed to mutter, "If you could possibly keep this between ourselves? Not mention it to anybody?"

"But suppose he tries again?" Now she did sound disapproving. "You can't just sit there and *let* him!"

Why not? I thought. What a simplification for both of us. But, of course, Zoë was right. I didn't want Ty to become a murderer. It would be so bad for his image. And though in plenty of ways and for many reasons I'd be glad to have my troubled existence put period to, I do hate being taken by surprise; I'd find it too nerve-wracking, waiting for Ty to make his next pounce; like that awful game we used to play at school, Grandmother's Footsteps, where you try to creep up behind somebody, and they suddenly whip round and grab you. I didn't fancy the role of either creeper or grabber.

"No, I can't let him," I agreed sadly. "But now I'm aware of his intentions, don't you see, I can tell him that I know, and that will stop him, won't it. If he knows I know, and that other people may know—"

"Stop!" said Zoë. "It sounds like those awful books by Henry James. I never could make head or tail of them. But, I suppose, if you let Ty know that if something bad happens to you, I shall go screaming murder to the police—"

"Oh, I won't bring you into it," I said quickly. "I'll just say 'someone else—' "

"Ah, look." Her voice held considerable relief. "Here come the chaps. I gave Odd Tom a note for them. They're very good—I knew they wouldn't be long." The relief, I thought, was due not only to our rescue but to the termination of this awkward dialogue. Zoë stood up and waved to the Greeks.

It was not really a beach buggy they drove, but a kind of bulldozer.

"Zoë!" I got to my feet and gave her a hug, embarrassed but warm. "I'll never forget what you did. It was—"

"Oh, pooh. Forget it." But she laughed; the awkward moment eased. The two cheerful Greeks brought their cumbrous vehicle to a halt and lifted me aboard.

In ten minutes we had rumbled back along the beach to Glifonis Harbour.

10

PAT Limbourne came quickly into the kitchen of Number 2, where Shuna was inventing an algebra jigsaw puzzle. Odd Tom had cut the pieces for her, and she was making up values for them.

"Do you know where Aunt Elspeth is?"

Shuna looked up with wide eyes at Pat's tone; but her own life was so packed with occupation that she seldom pried into the affairs of adults; she said, "Out in the garden. On the top terrace," and returned to her calculations.

Pat strode up the rock steps and found Elspeth upended among a patch of infant vines. She said abruptly, "Olga's dead."

"*No!*" Shocked, Elspeth sat back on her heels and, with an earthy hand, pushed the cloud of white hair from her eyes. "*How?*"

"Some of the Greeks found her. Down on the shore. There'd been a landfall—you know how treacherous those cliffs are—she was found underneath a lot of clay and shale. Dmitri saw her foot sticking out."

"Oh, my Lord," Elspeth muttered. After a moment she

added, "There was no sign of any other person? She was by herself?"

"Apparently so. Looking for fossils, the Greeks assumed."

"She did say something about fossils—I heard her," Elspeth remembered. "Oh dear—how dreadful. Poor silly Olga. *Not* a good advertisement for Glifonis."

"Fortuneswell certainly won't be pleased," Pat commented drily. "Lucky it was his office who recommended her."

Elspeth's brow puckered. She said, "It's queer, though— When was her body found?"

"Half an hour ago. But it must have been there all night. There'd been a couple of tides."

"She wouldn't have gone hunting for fossils in the dark."

"Hardly," agreed Pat in a neutral voice.

"So when could she have gone?"

"Well, I suppose the coroner will work it out. There'll have to be an inquest, obviously."

"Oh, *dear*— Well, I've told Shuna dozens of times to stay away from those cliffs," Elspeth said distressedly. "So this will be an object lesson. Do you think the child will be very upset?"

"Can't say. Olga was all over *her*—but I don't really think it was reciprocal."

"No, she likes Cat Conwil better," Elspeth agreed. "But Olga had known her mother—"

"Let's not get sentimental. Shuna isn't even aware of that."

"No, I suppose you are right. Oh my goodness, what a horrible thing to happen here. *Bother* Olga. That girl always was a troublemaker— I suppose I had better go down and clear out her house," she added. "If I know her, it's probably in a horrible state—"

Pat looked doubtful. "Wouldn't it be better to wait till the authorities arrive? You aren't supposed to meddle with dead people's effects."

But Elspeth was determinedly collecting her gardening tools into a wooden trug.

"Who's dead?"

Shuna had wandered into the garden carrying a sonar measuring tool. "I'm going down to help Father Athanasios measure out his graveyard," she said. "Who's dead?"

"Olga Laszlo is, I'm afraid," said Pat. "The Greeks found her body under a fall of rock at the foot of the cliff."

"She must have been digging for fossils."

"Well, we warned *you* not to. Now you see why," Pat said flatly.

"Yes. Anyway Father Athanasios will be pleased. Now he'll have somebody to put in his graveyard." Impressed by this possibility, Shuna wandered indoors again.

After putting away her garden tools among the ski's and crossbows in the shed, Elspeth followed, and found Shuna carefully marking an enclosure "Cemetary" on the map of Fridayland.

"Do you want to come down the hill with me? I'm going to tidy Olga's house and you can go on to the church."

"All right."

As they walked down the causeway, Shuna inquired, "What happens to people's brains when they die?"

"Their souls go to heaven," said Elspeth firmly. "And the physical part of the brain dries up and turns to dust. And all the things they have invented or written live after them—like Shakespeare's plays and Einstein's theories."

"I'm going to invent a new mathematical theory that will live after *me,*" said Shuna. After a moment she added, "What will it be called?"

Elspeth, whose mind was preoccupied with many problems, suggested, "How about the Fridayland Theory?"

"No!" Shuna's voice was disgusted. "That's silly! Friday-land is just a game!"

"So it is. Well; let's wait till you've completed your theory before you give it a name."

"All right." Mollified, Shuna inquired, "So, has Olga's soul gone to heaven?"

"I really couldn't say," Elspeth replied rather grimly, turning in at Olga's front door.

11

A couple of Greeks, Dionisios and George, carried me up from the beach as far as the Ladies' house. There I asked them to put me down, as I wished to use the telephone. They did so, promising to return and carry me the rest of the way whenever I sent for them. Then they hurried back down the hill. There had been some kind of commotion taking place by the harbour, at the other end of the beach, and they wanted to be in on it. The Greeks usually had some kind of commotion going.

I hobbled indoors, finding the front door wide open and the house empty. This must mean that the Ladies were not far away, but provided, I thought, an excellent opportunity for me to phone Ty. Tactful and considerate though they were about retiring to the front room while one held a conversation, their presence so close at hand gave rise to some constraint always; and what I had to say this time was definitely not for the public ear.

It took me a while to find the local telephone book, buried under a mass of seed catalogues, old newspapers, plastic

carrier bags and hanks of garden bast. With regrettably un-
steady hands I finally dialled the number of the Close Hotel.

"Close Hotel, good afternoon?"

"Can I speak to Lord Fortuneswell?"

"Who?" said the bored young voice and continued a conversation: "Well, I said, if he can't come *then,* why can't he
come later? And do you know what she had the nerve to say?
—*Who*'d you say you wanted?"

"Lord Fortuneswell."

"Fordsall? Haven't *got* anyone of that name."

"Fortuneswell."

"What?"

I spelt it out. *"F* for Freddy, *O* for orange—"

"Oh, Fortuneswell. Room 12, hold on . . ."

A long, long pause, with clicks and rattles. I waited, my
hands sweating so badly they could hardly grip the receiver.
The pain in my back was dire. I wondered if I would be able
to speak at all. Sometimes my throat dries up entirely and I
can only open and shut my mouth like a goldfish. (Mercifully,
it has never done that on stage.)

At last I heard a ringing, then a click. Then a voice, familiar but calm and remote: "This is James Tybold, Lord Fortuneswell. I am out at present. If you care to leave a message,
wait for the tone . . ."

I felt both deep disappointment and profound relief.
There need be no confrontation, thank heaven. I could just
leave my message and withdraw. And yet, and yet, in a way I
was sorry not to be able to tell him face to face—ear to ear—

"James?" I said. "Listen, this is Cat speaking. I didn't—I
didn't wait to study your conceptual art." (Choosing my
words with some care because, after all, anybody may play
over a taped message.) "I'm back in Glifonis now, at Miss
Morgan's house. Listen, James: *Don't bother about me!* I think I
know what's in your mind, but—honestly—it isn't worthwhile. You see, all you need to do is *wait.* I'm, I'm not well,

not at all well. Can you understand what I'm trying to tell you? The wrong thing, the really wrong, dishonest thing I did in marrying you, the crucially important fact that I did keep from you, was that I'm ill, not at all in good health. In fact I suffer from so many terminal illnesses that you could use me for a medical textbook. I know I shouldn't have kept this from you—but, well, that's it. So—so you see, it's just not worth your while taking any *action*—like, like divorce, for instance—it would just be a lot of needless scandal and publicity. *You* don't want that—do you? And I—I don't want you doing something that you'd have a lot of cause to regret . . . Okay? Do you understand me, Ty? I'm not going to be around long enough to make what you planned worth doing. Love, Cathy," I ended, and replaced the receiver with wet, shaking hands.

Only then did I realise that Miss Morgan had pottered in from the next room and was stuffing a bundle of laundry into the capacious washing machine.

"Poor, poor thing," she was muttering, half to herself, half to me, "Still, there's no sense leaving dirty washing down there in the house—is there?" Her pleasant wrinkled face was all drawn sideways with bother and worry. She had not, I thought, in huge relief, paid the slightest attention to what I had been saying.

"Hello, Miss Morgan, I'm sorry, I just walked in and used your telephone—"

"That's perfectly all right, my dear, that's what it's intended for. Oh, by the way, there was a message for you earlier—somebody phoned and we went and looked for you, but you weren't at home, so he said he'd ring back later."

"Who was it? Not—not my husband?"

"No, no," said Miss Morgan. "I'd know *his* voice. This was a man, but he didn't leave his name."

"Joel, perhaps. Or Ralph."

The child Shuna came in carrying a black plastic gadget that looked like a massive, complicated torch.

"Father Athanasios has gone into the church to say a lot of prayers for Olga," she reported. "Honestly, I don't quite understand him. Because he says that Olga's talking to God *now,* so, if she is, why does he need to say prayers for her?" She turned to me. "Do *you* think Olga's talking to God?"

I stared at her in petrifaction.

"You hadn't heard?" said Miss Morgan.

"No—?"

"Olga got killed," Shuna told me.

"Killed?" I could only just squeeze the word from my dry throat.

"The cliff fell on her. She must have been down at the bottom, looking for fossils."

"How awful," I said slowly. "How *awful.*"

It couldn't be a coincidence; could it? Two of us in one day—if Odd Tom hadn't warned Zoë—if Zoë hadn't come and dragged me away—

"So, do you think Olga's talking to God now?" persisted Shuna.

I thought of Papa. Don't interrupt, Catherine, I am talking to the Lord.

"Frankly, no," I said sadly.

"If she is, God's listening to a lot of malicious tittle-tattle," muttered Miss Morgan. "Now, Shuna, it's time for your piano practice. Go upstairs, and let me hear plenty of scales and exercises before you start the Italian Concerto. A *lot* of scales."

"All right," said Shuna equably, and pattered off up the stairs. A rattle of capably played exercises followed.

Miss Morgan said to me, "I'm so sorry. I didn't realise you hadn't heard about Olga."

"That's all right," I answered mechanically. "It was just

such a shock—I—I'd been out on the cliffs, I suppose at the time when they found her, taking a walk with my husband."

Miss Morgan stared at me. She said, "I don't think *that* was very wise."

"No. It wasn't. But it turned out all right." Or it will be all right, I thought, when he gets my message. Absently picking a paper clip out of the fruit bowl and putting it in my pocket, I asked her, "Could you be terribly kind, Miss Morgan, and just give me a hand back to my house? To tell the truth, I feel a bit bushed."

"Of course, my dear."

She escorted me back home. The front door was unlocked. "That's odd," I said. "I could have sworn I locked it."

Miss Morgan was mildly concerned. "Better check around. Does anything seem to be missing? Though everybody is perfectly honest in the village," she added. "We leave ours open all the time, as you know."

Nothing was missing, so far as I could see. Most of my belongings were still packed in suitcases. Some papers, I thought, might have been taken out of a folder, my extra lines for *Rosy and Dodo.* "Why would anyone be interested in them? Nobody would keep money in a folder?" But I was in such a disorganised state that I wasn't certain I'd left them in it. I am not orderly. And Odd Tom had turned up just before I left the house, so I hadn't tidied it— What a long time ago that seemed. A notebook, perhaps, might be missing?

"What was in it?" asked Miss Morgan. "Lists of things you mean to do? Diary?"

"Good heavens, no. I don't respect my life enough to keep lists in a *notebook.* On the backs of envelopes . . . What was in it? Ideas for plays, I think. But it may not even have been here. I'm in a terrible muddle."

She looked dissatisfied. "It's not a good idea for you to be on your own in this house," she muttered. "Perhaps you should come to us again—"

"But—good heavens—I'm much, much better than I was. Tom gave me another going-over this morning—he's a marvellous little man—"

"Yes. He is." But at the mention of his name she looked, if anything, more bothered. "Well. Give us a shout if you need anything. Or wave a scarf on your terrace—we can see it from our back window. It's just across the road really. Have you plenty of food?"

"Yes, the freezer's packed, thanks to Miss Limbourne."

"Pat," she said absently. "Do call us Pat and Elspeth. I know! The dog whistle!"

"Dog whistle?"

"The sound carries for miles— We used to have a Jack Russell with a very wandering disposition," she added obscurely. "I'll send Shuna with it. Good-bye. Do lock up."

And went off at a brisk pace.

I sat brooding about Ty. Abandoning me on the artillery range, I now realised, was only the last of a series: Almost certainly it could be assumed that his had been the intention behind the fire in the house; Parkson could have arranged that, or possibly Ty himself (at this point I remembered something Odd Tom had said about seeing my husband which, at the time, I had written off as fantasy); and then, in Venice, my fall—had that been accidental or contrived? Ty had grabbed me, but had he in the first place twitched me off balance, right by the Grand Canal? Then . . . I went on slowly remembering . . . back at the hotel he gave me a whole saucerful of pills—which I straightway flushed down the john; what would have become of me if I had swallowed those?

In five minutes Shuna ran up, carrying a large brass article with a ring at one end.

"You twist here—" she demonstrated. "That makes the

sound louder. This way it makes it so that only dogs can hear; but that's not what you want, is it?"

"I certainly don't want all the dogs in Glifonis to come running."

"I don't think there are any," she said seriously. "The lord won't have that here. And I doubt if Arkwright would come . . . Do you think there are sounds that we can hear and dogs can't?"

"Very likely. And there may be sounds that *you* can hear and I can't."

She thought about that. "The voice of God, you mean?"

"Certainly; if you can hear that, it's more than I can."

"Well," she explained, frowning, "Aunt Elspeth says that when I get a mathematical idea, it's a message from the Holy Ghost. Because, otherwise, where do they come from?"

"I know exactly what she means."

"Like 'Kubla Khan.' "

"That came from opium," I suggested.

"Not only from opium. After all, lots of people take opium and they don't write 'Kubla Khan.' Sometimes—do you know?—it's as if you were pulling on the end of a piece of string, or cottonwool, and if only you could pull *hard* enough, the whole reel would unwind, and then you'd know everything!"

She gave me look of triumph.

"Well," I said, "I hope you'll be able to give a really powerful pull of that kind by and by."

"Oh, I think I shall. Now I'd better get back to my piano practice."

Off she ran, and I thought, the Ladies are doing a good job on little Shuna.

THE day crept on. Through the mist, which thickened perceptibly in the afternoon, I observed a great deal of unusual come and go. Cars pulled into the parking area above my house, dark figures of men in uniform tramped down the stepped causeway. Some of them presently returned at a slow pace, carrying what I presumed was a stretcher; but the scene was wavering and vague, like a procession of ghosts, I thought, glimpsed through a steamed-up window . . . I supposed I ought to feel some pity for Olga, but all I did feel was a kind of horror. I could imagine her sallow, haggard face staring upwards as the slab of muddy cliff-face toppled outwards above her—her attempt, too late, to run; but was that *really* what had happened?

About teatime a Police-Sergeant Bridger knocked at my door and came in to ask when was the last time I had seen Miss Laszlo? Last night at Miss Pitt's party, I told him, and he nodded; evidently this was what everybody had said.

"You had known the lady for some time, I understand?"

"Oh yes, for nine or ten years. Though we weren't close friends."

He nodded and wrote.

"Would you say she was a keen fossil collector?"

"To be honest, I never knew before that she was interested in them. But she did say something about fossils at the party last night—and she had dozens of interests, she was always starting off in new directions—"

He nodded and wrote. "I understand she had lunch with your husband yesterday?"

"So I've been told. They were old friends too."

"Do you own a shotgun, Lady Fortuneswell?"

"A *shotgun?*" I stared at him, startled to death. "Good heavens, no! But—but Olga wasn't shot, was she? I thought she was killed by a landslide?"

"I couldn't tell you that," he replied, shutting his notebook and snapping the elastic band round it. "We'll have to wait for the coroner's report," and he went out, closing the door carefully behind him, and leaving me filled to the brim with worry. I lay on my bed and tried to rest, got up, sat shivering, and presently brewed myself a cup of instant coffee with brandy in it.

If I were in a thriller, I thought, at this juncture I would be in a frantic state of mind. Ty has had several goes at killing me. Until I know he has received my message, I have every reason to suppose that he will try again. Perhaps, even after he gets the message, he'll go on trying? As long as I am alive, I represent a threat to him. But why? I promised not to tell about the scene with the old man. So—either Ty doesn't trust me, or that isn't his only reason for wanting to get rid of me.

I suppose he's incapable of trusting me, really. Or anybody else. Not being a signal example of trustworthiness himself, how could he believe in anybody's else's promise?

I suppose I have to bear that in mind.

What other reason might he have for wanting to dispose of me?

I went on reflecting intently and sadly about Ty. Our lovemaking had been a kind of peak, I supposed. From that point there would be nowhere to go but down. Ty could never put up with that; only the best was good enough for him. A descent from perfection would count as failure, and failure was intolerable. So any reminder of failure must be tidied away out of existence.

A certain indignation began to grow inside me.

On the whole, I am ready to take what comes. I inherit that from Masha. " 'That thee is sent, receive in buxomnesse,' " she read me once from a poem by Chaucer, and at the time I found it puzzling. *Buxomnesse?* What did Chaucer mean? But the word, with its cheerful acceptance, gradually began to make sense. It absolutely defined Masha, and her way of deriving nourishment and joy from the most unpromising circumstances.

Chaucer wasn't preaching morality, so much as pointing out that you may as well make the very best of what you are sent, because, sure as hell, *you aren't going to be sent anything else.* One life is the ration. Nobody gets two Wednesdays.

Now that whole verse rouses me like a trumpet.

So back to Ty. I didn't plan to sit and wait for him to despatch me. I wanted to make the best of my life so far as it went.

Ty had no right to deprive me of it, even if I was due to die next year of leukaemia, gangrene, and toxic waste. In fact, I thought crossly, it would be a lesson to him if I struggled on for another forty years in his despite.

How to stop him killing me? One of those elaborate chains of precaution, write a letter to my lawyer (except that I didn't have a lawyer) informing him that in the event of my death, etc., etc. Then write another letter to Ty, telling him what I had done?

All this would take time.

Another knock at the door made me start, but it was only Sophie Pitt, carrying a large envelope.

"Hi, dearie. The postman left this with me earlier; said you were out when he called. Taking your walk with Zoë, I suppose. Wasn't that a bit premature?"

She glanced at my ankle.

"Yes it was, but I came off lucky."

Sophie nodded vaguely. "The whole place is upheaved because of this wretched business of Olga Laszlo," she went on, and I blessed Zoë for her discretion. "Stupid fool of a woman, it's just the sort of thing that would happen to her."

Poor Olga, that will be her general epitaph, I thought, and said, "I'm having Ness with brandy, would you like some?"

Sophie accepted the coffee but wistfully declined the brandy. "The Pools are in a terrible state too," she remarked, "because your husband has given them notice."

"What?"

She looked at me rather severely.

"You didn't know?"

I shook my head. "He doesn't speak to me about professional affairs. And—and since we got back from Venice I've only seen him once—"

"Well," said Sophie, "I suppose, in a way, you can't blame him. Everyone knows that Fortuneswell has a complete down on any kind of drug abuse, and there was that boy, *visibly* on something—your husband had made it perfectly plain he wouldn't have anything of the kind going on here. So, it seems, he's given them a day to clear out—"

"A day! That's pretty drastic."

"Your husband appears to be a fairly drastic man, my dear. He was down below just now giving Pat and Elspeth the rough side of his tongue for having let the Pools come here." She drained her coffee and rose.

"Ty was *here?*" I said stupidly. "You mean today? Just now?" One of those figures that I had seen passing in the mist?

"At your friends' house," she said, nodding.

I found it almost impossible to believe her, but she went on, "I'd planned to phone my sister on the way up here. However, when I put my head round the door I saw that it wouldn't be a tactful moment, so I came on up to you. I'll get Dot tonight, she'll be at work by now." And Sophie left, with her majestic gait, drifting away through the mist like a ship in full sail.

If I had been worried after the departure of P. S. Bridger, I was a thousand times more worried now. Ty was *here,* at this moment, in the village? Had he ever been back to the Close Hotel? Or had he phoned it and received my message? Almost certainly not. Had he discovered that I was still alive? Had the Ladies told him that piece of news? What would he do next?

I felt as if a hand grenade had been tossed down somewhere quite close to me, and I was not certain, either where it lay, or if the pin had been removed.

Unthinking, I stared down at the envelope that Sophie had delivered. It was large, brown, dirty, crumpled; had been used before, refastened with plastic tape, and a new label stuck crookedly over the previous address. A printed logo, "Tagus," in the top left-hand corner, had been crossed out in ink, and "Cat Conwil, No. 1, Glifonis, Dorset," was written on the label in a slapdash, messy, vaguely familiar handwriting.

I opened the envelope with the usual difficulty, dragging away the various wrinkled layers of plastic tape, and found inside a worn stained bunch of old newspaper clippings held together by a safety-pin and accompanied by a grubby post-card.

"Dear Catherine: Since you do not appear to have been told the Lilias story I am passing these on to you. Then your dear husband can't have any more reason to try and put pressure on me, can he? Olga." Signed with a grandiloquent flourish.

The cuttings were yellow with age. I had time to read the first headline: HANDS HORROR; and the second: MUTI-LATED HEIRESS BLEEDS TO DEATH—then looked up to see Ty standing outside the back door.

Peremptorily, Ty rapped on the glass door, then rattled the handle. The door was locked. I had the key in my pocket.

My mouth went dry as the Sahara. The pain in my back was like a volcano just about to erupt. A fierce pang of tooth-ache shot through my jaw. Foolishly, like a nodding toy, I wagged my head at Ty. His face was formidable, his blue eyes blazed. Again he banged on the door and rattled it. Then, as I still remained seated at the kitchen counter, petri-fied, with mad thoughts running through my head—Blow the whistle? Run out of the front door? Lock myself in the bathroom?—Ty briskly pulled a key from his own pocket and began to insert it in the outer keyhole.

Still I remained in a state of suspension. I remembered a Kipling story about Kaa the python hypnotising a whole row of monkeys before he proceeds to swallow them. I felt just like those monkeys while I waited for the scratching click of Ty's key turning in the lock.

But it never came. To my total astonishment, Ty began slowly to stoop, as if he intended to take a closer look, through the glass, at the faded sections of newsprint spread out along the counter. Then he slowly crumpled, his knees bent, his head came forward and rested against the glass of the door. After a moment he slumped forward entirely, coming to rest in a fetal position, with his knees under him and his head sunk between his shoulders. The whole process had been so silent, so strange, that I thought, Is he doing this simply to terrify me? Or has he suffered some kind of fit? Or is it a mad act of penance? Though that seemed the most unlikely of the three possibilities.

Then I saw the prong sticking out of his back, between his shoulders.

After a long, frozen time I did hobble to the front door, throw it open, and blow the whistle as hard as I could.

12

"*WELL!*"

The two friends stared at each other across the door which had just slammed behind their visitor, and Miss Morgan drew a hand shakily across her brow.

"My dear, what a disagreeable scene. I am too old for such rodomontades. They affect my heart in a most unpleasant way." She had indeed gone very pale. "I always had some reservations about that man, as you know—"

"He's taken leave of his wits, if you ask *me*," said Pat gruffly. She was the more profoundly disturbed of the two. Fortuneswell had, after all, been her friend in the first place. "The man must obviously have had some kind of brainstorm. Carrying on in such a way—all that rubbish about *conspiracy* and betrayal of trust—"

"Very unpleasant," repeated Miss Morgan, nodding. "Unbalanced, I'd say."

"Just because we'd adopted old Ossie's granddaughter—and chose not to advertise the fact—I can't see what business it was—"

"Of his," agreed Elspeth. "To give us notice on such a flimsy pretext was perfectly outrageous—"

"Well, he did say it was because of the Pools as well. Whether he has any legal ground—"

"One would not wish to fight it in any legal *way,* however," said Miss Morgan distastefully. "Besides, to have the whole thing opened up would be disastrous for the child—"

Pat rubbed her forehead distressedly. "And then there's the question of his influence, now he knows who she is. *Most* undesirable—in his present state. That's what really bothers me. I can see his case against the Pools; now I've met them I'm sorry they came; Llewellyn's a decent chap, and he swore up and down that Alexander was clear, but *she—*"

"Is a little trollop. Well, no use fretting," said Elspeth, who had recovered her colour. "We'll just have to wait and see."

The piano practice ceased and steps pattered down the stairs.

Shuna came in. "I've finished! Can I go down to the harbour?"

"Yes, all right," said Elspeth after a moment's thought. "But put on your jacket. It's chilly."

"What was all that shouting about? He kept shouting Lilias, Lilias. Who's Lilias?"

"Nobody you know. And you aren't supposed to listen to other people's conversations. You were supposed to be practising."

"I was practising, but he shouted so loud I couldn't help hearing," said Shuna, pulling on her windbreaker. "I never stopped playing."

Elspeth stumped off into the garden, her face crumpled in perplexity.

"I don't like Lord Fortuneswell. He's worse than Black Marby," observed Shuna, tugging on a boot.

"Oh? Why, pray?" asked Pat after a slight pause.

"First he made a terrible mess of my battle arrangements and never even said that he was sorry. And now, do you know what he's done? Sacked Jannis and Dmitri without any notice. Just because they left a pile of rubble in the path so he couldn't get by. And they were supposed to have their tickets paid back to Greece, but he wouldn't, so the others are having to club together to help them. I think he's a bad man," pronounced Shuna, and she stamped on the other boot and walked towards the door.

"Don't stay down at the harbour too long," Pat called after her. "And do watch out for tractors—it's so foggy you can't expect them to watch out for you. And if you see Father Athanasios, invite him up for a grog."

"All right," said Shuna. "But the fog's not so thick now. Patches are quite clear."

The telephone rang. Pat picked up the receiver. "Glifonis? Yes, this is Miss Limbourne. No, I *don't* have any story for the Wessex *Chronicle*. No, it was an entirely accidental death. It was thought the lady may have been hunting for fossils—can't possibly tell you what time of day, no doubt the coroner—shotgun pellets? I've no idea what you are talking about. *Most* improbable . . . you'd have to ask the police that—No; I'm afraid not. No, that is quite out of the question. Ask the police. No, nothing more. *Good* day."

"Blasted newspapers have got on to the Olga story," she said crossly, a few minutes later, when Elspeth reappeared in the kitchen.

"It was bound to happen sooner or later." Elspeth washed earth from her hands, dried them vigorously, and said, "I think I'd better just go up and call on that little Cat. Don't like to think of her up in that house on her own while he's wandering about the village in this nasty unpredictable mood. I'll tell you what he reminds me of—one of those disgusting radioactive mixtures gone critical. So I'll just pop up and see if she needs anything. Perhaps stay with her for a bit."

"Good idea," Pat agreed. "It seems more than probable that Olga was making mischief between them."

"Whatever else *did* Olga do? Besides"—Elspeth twined a ravelled grey muffler round her neck—"Cat, silly girl, is a *shocking* hypochondriac. Did you know? It's not good for her to be alone for too long; she suffers from the most farfetched notions about the state of her health—"

"And how did you discover that?" But Pat's tone had a dry respect; she knew her friend's talent for spotting such foibles.

"Just put two and two together! Now don't forget the casserole. I'll be back in an hour or so.

But when Elspeth opened the door, they both heard the frantic shrilling of the dog whistle.

So, of course, the village filled with police again. But Elspeth reached me long before they came, hobbling up through the patchy mist, almost before I had taken breath for my second whistle blast.

"What is the matter, my dear? What has happened?"

"It's Ty," I stammered. "My husband. He's—he's dead!"

"Dead? My dear, are you sure? What happened? Was he taken ill? A stroke?"

"No—no—somebody *shot* him—there's a horrible thing sticking out of his back."

I had tried—stupidly—to pull it out. That had been my first impulse. But no way would it come. And it wouldn't have made any difference. Nobody could be deader than Ty was. So then I had knelt by him, gulping and sobbing useless tears of remorse, regret, and terror, until, after a while, it came to my head that Society would expect me to do something about the crumpled empty thing that had been menacing, furious, unpredictable Ty only half an hour before.

Elspeth took one look at me and said, "I'll make a cup of tea."

Which she did with great speed, putting in about two dessert spoonfuls of sugar. It was disgusting, but boiling hot, and it did stop my shivers, thereby giving me a chance to notice a new and terrifying pain, which began in the roof of my mouth on the right side and from there forked down into my right arm and my chest . . .

"Oughtn't we to call the police?" I asked, my teeth chattering against the rim of the cup.

"Pat will have done that already. I told her to do so as soon as I heard your whistle."

"But how did you *know?*"

"He'd been to see us—he was in a very peculiar mood— not rational, I thought—storming on about the Pool family (he's given them notice, you know, and us too)—and carrying on about poor Lilias Leyburn—it was plain he'd been breathing fire all over the village," Miss Morgan said placidly, "and I thought he might have driven some poor soul to violence."

"But why would someone *kill* him? In such a queer, awful way?"

Elspeth had been out to look at Ty's body, and returned with her lips pursed and brow puckered.

"Well," she said, frowning, pouring herself a cup of the tea she had made, "I do have a theory about that; the police will certainly think it's very farfetched and that I'm a fanciful, meddlesome old body." She gave a somewhat eldritch grin.

I went back to something she had said. "Lilias Leyburn? You mentioned her name. Who was she?"

"Oh, my dear. She was a poor girl—very, very brainy, but sadly unstable, I fear. She was at Larchmont—that was my little private school, you know, I was headmistress. Academically she did most brilliantly, but we *always* worried about her."

"Did—did—" a sudden piercing memory came into my mind. "Did she go on to Manchester University?"

"Yes, took a science degree. Pat had known her father, Ostin Leyburn, from way back—met him over some scheme he had for starting a factory at Weymouth—at first he couldn't get planning permission— Her mother had died, you see, poor child, when she was quite tiny, and I'm afraid her father *didn't* give her so much of his attention as he should have; he was so busy pursuing his career; a very successful man indeed—"

Was that why the old boy was so nice to me? I wondered. Because he had neglected his own daughter and felt guilty about her? How mixed our motives are. "One leg of mutton drives another down." Who said that? (And what a very peculiar expression it is).

Elspeth, frowning with disapproval, had swiftly tidied away all the newspaper cuttings, stuffed them back in the envelope and buried it deep in my underwear drawer. "Who sent you these? Olga? I might have known. There's no need for the police to see *them.* Olga had been a friend of poor Lilias, at one time."

"I was going to ask where she came into all this?"

"Well, I am very much afraid," said Miss Morgan, wearing a most headmistresslike expression, "that Olga, having found that your husband had been shortlisted for the Grand Knights of Whatever-it-was—she told us about that—and being aware of this sadly unhappy connection from his younger days—he had promised to marry the poor girl, I understand, but made not the least effort to keep in touch or look after her. And finally she died in that dreadful way—"

"Olga had been trying to blackmail him?"

"Well, yes, I fear so."

"What *happened* to Lilias Leyburn?"

I had not had time to do more than glance at the clippings before Ty appeared, and had not the least wish to look at them afterwards. I asked the question with an icy chill at the pit of my stomach.

"She vanished," Elspeth said slowly. "She had been on drugs at the university, and associated with a very wild set; then she just totally disappeared. It was thought at first that she must have died somewhere unidentified—they were a wealthy set—used to roam about Europe and the Near East. She always had plenty of money from her father. But when he died, it was found he had cut her out of his will. Assuming her to be dead, perhaps. The money was left in trust for scientific research and charitable purposes. The trust to be administered by your—by Lord Fortuneswell. Or James Tybold, as he was then."

"Yes."

"But then—after eight years or so—Lilias turned up again. Telling a most piteous and dreadful tale. It seemed that she had married a man—a citizen of some wild little Arab emirate—and he had taken her back to his own country. What she expected, goodness knows—the Garden of Eden perhaps—" Miss Morgan paused.

"Go on," I said, thinking of Papa and Shangri-la.

"What she found was a primitive mountain village, absolutely cut off, where for seven years she lived a completely menial existence—working in the fields, treated as a servant, without any rights, by her husband's elderly female relatives —of whom there were dozens—unable to leave—physically abused, beaten on her hands till some of her fingers were broken—"

Irrelevantly—no, *relevantly*—I remembered the grey velvet hands, with diamond watches on their velvet wrists.

"And she had worse experiences—still, no sense in going into all that," Elspeth said quickly. "But then, unbelievably, she escaped. A Swedish scientific film unit came by, the first

Europeans she had seen since she arrived, and she managed to hide herself, stowed away in their truck. When they got to Baghdad she told them her story, and the Swedish Red Cross flew her to Stockholm. And from there she got back to England—"

"What happened then?" My mouth was dry.

"She was pregnant by the time she got to England."

"By—by her husband?"

"No. She *had* had two children, in the village, but had to leave them behind when she ran away. No, by one of the Swedish scientists; with whom she had spent a night." Miss Morgan's tone withheld judgment on this. "She borrowed a car and went down to Knoyle, looking for her father, but he was dead by then. When she learned about the money she went into premature labour and was taken off to Ludwell Hospital, where she had a baby which had to be reared in an incubator. And then, somehow, she escaped from the hospital—"

"Escaped?"

"The place was scandalously understaffed. But then," sighed Miss Morgan, "what hospital isn't?"

"What did she do?"

"Found a doctor's car with the keys in, drove herself back to Knoyle. There's a workshop, it seems, among the outbuildings, with power saws and so forth—Lilias had used it when she was younger, had been fond of joinery as a child—she cut off both her hands with the circular saw, and bled to death. One of the maintenance men came to see why the lights were on, and found her."

"Oh my God."

I sat thinking about Lilias Leyburn. I wondered what she had looked like. What she had believed in. What she had thought, when she painfully made her way back to her childhood home, only to find that her father had died. Had she been angry with him for dying? We expect people we love to stay alive and look after us. And Ty—who had promised her father to look after her and see she came to no harm—how must he have felt about it? I wondered if he had become acquainted with Leyburn in the first place through knowing his daughter . . . He must have thought her long dead when she vanished. And then, to have her reappear, only to kill herself in that dreadful way—what a shock for him.

"Why didn't I hear about her death? It must have been in the papers?"

"It was hushed up very much—except in local press— naturally the hospital authorities were extremely keen to keep it out of the national news—and it reflected great discredit on them—"

"And so it would on Ty." Discredit is putting it mildly, I thought. But no doubt by that time Ty had influence, and friends with influence; they had been able to reduce the story to a sad unfortunate affair of a poor unbalanced girl who had come to grief.

Miss Morgan looked out of the window. "Ah, here come the police."

During the two hours that followed I was heartily glad of Miss Morgan's presence. Up to the moment of their arrival it had not occurred to me that I would be their natural first suspect. I had forgotten that in murder cases the spouse is always the likeliest killer. But this was soon borne in upon me by the tone in which they questioned me, the way they looked at me, the remarkably thorough way in which they went over the house, although I told them that Ty had never even set foot in it.

"You say he knocked on the kitchen door?"

"Yes."

"Why didn't you let him in?"

"I had no time to. I was sitting on a stool at the kitchen counter—before I could move he took the key from his pocket—and he was just going to open the door—when he fell forward—and I saw this thing sticking out from his back."

"Do you know what it is?"

"I haven't the faintest idea."

"I can help you there," Miss Morgan put in.

The detective inspector—Mattingley, his name was—gave her an annoyed look.

"Just a minute—miss—er, if you please. I'd rather you didn't—"

"No, but I *can* help you," she went on with calm authority, ignoring his protest. "It's a crossbow quarrel. And the reason why I can tell you that is because it is almost certainly one of mine."

"One of *yours,* Miss—?" Now he looked even more annoyed.

"Morgan," she returned placidly. "I live just next door down the hill, at Number 2."

"And you have a *crossbow?*"

"Yes; I used to shoot for Hampshire, you see; I haven't been involved in county archery for some years, of course, but I still keep a couple of bows."

"*Where?*" he snapped.

"Down there, in my garden shed."

"Is it locked?"

"Good heavens no. The door doesn't even *have* a lock. All the people around here are so honest!"

"Who knew that the bow was in the shed?"

"Everybody in the village, I should imagine," said Miss Morgan.

"Did you?" The inspector turned back to me.

"Well, no, I didn't, as a matter of fact. But I've only been here a few days," I said apologetically.

"Did you know Miss Olga Laszlo?"

"Yes."

"How long had you known her?"

"Ten years perhaps—I don't remember exactly."

"Where were you at the time her body was found?"

"Taking a walk with my husband on the cliffs."

"And last night?"

"Here, in this house."

"With your husband?"

"No, alone."

"Why was that? Where was he?"

"At the Close Hotel in Dorchester. So far as I know."

"Why? Why wasn't he here?"

"He prefers more comfortable surroundings. Preferred."

The inspector gave me a sharp look and said, "I understand that you and your husband had separated. Is that so?"

"We hadn't—decided—" I was beginning, but Miss Morgan again interposed.

"I don't think Lady Fortuneswell should answer any more questions except in the presence of her lawyer. Don't you agree, my dear?" turning to me.

"Yes," I said in relief, wondering whom to summon. It didn't seem a case for Ponsonby.

"Oh, very well," said Mattingley crossly, but then pounced on her. "Didn't this house almost burn down a few nights ago?"

"*Now* what nonsense have you picked up?" She smiled at him as if at an impertinent fourth-former. "There was a little smoke from a smouldering sofa cushion caused by faulty wiring. Mr. Laurence Noble was easily able to put it out."

"I'd like to telephone my lawyer," I said, getting up. "May I do that from your house, Miss Morgan?"

"Of course, my dear. I'll come with you."

"I will too," said Mattingley.

I wished again, on the way down, that my crutches were not in the back of Ty's car. But I still had Zoë's stick, and Miss Morgan helped me. Mattingley walked alongside, like a sheepdog—he had rather the look of a collie, sharp long nose, narrow eyes, with black hair slicked back. On the way we passed Odd Tom, pattering upwards, who gave me a wide-eyed anxious glance but went on his way, minding his own business.

The village, dusk now falling, was again overrun by police; Mattingley had left several at my house, taking it apart, no doubt, piece by piece; while others had been sent to reinterrogate the neighbours. Glifonis was in a state of siege.

I rang up Roger Blagdon, a friend of Joel's who had steered me through the niceties of the Pyramid contract, and by good chance caught him at home, about to go out to the theatre.

"Good grief, Cat," he said when he heard my tale. "Of course I'll come. Tonight?"

"No, no, Roger dear, tomorrow will be time enough. Go to your play."

"Are you sure? It's only Ibsen. *Little Eyolf.*"

"Go see it. I'll be fine till tomorrow."

"Don't answer a single question till I get there," he said.

So the police took me into custody and I spent a night in a cell. I have passed many more uncomfortable ones in provincial hotels.

13

IN the night I woke from a frantic dream of Ty's hands murderously tight round my neck, and was hugely relieved to find myself in comfortable police premises.

I had let out some kind of desperate yell, and a head came poking round my door to ask what was going on.

"Nothing. I just had a bad dream. Sorry to have disturbed you."

"That's all right," said the head amiably, and was withdrawing again when I asked, "By the way, on what grounds am I here? I've not been charged with anything, have I?"

"You are here for your own protection," stated the head. "Inspector Mattingley thought it best. Too many funny goings-on in that place, Caundle Quay."

Well, that was all right by me. I rolled up again snugly in my warm police blankets, with a wonderful carefree feeling of being in official hands. It seemed highly ironic to be suspected of Ty's murder when, without a shadow of doubt, he had had a number of calculated tries at polishing *me* off.

All in all, I thought sadly, it seemed fated that I should live and Ty should not, so I might as well absolve myself from blame in the matter of his death; somebody else felt for him a lethal ill will and had loosed the deadly dart. Well: Supposing I was tried and convicted of the crime, I thought lightheartedly, it would be up to H. M. Prisons to nurse me through my various terminal illnesses; I could just relax and let them get on with it. While the individual who really killed Ty—with ample justification, doubtless—could just make the best of the situation; I bore them no grudge. Perhaps it was the unhappy Pool boy; I did hope very much that it was not Odd Tom. Old Elspeth had said—hadn't she?—something about a farfetched theory; I wondered what it was and how Inspector Mattingley would receive it. Not favourably, I'd guess, judging from his general demeanor to the Ladies. Plainly he had them down in his book as meddlesome spinsters of the worst breed.

I drifted back to sleep and dreamed of Masha larding a chicken with garlic and saying thoughtfully, "It can't, you know, it *can't* be right to stab a body, even a dead one," and Fitz replying, "No, that's why I'm going to become a vegetarian." Half waking again, I remembered all those ingenious kitchen gadgets Fitz had given her in his teens to ease her lot: the pressure cooker, the apple-chopper, the Mouli mixer, electric tin-opener, magnetic pot holders, the tiny immersion heater for one cup of coffee, the various appliances for extracting corks from bottles, the blender, the steam iron. "Oh, darling boy, how *good* you are to me," she said with overflowing gratitude on each occasion, and there they all were at the back of the pantry, gathering dust, while she went on using her little old kitchen knife, worn bent pans, and pot holders made from Papa's shirts when they grew thin and frayed beyond patching and turning the cuffs. But what she valued beyond praise, beyond speech, was Fitz's goodness to Papa: his endless, endless patience and kindness when Papa attempted to pick up two things at once while holding a third; when he somehow contrived to lock himself in the bathroom and drop the key; when he got in a terrible muddle with his buttoning and unbuttoning; when once, with a sudden piteous effort at generosity he tried to give Fitz a pound note with one hand but quickly lost it again with the other hand in his waistcoat pocket; at each of those moments Fitz would be ready, unfailingly kind, providing the necessary first aid and cheerful response. As he was, too, when Masha lost things. Growing older—perhaps in a kind of wordless protest?—she lost her possessions continually, half a dozen in a day, library tickets, her watch, her good glasses, National Savings Certificates, their TV license, the little worn purse Aunt Dolly had given her when she was sixteen, her chequebook; in hunting anxiously and distractedly about the house for one article she would come to the blank spot where something else ought to have been—her embroidery scissors, her little Zen book— and become diverted onto a secondary quest for that. Fitz always helped her search, but it was a never-ending process; at the end of the day it could be counted as a triumph if two things had been found; losing them, as Fitz said, seemed to be an exercise she continually set herself. But why, why? Each day, towards the close of her life, presented an impossible obstacle course, a challenge that she had to brace herself to meet.

We never did find the key of her desk . . . Perhaps she was trying to divest herself of her cares, her responsibilities?

On the day when she finally took to her bed, she summoned me by telephone. "Now listen," she said triumphantly. "I've done the washing and the ironing. If you could just put out the garbage—it's dustbin day tomorrow—"

Most people, I suppose, have a public persona and a private one. When in the company of others, they speak and move in chosen patterns adopted over years to reinforce the image they have decided to assume; while in private they pad about barefoot, pick their noses, eat voraciously and randomly with their fingers, sit straddle-legged, watch "Dallas" and read gangster novels. Don't you think that is true? Nearly everybody must have some secret self, removed, if only by a marginal distance, from the one offered to society. Yet with Masha I felt this was not so, could not be so; what you saw was what she was; her envelope was so transparent that any concealment would have been an impossibility; or rather, it would never have occurred to her that anyone would wish to conceal their real identity.

Poor Ty, what was his, Jim or Jas? I shall never know.

In the morning my little room seemed unnaturally dark; looking out of the window over the roofs of Outer Dorchester I saw the sky veiled in whirling grey flakes. Perfidious March had taken a plunge back into winter.

"Nasty storm," remarked the kind police lady, bringing me a breakfast ten times larger than my norm and a used copy of the *Daily Mirror*. "Half the roads in Dorset blocked."

"Oh dear," I said with foreboding. "What about Glifonis?"

"Caundle Quay? Cut off, love. All the power lines are down, too."

"Goodness, I hope they'll be all right."

I looked out at the scurrying flakes and felt a protective anxiety for my friends in the village and all those cheerful Greeks in their Portakabins; but then remembered the enormous freezer housed in the Ladies' utility room. No doubt they would manage very capably.

"They can drop food by helicopter if they run short."

"That's true . . . What about the roads to London?"

"A35 and A31 both blocked; they're working at clearing them but it'll be all day."

She went off leaving me to my sausages and toast, and I remembered how Masha used to love the treat of breakfast in bed, and how rarely she had it. Whereas I don't much like meals in bed, am always too worried about the possibility of mess and spillage. Which is why I don't look forward to my terminal illnesses with any enthusiasm. Those sybaritic repasts in the great gilded Venetian bed were something out of context, clean contrary to the regular warp of my life. And I owe Ty for them, I'm grateful that we had that time of nonsense together. He, poor dear, plainly felt just the other way; for him, afterwards, that interlude was like the wound of Philoctetes or the Fisher King, an oozing drain on his vital sources for evermore.

ROGER Blagdon came down by train; a horrible journey, he said it was, and took him over eight hours. He didn't reach Dorchester till nine at night, and came round to see me next morning.

Meanwhile I passed a long, dull day; a police doctor came and examined my wrist and ankle at one point but went away without discussing any conclusions he might have reached. He was a taciturn man.

So it was a pleasant relief to see cheerful, red-headed Roger.

"I'm terribly sorry about your hideous journey. How was *Little Eyolf?*"

"A thoroughly sick, nasty play! I don't want to see it ever again. Now, tell me the whole story. I've seen Joel, by the way; he's just back from Bombay. He sends his love and says he'll be down as soon as he's finished his assignment; he seems extremely worried about you."

I told Roger the whole story, my side of it at least.

"So Ty was trying to kill you, but someone else was trying to kill Ty."

"Someone did kill Ty."

"What about Olga Laszlo? Did Ty kill her?"

"It seems very possible. Hoping to shut her up."

"More than possible, probable," said Roger, who had done some scouting round before he came to see me. "The police found shotgun pellets in the cliff; that earth-fall was engineered in order to cover her body. There was a shotgun in the station wagon and the pellets match. Olga's head was bashed in by a rock, but that might have been done earlier. And they found an envelope from her, addressed to Ty, in his hotel room; also, at the Battersea flat, several plaster hands with her fingerprints on them, which had been sent to Ty anonymously."

"How disgusting." Any sympathy I might have felt for Olga evaporated at once. "So she had been blackmailing him."

"At least trying to soften him up for blackmail."

"She might have known it wouldn't work on Ty. But my goodness, Roger, how did you ever get all this out of the police so fast?"

"I have my methods," he said, looking smug. "There are lots of suspects besides you for his murder. The Goadbys, for instance—"

"The Goadbys?"

"A couple who have one of the houses in the village."

"Oh yes, the grey-faced man and fur-coated woman. Why in the world should they want to murder Ty?"

"One of Ty's business ventures was a new housing estate near Kettlewell. Their five-year-old child fell down an open drain in the foundations and was drowned. They claimed the area was insufficiently protected and brought a case, but Ty's lawyers were too good for them."

"How horrible."

"Goadby had made several unsuccessful attempts to see Fortuneswell. And his avowed intention, in coming to Glifonis, had been 'to get to grips with the chap.' He'd been heard to use those words. And there are the Pools, and Tom Stavely, who lost his home when the trailer site was demolished."

"Stavely? *Odd Tom?* Is that his name? I do so hope it wasn't him."

"He does garden work for Miss Morgan," Roger said, "and knew about her crossbow."

"Everyone knew about it. But she said she had some theory—"

"Oh yes, the police told me about that. They think it's really way out—"

"What is it?"

"This organisation that Fortuneswell might have been invited to join—"

"The Companions of Roland."

"What is it, exactly?"

"Founded by Charlemagne, I think, and has been going ever since. It's a secret society; Ty told me it was established to defend the Holy Sepulchre but now I think it's basically an industrialists' group, used for mutual advantage. Like Freemasons."

"Miss Morgan suggested they were angry that your husband accepted their invitation while concealing this very discreditable episode in his past, and so they took steps to eliminate him."

"Now that *is* farfetched," I agreed. "Why not just blackball him?"

"To discourage other frivolous applications."

"I hope they never invite me to apply for membership."

"I don't think women can apply— Do you want to spend another night in this place?" asked Roger, looking disparagingly round my bare little room.

"Not above half. There isn't much to read. Why? Can you get me out on bail?"

"My dear fool, you haven't been charged with anything.

The police say they took you in for your own protection. And now they know you can't have killed Ty—"

"They do? How do they know that?"

"Because of your wrist, idiot! No one with a recently broken wrist could winch up a hundred-pound crossbow."

The police surgeon might have told me that, I thought. But he was not a communicative man.

Roger helped me pack my things and drove me to the Close Hotel, where I took occupation of Ty's suite.

The police seemed relieved to see me go; I suppose they had been wondering how soon they could politely ask me to leave.

It was queer, sad, and ghostly to sleep in the hotel room with Ty's things still strewn about untidily as they had been left after a police search. I put them away in his case and, remembering that Ty preferred the bed nearest the window, slept in the other one. And, in the night, I dreamed of him crying out piercingly for his drowned friend.

I woke before seven next morning and switched on Radio Three—what luxury!—there had been no radio at Number 1, Glifonis—and caught a performance by Alfred Brendel of Beethoven's piano sonata Opus 109 and remembered with grief how Masha, who meticulously planned her whole week's work from one musical programme to the next, marked out beforehand in the *Radio Times,* had been stuck for an hour in the bathroom with excruciating pains and therefore missed Barenboim playing that same sonata, because there was nobody else in the house to switch on the radio. That was when—hearing of the episode by sheer chance—I knew she must be moved to a nursing home.

"Roads in the South are now mostly cleared after yesterday's freak blizzard," said the announcer on the eight-thirty news. "But flood warnings are in operation as the melted snow fills rivers and drains. The body of a man was found in a barrel at Poole Harbour. Foul play is not suspected."

Oh God, I thought with foreboding. *Please* don't let it be Odd Tom.

Roger drove me through slushy, squashy lanes back to Glifonis, and then returned to Dorchester for more police business. The sun gleamed, almost unbearably bright, on melting crystals and rivulets cascading down steep banks between clumps of flashing brambles. It was a joyful, brilliant, distracting day. The birds were busy shouting their heads off. Everything heralded spring.

But Glifonis was in mourning.

One could tell that instantly. The Greeks, with their loads, plodded in silence up and down the zigzag hill. The blue and white flag down by Father Athanasios's church flew at half-mast. Despite the sunshine, the whole place seemed shrouded in sadness. A knot of black crepe had been tied to the brass knocker on the door of Number 2. And old Elspeth answered the door with her face drawn into lines of sorrow.

"Poor, *poor* little man— No, it was just exposure, natural causes. The bitter cold was just too much for his heart. He'd told me once the old ticker wasn't all it should be—but he was so independent. We'd begged him to let us try to get him a cottage here—or a council house—but no, he wouldn't have that. He said that a whole house would be more than he wanted. Oh, well"—she wiped her eyes—"I suppose now the police will find it convenient to decide that he killed that unpleasant man—sorry, my dear, your husband—and they'll stop fussing around everybody else, which will be a good thing, I suppose. Tom wouldn't mind at all, he'd think that funny."

"You don't believe he did it, then? Nor do I."

"My dear, I'm quite positive he didn't do it." She darted me one very shrewd glance from tear-reddened eyes.

"Miss Morgan—there's something I'd like to ask you— Where's Shuna?"

"She and Pat are down with Father Athanasios, organising Tom's funeral service."

"Was Shuna Lilias Leyburn's child?"

"Yes, of course." Glancing about, as if walls had ears, Miss Morgan went on rapidly, "Ostin Leyburn's elder sister, Mrs. Mulready, had the care of her at first. But then, you see, her arthritis got so terribly bad that she had to go to a warmer climate. And died there. And there really wasn't anybody else. So we said we'd be happy to take charge of her."

"And you've done a wonderful job—"

"But how long we can go *on,* my dear—how long would it be *suitable*— After all, I am seventy-five and Pat is sixty-five, the child really needs younger company—"

"What I was going to say was—I suppose in time I shall come in for some of Ty's money. I don't mean to keep *any* of it—I have no right to it and don't want it—but that child does have a right to it—"

"Yes, yes, of course—yes, yes, well, we'll see!" Miss Morgan gave me several very bright-eyed nods. "Lots of cash not at all good for the young, much better put it in a trust, something like that, don't you agree? For later on, if she wants to do research. We'll talk about all that. Now: would you like a cup of coffee, my dear?"

"No, that's very kind of you but I think I'd better go and tidy my house. Probably the police have left it in a terrible mess—"

"We do *hope,* my dear, that you will stay on in Glifonis? That you haven't been put off the place by your experiences here?" Another of those shrewd, birdlike glances.

"Oh, no. No, I do like it here, very much. Though I shall miss Tom. No, I'd like to stay here, at least part of the time."

"That's good. That's very good. We'll find plenty of things for you to do here." She patted my arm—two quick taps. And I leaned forward and removed a tiny yellow disc, the size of a pinhead, from her collar.

"Oh, those things. They get everywhere. They are the protective caps, you know, from my hearing-aid batteries. Wonderful devices! Without it, I would not have been able to hear you blowing that whistle."

I walked slowly back up the hill, missing Odd Tom every step of the way. I must learn the rest of my part, I thought. In two days, shooting was due to begin again. I must go into Dorchester and get my hair done. Tie the strands of life together. Furbish up the Rosy mask a bit. Plato was quite right, I thought. Didn't he say that acting was morally bad? That you take on the persona of those sinful characters you are depicting, and are thereby likely to come to grief? I took on the character of Rosy and I came to grief.

The door of Number 1 was unlocked. As usual, I thought. *Now* who has been in, prowling about? Or did the police carelessly fail to lock up? No, some person was inside, for, as I put my hand to the latch, the door flew open.

"Fitz!"

"Old Cat!"

We hugged and hugged each other, and laughed, and hugged again.

"But why didn't you let me *know,* why didn't you tell me you were *coming?"*

"I did call that number you gave me and got some old duck, but I thought I wouldn't leave a message, as I was in transit, it seemed simpler just to come; and then at Heath Row, of course, we found all the lines were down, so the only thing was just to drive here—"

Vaguely I remembered Elspeth saying at some point that a man had left a message, but I assumed that it was Joel.

"So down we drove," said Fitz, "but of course the blizzard slowed us."

Us?

He drew forward someone from behind him. Tiny, frail, blonde, waiflike: Rosy in miniature. Scared, bewildered blue eyes; and looked as if she never had an idea in her entire life.

"This is Polly," said Fitz, proud, shy, tremendously protective. "We got married last Wednesday."

I suppressed my silent scream: *What about your fellowship? What about your job?* What about your career, your new philosophical concept? I said the proper things, My darlings, how wonderful, tell me all about it, tell me how you met, let's open a bottle of champagne.

Presently they left to find themselves a hotel room in Dorchester—they could have had the Pools' house but I felt that would be unlucky—and to arrange for a celebration dinner that evening. "I'm really sorry about Ty," Fitz said, giving me a straight look. "But I guess it was all for the best, really? I hope it was fun while it lasted?" and I said yes, on the whole it had been, great fun while it lasted, thinking in what simple terms the young view life. But perhaps that is all for the best, too.

"We'll be back to pick you up at seven then— Is this your cat?" Fitz said in the doorway. "He does howl, doesn't he? A strain of Siamese, perhaps?"

"I wouldn't know. No, he isn't my cat. Or, well," I said, thinking again, "perhaps he is."

"The postman came, while we were waiting. Told us about the key under the flowerpot. There's a letter for you on the counter."

And Fitz ran back to me, as Polly started up the hill, to say in a breathless, urgent undertone, "Polly's an orphan. Got a bad learning problem—several, in fact. She's going to need a lot of looking after—"

I thought of the puzzled blue eyes, regarding me with alarmed mistrust.

"Darling boy—you don't think you ought to be getting on with your *own* life?"

"But helping Polly is going to *be* my life," he said, gave me a swift hug, and ran after her.

Perhaps, I thought, she believed me to be a murderess.

THE letter was from Joel.

"Dear Cat, I'm terribly sorry about Ty. I hope you aren't too shattered. Listen, dear heart—why don't we get married? I know I've asked you before and you said it wouldn't work, but now I'm asking you again. I worry about you! Look at the things you get yourself into! *Someone* ought to take care of you. Do think seriously about this. Much love, Joel."

After I had fed Arkwright, and he had settled down beside me on the sofa, I began writing an answer to Joel, on a pad on my knee.

"Dearest Joel, you are a darling to suggest it, but it really *wouldn't* work. I do appreciate your suggestion, but I don't get on with your friends and they would find me a dreadful bore. Let's just go on the way we are, eh? without putting constrictions on each other? You are my very best friend. I hope I see you soon. Love, Cat."

Absently I removed a tiny yellow leaf from Arkwright's glossy fur and dropped it into the fire Fitz had thoughtfully lit. For a moment I thought it was one of Miss Morgan's hearing-aid battery stickers. They did, as she had said, get everywhere. There had been one on the crossbow bolt projecting from between Ty's shoulders. But that meant nothing. It was Elspeth's bow after all.

I had removed it, just the same.

What was the name she had given that lethal thing?

A quarrel, that was it. Such an odd term.

PAT and Shuna came into Number 2 and sat down, pale and silent and unwontedly idle.

"Let's have a glass of sherry, Bets."

"All right."

"Can I have some?" asked Shuna.

"Certainly not. Apple juice for you."

"It's going to be a very good funeral, Aunt Elspeth. All the Greeks are going to take it in turns carrying Odd Tom's coffin in a procession from the top of the hill. I'm glad Olga made that will saying what to do with her ashes, aren't you? It's much nicer that Tom will be the first in the graveyard."

"Scattered at sea," remarked Elspeth crossly. "Preposterous! Just like her silly self-importance."

"What about Lord Fortuneswell? What about him?"

"When somebody has been murdered, the police hold on to the body until they are sure who did the murder. They keep it in a refrigerator."

"So they may have him forever." Shuna looked a little anxious. "Poor thing, he will be rather cold." Her face clouded still more. "Aunt Elspeth, what do you suppose has happened to Arkwright? You don't think *he* died too, do you?"

"There's no reason to suppose so," said Miss Morgan decidedly. "He will very likely turn up. Cats take care of themselves very well, remember. Why don't you go out, and have a look round for him?"

"All right."

Shuna stood up slowly, without her accustomed alacrity. Then, brightening a little, she said, "I could go and see Lady Fortuneswell. She must be feeling a bit sad, with her husband dead. Even if he was very nasty."

"All right. Do that. Very good idea," said Pat briskly.

When the child had gone out, she added, "Really that man didn't get killed a moment too soon. Whoever did it deserves a public vote of thanks. Well"—glancing at her watch—"I'd better get off to the school board meeting." She stood, drained her glass, gave her old friend a comradely look, and went out.

Elspeth waited a moment or two, then, sighing, stumped out to her multifarious garden jobs. She would miss Odd Tom sorely—dear, *good* little man—but, she thought, how entertained he would have been at the notion that the police chose to consider him a murderer. Won't do no harm, he would say. Welcome to think that if they've a mind to.

Slowly, Miss Morgan began crumbling the damp warm soil to a fine tilth.

SHUNA loitered up the hill, stopping at every corner to study the rivulets running down between the marble slabs, and to call, unavailingly, for Arkwright. Down by the church, she saw, the Greeks were clustered, busy as bees getting the building ready for Odd Tom's funeral. I must remind Aunt Elspeth about going into Dorchester to get flowers, Shuna thought. Odd Tom liked daisies best, he told me so. This was a great big field of daisies, once, when he and the Missus first moved here. Daisies are the best, he said, because they come in summer when it's warm. I wonder if you can get daisies at a flower shop. Aunt Elspeth will know. *Won't* Tom be pleased to see the Missus again.

Absently, her mind moving back to integers, she stooped and picked up a paper clip which Mr. Vassiliaides the architect must have dropped, which had lodged between two of the marble steps.

Then she went slowly on to tap at Lady Fortuneswell's door.

About the Author

Joan Aiken is the daughter of American poet Conrad Aiken. Born in England, in Rye, Sussex, she was educated at home by her mother until the age of twelve, when she attended Wychwood, a small progressive boarding school in Oxford. She began working for the BBC at an early age; she has been Librarian in charge of documents for the United Nations London Information Centre, Features Editor at *Argosy* magazine, and had a brief stint as an advertising copywriter, before turning her hand to writing full-time.

Ms. Aiken is the author of some seventy books, for adults as well as for a juvenile audience. Her novels are acclaimed internationally. A Mystery Writers of America Award-winner, she is also the recipient of the Guardian Award for children's literature for three books: the classic *The Wolves of Willoughby Chase* (for which she also won the Lewis Carroll Award), *Nightbirds on Nantucket,* and *Black Hearts in Battersea.* Her adult novels include *The Girl from Paris, Mansfield Revisited,* and *If I Were You.*

Ms. Aiken is the mother of a daughter and a son; she and her husband divide their time between Sussex, England, and Greenwich Village, New York City.